The HIGHEST OF HOPES

Books by Susan Anne Mason

CANADIAN CROSSINGS

BOOK TWO

The HIGHEST OF HOPES

Susan Anne Mason

BETHANYHOUSE
a division of Baker Publishing Group
Minneapolis, Minnesota

© 2019 by Susan A. Mason

Published by Bethany House Publishers
11400 Hampshire Avenue South
Bloomington, Minnesota 55438
www.bethanyhouse.com

Bethany House Publishers is a division of
Baker Publishing Group, Grand Rapids, Michigan

Printed in the United States of America

Library of Congress Cataloging-in-Publication Data
Names: Mason, Susan Anne, author.
Title: The highest of hopes / by Susan Anne Mason.
Description: Minneapolis, Minnesota : Bethany House Publishers, a division of
    Baker Publishing Group, [2019] | Series: Canadian crossings ; #2
Identifiers: LCCN 2018034293| ISBN 9780764219849 (trade paper) | ISBN
    9781493417254 (e-book) | ISBN 9780764233173 (cloth)
Subjects: | GSAFD: Christian fiction. | Love stories.
Classification: LCC PR9199.4.M3725 H54 2019 | DDC 813/.6—dc23
LC record available at https://lccn.loc.gov/2018034293

Unless noted, Scripture quotations are from the New Revised Standard Version of the Bible, copyright © 1989, by the Division of Christian Education of the National Council of the Churches of Christ in the United States of America. Used by permission. All rights reserved.

Scripture noted NIV is from the Holy Bible, New International Version®. NIV®. Copyright © 1973, 1978, 1984, 2011 by Biblica, Inc.™ Used by permission of Zondervan. All rights reserved worldwide. www.zondervan.com

This is a work of historical reconstruction; the appearances of certain historical figures are therefore inevitable. All other characters, however, are products of the author's imagination, and any resemblance to actual persons, living or dead, is coincidental.

Cover design by Koechel Peterson & Associates, Inc., Minneapolis, Minnesota/Jon Godfredson

Author is represented by Natasha Kern Literary Agency.

19 20 21 22 23 24 25   7 6 5 4 3 2 1

For my dear friends since high school,
Michelle and Colette. Thank you for your love
and support and our monthly tea dates!

And to my cherished friend, Katarina,
who passed away ten years ago. It's a comfort
knowing you're cheering me on from above!

Be strong and take heart,
all you who hope in the LORD.

Psalm 31:24 NIV

PROLOGUE

Late May 1919

Emmaline Moore stepped up to the ship's railing and peered through the mist to catch her first glimpse of the Nova Scotia shoreline now becoming visible. It was a most welcome sight after a week at sea.

A week since she'd left her home in England to embark on this journey.

Six weeks since she'd found her beloved grandfather dead on his bedroom floor.

Two weeks since she'd sold Grandad's watch shop and handed over the key to the new owner.

All because of a packet of letters she'd found in his desk that had turned Emma's life upside down.

She shivered and pulled her collar up around her chin. Beside her at the rail, Grace Abernathy, a friend she'd made on the voyage, turned to give her a wobbly smile. Emma's emotions too were running high—sadness at leaving the people she'd met on the ship and nervousness as to what the future would hold for her now.

"Are you still planning to spend a few days in Halifax before heading to Toronto?" Grace asked.

Emma glanced farther down the rail to where Jonathan stood gulping in the sea air. Her dear friend and traveling companion had suffered extreme seasickness the entire journey and still looked ready to empty the contents of his stomach over the side of the ship. "I think we have to. Not that the ship's doctor isn't competent, but I won't be satisfied that Jonathan's truly all right until another doctor pronounces him healthy. Plus, he'll need a few days of rest to get his strength back before we set off on the next leg of the trip."

"Of course. You must put his health above everything right now." Grace gave a slight shrug. "I would have loved the company on the train though. Quinten's not sure where he's headed, but he has some sleuthing to do in Halifax first."

Quinten Aspinall, another kindred soul searching for family members in Canada, was a true gentleman who had served as their protector during the voyage, keeping away unwanted attention from other males.

Emma smiled. "Perhaps we'll all meet up in Toronto once we get there."

"Perhaps we will." Grace turned to face the water, but not before Emma caught sight of tears welling in her friend's eyes. She reached over to squeeze Grace's arm, silently offering up a prayer for her well-being.

The ship's horn sounded as a warning to prepare for docking.

Emma's heart pumped harder in her chest. They'd reached Canada, the country that would hopefully become her new home. What would she find here? A welcoming family or further rejection?

She cast a guilty glance at Jonathan, who looked her way and waved. She managed a brief wave in return. What would he do when he learned that her intention for the trip was not exactly as she'd indicated? She'd kept one important detail of her plans to herself. One she knew he'd do everything in his power to thwart, and because of that, she couldn't tell him until the timing was right.

Resolutely, Emma pushed away the twinge of guilt. After all, Jonathan was the one who'd insisted on coming with her. She'd been perfectly happy to make the trip alone, but he wouldn't hear of it. Even his Aunt Trudy had joined his petition to keep her from going, but when she realized Emma would not be swayed, Trudy had supported Jonathan's decision to travel with her. Unable to fight the both of them, Emma had finally relented, secretly a bit relieved to have his company. Jonathan's presence aboard the ship had provided her a great deal of comfort—it helped knowing her best friend was in the cabin down the hall. All she could do now was pray he'd forgive her when he learned of her true intentions.

Another blast of the horn shook Emma from her thoughts. She squared her shoulders as the ship slid closer to the dock, vowing to put all regrets behind her. There was no point in looking back. The past was filled with nothing but loss and grief. It was time to look ahead to a future that brimmed with possibilities.

Soon, with God's blessing, she would embark on a new life with a family she'd never met, but who, Emma prayed, would accept her graciously into their fold.

Maybe then the emptiness inside her would finally be filled, and at last she'd feel whole.

CHAPTER I

JUNE 1919

There was no turning back now!

The shrill scream of the steam whistle signaled the locomotive's departure from the last stop before they reached their ultimate destination of Toronto. Emma gripped the wooden armrests until her fingers ached, though it did little to rid her body of the tension building within her. Perhaps it was due to stress and fatigue, but on this final stage of her long journey, a cloud of doubt had crept in to plague her.

Had she made the worst mistake of her life, selling everything she owned to journey halfway across the world? For the first time since leaving England, Emma feared she may have.

Smoke billowed past the passenger car windows, momentarily masking her view of a sparkling blue lake amid the rolling countryside—not quite as scenic as the landscape in Wheatley, but certainly prettier than she'd imagined. Emma smoothed her hand over a stomach that was roiling with a mixture of anticipation and dread. She had no idea what to expect upon her arrival in Toronto, and the very real fear that she'd placed too great an importance on this trip continued to nag at her—as well as the uncomfortable feeling that she hadn't really consulted with

God before making her impulsive decision. What if Jonathan was right about giving her father fair warning before simply appearing on his doorstep? What if her father wanted nothing to do with her?

Emma leaned back and took a deep breath. Nothing would be gained by this tiresome worrying. Only time would tell whether her journey would be worth leaving everything behind—or not.

In the seat beside her, Jonathan slept with his head against the window. He still looked somewhat green, a color that seemed to haunt him since their ocean crossing. Who knew he would make such a poor sailor? Despite the doctor's pronouncement that he was fine, their six-day sojourn in Halifax had done little to restore Jonathan's equilibrium, and the extreme jostling of the train for the past two days had only exacerbated his condition. Because of the constant nausea, he'd barely been able to keep down more than a few saltine crackers and tea and had slept most of the time.

A door opened at the far end of the car, and a man in a conductor's uniform entered. He stopped at the first seat and requested to see the occupants' tickets, as he'd done after every new stop.

Several rows ahead, a young girl slipped away from her mother and darted into the aisle. Despite the jerky movement of the train, the girl managed to race toward Emma, a grin of triumph lighting her face.

She came to an abrupt halt at Emma's seat and stared, eyes dancing. "Hello. My name's Sarah. I like your hat."

Before Emma could reply, a bearded man approached. "Sarah, you must stay where your mama and I can see you." He lifted the girl into his arms and dropped a kiss on her cheek. "Come now. You can give the conductor our tickets."

Sarah threw her arms around the man's neck. "Then can I have some candy, Papa?"

The man chuckled, gazing at the child with such adoration

that Emma's throat tightened. "If you promise to stay in your seat, you may have a peppermint," he said.

Emma watched them until they disappeared from view, but the image of the man's expression as he held his daughter remained seared in Emma's mind, igniting a flicker of hope.

She'd traveled four thousand miles to receive a look such as that.

When the conductor reached them, Emma handed him the tickets. "How much longer until we reach Toronto?"

The man's expression brightened as he met her inquiring gaze. He appeared to be a little older than Jonathan, perhaps twenty-five or so, but his uniform gave him an air of authority. "About three hours, miss."

"Thank you." She bit her bottom lip. Only three hours until she'd disembark in the city where Randall Moore had been living for the past twenty-two years. Twenty-two years that Emma had believed her father to be dead. Was she daft to come so far in search of him without writing first?

Jonathan seemed to think so. He'd tried to get her to postpone her trip until she'd contacted Randall. However, the fear that her father would reject her before she'd even had the chance to meet him had spurred her to take immediate action. A letter could be ignored, but it would be a lot harder to dismiss her when she was standing right in front of him.

"Are you all right, miss?" The conductor peered at her, a concerned frown wrinkling his brow. "You're not feeling ill, I hope." He glanced over at her companion, perhaps fearing she had succumbed to motion sickness as well.

Emma managed a smile. "I'm fine. Just a bit nervous is all."

"Heartier than your husband, I see." He chuckled as he punched their tickets.

"He's not my husband," Emma replied quickly. "Just a dear friend who was good enough to accompany me on this trip."

Curiosity animated the man's rugged features. "First time to Canada?"

"Yes." She squeezed her gloved hands together on her lap. "I'm here to . . . visit some relatives I've never met before."

The train jerked as it rounded a bend, and the conductor grabbed the back of the seat to steady himself. "I'm sure they must be as excited as you are. I know I would be to have such a lovely guest arriving." He winked at her. "As much as I'd love to hear more, I'd best get back to work. Enjoy your stay in Toronto." He tipped his cap and set off down the car.

"Already breaking hearts all over the country, I see." Jonathan's wry voice brought heat to Emma's cheeks.

"Don't be silly. He was just being friendly. Like all the Canadians we've met so far."

Jonathan opened one eye to give her a disbelieving look. "I doubt they'd be as friendly if I were traveling alone."

"Go back to sleep, Grumpy Gus. You have three more hours until you're free of this torture."

Jonathan shifted in his seat, straightening to look out the window at the passing countryside. "It's not so bad. Better than being on that ship." He turned to look at Emma. "I suppose our first order of business when we arrive will be to secure lodgings."

Emma nodded. Her thoughts flew back to her safe little room above Grandad's watch shop and a wave of homesickness hit hard. What if things went wrong here? There was no cozy flat to go back to. No suitor waiting in the wings either. Her last letter to Lord Terrence had made sure of that.

"Should we try the boardinghouse Grace mentioned?" Jonathan's voice brought Emma out of her musing. "It will likely be more reasonable than staying at a hotel."

"That sounds like a good place to start." Although the impatient part of her wanted to delve right into locating her father, practicalities had to be considered before that could happen.

"And if there's no room, perhaps the landlady could refer us elsewhere." Jonathan's brown hair was sticking up in all directions from being plastered against the window for most of the morning. A shadow of a beard hugged his jaw, which was unusual for Jonathan, who normally prided himself on being impeccably groomed. Further proof that he still wasn't feeling up to par.

Emma pointed to his wayward tufts. "You'd better freshen up or you're likely to scare the proprietress off. You look like an outlaw right now."

He scowled at her as he ran his fingers over his jaw. "You try shaving in a room smaller than a closet. Besides, with this constant motion, I'd likely slit my throat."

Emma forced a laughed. "I'm sure there will be a restroom at the Toronto station. From what I hear, it's quite the grand place."

"It is indeed." The man seated across from them lowered his newspaper. "Recently renovated and everything. You can get a great shoeshine there," he said to Jonathan.

"Sounds like you know the place well."

"I travel for business, so I've spent my fair share of time waiting for trains there." He smiled. "I'm Stan Olsen. Born and bred in Toronto. If I can be of any help, let me know."

Emma restrained herself from barraging the poor man with questions. In a city the size of Toronto, chances were slim that he'd ever heard of her father.

Jonathan shot her an inquiring look, then leaned forward. "As a matter of fact," he said, "we're looking for someone. I don't suppose you know a man named Randall Moore?"

The man's brows rose. "Not personally. But most Torontonians know who he is." He turned the newspaper back to the front page and handed it over. "Just finished reading an article about him. Bottom right-hand column."

Emma's pulse raced. "Not in the obituaries, I hope."

"No. He's very much alive and kicking." The gentleman's eyes held a trace of amusement.

"I'm almost afraid to ask what that means." Jonathan held the paper between them so Emma could see it.

The headline of the article read *Mayoral Candidate Randall Moore Ramps Up His Campaign*.

Emma exchanged a look with Jonathan, then bent closer to read the smaller print.

> Despite his recent defeat in the Toronto mayoral race, Professor Randall Moore has kicked off his next campaign with a bang. In light of the close finish in January's election, it's apparent that public support for Moore is reaching an all-time high. "Tommy Church can't win forever," Moore stated. "And I intend to be the one to unseat him."
>
> The University of Toronto professor's bold declaration has issued a clear challenge to the mayor. If Moore's popularity continues, it seems he might indeed unseat Mr. Church in the next election.

Emma's mouth fell open. "He's running for mayor? Isn't that a rather mammoth undertaking?"

Mr. Olsen nodded. "A lot of time and money go into the campaign, especially for a candidate trying to unseat the current mayor who's been elected three years in a row." He crossed his arms over his chest. "What do you want with Randall Moore?"

Emma laid the newspaper on her lap. It wouldn't be fair for anyone else to learn about her visit before she had the chance to meet her father. "He's a . . . distant relative. I promised I'd look him up when I got to Toronto." She made to hand the paper back, but the man waved it off.

"You keep it. You might want to save that article for your family back home."

"Thank you." She folded the paper and placed it in her handbag.

Mr. Olsen didn't need to know that she had no family left. That Grandad was gone, leaving her with nothing but lies and deception.

Emma swallowed the hurt that rose in her throat.

She only prayed that once she met her father, he would provide her with answers to the questions that haunted her. Otherwise this arduous voyage would all be for naught.

Jonathan entered the dining car of the train and steadied himself with a hand to the wall. A low din filled the room. Seated at the cloth-covered tables, various passengers chatted over plates of food, their conversation punctuated by the clink of silverware and china.

Jonathan's stomach, however, rebelled at the variety of smells that assaulted him. Bacon, beef, and a hint of barley soup. He wished he were up to eating something solid, but tea seemed the only thing that could ease the constant nausea that had plagued him since leaving the shores of England.

He made his way to the bar, where a large balding man in an apron was wiping the counter. Jonathan sat down in one of the chairs. "A cup of Earl Grey tea, please."

The man blinked. "How about orange pekoe?"

"That will do. Thank you."

The fellow turned, lifted a pot from behind him, and grabbed a cup with the other hand. He studied Jonathan while he poured the hot beverage. "Didn't I see you in here this morning with your wife? Couldn't help but notice her." He winked at Jonathan.

Jonathan had been in with Emma for breakfast but had only been able to get down a few swallows of tea. "She's not my wife. Just a very good friend."

"Oh, I get it." The man waggled his brows.

Jonathan held back a groan. He'd come on this voyage to keep Emma safe, not sully her reputation. "No, sir. I don't believe you do. Emma considers me a brother." He poured some milk into the tea and took a quick sip. "Not that I'd mind changing that opinion."

"A brother, eh? You must have known each other a long time."

"Indeed. Since the age of ten when I moved next door to her. Emma and I were both orphans—or so she thought at the time." He lowered his cup. "She helped me cope with the loss of my family. We've been best friends ever since."

The man peered at him. "I'm guessing your feelings changed once you got older?"

"For me, yes. But not for her. I'm trying to figure out how to remedy that." Jonathan shifted his gaze to the counter. Why had he just spilled his innermost thoughts to this hefty stranger with coffee stains on his shirt?

"Ah, unrequited love. I totally understand." The big man's belly hung over the bar as he leaned forward, ready to share a confidence. "There was a girl in my hometown. Never could get her to notice me. Hope you have better luck, pal."

"You and me both, sir." He raised his cup in a mock salute and drained the contents, then rose to make his way back to the next car.

Emma had taken his spot by the window and was dozing in the seat, her long lashes a dark smudge against her skin. Jonathan sat beside her and inhaled deeply. The stuffy air in the train did nothing to help his stomach, nor could it calm his worry.

His dearest friend was in for a huge disappointment, and Jonathan had no idea how to prevent the crushing blow she would soon receive. Emma seemed blinded to the fact that her father did not appear to want her in his life. If he had, he would have made more of an effort to contact her. More than a handful of letters that Emma had never received until the day she'd cleaned out her grandfather's desk.

Yet Jonathan couldn't blame her for wanting to meet the man. He just wished she'd waited to correspond with him first, to better ascertain the chance at being well received, but she claimed she needed the element of surprise in her favor. From Jonathan's experience, the sort of surprise she had in mind rarely worked out the way one intended.

Something he would do well to remember himself.

He reached up to pat the breast pocket of his jacket where the envelope that held his future rested. A measure of guilt weighed on his conscience at keeping this information from Emma. But if he'd told her before they left, she would have demanded he stay behind. He'd had a hard enough time convincing Emma that Aunt Trudy would be all right without him for the summer. In truth, Jonathan hated leaving his aunt to manage her dress shop alone, especially after just returning from four years at war, but in the end, he'd had no choice. There was no way he could allow Emma to travel halfway across the world alone.

His news could wait for a more opportune time. In fact, if everything went according to his expectations, they might be on a ship home within a few weeks. He pressed a hand to his still tender abdomen. Not a trip he was looking forward to, but it would be worth the seasickness to have Emma home where she belonged.

With him.

Jonathan snuck a glimpse at Emma's profile as she slept. Dark curls framed her heart-shaped face, and her pert nose was peppered with light freckles. But it was her stunning blue eyes that captivated him the most. Those eyes could turn from mischievous to furious with little warning, reflecting every thought and emotion that flitted across her delicate features. He still found it difficult to comprehend how the girl he'd grown up with—the one he used to view as a little sister—could have turned into the woman who had captured his heart so completely.

Yet the question remained. How would he ever get Emma to see him as anything other than her best friend and surrogate brother?

Jonathan rubbed a hand over his whiskered jaw. He must look a sight after being sick the whole voyage over. He'd thought he could use the time on the ship to get closer to Emma, to reestablish their bond that was somewhat strained after the war. And then there was her relationship with some baron that had started near the end of the hostilities, while Jonathan was recuperating in France. Thankfully, she'd come to her senses and written to Lord Terrence the Terrible—as Jonathan had secretly taken to calling him—before they set sail, turning down his proposal of marriage. One less obstacle for Jonathan to overcome.

However, he would now have to make up for lost time and begin to woo the woman he was determined to make his wife.

If only he could be sure there was a chance Emma would one day reciprocate his feelings.

CHAPTER 2

"I'm terribly sorry, but I don't take gentlemen boarders." Standing in the doorway of the boardinghouse, Mrs. Chamberlain, the gray-haired proprietress, gave Emma a sympathetic look, then turned to Jonathan. "You might try the YMCA on College Street. They have a very nice facility there."

Emma's spirits sank. She'd barely seen Jonathan on the ship. Now he wouldn't be able to stay at the same boardinghouse? With a determined huff, she grabbed her valise off the porch. "Could you recommend another establishment nearby that would take us both?"

Mrs. Chamberlain's eyes narrowed as she studied them. "Are you two related?"

"Not by blood, but we grew up together. Jonathan's practically my brother. I can vouch for his good character." It wasn't as if the woman had cause to mistrust him. With his freshly shaven face and clean shirt, Jonathan appeared eminently respectable.

The woman smiled. "I have no doubt you're a fine young man, Mr. Rowe. But my other boarders are all women, and they wouldn't feel comfortable sharing facilities with a man."

"I understand." Jonathan laid a hand on Emma's shoulder. "You get settled here, Em, and I'll find somewhere else to stay."

"No." Emma tightened her grip on the bag. "We'll find a place together."

Jonathan shook his head. "It's getting late, and you're exhausted. I'll check out the YMCA and come back to get you in the morning."

Despite her brave front, the burn of tears bit the back of Emma's eyes as the toll of the past two weeks caught up with her. She clamped down on her bottom lip that had begun to tremble, unable to speak a word.

Mrs. Chamberlain wiped her hands on a towel that hung from the waist of her apron and stepped onto the front porch. "How are you at yard work, Mr. Rowe?"

"I can get by. Why do you ask?"

"My grounds keeper recently quit—as you can tell by the length of my grass—and I'm having a difficult time finding a replacement." She tilted her head, her gray eyes matching her tight curls. "If you care to take the position temporarily until I find a new man, you can stay in his old quarters above the garage."

Emma's heart pinged with hope. She turned to Jonathan with a beseeching look.

"That seems like a fair proposition," he said slowly. "Just how much work would this entail?"

"No more than a few hours each day, I'm sure."

"Very well. I'll take it."

Emma's shoulders sagged with relief. She wouldn't be alone. Jonathan would be nearby if she needed him. "Thank you, Mrs. Chamberlain. We appreciate it very much."

"Glad I could help." She smiled at Emma. "You may take your bags upstairs to the third floor. Second door on the right. I'll get Mr. Rowe the key to his quarters."

Emma picked up her valise and stepped inside. "Oh, can you tell me if Grace Abernathy is staying here? We met on the

22

boat from England. She was the one who recommended your establishment."

A faint shadow crossed Mrs. Chamberlain's features. "I'm afraid you just missed her. She took a job as a nanny and moved out."

"That's a shame. I'd hoped we'd have more time together."

"You and me both, dear." The landlady smiled. "But Grace has promised to come back on Sundays if she's able. Maybe we can all attend church together."

"I'd like that very much."

The thought cheered Emma as she climbed the stairs to the third floor. Upon entering the room, she found it to be decorated in lovely shades of pink and rose with a cozy window seat that overlooked the street below. Emma eyed the quilt-covered bed with longing. Perhaps tonight she'd have a full night's sleep, the first real one since she'd found the pack of letters among her grandad's belongings and learned that she wasn't an orphan after all. The unfamiliar hurt and anger still simmered beneath the surface at the thought of her grandparents' betrayal. How could the two people who'd raised her since infancy lie to her like that and keep her from her father?

She hated being mad at them, hated that they weren't alive to explain their reasons for hiding the truth from her. But one way or the other, Emma planned to find out what had transpired after her mother had died and why her grandparents had felt the need to perpetrate such a deception.

Filled with renewed resolve, Emma unpacked and freshened up with the water in the pitcher on the nightstand, then went in search of her landlady.

It stood to reason that if Randall were running for the mayor of Toronto, Mrs. Chamberlain would know something about him. And Emma needed every tidbit of knowledge she could dig up before she met the man.

After all, knowledge was power, was it not?

Jonathan climbed the rickety wooden steps to the living quarters above the building that Mrs. Chamberlain had called the garage. A misnomer for sure, since he doubted the building had ever housed a vehicle of any kind. It now served as a large storage area for a variety of tools. Clearly the former caretaker had been a master of all trades. Jonathan hoped he hadn't exaggerated his skills too much and could do the work required to earn his keep.

Using the iron key, Jonathan fiddled with the lock until the door opened, then entered the apartment. A wall of musty air met him the moment he stepped inside. Immediately he crossed to the small window at the front of the room, flipped the latch, and pushed up the sash. Then he took a look around the space.

It was sparsely furnished with a round table and two wooden chairs, a cot against the far wall, an armchair, a table, and a lamp. Lacking a kitchen and a restroom, the place was not ideal; however, in order to remain near Emma, he would make do with the inconvenience of using an outdoor privy and taking his meals in the kitchen with the cook.

His gaze fell on a black wood stove in the corner. Beside it, a basket contained the remnants of kindling. Jonathan forced his feet to cross the room. He supposed there had to be some means to heat the quarters, given the harsh Canadian winters. With any luck, though, it would now be warm enough that he wouldn't need to light it.

Beads of perspiration popped out on his forehead. Ignoring his discomfort, he forced himself to grasp the iron handle and open the door. The interior had been swept clean of debris and ash, yet the lingering odor of burnt wood caused a spasm in his chest. He banged the door shut and rose, willing the flood of memories to fade. He would not have an episode now. He inhaled deeply and exhaled through his mouth. Usually fireplaces and wood stoves didn't trigger this type of reaction, but ever since the war, the tremors had come back with a vengeance, brought on by seemingly innocuous circumstances. The worst part was never being able to predict when they'd hit.

Jonathan crossed the room and deposited his bag on the floor by the bed. Since there wasn't much he could do here at the moment, he supposed he should find out exactly what work would be required of him. He left the room and returned to the rear door of the boardinghouse, hoping he wasn't breaking any rules of etiquette by entering the kitchen without permission.

A stout woman stood at the large stove, stirring a pot. The delicious aroma of freshly baked bread and boiled beef filled the air. Jonathan's stomach growled, the first sign of an appetite since he'd boarded that dreaded ship. Judging by the way his ribs protruded, he must have lost weight on the trip. He intended to make up for it as soon as possible.

"Hello," he called out, not wishing to startle the woman.

The cook turned to peer over her shoulder, her rhythmic stirring never faltering. Under her white cap, where wisps of gray hair stuck out like porcupine quills, lines furrowed her brow. "Who are you, and what are you doing in my kitchen?"

"My name is Jonathan Rowe. Mrs. Chamberlain hired me as the temporary grounds keeper."

The woman's frown relaxed. "I see." She looked him up and down as she wiped her hands on her apron. "I'm Mrs. Teeter, the cook here. I assume you're looking for something to eat." She shot a glance at a clock on the wall. "Dinner is over, but I can rustle you up some bread and cheese and maybe a little beef."

"That would be most kind. Thank you." Jonathan gave a small bow. "We've been traveling for weeks it seems."

"We?" The woman opened the icebox and removed a round wheel of cheese.

"My friend and I. Emma is staying upstairs."

At the disapproving set to her mouth, Jonathan rushed to help her carry the food. "Emma and I grew up together. She looks on me like a brother." He was getting very tired of explaining that. But for now, it seemed to be working in their favor, considering it was unusual for an unmarried woman to travel with a male who wasn't a relative.

"What brings you to this side of the world?" Mrs. Teeter pulled out a loaf of bread and grabbed a large knife.

"Emma has come to visit some . . . distant relatives." He gestured vaguely with one hand.

"And you?" She squinted at him.

"I'm just along to keep her out of harm's way." He gave the woman his most charming smile and was gratified to see a slight lift to her lips.

"Like a good big brother should." She arranged the bread and cheese on a plate. With a grunt, she went back to the stove where she scooped a bit of beef from the pot. She handed him the plate, and then poured out a cup of black coffee.

Jonathan didn't have the heart to tell her he preferred tea. "I do plan to look up a friend of mine while I'm here. We met in the military infirmary in France while we both recovered from our injuries. He made me promise to look him up if I ever came to Toronto." Jonathan prayed Reggie was doing well. He'd been more severely injured than Jonathan, deemed unfit for combat, and sent back to Canada.

Mrs. Teeter paused to study him. "You fought in the war?"

"Yes, ma'am." He broke off a piece of bread and chewed the hardened crust. "I was wounded near the end. Spent the last few months in hospital."

"You were one of the lucky ones, then. To make it home alive."

A sheen of moisture appeared in her eyes. "My poor nephew wasn't as fortunate." She bent her head and swiped the back of her hand across her cheek.

Jonathan frowned. "I'm terribly sorry for your loss." How many times had he repeated that phrase since the war had ended? And why did he feel so guilty that he had lived while others had not? He tried to swallow the bread that had lodged in his throat, washing it down with a quick sip of coffee. He fought to keep the grimace from his face. How did people drink this tar?

"Philip was a good lad. The apple of my dear sister's eye. I don't know how she'll go on without him." A huge sigh escaped the woman's pinched lips.

Jonathan nodded. "I lost my good friend, Danny, as well as many fellow soldiers, so I understand a little of what you're feeling. When I got back, I had to face Danny's widowed mother and give her his few belongings. Never had to do a harder thing." Visions of Danny's body draped in a white sheet danced behind Jonathan's eyes. He took another swig of the thick brew in an attempt to dislodge the ever-present lump in his throat.

Mrs. Teeter went to the icebox and took out a plate. She cut a large slice of pie and brought it over to him. "Any man who'd fight for his country is a gentleman in my eyes, Mr. Rowe." She laid a fork beside the plate.

"Thank you. Apple pie is a luxury I've had to do without for the past four years."

She went back to stirring her pot. "Tell me, do you have much experience being a grounds keeper?"

"A little," he said cautiously.

"After you're done eating, I'd like to show you the vegetable garden out back. I've planted most of the seeds, but I'd be glad to turn the upkeep over to you."

"Certainly." The tight muscles in Jonathan's stomach finally

27

relaxed, as though he'd just passed a test of sorts. If tending a garden would keep him on the cook's good side and assure him of a constant supply of food, he'd happily learn all he could about growing vegetables.

Especially if it meant he could be near Emma.

CHAPTER 3

When Emma had questioned her landlady about Professor Moore and shown her the return address on his last letter, Mrs. Chamberlain had known the exact area where he lived and had given her directions.

"It's a very fancy neighborhood," the landlady told her. "Lots of doctors and lawyers live there. Is the professor a relative of yours?"

"He is." Emma had smiled brightly and put away the letters, hoping Mrs. Chamberlain wouldn't question her further. "I only hope he still lives at the same address. I suppose I'll find out soon enough."

"No need to worry. I'm sure a public figure like Randall Moore won't be hard to track down."

Now, as Emma made her way up to her father's front door with Jonathan beside her, nerves threatened to swamp her. Perhaps she should have taken more time to prepare for this initial meeting, as Jonathan had suggested. But she'd been loath to waste one more minute, knowing she was so close to the man who had fathered her.

To the one person who could fill in the missing pieces of her life.

"This place looks fit for the king of England," she whispered.

Twin columns flanked the front entrance of the tall redbrick home, which stretched half the length of a city block. Back in their English village, they could have fit four cottages in the same space. All around the house, the landscaping looked professionally tended, with its well-manicured bushes and flower beds just beginning to bloom.

"It does indeed." Jonathan stretched his neck to look up at the building. "A far cry from our flats above the shops back home."

Suddenly Emma was very grateful that she'd used some of the profits from the sale of her grandfather's watch shop to buy a new wardrobe for her trip. At least in her best blue dress and matching jacket she wouldn't feel like a poor relation from the homeland, looking for a handout.

She drew in a deep breath, willing a courage she didn't feel.

"We don't have to do this now." Jonathan's warm hand at her back steadied her. "I still maintain it would be better to wait. Give more thought to this first meeting."

"No." Emma lifted her chin, her fight returning. "I haven't come this far to back out now." She grasped the iron knocker and rapped it sharply against the door, then stood back to wait. At last the door opened.

A large-boned woman with heavy brows stared out at them. "Can I help you?"

"Is Professor Moore in, please?" Emma barely managed to keep her voice from quivering.

"He's in the middle of dinner with his family. You'll have to come back another time." The sour-faced housekeeper frowned at Emma as though scolding her for the interruption.

"I'm sure he'll want to see me," Emma said. "I've come all the way from England. Perhaps we might wait in the parlor until he's finished?"

The woman's brows crashed down. "I think not. You'll have to come back tomorrow. Better yet, call and make an appointment."

The door closed in front of Emma's nose with an audible slam.

Scowling, she turned to Jonathan, not even attempting to hide her frustration. "How rude. All the other Canadians we've met were so polite." She crossed her arms and tapped one foot on the cement porch, trying to decide what to do next.

Jonathan took her gently by the elbow. "Let's go back to Mrs. Chamberlain's," he said in his ever-patient voice. "We'll try calling tomorrow."

His soothing tone, one meant to cajole her to his way of thinking, had little effect. She was not inclined to give up so easily. It simply wasn't in her nature. Whirling about, she knocked loudly once more.

"Emmaline." Jonathan's low growl from behind her did nothing to diminish her resolve.

The door flew open again, and the cross housekeeper glared at them. Before she could say a word, Emma pushed by her into the vestibule. If the woman wanted rid of her, she would have to throw her bodily into the street.

"I've decided that Uncle Randall would be terribly disappointed to learn you'd sent us away. We don't mind waiting until he's free, do we, Jonathan?" She turned to look over her shoulder at Jonathan, who glowered at her as he usually did when peeved by her behavior.

"Please excuse my friend's . . . enthusiasm." He bowed to the flustered housekeeper. "She's a trifle impatient, I'm afraid."

"Did you say Professor Moore is your uncle?" the woman demanded.

"I suppose that's not entirely accurate." Emma gave her a bright smile, one that had always gotten her way with Grandad. "But a relative is a relative, is it not?" She peered down a hallway past a set of open double doors that likely led into the parlor.

The woman looked from Emma to Jonathan and heaved a

loud sigh. "Very well, you may wait in here." She gestured to the doorway. "What are your names, please?"

Emma gulped in a long breath as she hesitated on the threshold of the large room. "Miss Emmaline Moore and Mr. Jonathan Rowe," she said.

"Please have a seat." The clearly disgruntled servant marched down the hall.

Emma walked over to a gold brocade sofa, where she sank onto the cushions, her legs unsteady beneath her.

"Breathe, Em. You don't want to faint before you meet him, do you?" Jonathan crouched in front of her, rubbing her hand between his fingers. His brown eyes studied her with concern as though he were afraid she might fall apart.

"No. That wouldn't do at all." She inhaled and slowly exhaled, willing the nerves to quit jumping in her stomach. Could she really be about to meet her father for the first time, after all these years? Would he be stoic and reserved as most British tended to be, or overcome with joy to see his infant daughter all grown up?

Jonathan's encouraging smile warmed her more than his hands could. If only her father would one day look at her that way. Like she meant everything in the world to him.

Loud footsteps sounded on the tiled floor. Emma's heart hammered loudly in her chest. She squeezed Jonathan's hand as he helped her to her feet. She needed to be standing for this moment.

Seconds later, her father appeared.

Emma could only stare at the imposing figure in the doorway. Nothing in her imagination had come close to this larger-than-life presence.

Randall had jet-black hair, very similar to her own, except that his was swept back off his forehead with no hint of her curls. His temples were sprinkled with threads of silver, the only clue to his age. Otherwise he could pass for a man in his twenties, so tall and fit did he appear. He'd obviously donned his jacket in some haste, as the buttons were left open, revealing a striped waistcoat beneath.

Very slowly, he moved into the room, his eyes not leaving her face. As he came closer, Emma saw he had the same vivid blue eyes as she. There could be no denying the authenticity of their relation.

"Emmaline?" The color had drained from his face, leaving it almost ashen. "Is it really you?"

Jonathan's hand gripped her elbow, giving her the support she needed. Several more people appeared in the doorway, but Emma remained focused on the man before her.

"It is." She forced her quivering lips into a smile. "I believe I'm your long-lost daughter."

Jonathan flinched at the blunt manner in which Emma blurted out the information to the strangers in the room. Whatever happened to the tactful manner he'd suggested she use to break the news?

A slight cry came from behind Mr. Moore, as a tall, elegantly dressed blonde pushed forward.

"What kind of vile prank is this?" she demanded.

If not for the shock of the moment, Jonathan was certain she would be a handsome woman. But now, her face contorted with suppressed anger, she appeared almost frightening.

Emma, however, did not shrink back. She tilted her chin in that adorably frustrating manner of hers. "This is no prank, I assure you. I've traveled a long way to meet my father, a man I'd long believed to be dead, and whom I only recently learned was in fact alive." She focused on Randall. "I hoped he would be as happy to meet me as I am him."

A tense silence hummed in the room. A fair-haired girl who looked to be around seventeen or eighteen came farther into the parlor, pushing a younger girl in a wheelchair. Both stared at Emma.

Everyone seemed to be waiting on the professor to say something, to take charge of the situation, but he appeared to be in a trance.

The woman, likely Randall's wife, tugged on his arm, her brows swooping downward. "Tell the girl she's mistaken, Randall."

The girls watched their parents with undisguised curiosity.

"I . . . that is . . ." He blinked rapidly as though he could dislodge the sight before him.

"I know just how you feel." Emma moved toward him. "I was at a loss for words too when I discovered your letters in Grandad's desk after he died. But once I recovered from the shock, I knew I had to find you. To see you with my own eyes." A smile trembled on her lips. "Now that I have, you can't deny the resemblance between us."

"No," he whispered. "I certainly cannot."

"Are you saying she really is your daughter?" The wife's mouth gaped open, and her nostrils flared like a bellows fanning a flame.

He huffed out a great breath. "Yes, Vera. It appears so."

The woman pinched her lips together and moved to sit in one of the upholstered wing chairs. "I don't believe this."

Emma fished around in her handbag. "I brought a copy of my birth certificate. In case there was any doubt." She pulled it out, unfolded it, and handed it to Randall.

A shadow crossed his features as he scanned the document. Then he handed it to his wife. "It's legitimate."

"How do you know? She could have forged it." Vera barely glanced at the parchment.

"It's the original document I received after . . ." He cleared his throat. "After Emmaline's mother died."

For a moment, Jonathan felt sorry for the man. He seemed to be truly distraught, remembering his wife's death and the events that had surrounded it.

"Does that mean she's our sister, Papa?" The younger daughter propelled her wheelchair forward, curiosity lighting her elfin features. She wore her hair in two plaits tied with blue ribbons at the ends and appeared to be about twelve years old.

"She's your half sister, yes."

The girl turned to Emma with a grin. "I'm Marianne. And this is Corinne." She pointed to the girl beside her.

"I'm pleased to meet you both," Emma said. "I've always wanted a sister. How delightful that I now have two."

Jonathan looked at Corinne, who stared at Emma with open hostility. *Oh, Emma, love, guard your heart. You have no idea how these people will react to your presence.*

"I, for one, do not need another sister." Corinne's chin quivered. "Papa, I don't understand. How can she be your daughter too?"

Randall straightened his spine and seemed to pull himself together. "It's a long story, sweetheart. One that will wait for tomorrow. Now please take your sister upstairs."

"But I want to—"

"Do as I say."

"Yes, Papa." Corinne ducked her head and grasped the handles of the wheelchair.

"Good night, Emma," Marianne said. "I hope I'll see you again."

"I hope so too." Emma patted the girl's arm before Corinne wheeled her away.

As soon as they'd left, Randall focused his attention on Emma. He released a long breath. "I wish you had given me some warning that you were coming. Given me time to prepare my family."

For the first time, Emma seemed to lose her confidence. "I . . . I'm sorry. I thought it would be a wonderful surprise. I had no idea you hadn't told your family about me."

At the quiver in her voice, Jonathan draped a protective arm over her shoulder. "You'll have to excuse Emma's enthusiasm, Mr. Moore." He smiled. "She simply couldn't stand to delay another minute."

"And who exactly are you?" Randall frowned at him. "Her husband?"

How Jonathan wished he could answer in the affirmative. "I'm Jonathan Rowe, sir. Emma and I grew up together." He would have offered his hand if he had any expectation the man would accept it. But Randall was clearly too overwhelmed at the moment.

Randall glanced at his wife's rigid form, then back to Jonathan. "I hope you understand why I must ask you both to leave. I need time with my family to explain everything."

Emma gasped, her eyes wide with disbelief. "But I've only just arrived. We have so much to discuss."

Jonathan's heart ached for her. She'd never once imagined that she wouldn't be welcomed with open arms.

A muscle in Randall's jaw jumped. He stared at her and shook his head. "I'm sorry."

Emma's frame grew still beneath Jonathan's arm. Her hopes of a long-awaited happy reunion were sinking faster than the ill-fated Titanic. He needed to do something to salvage the situation.

"I understand this is a difficult situation, sir," Jonathan said. "We're staying at Mrs. Chamberlain's boardinghouse on Jarvis Street. You can contact Emma there when you're ready." He nodded at Mrs. Moore seated by the fireplace, then tugged

Emma across the room. If he didn't get her out of here now, her stubborn nature would take over, and there would be a scene. An ugly one at that.

Thankfully, she let him guide her to the entranceway.

The housekeeper, who must have been hovering nearby, hurried to open the front door for them. "Next time be sure to call first."

The door banged shut behind them.

Emma descended the stairs to the brick walkway below, her feet as numb as her emotions. Her father hadn't been the least bit happy to see her. In fact, he seemed almost resentful that she'd come to his home without permission.

A shudder went through her as her pent-up emotions began to unravel.

"Come here." Jonathan pulled her against his chest and wrapped his arms around her. "I'm sorry, love. That could have gone a whole lot better."

Emma laid her head against his shoulder, allowing the familiar scent of his spicy aftershave to soothe her spirits. She sniffed and wiped away a tear before it could fall. "You were right, Jonathan. I should have listened to you and given my father some warning before simply showing up on his doorstep."

"Um-hm. But then again, when have you ever listened to me?" He chuckled.

She let out a shuddering breath that ended on a half laugh. Jonathan always had a way of making her feel better.

"I'm sure it will go more smoothly the next time you see him." His voice was comforting, as was the hand that rubbed her back.

Emma accepted the handkerchief he handed her. She blew her nose and firmly shook off her disappointment. She would not allow this initial rejection to put her off. Once the family got used to the idea, they would want to get to know her and welcome her into their fold. She certainly would if their roles were reversed.

"The good news is I have two sisters. Marianne and Corinne. How wonderful is that?" She dabbed at her eyes. "I'm sure it's only a matter of time until my father comes around."

"I hope so, love."

Jonathan's doubtful expression only fueled her determination. "I'll make certain of it. Perhaps a shopping trip is in order. I'll get gifts for everyone."

"You can't buy their love, Emma."

"Maybe not, but it couldn't hurt. I should have thought of that in the first place." She linked her arm through his and they began to walk, her momentary despair fading as she focused on a new plan. "There's more than one way to win my father over. I'm sure I'll figure something out."

Jonathan blew out a breath. "That's what I'm afraid of."

Emma laughed at his wry expression. "Admit it, Jonathan. You missed me while you were gone."

"Of course I missed you." He turned to lock his eyes on hers. "The memory of your face was the only thing that got me through the horrors of that war."

For a moment confusion reigned, then she shook her head on a laugh. "You always did like to tease me."

"On the contrary, I've never been more serious. I needed something to cling to out there." His features remained unusually somber.

Once again, Emma wished she knew what had happened to him during his time abroad. Six months ago, he had returned from the war a changed man. She missed the perpetual twinkle in his brown eyes and his mischievous sense of humor. One of the reasons she'd agreed for him to come with her on this trip was that she hoped it might help dispel the ghosts that haunted him and facilitate the return of his cheerful demeanor.

"All that matters is that you made it home in one piece." She squeezed his arm. "I'll be forever grateful to God for bringing my best friend back to me."

He regarded her with an unreadable expression for several seconds. "What about Danny?"

A stab of guilt rose in Emma's chest at the mention of her late fiancé. Was she a horrible person to be relieved that Jonathan had survived the war? That while she mourned Danny with one breath, she praised God with another for sparing Jonathan?

"I cared a great deal for Danny," she said slowly, "but the truth is our relationship never came close to the friendship you and I share. I doubt any ever could." She paused and then, with a deliberate grin to diffuse the situation, gave him an elbow to the ribs. "Unless you fall madly in love with some girl and forget all about me."

"That will never happen, Emma." A fiery intensity lit his eyes as he laid his hand over hers.

Emma's stomach gave a nervous jump, and she almost pulled her hand away. What was the matter with her? This was Jonathan. Why was she reacting so strangely to him?

Her emotions must be on edge after the long voyage and the drama of meeting her father for the first time.

Of course that was it. What else could it be?

CHAPTER 4

Randall closed the door to his study and leaned back against the wood. Even with his eyes closed, nothing could erase the image of his wife's furious face. That was one conversation he never wanted to repeat.

What a fool he'd been to hide his past from her. But in all honesty, he never once imagined his daughter crossing the ocean to seek him out. As far as he knew, she wanted nothing to do with him. In all these years, she had never acknowledged his letters nor made any attempt to contact him. Not even for money.

So what on earth had brought her here now?

"I've traveled a long way to meet my father, a man I'd long believed to be dead, and whom I only recently learned was in fact alive." Emma's jarring words came back to him. Her grandparents had told her he was dead? He knew the Bartletts blamed him for Loretta's death, but to tell Emma such a lie seemed low even for them.

Randall crossed the room to the table that held a decanter of his favorite whiskey. With unsteady hands, he poured a good amount into a glass and took a long swallow, welcoming the burn at the back of his throat. It was imperative to gain control over his emotions if he were to view the situation with clarity. But faced with the child he'd all but abandoned over twenty years ago, the floodgates of guilt had opened, unearthing all the toxic emotions he'd thought long buried.

Especially the pain of Loretta's last words. *"Take care of our daughter, Randall. Make sure she knows how much I love her."*

Randall raked a hand over his jaw. "I'm sorry, Loretta," he whispered aloud, as though she could hear him. "Sorry I wasn't the man you believed me to be."

He sat down at his desk and dropped his head into his hands.

The vision of his beautiful daughter, with her dark hair and blue eyes so similar to his own, haunted him. Part of him longed to see her again, to spend time with her, get to know the woman she'd become. But his more practical side cringed at the scandal her arrival could mean for his political career at this crucial time in his campaign. He could only imagine the backlash if the press ever learned that the self-proclaimed family man had abandoned his infant daughter, fled the country, and left her behind.

What manner of cad would do such a thing?

Randall drained the rest of his glass with one gulp. He had absolutely no answer to that question. And until he could figure out a suitable reply, he'd have to avoid seeing his daughter again.

If only he could erase the memory of the hurt in her eyes as she'd walked out the door.

The houses along Forest Hill Road burst with the color of newly budding flowers, yet Corinne barely noticed them as she strode along the walkway. Normally the approaching summer put a lightness in her heart and a spring in her already jaunty step. But today, as she walked through her neighborhood, too many unwelcome thoughts burdened her mind, so that not even the beautiful weather could lift her spirits.

Ever since that mysterious woman had shown up at their

home claiming to be Papa's daughter, her father had not been himself. And Mama had taken to her room, barely speaking to anyone.

When Corinne had tried to question Papa about the woman, he'd put her off, saying he didn't wish to discuss the matter. Now almost twenty-four hours had passed, and Corinne would not be ignored any longer. She would demand to know what was going on. If not for her sake, then for Marianne's. Her little sister had latched on to the idea of another sibling faster than a pickpocket snatching a wallet. She'd even begun to spin all sorts of silly fantasies where they welcomed this foreigner into the heart of their family.

Corinne shuddered at the thought. The last thing she needed was another sibling, especially one as striking as Emmaline with her raven curls and mesmerizing eyes. After Marianne's illness and subsequent paralysis, Corinne had enough trouble overcoming feelings of being forgotten. Invisible. Though she understood the need to put her sister first, Corinne was looking forward to finally being the focus of her parents' attention at her upcoming high school graduation. She'd worked hard to achieve top marks in order to make her parents proud. She could already picture the joy on their faces as she received her diploma.

Mama was planning a party in her honor, and all the well-to-do families in the city would be invited. Plenty of eligible young men would attend, but truly only one man mattered to Corinne. She would let nothing ruin her chance to be the belle of the ball for once.

Maybe then Will Munroe would finally take notice of her.

With determination, Corinne turned onto the walkway that led up to her house, strode around to the rear door, and entered the kitchen. She didn't often come in this way, only when she was trying to avoid her parents. She hung her wrap on a peg by the door and scanned the room for the cook or any of the maids. Thankfully, the kitchen was empty, though the lingering scent of baked apples told her that Cook had already prepared tonight's dessert.

Corinne headed down the hall that led to her father's study. This time she would insist he answer her questions. After all, she wasn't a child any longer, having just passed her eighteenth birthday. And she would not be kept in the dark about a long-buried family secret. She deserved to know the truth.

They all did.

The door to the study was slightly ajar, and as Corinne approached, voices drifted into the hall.

"This is a most unfortunate turn of events, Randall. Right at a time when your popularity is at its peak." Grandfather Fenton's voice oozed displeasure. "This girl could ruin everything. Voters won't take kindly to a man who appears to have abandoned a child, no matter how long ago it was. I cannot stress enough the importance of keeping this information out of the press."

"Do you not think I know that?" Papa snapped. "That's why I've brought you both here. To help me strategize my next move."

Both? Who else was with them? Could it be . . . ?

"If I may, sir, perhaps we could let it be known that your *niece* is visiting from abroad. After all, isn't that how she first introduced herself to your housekeeper? That way the girl's presence would create no idle speculation."

Corinne's heart gave a flip. There was no mistaking that baritone.

Will Munroe had been working as her father's assistant at the university for more than two years now. In addition, he was one of Papa's best campaigners during his run for mayor. Will had always been polite whenever they came in contact, but lately Corinne dared hope that he'd begun to notice she was no longer a child. She smoothed a hand over her hair, wishing she'd taken time to freshen up after her walk.

"I agree," Grandfather said. "That might be the best approach."

"But can we be sure Emmaline will go along with the idea?" Will asked.

"I couldn't say, since I've only met her once for five minutes." Exasperation crackled in her father's voice.

"Perhaps you should pay her a visit," Grandfather said. "Make it clear in no uncertain terms what is expected of her."

"And if she doesn't agree?"

"Let's not worry about that just yet. If she's looking for money, that might be one way to keep her quiet."

Corinne put a hand to her mouth. Was that woman blackmailing Papa?

"Speculation is pointless. We won't know until I talk to her. I'll make arrangements to meet with her tomorrow."

At the sound of chairs scraping the floor, Corinne quickly tiptoed down the corridor and slipped into the parlor, where she picked up her embroidery and took a seat facing the hallway. When footsteps sounded minutes later, she looked up.

"Good evening, Miss Moore." Will stood in the open doorway, smiling at her. He looked very handsome in his dark jacket and linen shirt, with his chestnut hair sweeping his brow. "I hope you are faring well."

"Very well. And you?"

"Excellent as always, thank you."

"My father has you working late today. Don't tell me he's obsessing about the next election already." She gave a light laugh, but her hands trembled. Why did she always sound like a ninny when she tried to talk to Will?

His lips twitched. "With just cause. The campaign is already well underway. We need to plan our moves carefully if we wish to unseat Mayor Church." He hovered on the threshold, his green eyes studying her as though waiting for her to say something more.

Corinne set her needlepoint aside and rose. "Would you care to join me for some tea or coffee?" Her palms grew damp. Would he think her invitation too bold?

"That's most kind of you, but I must be getting home. My mother is expecting me."

"Of course. Forgive me."

The oldest of six children, Will had taken on the responsibility of providing for his family since his father's death five years ago, a sacrifice Corinne admired greatly. The fact that he was needed by his family had kept Will from going to war, which was an added benefit in Corinne's view, and likely in Mrs. Munroe's as well.

"There's nothing to forgive, Miss Moore."

"Please, you must call me Corinne." She took a few steps closer. Close enough to see the golden flecks in his green eyes.

"Very well, Corinne, thank you for the invitation. Perhaps another time." He smiled and gave a slight bow. "Good evening."

A sigh escaped her as Will disappeared down the hall. Would he ever feel comfortable enough in her presence to let his guard down? To speak the secrets of his heart that sometimes shone in the depths of his eyes? Or would he consider a friendship with her a betrayal of her father's trust?

Corinne waited until the front door closed before venturing back to her father's study. Papa must still be inside with Grandfather. Maybe if she confronted them both, one of them would tell her how Papa could possibly have a grown daughter they'd never heard of and why she had turned up here now.

With purpose, she approached the door and knocked. Immediately the murmur of voices stopped.

"Come in."

Corinne lifted her chin and entered. The comforting smell of her grandfather's pipe tobacco gave her courage. She looked from one man to the other. "May I speak with you both?"

"Corinne." Her father frowned. "It must be important for you to disturb our meeting."

She didn't miss the note of censure in his voice. "It is." She came forward and took a seat across from Papa's desk. "I want to know more about that woman who came here the other day. Is she your daughter, as she claims?" She held her father's gaze, aware that her grandfather had stiffened on his chair.

"The matter is no concern of yours, child," Grandfather said. "Your father will handle it."

"I beg to differ." Though quivering inside, she held her ground. "If this woman is related to me, I believe I have a right to know."

"I agree with Corinne." Mama appeared in the open doorway. "I think it's time for her to hear the whole story."

The coldness in her mother's voice sent chills up Corinne's spine. Mama could be a formidable woman when the necessity arose, and right now, her family's future appeared to be in jeopardy.

Papa sagged against the back of his chair. "Very well. Someone should get Marianne so I only have to repeat the story once."

"She's resting now. I'll fill her in later." Mama perched on the seat beside Corinne, while Grandfather hovered by the desk, his pipe clenched between his lips.

"Fine. Let's get this over with, shall we?" Papa glanced at Corinne. "I've already told your mother most of the details, and I don't relish reliving that part of my life again."

Grandfather set his pipe down. "I would actually like to hear the full story myself."

A vein in Papa's neck pulsed. At last, he nodded and cleared his throat. "Suffice it to say I was young and foolish and fancied myself in love with a girl whose parents did not approve of me."

"I still don't understand that part." Mama's brow furrowed. "You were from a good family. Studying law at Oxford. What more could they want?"

"I was Catholic—the wrong religion, according to her parents. And they didn't trust lawyers. Thought them all to be crooks. I had two big strikes against me."

"What happened next?" Corinne asked.

"I allowed myself to be swayed by my infatuation for Loretta, and though we were far too young, I gave in to her pleas and agreed to marry her. Soon we were expecting a child. But there were complications and Loretta died not long after giving birth to our daughter." A muscle twitched in Papa's jaw. "I had no means to raise the child on my own, so when Loretta's parents offered to take the baby, I felt it was in Emmaline's best interest."

"What about your mother?" Mama asked. "Couldn't she have helped you?"

Papa looked away. "My mother was not in good health herself. She couldn't take on the responsibility of an infant. Judith and Felix Bartlett were the best option."

Corinne frowned. "But I still don't understand why Emmaline thought you were dead."

Lines of displeasure formed around Papa's mouth. "It seems her grandparents thought it better that she believe I had died rather than tell her I'd moved to another country. I wrote several letters over the years, first to the Bartletts, then to Emmaline herself, but the only answer I ever received was a threatening note from Mrs. Bartlett."

"Did you ever go back to England to try and see the girl?" Mama asked.

"No. The Bartletts made it clear they wanted Emmaline to have no contact with me. I felt it better to leave well enough alone." Papa jerked to his feet and ran a hand over his jaw. "I never dreamed she would show up here out of the blue."

Grandfather folded his arms over his broad chest. "Do you think she's looking for money?"

"I doubt it, though the thought has crossed my mind."

"If she hasn't contacted you again, that seems an unlikely conclusion." Mama rose to pace the room.

"No matter. I've already decided to see Emmaline tomorrow and attempt to ascertain what she wants. I intend to impress upon her the necessity that her identity remain a secret."

Mama shook her head. "God help us all if she refuses to comply. It could be the ruin of everything you've worked so hard for."

"Let's not jump to the worst-case scenario, my dear. The least I can do is give her the benefit of the doubt. For now."

"I only hope your trust is not misplaced, Randall," Grandfather said. "I do not intend to let a youthful mistake on your part jeopardize the years it took to get you to this point in your career. Not when the mayor's seat is within our grasp."

Corinne straightened her spine. *And I don't intend to let another daughter usurp my rightful place in this family.*

Thankfully Corinne had her mother and her grandfather on her side. They seemed equally unhappy about this turn of events. And if they wanted Emmaline gone, Corinne had no doubt that the woman would soon be on a boat back to England.

Emmaline and her schemes would be no match for Harcourt Fenton and his daughter.

CHAPTER 5

Jonathan mopped the sweat from his brow with his handkerchief, then took a moment to survey the results of his labor. All the dead leaves and other debris from the winter sat in one large pile on the back lawn. The flower beds around the perimeter of the property now looked neat and tidy. He bent to scoop some of the leaves into a large bushel basket he'd found in the garage.

As soon as he finished here, he planned to find Emma and convince her to go on an outing with him. It had been two days since she'd confronted her father and all she'd done in the interim was mope around Mrs. Chamberlain's parlor on the off chance that Randall would call. Jonathan didn't have the heart to tell her that her father might not contact her and that Randall likely hoped she would give up and return to England.

A sentiment Jonathan had to admit he shared. But knowing Emma as he did, he doubted she was ready to quit just yet.

After he'd finished tidying the yard and had stored the tools in the shed, Jonathan changed into a clean shirt and pants and headed into the house. Thankfully, the women boarders had gotten used to seeing him working around the property, and Mrs. Chamberlain had given him permission to come into the parlor to visit with Emma.

As he entered the cozy room, he noted with relief that only

Emma and their landlady occupied the space. He wouldn't have to waste time making small talk with the other boarders. Not that most of them weren't perfectly nice women.

It was just that he only had eyes for one particular resident.

Mrs. Chamberlain looked up from her sewing as he came in. "There you are. I hope you're ready for a break, young man. You've been working hard all morning."

"As a matter of fact, I am. I came to ask Emma if she'd fancy a walk."

"A splendid idea," the landlady exclaimed. "The fresh air will do her a world of good."

Emma scowled and set aside the book she'd been reading. "But what if my . . . uncle calls while I'm out?"

She hadn't told their landlady the true nature of her relationship to Randall yet, saying she didn't feel at liberty to do so until she made a better connection with her father.

"Not to worry. I'll take a message and make sure he knows you're eager to hear from him." Mrs. Chamberlain rose from her chair and approached Jonathan. "But you must be parched after all that work. How about a glass of iced tea before you set out?"

"Thank you. I'd appreciate that."

A few minutes later, Mrs. Chamberlain returned with a tray and three glasses, which she set on the table in front of them. "So, tell me a little more about yourself, Jonathan," she said as she handed them their beverages. "You said you and Emma grew up together. Did you live with her family?"

Jonathan cast a quick glance at Emma, who still seemed out of sorts. "No. I lived next door with my Aunt Trudy."

His mind flashed back to the first day he'd met his eight-year-old neighbor. Jonathan had gone down to the river, consumed with grief and anger over the loss of his family and at being sent so far away from London to live with an aunt he barely knew. He'd been hurling stones into the water in a futile attempt to relieve his volatile emotions when an elfin girl with big blue eyes approached him.

"It's more fun to skip stones over the water than just throwing them that way," she'd announced.

Humiliated at being caught crying, Jonathan had scrubbed at his damp face and tried to ignore her. But she continued to stare at him curiously.

"You're the boy from next door. I'm Emma. My grandad owns the watch shop." She picked up some flat stones and skipped one out over the water.

Jonathan pretended not to be impressed by her skipping ability. Craving solitude, he moved farther down the bank.

She followed. "I'm sorry about your family," she said. "I'm an orphan too, so I know how you feel. It's lousy not having parents or brothers and sisters." She stared out over the water, pushing unruly strands of hair off her forehead.

Something about the matter-of-fact statement eased the tension in Jonathan's belly. They stood for several quiet moments, watching the ripples fan out over the surface. Then suddenly she jumped off the bank and waded knee-deep in the water, heedless of her now-wet clothing. With a shriek and a splash, she turned, holding her clasped hands high in the air. "Bet you never caught a frog with your bare hands before."

He thought she must be joking, but sure enough, a long greenish leg twitched between her dripping palms. When she climbed back onto the grass and handed him the bewildered amphibian, he couldn't help but laugh. Just like that, they'd become inseparable, and the river their favorite place to escape for some solitude.

"Jonathan and I had a lot in common." Emma's voice broke into his thoughts. "We were both orphans with no siblings. My grandmother and his Aunt Trudy were close, and our two families often had dinner together. It was inevitable that we'd become best friends." She turned to smile at Jonathan.

"How nice that you had each other for company." Mrs. Chamberlain set her glass down, a faraway look on her face. "I used to be close to my sister before I came to Canada."

"Did you grow up here or in England, Mrs. Chamberlain?" Jonathan asked. Judging by her faint accent, she'd lived in Canada for a long while now.

"Please, you must call me Mrs. C. All my boarders do." She smiled. "I came to Canada when my sister and I were still young. But ours was not a happy childhood. I won't ruin the day by talking of it now." With a determined set to her mouth, she rose from her seat and gathered the dishes. "Besides, you two must be getting on with your walk before the day is gone."

Clearly the conversation was over, and Jonathan was not one to pry.

"Where do you suggest we head, Mrs. C.?" He took Emma's hand and helped her up from the sofa.

"A walk along the water is always nice."

"Or . . ." Emma bit her bottom lip, her mind obviously spinning. "How about the university? I understand the grounds are lovely."

"Yes, indeed," Mrs. C. replied. "The buildings have beautiful courtyards with lots of shade trees. Your uncle works in one of those buildings, though I'm not sure which one."

Emma's face brightened. "That sounds perfect. Just let me get my hat and I'll be ready to go."

Jonathan held back a groan. He knew that expression. She had something up her sleeve for sure. But at least her mood had improved, and if that's what it took to make her smile, then he would gladly put up with her schemes. Besides, he wouldn't mind seeing the campus. From the way Reggie had described it during their conversations at the infirmary, it did sound lovely.

Not long after, with the directions to the university memorized, Jonathan escorted Emma down Jarvis Street. She looked every inch the lady in her light blue walking suit, with her matching hat perched at a jaunty angle atop her dark curls. He had to force himself not to stare.

She cast him a sideways glance as they walked. "All that talk of the past has made me a trifle homesick. Have you heard from Aunt Trudy? Any word on how her shop is doing?"

"I haven't heard anything yet, but I'm sure she'll write soon." He raised a brow. "Though you might be more likely to get a letter than me, since she knows you'll write back immediately."

Ever since Emma's grandmother passed away, Aunt Trudy had taken Emma under her wing. The two had always gotten on famously, a bond that only became stronger while Jonathan was away at war.

"Well, we all know how deplorable you are at writing letters," Emma said. "By the way, how are you faring in your cubbyhole above the garage? It sounds rather barbaric to me. Nothing more than a bed and a table from what I understand."

"It's comfortable enough. After sleeping in a foxhole, anything else seems like a palace by comparison." He forced a laugh to cover the underlying revulsion his comment evoked. The mere word *foxhole* conjured up the worst nights of his life—cold and wet, shivering in his damp boots and uniform, praying for the rise of the morning sun.

"Was it really so terrible there?" The sympathy in Emma's voice reminded him exactly why he never spoke of the war.

"It was. But it's not something you need concern yourself with."

"Of course I'm concerned. You haven't been the same since . . ." She left the rest of her thought unfinished.

Jonathan stiffened. There was no denying the war had changed him, but he thought he'd done a better job of hiding it. Apparently not. "All the more reason not to speak of it. Now, why don't you tell me what you're really up to on this outing?"

She scrunched her nose and looked ahead. "I'm not up to anything. I simply thought it would be nice to see where my father works."

"You're not going to barge in on him again, I hope."

She set her jaw and continued walking.

"Emma, you said you were going to give him time to adjust to the idea of a new daughter."

"I have. I just didn't specify how much time."

Jonathan released a slow breath, inwardly preparing for whatever might come next.

Knowing Emma, that could be anything.

Emma stepped through the high stone archway onto the path that traversed the university grounds. "Oh, this is so beautiful. You can almost smell the history here."

"Indeed." Jonathan squinted upward. "It's as picturesque as Reggie described."

Emma stopped to simply admire their surroundings and breathe in the clean air. Large elm and maple trees shaded the grassy area that flanked the path leading to the magnificent stone buildings. The stately architecture bore witness to the atmosphere of education and elegance, of pomp and circumstance. It was very reminiscent of some of the buildings she'd seen on a trip she'd taken to London with her grandparents.

"Speaking of your friend," she said. "Have you contacted Private Wentworth yet?"

Jonathan had told Emma about the wounded Canadian soldier he'd met during his stay in the military infirmary and how he hoped to get to see him while they were here. His friendship with the brave young man was one of the only things about his time abroad that Jonathan had actually shared with her.

"Not yet. I'll have to borrow Mrs. C.'s telephone and try his number. I don't even know for certain that he's still in Toronto."

"Didn't you say he hoped to study at the university here?"

"He did. In his last letter, though, he was still waiting to be accepted. And he was having a hard time adjusting to living back with his parents."

Emma plucked a leaf from a bush as they passed and twirled it through her fingers. "Wouldn't it be funny if he was one of my father's students?"

Jonathan smiled. "I know it's a small world, but I doubt it's that small."

Emma strolled by the large rectangular windows. She could just imagine her father standing in front of a classroom of eager students, mentoring them in the ways of the law and economics. A feeling of pride swelled in her chest. Her father was someone important, a man of learning who helped shape the minds of the next generation. A man who hoped to become mayor of the city, where he could benefit even more people. A truly noble man, just as she'd pictured him.

The air wisped by her, bringing with it the sweet scent of roses. Above her in the trees, a sparrow called out for its mate. Emma smiled. Coming out in the fresh air had been the perfect cure for her slight melancholy. And seeing the place where her father worked definitely had given her fresh hope. It wasn't the end of the world that he hadn't been overjoyed to see her. He just needed some time to process her arrival. With a renewed sense of purpose, Emma set aside her disappointment and focused instead on what she could do to form a bond between them.

"I wonder which building my father works in."

Jonathan glanced over at her. "I suppose that would depend on what subjects he teaches."

"Economics and law, I think, according to an article Mrs. C. showed me in the newspaper." Emma squinted to read the sign by one of the arched doorways. "The Faculty of Mathematics. How many buildings are there, do you suppose?"

They continued along the path, nodding to several people they passed, presumably students on their way to class. She assumed professors would stand out by the long robes they wore, much like their barristers back home.

"Emma, let's sit for a minute." Jonathan pointed to a bench under one of the trees.

Frowning, she slowed her steps and huffed out a sigh as she smoothed her skirt under her. Was he trying to distract her from finding the right place?

"I hope you don't mind, but I haven't been off my feet since early this morning."

Oh. How thoughtless could she be? She felt a stab of guilt at being concerned only with her own agenda. "There's no rush. We have most of the afternoon ahead of us."

They sat for a few moments in silence, soaking in the atmosphere around them. There was a soothing nature about this place, almost like being a world apart from everything else.

"Something's been bothering me, Em." Jonathan stared straight ahead. "I've been trying to understand why you're so obsessed with your father."

Stunned, she turned to face him. "How can you ask me such a thing?" As someone who'd also grown up without his parents, he must understand how important this was. Learning her father was alive had changed everything for her.

In the bright sunshine, his eyes appeared more the color of whiskey than chocolate. "I don't mean now," he said. "I'm talking about years ago. Ever since you were young, you were fixated on him. Wondering what he'd looked like. If he had dark hair like you. Even making up stories about him. Never your mother. Only him."

Emma stiffened against the hard bench, heat rushing to her cheeks. "I don't know why exactly. I had pictures of my mother, and my grandparents told me stories about her, but I knew nothing at all of my father." She shrugged, as memories flooded back of the stories she'd made up to comfort herself about her departed father. "When Gran told me he'd died of a broken heart over the loss of my mother, it sounded so romantic. A tragic tale, like Romeo and Juliet."

Jonathan nodded. "I can see that."

"I used to comfort myself with that idea. I'd daydream about his romance with my mother, about a love so great that going on without her was impossible. And that if he'd lived, he would have loved me that way too." Her voice quavered.

Jonathan took one of her hands in his. "Don't you think your expectations might be a little unrealistic?" he asked softly. "You don't really know anything about Randall. There's a good chance he might not live up to your storybook ideal."

She released a sigh. "I've thought about that. And I'm trying my best to keep an open mind." She looked up at him. "I've prayed hard every day since I found those letters, trying to reconcile my fantasy to the reality that maybe my father didn't love me—at least not enough to keep me." She drew in a shaky breath. "I only know I have to do everything I can to reach out to him. And I have to believe he'll come around eventually."

"I hope so, Em. I truly do. You deserve that type of man in your life." He raised her hand to his lips and smiled into her eyes.

Her heart fluttered strangely. She'd never shared her innermost thoughts of her father with anyone before, certain that her friends would make fun of her romantic views. But Jonathan had been nothing but caring and sympathetic. As always.

"Shall we continue our walk then?" he asked.

She wet her suddenly dry lips and nodded.

"There are a few more buildings over there." He helped her to her feet.

Grateful for his attempt to return the conversation to normal, she fell into step beside him and shook off the tension as they walked.

When they reached the next building, the sign out front read *The Faculty of Law*. Emma's pulse gave a nervous leap. For all her brave talk moments ago, she hesitated. Did she dare go in?

She glanced at Jonathan. "I suppose it couldn't hurt to walk through the halls," she said. "Just to see what it's like inside."

He pinned her with a stern look. "Only if you promise not to make a scene. You don't want to make matters worse."

She opened her mouth to protest that she'd never do such a thing, but then stopped. As usual, he had a point. "I'll be on my best behavior."

He studied her for a moment and then, seemingly satisfied with her sincerity, opened the heavy wooden door. "After you."

She entered the building and found herself in a wide corridor. The walls were lined with official portraits, likely of prominent men who had hallowed these halls. Would her father be honored this way one day? Certainly if he were ever elected mayor, he would.

They came to a staircase on the left that led upward, but Emma continued down the corridor until it opened into a reception area. A middle-aged woman sat at a plain wooden desk. The sign in front of her indicated that she was Mrs. Anderson, Receptionist for the Department of Economics.

She looked up as Emma approached. "Can I help you?" she asked.

For a split second, Emma considered her possible responses. "Good afternoon. I'm looking for Professor Moore's office."

"It's on the second floor." Mrs. Anderson scanned Emma from top to toe and frowned. "If you're here for the interview, you're much too early."

Emma blinked. "I'm afraid you're mistak—"

"Professor Moore clearly indicated he wouldn't be available until after his last class finishes at four o'clock." The woman's nostrils pinched.

Jonathan came up beside Emma and gave her elbow a slight squeeze. "We're not here for an interview," he told the woman with a smile. "We're visiting from England and thought we'd stop by to see where Professor Moore works." He waved a hand to indicate the vaulted ceiling and arched columns. "Such a prestigious institution. The architecture alone is simply breathtaking."

The woman's face brightened. "Why, thank you. And I'm sorry for assuming you were the candidate for the personal secretary position. Are you relatives of the professor?"

Emma's mind raced. She didn't want to make the same blunder as she had at her father's house. "We are related, yes, but he left England shortly after I was born."

"Ah, I see the family resemblance." Mrs. Anderson seemed ready to ask several more questions about their connection. Questions Emma did not relish answering.

She looked at the clock on the wall. "I'm afraid we can't wait until he returns. We'll have to come back another time."

The woman slowly stood. "I'm sorry, I didn't catch your names."

"Forgive our lack of manners." Jonathan stepped forward, his hand outstretched. "I'm Jonathan Rowe, and this is Emma."

She shook his hand and then Emma's. "A pleasure to meet you. I'll be sure to tell the professor you came by."

"Thank you, ma'am." A feeling of dread rolled in Emma's stomach. She should never have come in here. Now her father would think she was trying to cause problems at his workplace.

"If you're still here in July, you must attend the rally." Mrs. Anderson lifted a piece of paper off her desk and handed it to Jonathan. "Professor Moore is already campaigning for the next election." She chuckled. "He's determined to become mayor one day."

Emma's thoughts spun. What a perfect way to see her father in action and maybe get a chance to talk to him again. If he hadn't contacted her before then, she would definitely be in attendance. Perhaps there would be other public events she could go to as well.

"Thank you," Jonathan said. "We'll keep it in mind." He tipped his hat, and with a hand to Emma's back, ushered her firmly down the hall.

Once they were outside, Emma let out a sigh of disappointment. "So much for seeing my father."

"You're lucky Randall wasn't there. He wouldn't take well to being put in an awkward position at his workplace."

"I suppose you're right." Emma turned onto the walkway. "Can I see that flyer?"

Rather reluctantly it seemed, he pulled it out of his pocket and handed it to her. She unfolded it and scanned the information.

"'The Great Debate. Friday, July 25th. 7 p.m. Come out and hear our own Professor Moore debate the Mayor of Toronto, His Worship Tommy Church. Freewill donations to the university and campaign contributions gratefully accepted.'"

Jonathan shook his head. "I know what you're thinking, and it's not a good idea."

"Why not? It's open to the public. Anyone can attend."

"Emma, if you insist on hounding the man, you could alienate him altogether. Besides, July is a long way off. Who knows where we'll be by then?"

It sounded like he was ready to hop on the next boat home, but Emma wasn't about to get into an argument over that.

She looked up at him and smiled sweetly. "You're right. It is a long way off. No sense worrying about that now." Carefully, she folded the flyer and tucked it in her handbag for safekeeping.

Because whether Jonathan liked it or not, she *would* be going to that debate.

CHAPTER 6

Jonathan gazed down into Emma's blue eyes. He could tell by her quick capitulation that she was only backing off to appease him. Yet there was no sense arguing over a future event they might not even be here to attend.

"Don't worry," he said. "I'm sure you'll see your father again before that."

"I hope so, but at least I have an alternate plan if need be." She fell in step with him as they continued across the grounds. "You will come with me, won't you?" She asked him with a feigned air of innocence as though she hadn't already made up her mind.

He sighed. "If we're here, then yes. And just to be clear, if we do go, we'll stay in the background and remain anonymous." As anonymous as a vivacious woman like Emma could be. Maybe he could drape her in sackcloth and tie her hair back in a kerchief. He almost laughed out loud at the thought. Emma would never consider a disguise, especially not one like that. "No causing a public spectacle. Agreed?"

"Agreed," she said meekly.

Jonathan raised one brow. He knew that tone. It was the one she used to mollify him until she got her own way. He'd never met anyone quite as stubborn or determined as Emma.

Which was one of the reasons, he was sure, that Felix Bartlett had never told her about Randall Moore. He knew Emma would set out on the first ship to Canada—alone, if need be.

Jonathan pushed back the rush of sadness that surfaced every time he thought of Felix. The man had been more than a neighbor. He'd become a mentor and surrogate grandparent to him. Just like Aunt Trudy had been for Emma after her grandmother died.

Jonathan still had a hard time believing Emma had sold the watch shop so quickly after Felix's death. He never thought she would part with it, but that was before she'd discovered her father's letters. Before she'd let Felix's perceived betrayal overshadow his years of devotion and before she'd allowed her misguided obsession with Randall Moore to overtake her good sense.

He glanced over at Emma as they walked.

Perhaps now was the right time for his news. Especially in light of this future rally she seemed determined to attend.

He pointed to a diner across the road. "How about a soda before we start the walk back?"

"Sounds lovely. I'm parched."

Five minutes later, they were seated side by side at the counter in the small restaurant, two cold glasses of cola in front of them. The hum of conversation around them competed with the clatter of cutlery and dishes.

"Delicious." Emma released the straw and smacked her lips with a giggle, then stared at him. "You're awfully serious all of a sudden."

He waited a beat, then looked her in the eye. "There's something I've been wanting to talk to you about, but I've been waiting for the right time."

Her face scrunched in that adorable way that made her nose crinkle. "What is it? Nothing's wrong, I hope."

"No. It's good news actually." He set his glass aside. "Right before we left England, I received word that I passed the entrance exams, and that"—he paused—"Oxford has accepted my application."

Just saying it out loud caused a thrill to shoot through his system. If anyone would understand how much this meant to him, it was Emma. He'd rarely talked to her about his family, a subject too painful to relive, but when he did, it was usually about the bookstore his father owned and his passion for education. His dad had always wanted to go to Oxford, but circumstances in his life had prevented it. Jonathan had vowed after the fire that he would one day fulfill his father's dreams. A dream that was now within his grasp.

Emma squealed, throwing her arms around his neck. "Oh, Jonathan. That's wonderful. I know how much you wanted this."

Though conscious of the other patrons' stares, Jonathan wrapped an arm around her waist, holding her against him for a moment longer.

Too soon, she pulled away, smiling widely. "When do you start?"

"Classes begin mid-August. I'm taking general sciences in the hope of getting into medical school one day."

Her mouth fell open. "I thought you wanted to study business. When did you decide on medicine?"

He paused to let his emotions settle before he answered. "After experiencing the carnage of war, I want to do something to help my fellow man." He still struggled with the violence he'd been part of, the lives he'd taken in order to save himself or a comrade. Nobody really won in a war, he'd learned. It ate at your soul long after the gunfire had faded.

"That's very noble," Emma said softly. "I'm so proud of you."

The light of admiration in her eyes scrambled his pulse, so

much so that he almost forgot why he'd told her his news in the first place.

"The thing is," he continued, "I need to be back before the school term starts, which means we have to leave by the end of July. The beginning of August at the very latest."

"Oh." Her smile suddenly dimmed.

Was it fair of him to ask her to cut her time in Toronto short? When they planned the trip, it had been understood they would stay the entire summer, but that was before he'd received his notice from Oxford. And again, if she'd known, she never would have agreed to him coming.

He pushed back his rising guilt and reached for her hand. "Emma, I think you should prepare for the possibility that your father may not come around . . . and that you might have to return home without the resolution you'd hoped for."

Her gaze slid from his, her mouth pressed into a tight line.

A cold feeling invaded his chest. "Emma? What is it?"

She closed her eyes for a moment, then released a breath and opened them again. The determined glint shining there did nothing to ease Jonathan's anxiety.

"I'm not going back with you," she said.

His lungs froze, momentarily trapping the air inside. "What did you say?"

"I'm staying here." She tilted her chin defiantly. "There's nothing left for me in England now that Grandad's gone. I need time to establish a relationship with my father and my sisters, and the only way I can do that is to build a life here."

Nothing left for me in England. Is that what she truly believed?

"What about me? Or don't I count for anything?" Jonathan clenched his jaw shut before he said too much. Before she saw that her words had shattered him. Ripped the proverbial rug out from under him.

Her features softened. "Of course, *you'd* still be there, but

I'm talking about blood relatives. All my family is here now. You understand why I have to stay, don't you?"

There was no way to answer that question truthfully, so he remained silent.

"Besides," she said quietly, "I can't afford to depend on you for my well-being. I learned that lesson the hard way when you went off to war." Her eyes changed from sorrowful to determined, and in that moment, he realized the toll the war had taken on her. It wasn't just Danny's death that had affected her. It was far more complicated than that.

Still, his mind reeled with hundreds of arguments to make her reconsider. "What will you do here? How will you make a living? The money from Felix's shop won't last forever, you know."

"I haven't figured out all the details, but I'm sure I'll be able to find work somewhere." She gave him a long look. "I won't change my mind, Jonathan. And before you say it, this is not one of my impulsive decisions. I've given it a lot of thought."

As the full enormity of her announcement hit him, hurt turned to raw anger. "You planned to stay all along, didn't you? And you never bothered to mention it. You just let me tag along like a faithful puppy."

"I'm sorry." A mixture of emotions flashed over her features. "I knew you wouldn't approve. That you'd try to talk me out of it."

All his plans to woo Emma—to one day hear her declare her love for him—evaporated quicker than the morning fog over an English moor. What a fool he'd been to ever think she might one day return his feelings, when all along she planned to put an ocean between them—forever. If she cared for him at all, she could never have considered such a thing.

"I guess there's no point in that, is there? Your mind is obviously made up." He jerked to his feet, dug in his jacket pocket for some bills, and left them on the counter. "We'd best head back to the boardinghouse. Wouldn't want to be late for dinner." He jammed on his cap as he strode out the door onto the sidewalk. Quick footsteps followed him.

"Jonathan, don't be angry. Please." She reached for his hand, but he stepped out of her grasp.

Her gut-wrenching plea struck hard at his aching heart. He wanted to tell her it was all right, that he understood her need to reach out to her family, but the lie stuck in his throat, refusing to be voiced.

Instead, he kept walking, unable to bear her distress, yet equally unable to soothe her. For if he took her in his arms to comfort her, he would no longer be able to conceal his true feelings.

And his pride had suffered enough damage for one day.

CHAPTER 7

Later, after the evening meal, Emma trudged up the stairs to her room, unable to shake the melancholy that dogged her. She'd hurt Jonathan with her careless words, and that was the last thing she wanted to do. He'd always been her staunchest friend, her most loyal ally, sticking by her through thick and thin.

Even when she'd started dating Danny, Jonathan's good friend from school, he never allowed that to change their friendship. The closest they'd ever come to a falling-out was the day Jonathan had enlisted in the war. She still shuddered every time she remembered the terrible scene she'd caused in front of Aunt Trudy and Grandad. The truth was, she'd been more upset that day than when Danny told her he'd signed up. But after all, she and Jonathan had been best friends since she was eight and he was ten. She'd only gotten close to Danny in the six months prior to the start of the war. Naturally her bond with Jonathan was stronger.

In reality, she could live without Danny, but not without Jonathan. He was her anchor, her rock, the steadying force in her life. When he left, she didn't know how she'd cope without him.

But she *had* coped. For four long years. Little by little, she'd created a shield around her heart to protect her from ever depending on someone to such an extent again. If the war had changed Jonathan, it had changed her too. When he'd enlisted, she'd felt abandoned. Now she was planning to do the same to him. She could only imagine what he was feeling after dropping everything to travel to Canada with her. And how much he'd suffered during the voyage over. She bit her lip, realizing he'd have to face the return trip alone. What kind of terrible person was she that she hadn't even thought of that eventuality? She wouldn't blame him if he booked a ticket on the next train back to Halifax.

What would she do then?

Her emotions swirled together into a toxic mix. She dropped onto the window seat in her room and stared bleakly out at the street below, trying unsuccessfully to erase the memory of Jonathan's wounded expression. The only other time she'd seen that stark look was when he'd arrived home at the end of the war. The initial joy of their reunion had been one of the happiest moments of her life.

But then she'd had to tell Jonathan of her new relationship with Lord Terrence. Jonathan had quickly masked his features, but not before she'd glimpsed the devastation on his face. Why would he be so pained by her possible engagement? Was it because he thought her disloyal to Danny, even though it had been almost a year since his death?

A light knock sounded on her door.

Her heart gave a leap. Perhaps Jonathan had come to tell her he forgave her and that he understood why she had to stay.

"Emma?" Mrs. Chamberlain's voice came through the door. "Someone's here to see you."

Emma crossed the room and opened the door. "Is it Jonathan?"

The woman's eyes were round behind her glasses. "No. It's Professor Moore."

All thoughts of Jonathan skittered away like dry leaves in the wind. Emma's heart thumped a wild rhythm in her chest. Her father had reached out to her at last. "Tell him I'll be right down. Oh, and might we have a pot of tea, if it's not too much trouble?"

"The kettle's already on the stove." Her landlady winked. "I'll have him wait in the front room for you."

As soon as Mrs. C. left, Emma quickly changed into one of her favorite dresses, one she'd kept despite her new purchases. It was a striped navy-blue linen with white trim. Grandad always said it made her eyes look even bluer. Then she dabbed a bit of toilet water at her wrists and smoothed her hair into place. With a final look in the mirror, she made her way down the main staircase.

Her heart hammered hard against her ribs as she neared the parlor, and she paused to whisper a prayer. *Please, Lord, let my father be more receptive to me today. Help me make him understand that I only want a chance to get to know him. That I don't mean him any harm.*

Pasting on a bright smile, she entered the room. Randall stood by the fireplace, staring at the framed painting on the wall above it. Emma knew it was Mrs. C.'s favorite piece, a depiction of the English town where she'd lived as a child.

"Twenty years later and I still miss the greenery," Randall said without turning. "That fresh smell of the meadows after a cool rain. The hint of smoke in the air from the chimneys. There's nothing here that compares to that."

Emma slowly crossed the room. "It's a slice of heaven, to be sure." She clasped her hands together and waited until he turned around.

He was dressed in a suit with a starched shirt and tie, as though he were going to the opera for the evening.

"Won't you have a seat?" Sudden nerves swamped her, making her hands tremble. She gestured to the sofa. The tea cart stood beside it, laden with a silver teapot and a plate of ginger snaps.

Did her father even like ginger snaps?

"Just a moment." He crossed to the pocket doors and pulled them closed.

Emma had never seen them shut since she'd moved in. Mrs. C. always wanted everyone to feel welcome to share the area.

"I hope you don't mind, but I need to ensure this conversation is not overheard."

His serious demeanor did not inspire much optimism. She perched on the edge of the sofa and lifted the teapot. "Do you take milk and sugar?"

"Milk, please. Just a splash." Randall took a seat in the wing chair across from her.

Emma forced her hand to remain steady as she handed him the cup. "I'm glad you came," she said. "I hope this means you've had time to get used to my being here."

"Not entirely." He studied her. "I'd like to know more about what prompted you to come."

She blinked. "I thought I explained that. I wanted to get to know you, of course." When he continued watching her with an expectant air, she set her cup down, searching for the right words, ones that wouldn't sound accusatory or put him on the defensive. "As you know, my grandparents raised me. After my grandmother passed away, it was just me and Grandad—until this past April, when he had a heart attack." She swallowed hard to keep her emotions at bay. It still seemed impossible that her hale and hearty grandfather was gone.

"I'd always believed that Gran and Grandad were my only family, until I was cleaning out our flat above the shop and found a box of letters. Letters from you." She met his eyes, hoping for some sort of acknowledgement, but he revealed no emotion. "You can imagine my shock to find out that you'd been alive all along and that they'd lied to me my whole life."

"That must have been quite distressing."

"More than distressing. I was devastated. Knowing my grandparents as I did, I could only assume they'd done it to protect me. But protect me from what?"

Randall took a quick sip of tea, avoiding her eyes, then set his cup down with a sigh. "Ask the questions you want. I'll do my best to answer them." He crossed one leg over his knee.

She licked her dry lips, struggling to know where to begin. "Why didn't you . . ." she almost said *keep me* but that made her sound like a stray puppy that no one wanted. "Why didn't you raise me after my mother died?"

He closed his eyes briefly. "It wasn't that simple. I was in my last year of law school. I had no means of providing for you at that time and would have had to hire a nursemaid." He paused. "Your grandparents offered to take you in, claiming it would be better for you. Though it pained me to do so, I knew they were right."

She braced herself for her next question, one that had the potential to wound her all over again. "But how could you move halfway around the world? If you'd stayed, we would have been able to have some sort of relationship at least. I wouldn't have grown up believing I was an orphan." She swallowed hard and gripped her hands together, mentally berating herself for appearing so needy.

Randall pushed up from his seat and stalked to the fireplace. "I don't know if I can make you understand how difficult it was for me at that time. Trying to cope with your mother's death. Dealing with your grandparents' resentment." A muscle jumped in his jaw.

Resentment? For what? Did they somehow blame Randall for her mother's death?

"I know they didn't approve of my mother marrying you." Emma frowned as a new thought formed. "Did they try to keep you from seeing me?"

Randall turned to pin her with a frank stare. "What do you think?"

As much as she wanted to defend her beloved grands, Emma could very well believe they had tried to keep Randall away from her. "Is that why you left England then?"

"In part." He shrugged, his brow tense. "When the opportunity arose for a fresh start in Canada, I jumped at the chance to put some distance between me and my past, thinking I'd finally be free of the guilt and pain."

"And were you?"

He fingered the cuff of his sleeve. "To some degree, yes. I threw myself into my work here at the university. Then I met Vera, and for the first time since your mother's death, I felt whole again."

Emma tried to ignore the pinch of pain around her heart. That he could so easily leave her behind and start a new family. If he truly loved her, shouldn't he have fought harder to be part of her life?

"Once you were old enough, I started writing to you, but when you didn't answer, I assumed you wanted nothing to do with me."

"I never knew," she whispered. "Not until I found your letters."

A minute of silence lapsed between them.

Then finally Randall said, "If it's any consolation, your grandparents must have believed you'd be better off thinking I was dead. That way, you'd never pine for me. Never wonder why your father didn't come to visit. In a sense, it was the kinder option."

Emma stared at the man for several seconds. "It's nice of you to defend them. However, I think fear was the greater motivation. They knew I'd want to look for you if I found out you were alive. Which meant I would leave them."

Randall moved from the fireplace and came to sit across from her. "Reliving the past won't get us anywhere. What I'd like to know is how you wish to proceed from here."

Emma twisted her hands together on her lap. She tried not to dwell on the fact that he showed almost no emotion. That he seemed to be treating this conversation as more of a business deal than anything personal. "I hoped we could get to know one another—as father and daughter. After all, you're the only family I have left." She met his gaze, holding her breath and praying not to be rejected again.

His steady look gave nothing away. "I'd like that as well," he said at last.

Emma's shoulders sagged with relief. He did want to include her in his life. Knowing that made everything she'd sacrificed to come here worthwhile.

"There are, however," he continued, "a few obstacles we must consider. First, my wife and daughters may take some time to accept you. It's not entirely their fault, since I should have told them about you long ago."

"Yes, you should have." Emma bit her lip. "Sorry. Go on."

"Second, there's the matter of my political career. Revealing your existence at this crucial time would only create undue problems—for me and for all the people who are helping me get elected."

Emma swallowed. "So you want to keep me a secret." Why did that hurt almost as much as an outright rejection?

"For now, yes. I thought we could use your idea and introduce you as my niece who's visiting for the summer."

"But doesn't everyone know you have no siblings?"

Randall's eyes narrowed. "How did *you* know that?"

She froze. Perhaps she could lie and say she'd looked up his records back home, but she wasn't very good at lying. She released a slow breath. "I went to see your mother."

Randall shot off his chair. "How do you know her?"

He acted like she'd committed some sort of crime. It was only natural she'd be curious about her grandmother.

"In that same box of letters, I found one from your mother, begging Gran to let her see me. I assume Gran refused."

Randall closed his eyes. When he opened them, deep grooves were etched around his mouth.

"Before I left," she continued, "I went to the address on the letter and found out she still lived there."

Randall grasped the back of an armchair. "She's alive?"

Emma licked her dry lips, not prepared for this conversation so soon. She thought she'd have time to work up to it once she got to know her father better.

"She was at the time," she said carefully. "However, the woman who was caring for her said she didn't have much longer to live." Emma paused, unsure how he would take the next part. "I got word of her passing just before we left England. I'm only glad I got to meet her before it was too late."

Randall's shoulders sagged, and an almost blank expression settled on his face. "No one informed me, but then I guess that was to be expected."

"She told me you two had a falling-out and hadn't spoken in years."

"That's one way to put it." Red blotches appeared on his cheeks.

"When she learned I intended to come to Canada to find you, she asked me to tell you she's sorry and that she forgives you." There, she'd done her duty and delivered Grandmother Moore's final message.

But instead of the relief she expected at this olive branch after so many years, Randall's mouth tightened into a grim line and his eyes darted around the room like a cornered animal seeking an escape. "I'm sorry. I have to go." He crossed to the parlor doors and pulled them open.

"Wait." Emma rushed after him. "Doesn't her apology mean anything to you?"

Anger leapt in the blueness of his eyes. "Our estrangement

was my mother's choice. She was the one who disowned me. It's a little late to grant me absolution now." He rammed his hat on his head. "We'll talk again soon. In the meantime, remember you're my niece. If anyone starts asking too many questions, just avoid answering them."

With that, he strode out of the house and down the walkway, leaving Emma more bewildered than ever about her mystifying father.

And no further ahead as to where she stood with him.

CHAPTER 8

Jonathan got out of the taxi, paid the driver, and stared at the small house before him. A modest abode, to be sure. And a far cry from the opulence of Randall Moore's mansion. According to Reggie, his parents had lived here for many years. His father had made a living as a butcher, peddling his goods in a place called Kensington Market. Reggie had promised to take him there if Jonathan ever came to visit.

Now, he paused on the sidewalk, praying for the right words to say to his friend. Praying that here, without the unifying factor of the war, their friendship would still be strong. Even though he and Reggie had served in different regiments, their similar experiences had drawn them together. And during the weeks of their recovery, the two had shared their hopes and dreams for the future.

Jonathan had told Reggie things he'd never told anyone. His guilt over not being able to save Danny. His phobia that stemmed from being the only survivor of the fire that had killed his family. And maybe most importantly, Jonathan had told Reggie of his true feelings for Emma.

The front screen door swung open and a man emerged, swinging a crutch out in front of him. Jonathan forced back a grimace at the flapping pant leg on Reggie's right side. Somehow, when he'd been in a hospital bed, it had been easy to ignore the lack of a limb, but now faced with the stark evidence, Jonathan could no longer hide from reality.

"Don't just stand there. Get up here and save me having to navigate the stairs." Reggie's booming voice brimmed with enthusiasm and laughter.

How could he joke about his handicap like that?

Jonathan jogged up the walkway and onto the porch. "Reggie, mate. It's great to see you again."

Reggie didn't answer but simply dropped a crutch and grabbed Jonathan in a one-armed hug.

Jonathan swallowed back the rise of emotion at the simple show of affection. When he moved back, Reggie's hazel eyes appeared as damp as Jonathan's.

"Look at you. You're practically a Romeo with all those waves." Reggie swiped a hand over Jonathan's head to muss his carefully combed hair.

Jonathan laughed, the tightness in his chest loosening. "And I see you've chosen to keep your army haircut."

"Old habits die hard." Reggie grinned and dragged his free hand over the short locks. "Besides, the ladies love the military look."

Jonathan shook his head, still laughing.

"Come and have a seat. Mom left us some lemonade before she went out." Reggie moved along the covered porch to two sturdy-looking wooden chairs. A pitcher of lemonade, two glasses, and a plate of cookies sat on the table between them.

"How are you getting on?" Jonathan asked as he took a seat beside his friend. "Is it any easier being back home?"

"A bit better. Still a little suffocating at times." He pointed to his missing leg. "Mom tends to hover and try to do everything for me, whereas Dad just tries to ignore it. I'll get my own place one day soon, but for now, this is best. For everyone." A shadow passed over his face, but he quickly smiled. "How about you? What brings you to this side of the world?"

Jonathan shrugged. "Emmaline. She came to meet her father. I couldn't let her travel all that way alone."

Reggie turned to pin Jonathan with a frank stare. "Have you finally told her how you feel about her?"

Tension snapped in Jonathan's neck. "No."

A beat of silence followed.

"What's holding you back, Jon? You said that was the first thing you were going to do when you got home."

Jonathan pressed his lips together. "It didn't go quite as planned."

"In other words, you chickened out." Reggie lifted the pitcher and poured them each a glass of lemonade.

Jonathan winced. He'd forgotten how blunt his Canadian friend could be. "I didn't think it appropriate since she was considering a marriage proposal from some rich bloke."

"Oh no. That's rough." He set the pitcher down with a thump. "Why didn't her fiancé come with her to Canada, then?"

Jonathan sipped the lemonade. The tartness burned the back of his throat. "Emma ended their relationship right before she left. I didn't really understand why at the time, but I do now."

"What do you mean?"

"Emma has no intention of returning to England. Never did. She admitted it only yesterday." His gut twisted. Would he ever get over the hurt of that revelation?

"You mean she let you come with her and then dropped that tidbit once you were here? That's pretty low."

It *was* a trifle selfish, Jonathan had to admit. But Emma never was one for thinking anything through. Had she hoped he'd stay in Canada with her? She hadn't known about his acceptance to Oxford when they'd embarked on this adventure. Maybe she thought she could convince him to stay too.

"So now what?" Reggie drained his lemonade in one long gulp.

Jonathan heaved a sigh. "I have no idea." He patted his jacket pocket. "Right before I left, I received my acceptance to Oxford. I have to be back by early August."

"That's great news." Reggie's smile dimmed. "But it only gives you about six weeks before you have to leave." He studied Jonathan. "If I know you, you won't give up. You'll stay until the bitter end, in case she changes her mind."

"I have no choice. As long as there's a shred of hope, I have to try." A breeze ruffled Jonathan's hair. Reggie's porch was indeed a pleasant place to sit. You could see all the activity in the neighborhood from here.

Reggie stared out across the street. "I suppose I'd do the same. If I had any hope at all."

The bitterness in Reggie's voice snapped Jonathan out of his own melancholy. "What do you mean? I thought Elsie was waiting with bated breath for your return."

Jonathan had actually been jealous of Reggie. The love that flowed from the letters his fiancée had sent, at least the snippets Reggie had read aloud to Jonathan, had made him burn with envy, wishing for such words of devotion from Emma.

Emma's letters had been wonderful, regaling him with the happenings in their town and stories of her grandad and Aunt Trudy. And of course, she said she missed him. But not like Elsie had missed Reg.

"She decided she couldn't marry a man with one leg." Reggie pressed his lips together. "Can't say I really blame her."

"Are you joking?" Jonathan jerked up from his chair. "What kind of woman abandons the man she loves when he's injured?" He banged a fist on the railing, outrage for his friend evoking an almost violent reaction within him. How could she be so fickle? Either you loved someone or you didn't.

He drew in a shuddering breath, recalling his stunned reaction when he'd arrived home to Emma's announcement that she was considering marriage to a man named Lord Terrence. Danny had barely been gone a year and she'd already taken up with someone new. Were all women so disloyal? Jonathan clutched the wooden rail until his forearms burned.

"Hey, no need to dismantle the porch." Reggie's voice held a trace of humor. "I appreciate your anger on my behalf, but I've made my peace with the whole situation."

Jonathan turned to stare at him. "You just gave up?"

"You can't force someone to feel something they don't." He shrugged. "Turns out Elsie wasn't the right girl for me after all. I have to believe God has someone else in mind. Someone who's better suited." He gave a lopsided grin. "One who can put up with my quirky sense of humor. I realized soon after I returned that Elsie's really lacking in that department. And I couldn't spend my life with a woman who wasn't able to appreciate the lighter side of life."

Jonathan's lips twitched. "You always said: 'If you can't laugh at what life hurls at you, you might as well quit.' Your humor was one of the things I truly admired about you those first days in the infirmary."

Reggie laughed. "Face it, Rowe, I saved your sanity in that place."

"You did indeed, my friend." He smiled sadly. "So, what are you going to do now?"

Reggie's countenance brightened. "I'm taking a few summer courses at the university. And come the fall, I'll be enrolled full-time."

"That's wonderful news. I know you were hoping for that."

"Even better, the army's going to cover my tuition."

"Smashing."

Reggie laughed out loud. "I've missed those crazy British

sayings of yours. Hey, while you're here, why don't you sit in on a few classes with me?"

"Is that allowed?"

"Sure. Besides, no one's going to question a war veteran with one leg. And who knows, you might meet a girl. If that doesn't make Emma take notice, nothing will."

Jonathan shook his head. "You're incorrigible. But I might take you up on the classes. It would be interesting to hear lectures for comparison to Oxford when I go home. What courses are you taking?"

"History and English Literature."

"Not as exciting as science, but I'll try to stay awake."

Jonathan grinned as Reggie bellowed out his signature laugh.

One thing was certain, he'd made the right decision in coming here today. Though Reggie had every right to be depressed, his friend's optimistic nature had fueled Jonathan's own sense of hope for the future.

If Reggie could accept the loss of his leg and of Elsie and still trust his future to God, how could Jonathan do any less?

Later that afternoon, Jonathan's good mood vanished when Mrs. C. told him Emma had left without saying where she was headed and that she'd been gone for hours. The fact that Emma hadn't mentioned anything when Jonathan had seen her for a brief moment after breakfast made his head pound.

She must still be annoyed with him for the way he'd reacted to her news that she intended to stay in Canada. In truth, he had behaved badly. He'd been avoiding Emma, nursing his wounded pride. Waiting for her to come and apologize for deceiving him, for allowing him to travel halfway across the world under false pretenses.

Now, she was off heaven knew where by herself. Was it even safe for a young woman to walk alone in this city?

He paced the walkway in front of the boardinghouse, his anxiety mounting with each moment that passed. At least he was fairly certain she'd gone to see Randall Moore, and if so, she'd be safe there. When Mrs. C. informed him that the professor had paid Emma a visit, Jonathan didn't know how to feel. Happy for Emma or upset that she hadn't told him about it?

Was she already distancing herself from him, knowing he would soon return to England without her?

His chest constricted at the mere thought of never seeing her again. Never hearing her lilting laugh or feeling the warmth of her hug.

One thing had become very clear to him after his talk with Reggie. He needed to forget about his pride and put all his energy into wooing Emma. He couldn't give up without a fight. Not until he was on the ship headed back to England alone.

Now, if only she'd come back from wherever she went, they could clear the air between them.

The sound of an approaching vehicle pulled Jonathan from his tortured thoughts. A taxicab stopped at the curb in front of the boardinghouse and Emma alighted, several bags in hand.

Instant relief flooded his chest.

When she looked up and saw him, her entire face brightened. "Jonathan! You'll never guess what's happened."

His tense muscles relaxed. Trust Emma to completely overlook their disagreement. But right now he didn't care. He was too happy just to see her.

"Something good, I take it." He came down the walkway to meet her.

"Something wonderful." She flung herself into his arms, bags and all, and hugged him.

For a moment, Jonathan went still and simply breathed in the floral scent of her favorite perfume. How he wished he could hold her like that forever.

Too soon, she pulled back and laughed. "You are looking at Professor Moore's new personal secretary. I start tomorrow."

"What? How did that happen?"

"Let's go for a walk, and I'll tell you all about it." She set her bags on the porch, then returned to hook her arm though his, a smile creasing her face.

At that moment, she could have led him off the cliffs of Dover and he'd have cheerfully followed. "How did you talk your way into this one?"

She tilted her head, the feather from her hat almost tickling his chin. "My father came to see me yesterday. For the most part, the visit went well. Although he wants me to pretend to be his niece in order to protect his political reputation."

Jonathan frowned. "I don't like it, Em." It was bad enough that Moore had rejected her as an infant. Now he wanted to pass Emma off as his niece?

"I'm not wild about it either, but don't worry, I plan to wear him down. Sooner or later, once he realizes I'm here to stay, he'll have no choice but to acknowledge me as his daughter."

Barbs of pain spread through Jonathan's body. How he wished she weren't so set on staying in this country. "So, after your talk, he offered you a job?"

"Not right away. I came up with the idea this morning. What better way to be close to my father and learn about his career than to work with him?"

They turned a corner onto the next block.

"Let me guess. You went over unannounced?"

"I did." She seemed completely unapologetic about it. "And when I told him my idea, he thought about it for a few minutes and then questioned me about my qualifications."

He glanced over at her as he guided her around a large crack in the sidewalk. "You have no experience as a secretary." Surely, she hadn't fibbed about that.

"No, but Randall placed great value on my work as Grandad's bookkeeper. He said it gave me the skills necessary to work in an office. Once I told him I'd take some secretarial courses, he agreed to give me a try."

"Why would he do that? Wouldn't he want someone more experienced?" A niggle of suspicion wound through Jonathan's chest. It didn't make sense for the man to hire someone without the proper credentials. Was it his way of controlling Emma's actions?

"Why, to get closer to me, silly." She laughed again. "And if it doesn't suit either of us, we've agreed to let the other know."

"I suppose it makes sense when you look at it that way." Jonathan shook his head, still not completely convinced. "Randall's attitude must have changed quite a bit since our first meeting."

She grinned, her eyes lighting up. "I think he's coming around to the idea of another daughter. And that's not all. He's invited us both for dinner tonight with his family. Isn't that wonderful? I'll get to spend more time with my sisters."

The excitement on her face worried Jonathan. Emma gave away her heart so freely. He feared she was doomed to have it crushed again tonight.

"I'm glad you're so enthused, Em. But you should prepare for your stepmother and your sisters to be less accepting. It could be somewhat tense at the dinner table."

"There you go again with your gloomy predictions. I, on the other hand, choose to believe that my charming personality will win them over before dessert is served."

When she looked up at him and winked, it took all his will-power not to kiss her.

Instead, he laughed. "They have no idea what they're in for, Emma love. None whatsoever. But if anyone can captivate them, I'm sure it's you."

CHAPTER 9

Despite her boasting to Jonathan, Emma found herself beset by a severe case of the jitters as she got ready for dinner with her father's family.

What if her sisters despised her? What if her stepmother refused to speak to her? What if they swayed her father's opinion and made him rescind his offer of employment?

Seated at the vanity in her bedroom, she brushed her hair with vigorous strokes and stared at her reflection in the mirror. "That's enough of that, Emmaline Moore. You have never backed away from a challenge, and you're not going to now. You will win them all over, if not with your charm, then with the gifts you're bringing."

Thankfully, she'd fit in some shopping that morning after leaving her father's office. With the gifts now wrapped and ready to go, Emma turned to her closet, still undecided as to what to wear. She wanted to look nice, yet not overly fancy. At last, she chose her new purple brocade with a lace bodice.

She'd just finished fastening a string of pearls at her neck when a knock sounded on her door.

"May I come in, Emma?" her landlady called from the hall.

"Of course, Mrs. C."

The woman poked her head around the door. "Jonathan is

waiting downstairs for you, dear." Her eyes widened. "Don't you look lovely. That shade of mauve looks wonderful on you."

"Thank you. I hope my fa—uncle thinks so too."

"How could he not?" Mrs. C. smiled as she came into the room. "I'm so glad you're going to get the chance to visit with his family."

Emma bit her lip and twisted a curl around one finger, sudden insecurities taunting her. "What if they don't like me?"

Mrs. C. draped a comforting arm around Emma's shoulders. "Just be yourself and they won't be able to help but fall in love with you." She squeezed her shoulder. "Come on, now. That young man of yours is waiting—and looking mighty dapper, I might add."

Emma's pulse fluttered, imagining Jonathan in a suit and tie. He always could turn every girl's head when he entered a room. Like the time he'd arrived at her graduation, dressed to the nines, with a bouquet of flowers for her. All her friends had practically swooned at the sight of him.

She lifted a quiet prayer of thanks that he would be with her tonight. His presence would give her confidence and keep her calm. With one last look in the mirror, she straightened. "You're right, Mrs. C. I need to believe in myself and trust in the talents God gave me." And hopefully use them to impress her father and his family.

After pinning on a small feathered hat, she grabbed the jacket that matched her dress, her handbag, and the gifts, and descended the stairs to the main level.

Jonathan appeared in the foyer as soon as her foot hit the tile. His smile froze, and he simply stared. "You look beautiful, Em."

For no good reason, heat scorched her cheeks. What was wrong with her? Jonathan had complimented her many times in the past. But why did it feel different this time? "Thank you. You look rather dashing yourself."

And he did. His crisp white shirt stood out against the dark wool of his suit. But it was the way he'd parted his brown hair on the side and slicked it back from his forehead with pomade that made him look so handsome.

He set his bowler hat on the hall table and came toward her. "Let me help you with your wrap." Before she could utter a word, he took it from her and held it out.

Emma placed her bags on the hall bench and allowed him to help her into the jacket. He tugged it up over her shoulders, then in a deliberate move, lifted her hair and gently pulled it free from the collar. As he settled her curls over her shoulder, his hand brushed her neck.

A cascade of tingles shot through her body. The air seemed to knot in her lungs, making breathing a chore.

"Ready?" he asked.

She could only nod, since her tongue refused to cooperate. Clearly, she was nervous about the dinner tonight or she wouldn't be reacting so strangely to her friend.

Jonathan put on his hat and held out his arm for her. "Your taxi awaits, m'lady."

He gave her a silly grin, and she laughed, easing the tension in her muscles.

She gave a mock curtsy and took his arm. "Why, thank you, kind sir. Do lead on."

Just like that, everything went back to normal between them.

Twenty minutes later, Jonathan helped her alight from the taxi in front of her father's house. This time when Emma knocked at the door, the housekeeper greeted them as proper guests.

"Good evening, Miss Moore, Mr. Rowe. Please come in."

"Thank you." Emma stepped into the vestibule.

The woman pointed to Emma's shopping bags. "May I take those for you?"

"No, thank you. I'll bring them with me."

"Very well. Right this way, then."

Emma expected the woman to usher them into the parlor. Instead, she led them farther down the hall, through a sitting room to a set of French doors that led outside.

"The family are having cocktails on the terrace. Follow me." The woman preceded them onto a back verandah that overlooked a well-manicured lawn and garden. Nothing as marvelous as the gardens back in England, but respectable just the same.

The family sat around a long wrought-iron table. All heads swiveled in her and Jonathan's direction.

"Miss Moore and Mr. Rowe, sir," the housekeeper announced, then slipped back inside the house.

Right away, Randall rose from his chair. "Emmaline, Jonathan. Welcome."

Emma swallowed and pasted a smile on her face. At least her father seemed happy to see her this time. "Hello, everyone. It's lovely to see you again."

The faces were a blur at first, but gradually they came into focus. The sour face of her stepmother, a frowning Corinne, a younger male and an older gentleman Emma had never met before, and finally, the cheerful smile of the darling Marianne.

"You know everyone except these gentlemen. This is my father-in-law, Harcourt Fenton." The older man nodded. "And this young man is Will Munroe. He works with me at the university."

Will smiled. "A pleasure, miss."

"Likewise. And this is my dear friend, Jonathan."

Jonathan stepped over to the table and shook each man's hand, engaging them in small talk.

Vera offered them refreshments, which they politely refused. Emma wanted to keep a clear head about her.

Marianne rolled her chair over, her face alight with excitement. "Emma, I'm so happy you're here. You must sit beside me at dinner."

"I'd love to."

"The seating is already arranged, Marianne." Vera rose from her chair, looking every inch a queen, from the icy tilt of her chin to the top of her upswept hair.

The child's smile faded. "Yes, Mama."

Emma bit her tongue to keep from protesting. Would Vera forbid Marianne from being friendly with her? Emma lifted her arms so the bags in her hands rustled. "I have gifts for everyone," she announced cheerfully. She moved forward and crouched in front of Marianne, handing her one of the small parcels. "This one's for you. I hope you like it."

"For me?" The girl's hazel eyes lit up. "I love presents."

Swiftly, Emma rose, and before Vera could object, delivered a gift to Corinne, to her father, and lastly to Vera herself, who looked as if Emma were handing her a piece of rubbish.

"I'm sorry," Emma said to Will and Mr. Fenton. "If I'd have known you'd be here I would have found something for you as well."

Mr. Fenton said nothing, but Will laughed. "No apology needed, Miss Moore."

"Please, everyone must call me Emma."

A squeal from Marianne had Emma whirling around. The girl held up the silver heart necklace she had bought her.

"I love it, Emma. Thank you."

"You're very welcome."

Emma had gotten all the women similar necklaces and her father a pair of cuff links.

Corinne opened her package and looked up without expression. "Thank you. It's very nice."

Emma's heart sank a little. She'd really hoped Corinne would start to like her.

"The cuff links are beautiful." Her father came forward with a smile. "You didn't have to spend your money on us like this."

"It was my pleasure." Emma turned to look at Vera.

The woman had set her gift on the table and made no move to unwrap it.

"Vera, darling, aren't you going to open yours?" Randall, as he'd suggested Emma call him, held out the box to his wife.

"Yes, of course." She undid the wrapping and picked up the necklace. "It's lovely. Thank you."

Emma forced a smile at the false remark. "It's not much, but I wanted to give you something to show you how happy I am to meet everyone. I hope as we become better acquainted, we can all become friends." She held her breath, waiting for their reaction. Her palms grew damp at the stony stares from Vera and Corinne.

Her father gave a tight smile. "I'm sure we all would like that."

"I feel like we're already friends." Marianne's sweet voice warmed the cold place in Emma's heart that yearned for acceptance and love.

She bent down and kissed the girl's cheek. "So do I."

A maid appeared on the terrace. "Dinner is ready."

"Thank you, Ellen," Randall said, then turned to everyone else. "Shall we head inside?"

Marianne grasped Emma's hand. "Maybe after we eat, I could show you my bedroom."

"I'd love that." Emma thanked God for the open spirit of this wonderful child, who by all rights could have been a dour, bitter person, being confined to a chair as she was. But Marianne was the exact opposite: cheerful, sweet, and kind.

Looking down at the girl's bright smile, Emma vowed to follow her younger sister's example and use a sunny demeanor to win over the other members of her family.

Corinne took a sip of water while casting a surreptitious glance across the dining room table at Emmaline. What made the woman think she could buy their affection with her silly trinkets? Did she not realize by now that Papa could buy hundreds of such necklaces?

Will laughed at something Emmaline said. Corinne set down her goblet before she snapped the delicate stem in two. That trollop had been flirting with Will from the moment they sat down—a fact that seemed to bother the mysterious Jonathan almost as much as it did Corinne, judging from the scowl on his face. What exactly was the relationship between those two? Emma had said he was a dear friend, but Corinne doubted Jonathan viewed their relationship the same way. How could he not be lovelorn over such a beautiful creature?

She tucked that nugget of information aside for the time being.

At the head of the table, Papa rose and asked for everyone's attention.

Corinne's stomach clenched. Something told her she wouldn't like whatever he was about to say.

"Thank you all for being here tonight and helping me welcome Emmaline and Jonathan. We're glad you both could join us and thankful that you have overlooked our less-than-gracious first meeting." Papa chuckled somewhat nervously, while everyone else squirmed in their seats. "Emmaline and I have been speaking, and we've decided that in order to get to know each other better, we need to spend more time in each other's company. As luck would have it, the perfect solution came to mind." He paused in a dramatic fashion, as he often did while giving his political speeches. "And so I have hired Emma to be my personal secretary at the university."

Corinne's back muscles seized. This could not be happening. She'd been certain her father had been waiting until after her graduation in a few weeks to offer *her* the position. And she'd planned to accept wholeheartedly for two very good reasons. Not only would it give her more time with her father, but it would also afford her the opportunity to see Will every day. That alone would be worth doing a job that didn't exactly excite her.

But now, without even discussing the matter with any of them, Papa had blithely given the position to a stranger.

A stranger masquerading as family.

A murmur of surprise rippled around the table. Mama scowled, lines of disapproval creasing her forehead. Grandfather wore his thunderous expression, which proved he hadn't been privy to Papa's decision either. Though to be fair, as Papa's campaign manager, her grandfather really had no say over Papa's workplace—only over matters pertaining to politics. Corinne flicked her gaze to Will, who did not appear displeased, only somewhat bewildered.

"What kind of office experience do you have, Miss Moore?" Grandfather asked in a tone that indicated he was not impressed.

Emma turned to him, smiling. "Please call me Emma, sir. As I told my father . . ."

Corinne coughed on a swallow of water. How dare she call Papa her father? She'd known him all of five minutes.

". . . I've never worked in an actual office before. But I have a good deal of experience working with the books in my grandad's watch shop."

"Which I'm certain will make her easy to train in this position." Papa turned his attention to Will. "That's where you come in, Will. I am putting you in charge of Emmaline. I can think of no better mentor than you to show her the ropes."

Will's cheeks turned bright red. "Thank you for the vote of confidence, sir. I'll do my best."

Once again, Emma beamed a smile at Will.

Corinne bit the inside of her cheek to keep from screaming.

She should be the one spending time with Will every day. Not this attractive viper with her sapphire eyes and raven hair, who would likely steal him away from her.

Corinne tossed back the rest of her water in one gulp. Drastic measures were needed in order to get this woman out of their lives.

She would have to come up with an idea very soon, before Emmaline ruined every plan Corinne had for the future.

CHAPTER 10

Jonathan studied the faces of the people around the long mahogany table, attempting to gauge their responses to Professor Moore's announcement. Not one person, other than perhaps Marianne and Emma, seemed at all pleased with the news.

Will Munroe appeared perplexed but not entirely hostile about the situation. Mr. Fenton, on the other hand, seemed ready to explode, as did Mrs. Moore. But curiously enough, it was Corinne, with her cheeks blazing red and her nostrils flaring, who seemed the most visibly upset. Why would she care who her father hired as his secretary?

Will leaned his head toward Emma, who gave him a blinding smile.

An instant clutch of jealousy hit Jonathan hard. He turned to hide his reaction, and his gaze landed on Corinne. She stared at Will and Emma with eyes that glittered with an unnamed emotion. A stir of recognition moved in Jonathan's chest. Did Corinne have feelings for Will Munroe? Perhaps that was why she was unhappy about Emma working with Randall.

Jonathan released a slow breath. One more obstacle for Emma to overcome in establishing a connection with her sister. He would have to speak to Emma about his concerns and ask her to watch her interactions with Will, especially around Corinne. Jonathan shifted in his chair. Somehow he would have to have that conversation without sounding like a jealous fool.

"Whose idea was this, darling?" Vera Moore's cool voice drew Jonathan's attention back to the table.

Randall smiled at his wife. "It was mutual and seemed a natural solution to both our needs. You see, Emma is not just visiting for the summer. She plans to stay in Toronto permanently and will therefore need a way to earn her keep."

A bomb detonating in the dining room could not have produced a more devastating effect. Vera's cup rattled to her saucer. Tea sloshed over the side and stained the pristine white tablecloth. Mr. Fenton's eyes bulged as though having a fit of apoplexy. And Corinne bolted up from her chair so fast she jarred the table. Two of the crystal glasses toppled, knocking over the candelabra in the center. For a brief moment, the sparks from the many candles seemed to stutter, as though unsure what to do next. Then the flames found purchase in the tablecloth, shooting greedily outward to consume all in their path.

The air left Jonathan's lungs while his blood turned to molasses—solid and unyielding, clogging every artery. Visions of his childhood home ablaze in the cold chill of the night rose up from the depths of his memory. He sat frozen to his chair while chaos erupted around him. The women screamed. Men shouted. Servants rushed into the room.

Yet Jonathan could do nothing but stare into the bright flames of death as they raced toward him, surely to claim now what they should have taken that night when he was a child, and again more recently on the battlefield in France. He'd known it was only a matter of time before the wrong would be righted, that the universe would correct its mistake at leaving Jonathan alive. Now he would receive his just punishment for his cowardice at letting Danny perish in the inferno.

"Jonathan! Get up!" Emma's voice barely penetrated the haze engulfing him.

Hands clutched at his arms. Soldiers dragged him back while others rushed by him to haul Danny's charred remains from the receding flames. His friend's blackened face and smoldering body would be forever etched in Jonathan's memory.

A loud crack sounded, and a sharp sting shot up his cheek. He shook his head and blinked up at Emma. Had she just slapped him?

Her anxious eyes stared at him, blocking his view of the orange glow. "What's wrong with you?" she cried. "Get up!"

Slowly, he rose from the chair, his legs wooden and unbending. Emma tugged him by the hand out into the hallway where he leaned heavily against the nearest wall. Sweat poured from his forehead into his eyes and onto his lips. His body shook with tremors he hadn't experienced since . . .

"Are you all right? Jonathan, talk to me." Emma patted a handkerchief to his face, blotting the moisture from his cheeks.

His mouth couldn't form the words. He shook his head and drew another tortured breath into his lungs.

"Is he injured?" Professor Moore's concerned voice sounded over Emma's shoulder.

"He's fine. Or he will be in a few moments." Emma continued her ministrations to his face and neck. "He has a dreadful fear of fire due to a traumatic event from his childhood."

Jonathan glanced up at the frowning man. "Sorry," he managed to croak out.

"As long as he's not hurt, that's the main thing." The professor snapped his fingers at one of the maids coming out of the dining room. "A glass of water for Mr. Rowe. Right away, please."

"Thank you, Randall." Emma smiled up at the man as though he'd performed a miracle.

"The fire is out," Mr. Fenton announced to everyone in the hallway. "No real harm done."

Vera threw out her arms. "What do you mean, no harm done? The crystal is broken. The candelabra is ruined. And that was my best damask tablecloth."

Mr. Fenton glared at her. "Those are all replaceable items, daughter."

"Well, Corinne is distraught." Vera lifted her chin. "I've sent her upstairs for the evening. And Marianne as well. They don't need to be exposed to such . . . calamity."

"Corinne wasn't hurt, was she?" Emma asked.

The anxiety in her tone made Jonathan suck in a breath. Didn't she realize that Corinne's own hostility had started this whole chain of events?

Randall laid a hand on Emma's shoulder. "She's fine. More likely embarrassed at having caused such a fuss."

Emma frowned. "Maybe I should go and speak with her."

"That would only make matters worse." Vera pulled Randall's arm away from Emma as though she might contaminate him. "Haven't you caused enough turmoil for one evening?"

Emma's lip trembled. "I-I'm sorry."

Jonathan pushed away from the wall. This woman would not bully Emma, not while he still possessed most of his faculties. "The fire was not Emma's fault, Mrs. Moore. And I would thank you to speak to her in a kinder manner."

"If it's kindness you're looking for, then go back to England where you belong."

A loud gasp sounded from behind the group.

"Mama, why are you being so mean to Emma and Mr. Rowe?" Marianne wheeled toward her mother.

"Marianne." Vera's hand went to her throat. "What are you doing down here? I thought Corinne brought you upstairs."

"I came back down in the elevator. I was worried about Mr. Rowe."

The child's sincere empathy touched Jonathan's heart. How did such a disagreeable woman raise such a wonderful girl? He smiled at her. "I'm fine. Thank you, Miss Marianne."

Emma went to kneel beside the girl's chair. "You mustn't blame your family for their reaction. My existence has come as a great shock to everyone. Give them some time to get used to me."

"But I'm afraid you'll go away if they're mean to you." The girl's eyes brimmed with tears. "I don't want you to leave."

"I'm not going anywhere. I promise." Emma leaned in to brush the girl's tears away and kissed her cheek. "How could I leave now that I have a little sister? Two sisters, in fact."

"Corinne isn't happy you're staying." The child's frank statement hung in the air.

"She'll have to get used to the idea." Professor Moore gave his wife a pointed look as if to say *you too* and patted Marianne's head. "Now off to bed with you. I'll have Cook bring you and Corinne some warm milk and cinnamon."

"Yes, Papa."

Emma bid the girl good-night, then turned to Jonathan. "Perhaps we should go as well."

As exhaustion began to set in, Jonathan's muscles grew lax. "I think that would be best." He straightened his jacket and pulled himself up to his full height, wishing he could escape the mortification swamping him. How feeble must he appear to Emma and her family?

The other men, even the elderly Mr. Fenton, had jumped into action to douse the flames and get the women to safety.

Jonathan had gone into a state of shock.

"Thank you for your hospitality." He gave a curt bow and headed to the foyer.

Behind him, Emma said her good-byes.

The housekeeper appeared with his hat and Emma's wrap. "Good evening, sir."

"Good evening." Jonathan jammed his bowler on and rushed out the front door. Immediately, he gulped in a lungful of fresh air.

Soon, if he was fortunate, he'd fall face first onto his cot over the garage and try to pretend this night had never happened.

"It's getting worse," Emma said quietly on the cab ride back to the boardinghouse. She'd debated saying anything, knowing Jonathan's pride must be damaged at having displayed such weakness in front of her family. But she'd kept quiet for too long, always afraid to upset him or cause him any more distress. Now there was no way to avoid discussing what had just happened.

Jonathan stared out the window. "What is?"

"Your fear of fire. It's never paralyzed you like that before."

His jaw tensed, but he said nothing.

The need to comfort him, to make it all better, became a physical ache. She laid her hand on his arm. He flinched and pulled away.

"You've no reason to feel ashamed, Jonathan. After losing your family in that fire, you can't help your reaction."

Silence.

"But why is it getting worse now, all these years later?"

He stiffened against the seat.

She recognized the withdrawal, the tension that radiated off him in waves. Tension that had followed him back from combat. A sudden thought struck. "It's the war, isn't it? Did something happen there that involved fire?"

"Leave it alone, Emmaline."

Frustration bubbled up within her. Why was he being so

stubborn? "You can't keep everything bottled up inside. You have to get it out or it will . . . consume you."

He glared at her. "Do you think I wish to rehash the worst experience of my life?" Beads of perspiration dotted his forehead.

"Of course not. But you haven't been the same since you returned. I thought given enough time you'd recover, regain your sense of humor and your easygoing nature, but instead you're getting worse." She took a breath. "What happened, Jon?"

"You don't want to know."

"Yes, I do. I want to help you. I miss my friend."

A growl escaped his lips. "If that's true, then why are you planning to put an ocean between us? You don't seem to care that we'll likely never see each other again."

Emma closed her eyes on a wave of remorse. Never had she felt so torn, so divided in her loyalties. Why couldn't she have her family and Jonathan too? But he would never leave his Aunt Trudy to live in Canada. He felt he owed her everything after she took him in. In addition to that, there was Oxford.

"Of course I care," she said at last. "It kills me that in order to be with my family, I'll have to leave you." She pressed her lips together, and before she could stop herself, added, "But you left me first. Four years ago. To go off to war, of all places."

Her stomach churned with the resurgence of old resentment and hurt, reliving that horrible day when she'd watched him board the train, dressed in his uniform, not knowing if she'd ever see him again.

He'd left her alone, except for Grandad and Aunt Trudy, who were both getting on in years. Often the two would be so engrossed in their own friendship and their own careers that Emma felt like an outsider. She'd vowed during those four lonely years that she would never become so dependent upon another person again. Never rely on anyone so much for her peace of mind.

Perhaps she was leaving Jonathan before he could hurt her again. Better to make a clean break on her terms.

"You make it sound like I went away on vacation," he said tersely. "I was fighting to protect my country, including you and everyone else I care about."

He made it seem so logical, so noble. Yet there was nothing logical about her emotions. If he'd been forced to go, it would be different. But to make the conscious choice to enlist the moment the prime minister had declared war felt too much like abandonment to Emma.

However, to rehash the argument now would serve no purpose.

"You're trying to get me off topic. If you won't discuss the war with me, you should find someone you can talk to. Someone who might understand what you're going through. Maybe a fellow soldier?" She paused. "What about your friend, Reggie?"

"No. He's been through far worse than me. It wouldn't be right to heap my problems on him."

"All right. Then maybe a stranger might be easier to talk to."

In the darkened back seat of the taxi, she sensed him capitulating. His shoulders sagged. "I'll think about it. Maybe when I get home, I'll go to the veterans' office and find someone through them."

Emma swallowed the lump rising in her throat. "That's a good idea," she managed to say.

He sounded as though he were leaving tomorrow. But the reality remained that whether it was tomorrow or several weeks from now, it was only a matter of time until he left her again.

And when he did, Emma needed to be certain she would survive it.

CHAPTER 11

As much as Corinne would have liked to stay in bed and wallow in her misery after the previous night's fiasco, she knew Papa wouldn't allow it. Therefore, she rose and dressed, the same as any other morning, and descended the stairs for breakfast at precisely seven thirty, mentally preparing for the chastisement to come.

Papa would never cause a scene in front of their guests, but he would definitely berate her this morning for her outburst and her carelessness that had caused the fire.

When she passed the darkened parlor, a figure emerged from the shadows.

"Corinne?"

She froze. "Will. What are you doing here?"

"Your father asked me to come by first thing this morning. But after our meeting, I stayed behind because I wanted to make sure you were all right. You seemed . . . overwrought last night."

Heat climbed up her neck. She focused her gaze on the carpet. "I'm sorry. I made a fool of myself in front of everyone."

He stepped closer. "Not at all. Your reaction was justified, given the circumstances." The compassion on his face seemed sincere. "It's not every day you have a stranger turn up, claiming to be your sister. And then to find out she intends to stay here and work for your father—well, it's no wonder you were upset."

Her pulse thrummed as hope surged through her. Could Will actually care about her? His concern certainly suggested he did.

She raised her head to stare into his sincere green eyes. "Do you find this situation as intolerable as I?"

He gave a shrug. "I'm not emotionally involved, so no. I'm able to look at the matter somewhat objectively. Still, I do realize the complications this new addition to the family might create."

"In more ways than one," she murmured.

"Try not to worry. I'm sure everything will settle down soon."

"Are you really going to train her?" She prayed he would refuse. That he would tell her father how ridiculous it was to hire Emmaline in the first place.

"If your father says so, then I shall. He is my boss, after all."

If only Will had the courage to defy her father. But then, she'd yet to meet one person who could. She pressed her lips together. "Please be careful. I don't trust her. I fear she's here for some hidden agenda."

And what if that agenda included Emma claiming Will as hers? Corinne could not allow that to happen.

"Don't worry. If I discover anything untoward, I will let your father know immediately." He took hold of her hand and raised it to his lips, his eyes trained on her face.

She couldn't seem to breathe. Couldn't tear her eyes from his.

"Take care and try not to worry. Everything will be fine." Gently he released her hand.

She pressed it to her chest where her heart beat a wild refrain. "Good-bye," she whispered.

He tipped his cap with a wink and headed toward the front entrance.

How could such a tiny gesture make her head spin? She leaned her back against the door, unable to stop the smile that spread across her face. For the first time, she had a tangible hope that Will Munroe might feel the same way about her.

Corinne waited in the dimly lit hall for several moments until her system settled. She couldn't afford to swoon over a kiss to her hand. She needed all her wits about her to face her father.

Minutes later, she entered the dining room where her grandfather sat, sipping his coffee. Luckily, the room was none the worse for wear after the incident the night before. Only a faint scent of burnt cloth lingered.

"Good morning, Grandfather. Where is everyone?"

He looked up from his newspaper. "Corinne. Glad to see you're feeling better after last evening's . . . events." He folded the paper and set it on the table. "Your father had a meeting with Will and has now gone upstairs to speak to your mother. Which worked out well since I wanted to talk to you in private."

Corinne hesitated by her chair. "If this is about the fire . . ."

"Sit down, child. We don't have much time. I want to talk to you about this Emmaline."

Her stomach clenched. Would Grandfather be the one to chastise her then? She pulled out her chair and sat down.

"I won't mince words. Your mother and I are both very concerned about this woman's motive for coming here. Your father is understandably torn by her arrival and, as such, is not thinking clearly. We, as his family, need to work together to protect his reputation."

Corinne nodded, relief flooding her system that she was not in trouble after all. At least not for the moment. And she had an ally—one with a plan. "I agree, Grandfather. Most wholeheartedly."

"Good. Then I can count on your support?"

"Certainly. Whatever you need me to do, I will."

Grandfather gave her a most approving look. "For the time being, just keep your eyes and ears open. Be alert for anything suspicious." He leaned across the table and lowered his voice. "And if you could hide your animosity for now, that might be helpful. In fact, if you could convince Emmaline that you'd like to get to know her better, perhaps she might let down her guard and confide in you."

Her stomach dropped. Pretend to like this woman who was out to steal her place in the family? "I don't know if I'm that good of an actress, Grandfather."

"Nonsense. You can do anything you set your mind to."

Corinne reached for the teapot and poured herself a cup. Her grandfather's confidence was both uplifting and worrisome. What if she failed to live up to his expectations?

"Do you think you can put aside your personal feelings, for your father's sake?"

She unfolded a napkin, then set it on her lap and looked over at him. "I'll do my best."

Grandfather nodded, satisfaction glinting in his dark eyes. "Good girl. Between you, me, and your mother, we should be able to keep Randall from losing his career."

Corinne forced a smile for her grandfather's sake. Politics were of no real importance to her. She was far more concerned with making sure Will Munroe didn't lose his heart to that English vixen.

And Corinne was prepared to do whatever it took to make sure he didn't.

Emma shaded her eyes against the morning sun as she stared up at the ivy-covered walls. Somehow today the law building seemed much more imposing than it had the day she and Jonathan had come here. Today, she was entering as a new employee at the Faculty of Law.

What if she couldn't perform her duties the way her father

expected? The last thing she wanted was to disappoint him. She needed to impress him, to show him she was smart and capable. Emma prayed that the experience she'd gained in Grandad's shop had prepared her sufficiently for this position and that she could pick up the other skills she'd need in short order.

She smoothed a gloved hand down her wool skirt and tugged her suit jacket into place. Taking a deep breath, she entered the main building. This time, Emma took the staircase leading to the second floor, followed the signs to the Faculty of Law department, and entered a frosted-glass door.

Inside, she found herself in a large room that contained several desks. The strong smell of coffee, ink, and parchment wafted in the air. She hesitated as several heads swiveled to look at her, and she clutched her handbag tighter, willing her heart to quit pounding so hard.

A man stood from one of the desks and came toward her.

Relief flooded her as she recognized Will Munroe's brown hair and engaging smile.

"Good morning, Miss Moore. Welcome to the Faculty of Law."

"Good day, Mr. Munroe." She grinned at him. "I hope I'm not late."

He glanced up at a clock on the wall, which showed three minutes before nine o'clock. "Not at all. You're right on time." He gestured for her to follow him over to the desks, where he introduced her to another man and two women. Emma did her best to commit their names to memory.

"This will be your desk. Professor Moore's office is right through there." He pointed to a closed door beside her desk.

"Does everyone here work for him?"

Will smiled. "Not directly. But we all work for the Faculty of Law. You, however, will report directly to the professor as his personal secretary. As such, you will be his right hand, assisting him in whatever he needs done."

"I thought that was your job."

He laughed. "Most times I feel like a jack-of-all-trades, but actually I'm a law student, working here part-time as a teaching assistant." He pulled out the chair for her. "You can put your handbag in one of the drawers, and there's a coatrack in the corner."

"Thank you." She set her bag on the desk and glanced nervously at the door. "Does my—the professor—want to see me?"

"I'm sure he will when he returns from his morning classes." Will gestured to the typewriter on the desk. "Do you know how to use one of these?" The hopeful glint in his eye made her spirits sink.

Could she really do this job?

"A little. Grandad had one in his shop that I used on occasion. But mostly he insisted on handwriting all his invoices."

"I'm sure you'll pick it up in no time." He moved some papers on the desktop. "These are two letters that need typing. You can start with that until the professor returns to give you a more detailed job description."

Emma smoothed her skirt under her and took her seat, trying not to feel the object of scrutiny from the others in the room.

"Any calls for Professor Moore come through here." Will pointed to the telephone on the left-hand corner of the desk. "You answer by saying: 'Good morning, Faculty of Law, Professor Moore's office.' You can write any messages on the pad there."

"That sounds easy enough." Emma's stiff muscles relaxed a fraction. Anyone could answer a phone and take messages. She'd done that plenty of times for her grandfather.

"If you have any questions while I'm gone, Doris will help

you. Won't you, Doris?" He smiled at the woman across the aisle, who looked to be several years older than Emma. She wore her shoulder-length brown hair curled under at the ends. A pair of large-framed glasses magnified her dark eyes, while red lipstick highlighted her wide mouth.

The woman nodded. "I'd be happy to, Mr. Munroe."

"You're a gem, Doris." Will grabbed some folders from one of the desks. "I'm off to teach my next class. I'll see you later." With that he bounded out the door.

Emma released the breath she'd been unconsciously holding and peered at the machine on her desk. Where to begin?

"The paper, onion skin, and carbon paper are in the top drawer," Doris said. "They usually like at least one copy of the letters for their files." She smiled kindly at Emma.

"Thank you. I must say this is all very new to me."

Doris rose and crossed the room. "You're from England, I take it."

"That's right."

"How'd you find out about the job opening? I didn't think the professor had even advertised it outside of the university yet."

"Professor Moore is my . . . uncle. He knew I was looking for work and offered me the opportunity." Emma peeled off her gloves and laid them on the desk. "I hope that doesn't color your opinion of me."

Doris shook her head. "It's no skin off my nose. I make it my policy to mind my own business and do my work. Unlike some of the people around here." She tilted her head toward the workers behind them.

Emma didn't dare turn around. The last thing she needed was to cause any kind of conflict on her first day.

"Don't worry, hon," Doris said with a laugh. "No one here bites. But if they do, just bite them right back." She sashayed back to her desk.

Emma opened the drawer and took out some papers, fitted them together as best she could, and threaded them into the typewriter.

"Here goes nothing," she muttered under her breath.

She only prayed that by the time the professor arrived, she'd have at least one perfectly typed letter for him to review.

Maybe then she'd begin to win his favor.

The lunch hour came with no sign of her father. Emma tried hard to hide her disappointment that he hadn't been there to welcome her on her first morning and hoped he wasn't purposely avoiding her. After the fiasco at the house, maybe he'd changed his mind.

But right before Will left for lunch, he assured her that the professor would be in sometime before one o'clock.

"You can take a break from twelve till one," he said as he put on his hat. "I won't be back until later this afternoon as I have classes."

"Thank you, Mr. Munroe."

He smiled. "Please, call me Will."

Doris rose from her desk soon after Will had left. "Are you staying here for your break?"

"I think so. I have a sandwich with me, so I'll eat at my desk."

Doris pinned a small hat on top of her head and took her purse from the bottom drawer. "I have an errand to run, but I shouldn't be too long. I don't expect anything important to crop up while I'm gone. It's usually pretty quiet."

"I'll be fine," Emma said, despite the flutter of nerves at being left alone to handle the office.

With a small sigh, she took the brown paper bag out of the drawer and unwrapped the chicken sandwich Mrs. Teeter, the boardinghouse cook, had made for her. Maybe if she was lucky, her father would come back soon and they'd have a bit of time together before the others returned.

About half an hour later, Emma heard footsteps on the stairs. She quickly patted a napkin to her mouth and shoved the remains of her meal into the drawer. She was typing steadily when a man walked into the office.

With a start Emma realized it wasn't her father. The stranger wore a beige trench coat and fedora and carried a brown leather satchel. He came to a sudden halt when he spotted her.

She summoned her most professional tone of voice. "Good afternoon. May I help you?"

"Aren't you a wonderful new addition to this stuffy office?" The man grinned at her and doffed his hat. "A new employee?"

"That's right." She tilted her head. "And you are?"

"Giles Wainwright at your service." He bowed and extended his hand. "I'm with the *Toronto Telegram*."

Emma leaned over the desk to shake his hand. "Nice to meet you. Do you have an appointment?" She forced a smile, out of her element with no one around to offer advice.

"Not exactly. But I was hoping to speak with Professor Moore. Is he in?"

"I'm afraid not. But he should be back within the hour."

He frowned. "I'm afraid I can't wait around that long." He fished in his pocket and drew out a business card. "If you could give him this and tell him that I look forward to an interview at his earliest convenience, I'd be most grateful."

"Certainly." A wave of relief spread through her, and she was thankful that she wouldn't have to entertain this stranger until her father returned. She set the card on her desk.

"I'm sorry. I didn't catch your name." His intense gaze made her shift uncomfortably on her wooden chair.

"Emmaline Moore."

His eyes narrowed. "Did you say Moore? As in Professor Moore?"

"That's right." She lifted her chin. "I'm his niece." The fib was getting easier to roll off her tongue.

"And right off the boat from Britain, I'm guessing. Is this a permanent job or are you filling in until they find someone else?"

Why did she feel as though she was being cross-examined?

The loud tap of high heels sounded in the corridor, and Doris entered the room with a flourish. Her smile turned to a scowl the moment she laid eyes on Mr. Wainwright.

"You!" She planted her hands on her hips. "You know better than to show up here. Get out now before I call security."

Emma's mouth dropped open.

Mr. Wainwright held up both hands. "Now, now. No need for hostility. I was just getting to know Miss Moore here."

Did Emma imagine the emphasis on her surname?

"Out." Doris pointed to the door.

Mr. Wainwright put on his hat and bowed to Emma. "Lovely to meet you. I hope we'll see each other again." Then he turned on his heel and disappeared out the door.

Immediately, Doris leaned over Emma's chair. "What did that snake want?"

"To speak to the professor. I told him he wouldn't be back for a while, and he gave me this." She held out the card to Doris.

She took the card and ripped it into tiny pieces. "I'm sorry. I shouldn't have left you alone on your first day."

"I don't understand. Who is this man, and why did you call him a snake?"

Doris walked over to her desk and sat down. "He's a reporter with one of the local papers, which isn't a crime in itself. But he's always on the lookout to dig up dirt on the professor. He was probably hanging around, waiting for a chance to sneak in while we were all out, hoping to catch the professor alone.

This isn't the first time he's pulled such a stunt." She tapped a pen on her desktop. "He sure was quick to take advantage of the fact that you're new here."

Emma struggled to make sense of the situation. "I don't understand. Why would he want to harm the professor?"

"He and his paper are supporters of Mayor Church, and Wainwright has made it his mission to do whatever he can to discredit the competition." She shoved her purse into a drawer. "But now you know. In future, he is not welcome here."

Emma blew a curl off her forehead. "What if he shows up and won't leave? What do I do then?"

Doris pointed to the telephone. "Pick up the receiver, dial nine, and someone in the security office will answer. Tell them Wainwright is here. They'll know what to do."

"But he seemed so . . . charming."

"So does a boa constrictor until it has you wrapped up tighter than a violin string." Doris smiled. "Don't worry, honey. Now that he knows you're onto his tricks, he won't bother you again."

An hour later, when her father finally strode into the outer office, Emma had filled a trash can with crumpled pieces of paper, proof of her many failed attempts to type a simple letter. Her fingers stilled on the keys as Randall came to an abrupt halt in front of her desk.

"Emmaline. Good afternoon." He blinked as though surprised to find her there.

"Good afternoon." How did one address one's father—or uncle—in the workplace? He looked very professor-like in his tweed jacket, a gold watch chain dangling from his vest pocket.

"I see Will got you situated. Give me five minutes, then come into my office, and we can discuss the job in more detail."

"Yes, sir."

Precisely five minutes later, Emma knocked on his door. She carried a notepad and pencil, not sure what would be required of her.

"Come in."

She walked into the room and halted, seeing he was on the telephone. He gestured for her to sit down on one of the chairs. She did so, trying not to listen to his conversation, and looked around the office while she waited. It seemed her father was a tidy person. The bookshelves were meticulously arranged with books of like height grouped together. His gleaming desktop held a telephone, a globe, a blotter, and an inkwell. In the corner by the window, a large fern hung from the ceiling by a heavy cord.

"Can you not cancel the appointment?" Randall's exasperated tone drew Emma's attention.

She glanced at him, attempting to study him unnoticed. He really was a handsome man. *Distinguished* would be a better word. With his dark hair and vivid blue eyes, he must have turned many a girl's head in his day. Including her mother's.

"Very well. Let me see what I can arrange. Perhaps Will can take her." Frown lines marred Randall's forehead. "Feel better, my dear. I'll see you at dinner." He replaced the receiver with a loud exhale.

"I hope nothing's wrong," Emma said cautiously.

"Nothing serious." He looked at her with a slight smile. "Vera is under the weather with one of her headaches and can't take Marianne to her doctor's appointment. Once Will returns, I'll see if his schedule permits him to do it."

Emma straightened on her seat. "I'd be happy to take her, if I can. I mean, I don't know exactly what it would require . . ." She bit her lip, feeling foolish. What did she know about transporting a girl in a wheelchair to her physician?

Randall studied her. "Actually, I believe it would be helpful if you could accompany Will. It would make Marianne and Will feel more at ease, I'm sure."

She brightened. "And if Will can't do it, perhaps Jonathan would help me. I presume you need someone to lift Marianne in and out of the auto."

"Precisely. Vera is used to doing it, but even she has trouble sometimes."

Emma hesitated. She longed to ask a hundred questions about her youngest sister but hated to appear nosy. Finally, her curiosity won out. "May I ask how Marianne came to be confined to a wheelchair? Was she born that way?"

At the look of misery that crept across Randall's features, Emma instantly regretted her question.

"Marianne was a healthy, happy girl up until three years ago. Her favorite game was chasing her pet rabbit around the yard. And skipping." He pressed his lips together. "Then she came down with polio, and for a while we didn't know if she would live or die. Paralysis seems a small price to pay to still have her with us."

"I'm so sorry. That must have been terribly hard on everyone."

"It was dreadful. Vera blamed herself for not realizing the seriousness of the illness sooner, even though the doctor assured us it wouldn't have mattered." Randall shook his head. "We are fortunate to have the financial means to see to her needs, like installing an elevator in the house and hiring a private tutor. Still, I constantly worry about her future."

"Is there no possibility she will regain the use of her legs?" Emma asked gently.

"Very little. She is working with a physical therapist at the hospital to strengthen her muscles, but it's a relatively new process and there's no guarantee of improvement. Vera and I deemed the possibility worth the time and money involved on the slim chance that it might help."

"Of course." Emma smiled. "If anyone can achieve the impossible, I believe it would be Marianne."

For a moment, the tension left her father's face and he smiled. "You're right about that. Our Marianne is indeed a special girl."

Emma's throat thickened. What would it be like to hear her father speak of her in such glowing terms? Perhaps if she continued to prove her worth to him, one day she would.

CHAPTER 12

Later that afternoon, Emma walked down the corridor of the children's hospital beside Will, who pushed Marianne in the wheelchair. This was definitely not how she envisioned spending her first day on the job.

The strong scent of lye soap and antiseptic hung in the air, burning Emma's nostrils. Nurses bustled from room to room, their soft-soled shoes barely making a whisper on the tiles. Emma peered into a waiting room as they passed, amazed to see parents and children of all ages inside. Some of the little ones played with toys, while others clung to their mothers, fear evident in their eyes.

In her wheelchair, Marianne smiled brightly, seeming unaffected by the sights or smells around her. "Thank you for coming with me, Emma. I can't wait for you to meet Dr. Stafford. He's so nice."

Emma marveled at Marianne's cheerfulness. Most children would not be looking forward to an appointment with their physician. But she seemed eager for it. "Your father mentioned that you also come here for physical therapy."

Marianne's smile dimmed. "That part I don't like. But I know my parents want to believe that one day I might walk again. So I do it for them."

Emma's heart tugged with a mixture of sympathy and pride. What a brave girl to endure obviously painful exercises to give her parents hope. "Would you like me to come with you sometime? I'd like to see what your therapy involves."

"I'd love that."

"Good. Let me know when your next session is and I'll arrange it with . . . I'll arrange for the time off work to go with you."

Marianne giggled. "Good thing our father is your boss."

"Marianne." Will lowered his voice. "If he ever heard you speaking like that . . ."

"I'm sorry."

"Remember, if the doctor asks, Emma is your cousin, not your sister."

Marianne sighed. "All right. But I still don't understand why it's such a secret."

Will stopped the chair and came around to face her. "You don't need to understand. Just know that your father's career might depend on this. And trust him to reveal the truth when the time is right." He stared at the girl until she lowered her eyes.

"Yes, Will."

Affection and admiration for this dear girl stirred in Emma's chest. "I think Marianne is old enough to understand the reason why Randall is doing this." When Will shrugged, Emma crouched beside Marianne's chair. "When I was a baby, my mother died, and my father—our father—didn't think he could raise me alone. When my grandparents offered to take me, he agreed. Some people might call that a great sacrifice." And it suddenly occurred to Emma that she had in fact come to view it as such. "But some people might think of it as a cowardly act, for him to abandon his child that way. And your father's opponents could use this information against him to make him look bad. Does that make sense?"

Marianne nodded thoughtfully. "So we're telling a lie to protect him."

"For now, yes."

"If you think that's the best thing to do, then I can pretend you're my cousin."

Emma squeezed her hand. "As long as you and I know that we're sisters, that's all that matters." She leaned in to brush a kiss to the girl's cheek. "Come on. We don't want to be late."

Nothing seemed to allay Jonathan's unease as he waited for Professor Moore in his parlor. Though he hated to admit it, Jonathan had been worried about Emma all day, wondering how she was getting on at her new job, and now that he couldn't seem to find her, he'd swallowed his pride and come in search of her. Or at least in search of someone who might know of her whereabouts.

He'd already embarrassed himself by showing up at the university, where a woman named Doris Ingersoll had told him that Emma and Mr. Munroe had left early on some errand for the professor. That had been several hours ago, according to Miss Ingersoll, and instead of returning to the boardinghouse to pace the floorboards until Emma returned, Jonathan decided to visit the professor himself to see what he could learn of the situation. It would also afford him a chance to speak with the man in private and hopefully ascertain his true intentions regarding his daughter.

The fact that the professor had given Emma this job didn't sit well with Jonathan. He feared the man had ulterior motives, though Jonathan couldn't imagine what they could be. Perhaps Randall didn't trust Emma completely and wanted her close by to keep an eye on her. In any event, having a frank discussion would hopefully alleviate Jonathan's concerns.

"Why hello, Mr. Rowe. How nice to see you again."

At the sound of a feminine voice, Jonathan shot to his feet.

Corinne Moore entered, laying an armful of books on a side table. "I was on my way upstairs and thought I saw someone sitting here. What brings you by?" She smoothed her hand down her dark blue skirt.

"I'm here to see your father."

"Alone?" One fair eyebrow rose as she scanned the empty parlor.

"Yes."

A slow smile bloomed. She came forward to loop her arm through his. "In that case, I'll make it my job to entertain you until Papa arrives."

An uncomfortable urge to flee rose in Jonathan's chest. "That's not necessary, Miss Moore—"

"Please, you must call me Corinne." She tugged him down onto the sofa, sitting much too close for comfort. "May I offer you some refreshments?"

"No, thank you." He attempted to remove his arm from her grip, but she held on tighter.

"Tell me, Mr. Rowe, or Jonathan, if I may, what have you been doing for fun since you arrived in Toronto?"

"Fun?" He blinked at her. Who had time for fun between his work at the boardinghouse and trying to keep tabs on Emma? "I've been on a few lovely walks around the city."

"That hardly qualifies as fun." She smiled up at him from under her lashes. "Do you roller-skate at all in England?"

"I haven't for some time. Though I did enjoy the sport in my younger years."

She trilled out a laugh. "You make it sound as if you have one foot in the grave. You can't be more than, what, twenty-five?"

"Not until later in the year."

"Then you're much too young to be so serious." She ran her

hand up his arm. "I would love to show you more of our city. How about a night of roller-skating at our local rink and milk shakes afterward?"

Jonathan squirmed on the cushions. That sounded far too much like a date. "That would be"—*tortuous*—"smashing. I'm sure Emma would enjoy it too."

Corinne's smile faded. "I thought we could go together, just the two of us."

"And that would go against my rules, young lady." The booming voice of Professor Moore had never been more welcome. He entered the room, frowning at this daughter. "You know my policy on dating."

"But, Papa, I'm eighteen. More than old enough to go on a date."

Randall looked at Jonathan. "No offense, Mr. Rowe, but you're still a stranger."

Jonathan quickly got to his feet. "Of course, sir. I'm sure your daughter was only being kind to a visitor and didn't intend it as an actual date." At least he prayed not.

"I hope you're right." He pinned Corinne with a hard stare. "Why don't you make it a group outing? With Emmaline and Will along, I'd feel much better."

Was it Jonathan's imagination or did Corinne seem to pale?

"That sounds brilliant," he said. "I'll ask Emma when I see her. And speaking of Emma, sir, that's why I'm here. Do you happen to know where she is? I stopped by the university and she was gone, apparently on some type of errand."

"That's right." Randall unbuttoned his jacket. "She and Will took Marianne to the hospital for her specialist appointment. My wife came down with one of her headaches and wasn't able to go. They should be back any minute."

Scowling, Corinne crossed the room. "Why didn't you ask me to go? I normally fill in when Mama can't make it."

"I knew you had an exam today, and with the end of the school year so close, I didn't want to jeopardize your excellent marks."

Corinne pressed her lips together in undisguised displeasure.

Randall clapped a hand on Jonathan's shoulder. "Why don't you join me in my study for a brandy while we wait for Emma? When she arrives with Marianne, we can make arrangements for the roller-skating excursion."

Jonathan bit back a sigh. It seemed Randall Moore was used to getting his own way in both personal and career-related matters. Jonathan might as well make the best of it since there didn't appear to be any other alternative.

Corinne gritted her teeth together as her father escorted Jonathan down the hall to his study. Once again, he'd overridden her desires and changed the circumstances to suit his own ends.

She'd wanted to get Jonathan to take her on a date. Alone. For two reasons. One, to perhaps learn more about Emmaline, per Grandfather's request. And two, as a catalyst to make Will Munroe sit up and take notice. To make him realize that if he didn't act soon, someone else would be waiting in the wings to claim her heart . . . and possibly her hand.

Now, thanks to Father, he and Emma would be joining them on their outing. And the beautiful Emma would monopolize both men's attention, leaving Corinne invisible once again.

Her grandfather's words came to mind. *"Get close to the girl. Get her to confide in you."* The very idea made Corinne's stomach twist.

But perhaps this roller-skating excursion could be salvaged. Perhaps she could still make Will jealous. And if she played her cards right, she might even get to spend some time in Will's arms on the rink.

If that meant pretending to be friendly with Emmaline, then Corinne would simply have to sharpen her acting skills.

Jonathan scanned Professor Moore's study in silent awe as he took a seat by the hearth. Two large bookcases flanked the stone fireplace, both filled with rows of identical-looking law books. At the far end of the room, a large oak desk and filing cabinet took up most of the wall.

Professor Moore moved to a table and uncapped a glass decanter. "Brandy?"

"Um, no thank you, sir. I don't care for spirits."

He raised a brow but poured some amber liquid in a glass for himself. "Water then? Or tea?"

"I'm fine, thank you."

The professor took a seat opposite Jonathan. "I'm glad to have this chance to speak to you alone. You seem very close to my daughter, and I'd value your insight."

Instant tension seized Jonathan's shoulders. As much as he'd wanted to talk to the man, Jonathan now couldn't remember what he'd planned to say. His heart beat double time, and a fine sweat broke out on his brow. No doubt about it, Randall Moore could intimidate a person with one glance.

"I wanted to know if Emmaline had a happy childhood." The unexpected wistfulness of his question took Jonathan by surprise. Randall raised his head, angst written on his face. "Did the Bartletts treat her well?"

"Yes, sir. They doted on Emma. She meant the world to them." He wouldn't mention that her childhood had been marred by the fact that she'd pined for the mother and father she never knew.

"I'm glad." The lines around the professor's mouth relaxed. "That makes my decision to let them raise her worth it in the long run."

"Did you know that Mr. and Mrs. Bartlett told Emma you were dead?"

"No. But it makes sense now why all my letters went unanswered." He took a sip and set the glass down on a side table. "I had assumed my daughter wanted nothing to do with me. That she hated me."

"I don't think Emma could ever hate anyone. She is one of the most compassionate, loving, optimistic people I know."

"I'm beginning to see that." Randall Moore studied him for a moment as he sipped his drink. "Tell me, Jonathan, how long have you been in love with my daughter?"

Jonathan jerked back in his seat. His first inclination was to vehemently deny the accusation, but then again, did it really matter if Randall knew? Perhaps Jonathan would find an ally in him. He met the man's frank stare. "We've always been close, like brother and sister, as Emma says. It wasn't until she took an interest in my best friend that I realized I felt something more. Emma and Danny were engaged just before we shipped off to the war."

"Engaged?" He frowned. "She would have been awfully young."

"About eighteen. But times were different then with the war starting." He paused. "We knew a lot of us would never return. It turned out Danny was one of them."

"I'm sorry. It must have been hard to lose such a good friend."

"Very hard." *In more ways than one.*

Randall tapped his fingers on the armrest. "I don't mean to sound insensitive, but what's holding you back now?"

Jonathan sucked in a breath and slowly released it. "Emma's always wanted a traditional family. Now that she's found you and her sisters, I think she wants it more than ever. To be honest, sir, I'm torn. I don't want her to have to choose between us."

"I see. So, the noble fellow that you are, you're willing to

124

sacrifice yourself to make her happy?" A hint of sarcasm coated Randall's words.

Why did he make it sound like such a cowardly thing to do? "Isn't that what love is about? Putting the other person's happiness above our own?"

"Sometimes." The professor stared at him. "In a perverse way, I thought I was doing that by giving Emma up. At the time, that idea helped ease my own guilt for abandoning her." He shook his head and pinned Jonathan with a serious look. "Don't make the same mistake I did. Sometimes we have to fight for the people we love."

The murmur of voices from the front of the house drew Randall's attention. "Sounds like they're back."

The two men rose at the same time.

However, Jonathan couldn't leave without one last plea. "Promise me one thing, sir."

"What's that?" The man's expression turned wary.

"Emma wants a relationship with you more than anything in the world. It would devastate her completely if you rejectd her again." He prayed he wasn't betraying Emma's confidence by telling her father that much. However, if it protected her from heartbreak, Jonathan would face the consequences of her anger.

Randall gave a clipped nod. "I'll do my best. That's all I can promise for now."

CHAPTER 13

Jonathan sprinted across the busy street beside Corinne, Will, and Emma, trying not to gawk like a tourist. The flashing sign for Ruby's Roller Palace bathed the sidewalk below with a reddish-orange glow. Corinne and Will continued toward the entrance, chatting amiably, but Emma came to a full stop, staring up at the lights as though heading to the guillotine.

Jonathan gave her a nudge with his elbow. "Relax. This will be fun."

He couldn't believe how much he was looking forward to this evening. When was the last time they'd done something enjoyable? Randall's words kept ringing in his head. *"Sometimes we have to fight for the people we love."* Maybe Jonathan wasn't one hundred percent ready to be so self-sacrificing. Maybe it wouldn't hurt to keep fighting to win Emma's heart.

"Easy for you to say," she said. "I haven't been on skates of any kind since I was ten years old. And even then my sense of balance wasn't the best."

"Don't worry. I'll catch you if you fall." Jonathan winked at her. "It could even be romantic."

Emma's eyes widened and her cheeks blazed crimson. Jonathan held back a grin. It was certainly entertaining to keep her off-balance, saying things she least expected. And once they were out on the rink, Emma would be physically off-balance too. He hoped it would afford him the opportunity to get close to her and, if possible, begin to woo her with his charms.

"Why couldn't Corinne have chosen a nice restaurant or a night at the theatre? Something less physical?" she groused.

"Perhaps she loves to skate."

"That she does." Will and Corinne stood before them, likely having come back to see what was keeping them. Will laughed. "From what I've heard, Corinne's an expert roller skater, as well as an ice skater in the winter."

"Oh, now ice skating is something I'd love to try." Emma's eyes lit with enthusiasm. "I've always loved the winter. I understand you get much more snow here than we do at home."

"We do," Will said. "You have to learn to love outdoor activities, like sledding and skiing, in order to make the most of the winter months. Otherwise, you'll end up feeling like a prisoner until spring. Isn't that right, Corinne?" He smiled at the girl beside him.

"True." A strong gust of wind whipped blond strands of hair across her face. She patted them back in place with red-gloved hands. "I feel bad for Marianne though. There's not much she can do in the winter since it's so hard to wheel her chair through the snow."

Emma's face softened. "That poor dear. What hardships she's had to endure."

"Which is why Papa is so protective of her." Corinne sent Emma a rather frosty stare.

Jonathan held back a sigh. Corinne seemed to be jealous of Marianne's instant attachment to her new sister. And also, if Jonathan's hunch was correct, jealous of Emma's burgeoning friendship with Will.

"Let's head inside, shall we?" Will motioned toward the door.

Together, they entered the dimly lit building. Jonathan

blinked, trying to adjust to the lighting. The smell of popcorn and cotton candy filled the air, along with the slightly sour odor of sweaty feet. The closer they got to the rink, the louder the piped-in music became.

Corinne led the way to a long counter, where a man greeted them. Will took out a few bills, given to him by Professor Moore before they left, and paid the required skate rental fee for everyone.

Although he was excited about the evening, Jonathan still had his reservations, but at least Emma was along so he could keep an eye on her. He knew she hoped she could make some headway with Corinne, yet something niggled at Jonathan as to Corinne's true motive for inviting him on this outing in the first place.

Corinne and Will, both clearly good skaters, whizzed onto the rink as soon as their boots were laced. Emma had trouble getting to her feet and held onto the wall in a rather undignified fashion.

Jonathan bit back a grin, knowing she would not appreciate him finding humor at her expense. "Let me get my legs under me with a few laps around the rink," he said, "and I'll come back to help you." He hated to leave her alone, but it wouldn't do Emma any good if he were as wobbly as she.

"I'm not going anywhere." She looked adorable in her bright blue jacket and matching hat.

Gingerly, Jonathan stepped out onto the rink, keeping near the wall until he gained his balance. When he finally felt confident enough, he glided out among the skaters. He'd finished one full lap when he felt a tug on his arm.

"There you are." Corinne wound her arm through his. "You're not so bad at this after all."

"It's been a long time, but it comes back pretty quickly." He twisted to look over his shoulder. "Where's Will?"

She frowned. "Skating with some girl from work." Corinne's fair hair streamed out from under the red tam she was wearing. She pulled Jonathan forward. "Come on, let's show them how fast we can go."

Before he could argue, she propelled him forward, closer to the center where the faster skaters flew by, and he was forced to concentrate on keeping up with her or risk being trampled. Clearly an expert, Corinne kept a firm grip on his arm while weaving them in and out of the crowd in time with the music. Gradually Jonathan found himself enjoying the rush of the air as they glided, and as his confidence grew, his muscles relaxed, allowing him to skate with more fluidity.

"See, isn't this fun?" Corinne laughed up at him as they turned a bend.

Jonathan caught a glimpse of a woman in bright blue gripping the side walls and guilt tugged at him. "It is, but I promised to help Emma."

"Let Will take care of her. After all, I asked *you* out this evening, and if it hadn't been for my father, we'd be here alone." She moved her face closer to his, and for an instant, Jonathan thought she was going to kiss him.

He pulled back and attempted to disengage his arm from hers. What had gotten into the girl? "There's Will now." Relief flooded him as he waved the chap over. "Will, take over here for me. I have to help Emma."

Ignoring Corinne's scowl, Jonathan made a quick escape and headed in the direction he'd last seen Emma.

The loud music finally changed to something slower in tempo, cueing the skaters to reduce their pace around the rink. Couples seemed to pair off, moving in time to the romantic song as though waltzing across a dance floor. At least for the

moment, Emma didn't fear being mowed down by the speed-sters. She released a breath and attempted to move away from the wall. There was no way she would stand on the sidelines while Corinne monopolized Jonathan. Not if Emma had anything to say about the matter.

Jonathan had promised to be right back, yet it seemed he'd forgotten all about her, becoming totally enthralled by skating with Corinne. At one point their heads had been so close, Emma was sure they were kissing—and in public no less. Had Jonathan lost his mind?

The fact that she was so annoyed by his behavior only irritated Emma more. She did not need Jonathan in order to have a good time. She would make her way on her own.

The heat of her anger shored her courage. Emma lurched around the oval rink, taking as much care as possible to avoid the infatuated couples. Where was Will? Perhaps he'd come to her aid and steady her.

"Emma! Wait up."

Startled, she turned to see who had called her, but in doing so lost her carefully held balance. Her arms flailed out in a wild attempt to right herself. Just as she braced for a hard landing on the cement floor, a pair of arms pulled her upright.

"I told you I'd catch you." Jonathan's voice sounded near her ear, his breath stirring the tendrils of hair that had escaped her hat.

"Jonathan." One foot slid out at a precarious angle.

"Steady now. Hold on to me."

His right arm clasped her around the waist and the other gripped her hand. The heat from his body enveloped her, along with the scent of his aftershave. When he looked down into her eyes, her legs suddenly felt like jelly. If not for his arms supporting her, she'd be a heap on the floor.

"That's it. One foot at a time. Just like you're floating."

Shivers rippled down her spine. What was the matter with her? Skating shouldn't make her this jittery.

"There you go. It's just like riding a bike. You never really forget how."

"Riding a bike is a lot easier than this." Her foot slipped and again she almost went down.

Jonathan tightened his grip and lifted her against his chest. To confound matters, her hat slipped down over one eye, along with several unruly curls. Jonathan slowed them to a gradual stop, then reached out to tip the brim of her hat back up. With one finger, he brushed the hair from her cheek. The intensity in his eyes stole her breath.

"Emma." He whispered her name with a longing that spoke to something deep inside her.

She stared at him as though seeing him for the first time. Her lips parted, and her gaze fell to his mouth. Everyone around them faded to the background. The only thing that registered was Jonathan's quick breathing and the heat from his body.

Ever so slowly, he lowered his head toward her. Emma's heart took on a crazy rhythm of its own, thrumming louder than the beat of the music. Her eyes drifted closed, anticipating the touch of his lips to hers.

Then an ear-splitting shriek pierced the air.

Emma jerked back and almost fell again. "That sounded like Corinne," she said. "We need to make sure she's all right. Randall asked me to watch out for her. He'll have a fit if she's injured."

A flash of disappointment crossed Jonathan's face, but he nodded and steered them across the rink. "Why is he so worried about her?"

"I get the impression Corinne has a rebellious streak. One he's determined to curb until she's married to an appropriate man." Emma snorted. "Clearly neither you nor Will fall into that category."

"Fine by me. I have no desire to be in the running for that position."

A bit of the tension left Emma's shoulders. Perhaps Corinne's feminine wiles were wasted on Jonathan, and he was merely being polite. She must have been mistaken when she thought they were kissing.

He slowed to a stop at the edge of a crowd gathered around a fallen skater.

Emma peeked through the group until she saw her sister on the ground. "Corinne? Are you all right?"

Corinne grimaced, clutching her leg. "No, I'm not."

"It's all my fault." Will hovered over her. "I distracted her." His cheeks blazed red, and he wouldn't look at Emma.

"Let's get her off the rink and see if she needs a doctor." Jonathan moved toward Corinne to help her up.

Right away Will swooped in. "I'll carry her." He gave Jonathan a pointed look, then bent closer to Corinne.

Emma watched the interplay with dawning awareness. Did Will have feelings for his boss's daughter?

"Get away from me." Corinne shoved Will hard. "You've caused enough problems already."

Will blinked in surprise and fell backward with a grunt. His legs splayed out in front of him, the wheels of his skates spinning in helpless circles.

Jonathan gave Will an apologetic shrug, then lifted the girl into his arms.

A bolt of heat flared in Emma's chest at the way Corinne draped her fair head against Jonathan's shoulder and clung to his neck.

Emma skated painstakingly over to Will, who had pulled himself to his feet and was brushing the dust from his pants.

"What on earth happened, Will?" She didn't think his complexion could get any ruddier, but she was wrong.

"Nothing. Just an accident." Will shook his head. "I have to make sure she's all right." He skated off, leaving Emma teetering.

A boy who looked about seventeen reached out to steady her. "Careful, miss. You seem a little shaky."

Under normal circumstances, Emma would have been insulted by his cheeky grin. But she was too preoccupied with getting to Corinne and making sure she wasn't badly hurt. "Thank you. Could you help me over to the benches, please?"

"Sure thing. Wouldn't want you to end up like that other girl." He grinned again.

"Did you see what happened, by any chance?" she asked as the boy steered her over to the exit.

"Did I ever! The pretty blonde threw herself at that guy in the tweed cap and tried to kiss him."

Emma clutched the fellow's arm. What would have possessed Corinne to do something so brazen? First, she seemed to be kissing Jonathan, now Will. "Are you certain?" Emma asked the boy.

"Sure am. She caught him by surprise, but he pushed her away. That's when she lost her balance and fell." He chuckled. "If it had been me, I wouldn't have turned down a kiss, that's for sure."

Emma couldn't believe it. No wonder Will looked so uncomfortable. Not only had he rejected Corinne's advances, but he'd been partly responsible for her fall.

They reached the nearest bench, and Emma sank gratefully onto the seat. "Thank you for your help."

"My pleasure." He gave a quick wave and skated away.

Emma scanned the area but couldn't see Jonathan, Corinne, or Will. She quickly bent to unlace her skates, knowing she'd get nowhere until her feet were on solid ground again. As soon as she found her shoes and shoved them on, she rushed to the counter to turn in her skates. Voices drifted out from an open door. Emma peered inside the tiny room, and her stomach dropped.

Corinne was seated with her leg up on a crate, her face contorted in pain, tears streaming down her cheeks, while Jonathan studied her swollen ankle.

Will stood behind him, his brow furrowed.

Jonathan looked up as Emma entered. "We'd better take her to the hospital. There's a good chance her ankle is broken."

CHAPTER 14

With the aid of a pair of wooden crutches, Corinne hobbled through the front door of her house, praying that Papa was out at one of his many meetings. She did not relish the fuss he would make over her injury. Nor the reprimand she would receive if he learned the real reason for her accident.

Her cheeks burned with mortification at the memory. Will's face, filled with horror, pushing her away as though she were a woman of ill repute.

But in truth would a woman of ill repute act any less brazen?

Corinne had obviously misread the signals she thought Will had been giving her while they skated in time to the romantic ballad along with all the other couples. He'd held her hand and looked at her like . . . like a man attracted to a woman. And knowing Will would be too noble to ever act on his feelings, she decided to take the first step.

Never did she expect such a blatant and painful rejection.

"Let me help you to the sofa." Emmaline came up beside her.

Corinne stiffened her back. Of all the people to witness her utter humiliation, why did it have to be Emmaline? She pulled her arm free of the woman's hold. "I can do it myself."

The front door opened and closed again. Corinne imagined the men had paid the cab driver and come in behind them.

She had to get away before Will tried to talk to her. She could not face him right now. Not with her ankle throbbing and her temples pulsing with the start of a headache. If she could just make it to the elevator—

"Miss Corinne." The housekeeper rushed into the hallway, wiping her hands on her apron. "What on earth happened?"

"I'm fine, Mrs. Beck. I just want to go upstairs and lie down." *Before Papa finds out.*

"What is all the commotion out here?" Her father appeared from the entrance to his study. When he caught sight of Corinne, his mouth turned down. "Corinne! What happened?"

"It's only a sprain, Papa. Don't make a fuss." He was certain to overreact and embarrass her, which was exactly why Corinne hadn't wanted him to find out, at least not while Will was here.

Jonathan stepped forward. "It was an accident, sir. It could have happened to anyone."

Papa scowled. "I'll call the doctor and have him come examine you at once."

Corinne held back a groan of frustration. "There's no need. I've already seen a doctor. Jonathan and Will took me to the hospital."

"What? Why did no one call to inform me?" Anger blazed in her father's eyes.

Corinne bit her lip. She should have known better than to say the word *hospital* in association with her injury. Ever since Marianne contracted polio and had spent so much time in the children's ward, her father panicked at the mere notion that something was wrong with either of them.

"There was no point in worrying you for nothing, sir," Will spoke at last. "If the ankle had been broken, I would have contacted you immediately."

A muscle in Papa's jaw pulsed, a true indication of his agitated state. She needed to diffuse the situation. "I really should lie down and raise my foot. The doctor said putting ice on it would help with the swelling and the pain."

Her father's attention swung back to her. "Of course. I'll take you upstairs right now. Mrs. Beck, please prepare an ice pack and bring it up to Corinne's room."

"Yes, sir. Right away."

Papa took the crutches and leaned them against the wall, then lifted her into his arms.

Before he could take a step, Will came forward, finally looking at Corinne fully for the first time since the accident. "I'm very sorry you got hurt, Corinne. I hope you'll be feeling much better in the morning."

Her heart hiccupped at the misery shining in his eyes. This wasn't Will's fault. She could admit it now. The blame lay solely on her shoulders. "Good night, Will. And I'm sorry too." She hoped he understood her message—what she was really sorry for—and that her apology would right any wrong between them.

Her father shifted her in his arms. "Thank you all," he said gruffly, "for taking care of Corinne and bringing her home. Please see yourselves out."

"I must say the professor's reaction was a bit extreme, don't you think? It was only a sprained ankle, after all." Jonathan situated his cap on his head more firmly as they walked. He'd wanted to call another taxi, but Emma had insisted on walking.

Will had headed off in the other direction, still obviously upset by the turn of events. Perhaps he was as nonplussed by Randall's reaction as they were and feared further ramifications.

"I suppose. But Randall admits he's overly protective of his daughters, or so he told me. I think it's due to Marianne's fragile state. He couldn't save Marianne from polio, so now he's overcompensating with Corinne."

Jonathan threw her a wry look. "Since when did you become an expert in human behavior?"

She laughed. "I'm no expert, but I have learned a lot from observing people."

"Really? Then what do you make of Will's reaction to the whole thing?"

"Actually, I have some inside information on that."

"What sort of information?"

"The young man who helped me off the rink told me what happened." She leaned her head closer as they walked. "He said Corinne threw herself at a man, presumably Will, and tried to kiss him."

Jonathan stopped dead in the middle of the sidewalk. "You're joking."

"I'm not."

"That cheeky girl. She tried the same thing with me a few minutes earlier."

Emma stared at him, her expression skeptical. "So you didn't kiss her?"

He stiffened and glared at her. "Emmaline Moore. Have I ever kissed a girl I barely know in public?"

"No. At least none that I know of." She smirked at him.

"You dare insult my character like that? I should challenge you to a duel."

She giggled and squeezed his arm. "You're too much of a gentleman for that. Or anything else really." She sighed. "I'm sorry I thought otherwise."

"You're forgiven." He smiled at her. "But back to Will and Corinne. What happened after she tried to kiss him?"

"According to my source, Will pushed her away and she lost her balance."

"No wonder Will looked so guilty. Poor chap. He's likely worried for his job now." He shook his head. "What a terrible position to be in. Kiss the girl and get sacked. Reject the girl, and he'll still likely get the boot."

Emma frowned. "I don't think my father is that heartless. From what I've seen, he thinks very highly of Will. It would take a lot for him to get rid of such a devoted employee."

"Perhaps you're right. I still can't quite figure out the dynamics of that relationship."

"Simple, really. Will is like the son he never had. He probably wishes I'd been a boy. Maybe then he wouldn't have left me behind so easily." Sadness washed over her features.

Before Jonathan could dispute her statement, she linked her arm through his. "Let's get home. I'll need a good sleep in order to deal with my father at work tomorrow. I'm sure I'll hear a lot more about it then."

Jonathan swallowed his arguments and followed her around the corner to Jarvis Street, his heart aching at the hurt that lay beneath the surface of Emma's brave façade.

Would Randall ever give her the love she desperately sought and heal the wounds that ran so deep?

Jonathan could only pray that one day he would.

The next morning, in a vain attempt to have her work pile finished before Randall came in, Emma forced her fingers to move as fast as possible across the typewriter keys without making copious errors. By all rights, her father would not be in a good humor, and Emma wanted to ensure that he would have nothing to add to his troubles.

"My, aren't we the eager one this morning, Miss Emma." Doris crossed the aisle between their desks to stare down at her. "Trying to set a record for most letters typed before ten o'clock? Or just trying to impress the boss?"

Emma deliberately took her fingers off the keys and looked

up. Doris wore an amused expression that softened her angular features.

"I wanted to get a head start, is all. I think it could be a busy day today."

Doris lifted one brow as if to say she didn't believe a word. But before she could challenge Emma further, the thunder of footsteps sounded in the outer hallway, and seconds later, Randall strode through the door. He didn't lift his head or speak to anyone in the room. His surly expression matched the slam of his office door.

"Good grief. What crawled under his skin this morning?" Doris smacked her chewing gum. "You'd better finish those letters and hope he doesn't call you in to take dictation. In that mood, you'd be lucky to get out with your head still attached."

Emma shrugged. "Don't worry. I don't know much shorthand yet, so that likely won't happen." She frowned and focused back on her typewriter.

She'd almost finished the letter when the professor's door opened abruptly. She jumped and her fingers hit a few keys at the same time.

"Miss Moore? Can I see you in my office?"

Emma bit back an unladylike word and ripped the paper out of the machine. "Yes, sir."

Seconds later she entered the office, notebook and pencil in hand.

"Close the door, please," Randall said without looking up.

Emma did as he asked and took a seat in front of the desk.

"How is Corinne feeling this morning?" she asked brightly in an attempt to lessen the tension that blanketed the room.

"I wouldn't know since she wasn't awake before I left the house." He raised his head and gave Emma a hard stare. "Now I want you to tell me the real story of what transpired last night."

Emma swallowed. What could she say that wouldn't get

either Will or Corinne in trouble? "I didn't actually see what happened. At the time, Jonathan was doing his best to keep me from falling on my behind." She gave a nervous laugh, but her father only stared.

"From what I can gather," she went on, "Will was skating with Corinne when something caused her to stumble. She went down before he could catch her, and I know he feels terrible about that." There, a plausible explanation that made Will look competent and Corinne an innocent victim.

"What else?"

"Jonathan and I heard the commotion and went to see what had happened. He and Will helped Corinne off the rink. After examining her ankle, Jonathan determined that she should be seen by a doctor." She shrugged. "That's when we took her to Toronto General."

"I see." Randall tapped his pen on the blotter in an agitated fashion, then leaned forward. "Is there something going on between Will and my daughter that I should know about?"

Emma fought to keep her expression neutral. "What gave you that impression?"

"The fact that Will couldn't look me in the eye last night. And the nervous way my daughter was acting. She couldn't get upstairs fast enough. That leads me to believe there was more to this little accident than everyone is saying."

Emma hesitated. She had the chance to share something with her father, to perhaps gain his gratitude for her candor, but by doing so, she would lose any chance of forming a bond with her sister. She let out a breath. "I don't know anything for certain, but if I had to guess, I'd say it's possible that Corinne has a crush on Will. Perhaps that made her clumsy around him?"

Emma waited for his reaction, praying that she hadn't got Will or Corinne in trouble.

He narrowed his eyes. "Has Will ever mentioned his feelings for Corinne to you?"

"Oh goodness no. We only ever talk about work. Nothing personal." She paused. "Although we did talk about Marianne's condition after we took her to see the doctor."

Randall nodded, his shoulders relaxing. "Will's always been very solicitous with Marianne. Treats her like a little sister."

Emma hesitated while Randall brooded. She'd always had a soft spot for romance, especially forbidden ones. Perhaps she could do something to further Will and Corinne's relationship.

"Will seems like a fine chap. And you're obviously fond of him. Would it be so terrible if he did have feelings for Corinne?"

Randall's gaze swung to her, then his eyebrows drew together in a frown. "Will is too old for her. And Corinne is much too young to be thinking of marriage. She has her whole future ahead of her."

"I beg to disagree," Emma said softly. "She's exactly the right age for such dreams." She paused. "I was engaged when I was Corinne's age."

Randall's gaze remained even, though one brow rose. "Did your grandfather consent to this?"

"Yes, because he thought highly of Danny. Danny wanted us to marry before he left for the war, but I didn't want to rush into it, so we settled for an engagement." She smiled sadly, thinking of the ring hidden in her suitcase. "He never made it back."

"I'm sorry. That must have been extremely painful."

Emma swallowed. Not as much as it should have been. "It was, though the years apart had made me realize I didn't love Danny enough to marry him. I'd planned to break our engagement once he returned home. Thankfully he never knew that."

"You seem quite mature for your age," Randall said. "Corinne is a different creature. Impulsive, rebellious, and, dare I say, a tad self-centered." Randall pushed his chair back and rose. "Vera wants her to find a suitable young man to marry. But I feel Corinne needs to learn there's more to life than being married. I want her to go to college, find a career she's passionate about." He paced back and forth behind his desk.

Emma leaned back in her chair. Who knew her father was so progressive in his attitude toward women? "I champion your belief that a woman can have a career. But is that what Corinne wants? Forcing her to go to college would be almost as bad as forcing her to marry."

Randall stopped and stared.

"What I'm trying to say is, doesn't Corinne deserve the chance to make her own decisions about her life?"

"What if she's simply not mature enough to make such an important decision and throws away her chance to have a fulfilling career?"

"I don't think that will happen. In any event, who's to say she can't go to college and date a boy at the same time? One doesn't have to preclude the other. Besides, the more you forbid it, the more enticing it will become."

Randall studied Emma for a minute. "You make a valid point. Perhaps I have been looking at this the wrong way. Perhaps making some concessions with Corinne might make her more receptive to my ideas."

She smiled. "Spoken like a true politician."

Randall threw back his head and laughed out loud.

Emma blinked, certain this was the first time she'd ever seen her father laugh. His eyes brightened and the strain about his mouth eased. He looked unburdened, lighter.

"You, young lady, are very wise for your years. Perhaps I've underestimated your talents." He resumed his seat behind the desk. "Instead of wasting your time on that infernal typewriter, I think I should utilize your skills elsewhere."

Emma smiled, basking in his unexpected praise. "Wherever I can be the most help. Perhaps on your campaign team?"

"Really? You surprise me. I didn't think you'd be interested in local politics."

"To be honest, I probably wouldn't be, except that you're involved."

He tilted his head to one side, studying her. "Let me give the matter some thought. In the meantime, I'd like to invite you to Corinne's graduation party."

A warm glow spread through Emma. "I'd love to attend—as long as Corinne doesn't mind."

"Good. Then I'll arrange it." The furrows in his brow eased. "In the future, feel free to provide any insight you think appropriate in dealing with Corinne. Lord knows I can use the advice."

"I'll do my best. Oh, and I did promise Marianne I'd go with her to her next therapy session, if that's all right."

"I have no objection, though I will have to discuss it with Vera."

Emma's hope dimmed. Likely Vera wouldn't allow her anywhere near Marianne.

Randall leaned across the desk. "Don't worry too much about Vera. Give her some time and she'll come around."

Emma smiled as she rose from her chair.

Hopefully by Corinne's graduation, Vera would realize that Emma meant her family no harm. That all she wanted was to be included.

And if Vera gave her blessing, maybe Randall would at last acknowledge Emma as his daughter.

CHAPTER 15

"How do you like this setup?" Seated in the university lecture hall, Reggie elbowed Jonathan in the side. "Is it as fancy as Oxford?"

Jonathan took in the impressive theatre-like seating that rose all the way to the back of the room so that everyone had a clear view of the speaker below. "Nothing can compare to Oxford," he replied dryly, "but this comes pretty close."

Reggie's laughter echoed in the large room. Jonathan ducked farther back in his seat. Like a true repressed Brit, Jonathan couldn't quite get used to Reggie's easygoing, boisterous personality.

Then the lecturer began to speak, effectively ending their conversation. An hour later, the man assigned readings, as well as an assignment for the next class, and then promptly strode out, leaving nothing but chalk dust in his wake.

"He sure doesn't hang around for any chitchat afterward," Jonathan remarked.

Reggie chuckled. "No, sir. If you need help, you have to make an appointment and go to his office." He picked up his books, tucked them in a bag that he slung over his shoulder, then grabbed the crutches from the seat beside him.

Jonathan suppressed the urge to help him up, knowing his

friend would take offense at the implication that he was an invalid. Sure enough, Reggie rose with little effort and situated the crutches under his arms. A piece of paper floated to the ground.

Jonathan reached to pick it up and frowned. "I'd almost forgotten about this."

Reggie looked down at the paper in Jonathan's hands. "The debate with the mayor. Don't tell me you're getting involved in local politics?"

"Believe me, I'd rather not. Unfortunately, I promised Emma." He pointed at the small photo. "That's her father."

"Randall Moore?" Reggie let out a whistle.

"Yes." Jonathan studied his friend. "Do you know him?"

"Just from the last election. I did go to hear one of his speeches." He shook his head. "Can't say I was impressed."

Tingles raced up Jonathan's spine. "What makes you say that?"

Reggie shrugged as he started down the aisle. "Seemed cold to me. And somewhat fake, as though he was putting on an act. I think that's why he lost."

Interesting. "You know us British. Cool and aloof."

"That may work in England, but if you want to win people over in this country, you have to be friendlier. You know, shake a lot of hands, kiss a lot of babies, and smile."

"True enough." Jonathan followed him into the hall, amazed at how fast his friend could travel. Once Reggie navigated the steps outside, he paused on the walkway below, the breeze fluttering his pant leg.

"You're quite an expert maneuvering around on those things," Jonathan said. "I can barely keep up with you."

Undaunted by the stares of the people passing by, Reggie laughed as they continued walking. "I should be by now with all the practice I get. Though I can't say I'll miss the crutches once I get my new leg."

Jonathan stopped dead on the path. "A new leg? That's wonderful. Will it be a wooden one?"

"It'll be a bit more sophisticated than what you're picturing, but yes. Wood and metal. I go for my first fitting tomorrow." Reggie gave him an apprehensive glance. "I don't suppose I could talk you into coming to the appointment with me? That way my mom won't feel obligated to go."

"At the military hospital?" The mere words conjured up awful memories of rows and rows of metal cots, filled with men suffering from all kinds of horrific wounds. The putrid smells, the groans and screams of the soldiers as the doctors made their rounds. It wasn't a place Jonathan ever wanted to visit again.

"Yeah," Reggie said. "I've been going there once a week for therapy. They try to toughen up the stump area so it will accept the new leg more easily." The tense expression on his friend's face told Jonathan it had taken a lot to ask for his help with the fitting.

There was no way he could refuse. Jonathan drew in a deep breath of fresh air and forced a smile. "I'm sure I can work my schedule around the appointment time."

"Great." Relief washed over Reggie's features. "Having a fellow soldier along will be much manlier. Especially since there's this cute nurse I'm trying to impress."

Despite his trepidation, Jonathan could only laugh. "Trust you to use the situation to your advantage."

The next day, Jonathan and Reggie took a streetcar to the military hospital on Christie Street. The doctor's office was located in the basement, which Jonathan thought rather odd, an opinion further reinforced as they walked to the farthest corner in the back.

"Does this chap not warrant a better office than this?" Jonathan squinted in the dim light of the hallway. "Seems rather dingy for someone as well regarded as you described."

"The doc is a bit quirky, but he knows his stuff. He was injured in the war too and now makes it his mission to help guys like me get back on their feet." Reggie grinned. "Literally and figuratively."

When they came to the end of the hall, Reggie knocked on the last door and waited until it opened and a man came forward.

"Private Wentworth. Good to see you. Come in."

"Hey, doc. I brought a friend of mine visiting from England. Jonathan Rowe, this is Dr. Clayborne."

The doctor was a good-looking fellow, although far too grim for Jonathan's liking. If he was trying to help veterans, a smile could go a long way. He shook Jonathan's hand.

"Jonathan served in the war too," Reggie said. "We met in the army infirmary in France."

Dr. Clayborne looked Jonathan up and down. "Are you here for treatment as well?"

"No, sir. I'm just here for moral support."

The doctor's face relaxed. "That's nice of you. First-time fittings can be a grueling affair." He gestured to the chairs. "Please have a seat. Dr. Fullman will be along any minute with the prosthetic."

When Reggie was situated on the exam table, Dr. Clayborne took his crutches and set them against the wall. He began to roll up Reggie's pant leg. "Not squeamish, are you, Mr. Rowe?"

Jonathan swallowed as visions of severed limbs and burned corpses flashed behind his eyes. "I don't believe so."

Still, beads of sweat popped out on his forehead, belying his statement. He took out a handkerchief to dab his brow and upper lip. This was ridiculous. There was not a hint of fire here. No threat of danger. So why was his body turning traitor on him?

He took a seat, but that only afforded him a more eye-level

view of Reggie's wound. The entire red, scarred end of his leg sat exposed before him. The doctor took a cloth and some type of solution and bathed the area.

Jonathan looked away, tried to focus on the chart on the wall as the smell of antiseptic filled his nostrils. Closing his eyes didn't help. All he could envision was the sea of bodies heaped one upon the other, missing arms, missing legs, riddled with bullet holes.

He jumped up from the chair. "Excuse me for a moment."

Then he fled from the room, almost crashing into a gray-haired man carrying a wooden leg.

He jogged down the hall to the staircase and up to the main floor, then out to the street. Leaning against the brick wall, Jonathan gulped the fresh air into his lungs. His heart hammered hard against his ribs. Sweat streaked down his neck and back, the hot sun not helping matters.

He bent over his knees, willing his equilibrium to return. Other than in his recurring nightmares, this type of reaction hadn't happened since the night he and Emma had dined at the professor's house.

"It's getting worse. You need to talk to someone." Emma's admonition rang in his head.

Jonathan knew she was right. He'd thought if he ignored what was happening, it would go away. But now the attacks seemed to sneak in at the most uenxpected moments.

Times when people were depending on his help.

Jonathan straightened. He had to pull himself together. Go back inside and be there for his friend. He mopped his face with his handkerchief and dragged in a few more deep breaths. Then he forced himself to walk back into the building.

When he returned to the room, Reggie had the leg attached and was gingerly attempting to take a few steps. Jonathan watched from the doorway, wincing inwardly every time his friend did.

"You're doing very well," the doctor said. "It might be helpful to use a cane for the first week or two until you get used to the new sense of balance."

"I guess practice makes perfect, eh, doc?" Though pale, Reggie grinned.

"Yes, in small measures. You don't want to irritate the stump too much. Give it time to get used to the device. Slow and steady will do. I'll give you a schedule for the first week as to how long to wear it each day."

Reggie glanced up and noticed Jonathan. "There you are. I thought you bailed on me."

"Sorry. Needed a bit of fresh air. Still have a hard time with hospital smells." How lame did that sound when his friend had far more reason to fear such institutions?

"Why don't you take the leg off now? I'll pack it up for you to take home. I wouldn't attempt wearing it on the streetcar until you've become quite comfortable with it." The doctor assisted Reggie onto the exam table.

Then he crossed the room to where Jonathan still hovered in the doorway, not quite committing to going back inside.

"Mr. Rowe, I hope you don't think me too forward," he said in a low voice so that Reggie couldn't hear, "but are you seeing anyone about your anxiety?"

Jonathan stiffened. "What do you mean?"

Compassion radiated from the man's eyes. "War neurosis, or shell shock as it's sometimes called, is nothing to be ashamed of. It's a very real condition—just as real as your friend's missing leg. Without treatment, it can become debilitating."

"I do not have shell shock," Jonathan bit out. Waves of heat shot through his chest. Did the man not realize the negative connotation associated with that term? Not to mention the stigma and the horrific treatments, like electric shock therapy. There was no way he was being subjected to that type of torture. "Thank you for your concern, doctor, but I'm fine." He expelled a breath. "The fact that I don't like hospitals doesn't make me ready for a straitjacket."

Dr. Clayborne studied him for several seconds. "Let me guess. You suffer from frequent nightmares and night sweats. You seem fine most of the time, but then out of the blue something will trigger a severe reaction. You can't breathe, the walls seem to close in, and your whole body shakes."

Jonathan's mouth fell open. It was as though the man had been following him around or spying on him in his room at night.

"I've seen many veterans come through these doors, all with varying types of injuries. The worst ones, the hardest to diagnose and treat, are the ones of the mind. Do you know how many soldiers survive the war only to take their own lives? Too great a number, I'm afraid. Please don't let your pride get in the way of seeking help." He laid a hand on Jonathan's shoulder. "If you ever need a name, I can recommend someone."

Jonathan tried to speak, but the words lodged in his throat, so he merely nodded.

The doctor reached in his pocket and pulled out a business card. "Here's my number. Call me day or night if you ever find yourself in trouble." The man's total lack of judgment or criticism was a welcome change. Perhaps shell shock wasn't such a stigma after all. Perhaps Jonathan wasn't losing his mind.

He swallowed and shoved the card in his pocket. "Thank you. I'll keep that in mind."

"The reason I know so much about this," Dr. Clayborne said with a half smile, "is that I suffer from it myself. A good doctor gave me tools that helped me learn to control my reactions, so I can at least work again." He shrugged. "If I couldn't, I think I'd really go crazy."

Jonathan's lungs expanded, as though a brick had been lifted from his chest. "It's good to know I'm not alone. Sometimes

I really believe I'm going insane, though I've tried to hide it from everyone."

"Hiding it is almost as exhausting." The doctor clapped him on the back. "Don't be afraid to admit you're having trouble. After what we saw on the battlefields, it's not surprising."

Jonathan nodded. "A good friend has been after me to see someone. I suppose it's time I did."

"The sooner you do, the sooner you'll start feeling normal again." He held out his hand. "Good luck, Mr. Rowe."

"You too. And thanks for what you're doing for Reggie."

As Jonathan stepped into the hallway to wait for his friend, a new sense of purpose filled him. If he were to have any future with Emma, he wanted to be whole again—needed to be whole again. If that meant talking to a professional, then that's what he'd do. He owed it to himself—and to Emma—to do whatever he could to heal the invisible battle wounds that plagued him.

CHAPTER 16

Jonathan wiped the soot from his face. Cleaning the fireplace was not one of his favorite chores, but when Mrs. C. asked him to do it, he couldn't refuse. She'd been so kind to him since they'd arrived. In a way, she reminded him of his Aunt Trudy. He hoped someone back home would help his aunt while he was here.

While Jonathan had been away at war, he'd counted on Felix, Emma's grandfather, to look in on her and assist her with anything she needed. But with Felix gone and strangers living next door, Jonathan worried that his aunt might not be faring as well as she should. Leaving Aunt Trudy was Jonathan's biggest regret, but his aunt had been adamant that he go with Emma.

He dumped a mound of ashes into a bin and frowned. The one letter he'd received from Trudy had been filled with overly cheerful stories of the village, which only led Jonathan to worry more, especially since he remembered that her meeting with a banker regarding an extension to her loan should have taken place by now. He resolved to pen a letter to her that evening.

Between worry over Aunt Trudy, his embarrassment at letting Reggie down at his doctor appointment, and getting nowhere with romancing Emma, Jonathan's mood was as gray as the ashes in the grate. He swept the remaining debris onto a dustpan and rose from the brick hearth. As he turned around, a burst of laughter met his ears.

"You look like one of the street urchins back home." Emma stood in the doorway, arms crossed in front of her.

He scowled and scooped the remaining ashes into the trash bin. Then he picked it up and crossed to the door. "Excuse me, please. I have to dump this out back."

Emma's eyebrows rose. "What's got you in such a foul temper today?"

"Frustration will do that to a man." He pushed past her into the hall and made his way toward the back door.

"What are you frustrated about?"

Jonathan almost groaned. Had he said that out loud? "Nothing. Don't mind me."

Frustration didn't begin to describe the complicated mix of feelings swirling inside him. For the past few days, he'd relived the moment at the roller-skating rink when he'd almost kissed Emma about a million times. Despite the impropriety of doing so in public, he still wished he had. Who knew when he'd get the opportunity again?

Clearly, though, Emma hadn't given the incident a minute's thought. Or at least that's how it seemed to him since she hadn't mentioned anything about it. Any time he'd tried to broach the subject, she'd found a way to avoid the conversation.

Which didn't bode well for any sort of romance between them.

He stepped outside, took the lid off the large trash can, and dumped the ashes inside. Then he banged the lid back on.

The door squeaked as Emma emerged.

He dusted off his hands. "What are you doing home from work already?"

"Corinne's graduation is today. Randall let me leave early to get ready."

"That's today?" His head really had been full of cotton lately.

"Don't tell me you forgot. You said you'd escort me to the ceremony and the party afterward."

He swallowed a sigh. "Of course. I just need to clean up." He looked down at his grubby clothes. "Do you want me to meet you there?"

"No need. I have to change too and fix my hair. I'll meet you on the front porch."

An hour later, when Jonathan and Emma arrived at Toronto's Academy for Girls, the school auditorium was packed with excited parents and siblings of the graduates. Jonathan guided Emma to a row of empty chairs in the back.

She frowned. "We won't be able to see a thing from here."

"There's not much choice unless you want to stand against the wall."

"Let me see if Randall saved us any seats. I'll be right back." She set her handbag on the chair beside him and marched up to the front of the room, heedless of the stares that followed her. In her stylish outfit with matching hat, she drew the eye of everyone she passed.

Jonathan leaned back against the seat, hat on his lap, and waited for her to return. He sincerely doubted Randall would have saved a spot for them up front. Not in light of his wife's obvious disapproval.

A few minutes later, Emma returned. "There's no space for us. Vera seemed horrified that I even asked about it, but Marianne was sweet. She's so excited to see her sister receive her diploma." Emma plopped down beside him. Then a slight frown creased her brow. "That reporter is here. I wonder why he's covering a high school event."

"What reporter?"

She turned to him, confusion in her blue eyes. "Did I not tell you about Mr. Wainwright? He came to the office my first day there, hoping I'd grant him an appointment with Randall. Luckily Doris came to my rescue and got rid of him."

Jonathan chuckled. "Doris sounds like quite the girl to have around." He'd told Emma about the day he'd gone looking for her in the office and had briefly met the formidable Miss Ingersoll.

"She is rather intimidating." Emma laughed. "But she's actually a sweetheart once you get to know her."

Jonathan glanced over the audience to the right side of the room. A man wearing a camera around his neck stood against the wall, staring at Emma. "Is that Wainwright?" Jonathan said under his breath.

"Yes." Emma's frown deepened. "Why is he looking at us like that?"

"I don't know. But I'd avoid him if I were you." Jonathan didn't like the speculative gleam in the other man's eyes as he dared to lift his camera and aim it in their direction. Jonathan shifted in his seat, putting his back to the man so as to block Emma.

"What are you doing?" she asked.

"Keeping you out of his line of vision. He's a bit too curious for my liking."

Emma shrank back in her chair. "Doris said he's always looking for ways to discredit my father. Do you think he knows who I am?"

"I doubt he knows anything for certain, but he may have his suspicions. And we are not going to give him anything to use as ammunition." He gave Emma a stern look. "Isn't that right?"

"I'm not planning on it." She sighed. "I guess it's a good thing we're sitting far away from my father after all."

Jonathan agreed with her and made a mental note to avoid Wainwright at all costs once the ceremony was over.

Emma walked into the ballroom of the King Edward Hotel and fought to keep her jaw from dropping. How much had her father spent to have Corinne's party in this magnificent place?

Chandeliers sent a cheerful glow over the room, where elegantly dressed men and women were chatting, drinks in hand. In the far corner, a four-piece band played soothing background music, while tuxedo-clad waiters circulated with trays of hors d'oeuvres.

Emma had never been anywhere so elegant in her life. She smoothed a hand down her silky green dress, suddenly feeling like a duck in the company of swans.

"Relax." Jonathan's voice sounded behind her. "You look beautiful."

She gave a nervous laugh. "How do you always know what I'm thinking?"

"I grew up with you, remember?" He took her hand and linked it through his arm. "Are you ready to face this crowd?"

"I suppose so."

"Good. Let's head inside."

They strolled into the room among the elegant tables garnished with black tablecloths and white napkins. Gleaming china, silverware, and crystal bore evidence to the expense of the occasion.

"I can't believe Randall is paying for a sit-down dinner for all these people. All for a high school graduation." Emma couldn't help but compare it to her own graduation day in her small high school. The principal had provided cake and punch in the school library for the graduating students and their parents. Her grandad, Trudy, and Jonathan had attended the brief ceremony. When she'd received her diploma, the pride on Grandad's face had brought tears to Emma's eyes. She still had the beautiful watch he'd designed for her, as well as the leather-bound journal Jonathan had given her. That one had long since been filled, and she'd completed at least three others since then.

"Look, there are name cards on the tables. Let's find ours." Jonathan tugged her out of her daydreams.

"Maybe we'll be seated near the head table." Emma didn't dare believe she'd be included with the family, but she hoped for a spot nearby.

She walked ahead and scanned the name cards on all the tables at the front of the room. Nothing. Frowning, she looked up and saw Jonathan waving at her. He pointed to one of the tables at the back of the room near the door, and Emma's stomach dropped. They'd seated her in the farthest corner, like a wayward child. Did her father know about this, or was it Vera's doing?

A ripple went through the attendees as Randall entered the room with Corinne on his arm, grinning like a proud father. Emma swallowed back the bitter taste of envy and focused on her sister. With her blond hair piled high on her head, Corinne looked as elegant as a princess. She wore a cream-colored gown with elbow-length gloves of the same shade. Jewels glittered at her neck and on her ears. Clearly in her element, the girl beamed at the group that had gathered to watch her entrance. Emma noted that she walked with no hint of a limp, so her ankle must be fully healed from the skating accident.

Behind Randall, Vera stood with Mr. Fenton, who pushed Marianne in her chair. Emma couldn't help but marvel at the change in Vera's appearance. Tonight, she looked ten years younger. Her hair was perfectly coiffed, and she was wearing a stunning peacock-blue gown with what appeared to be real sapphires at her throat. As she moved through the room, she smiled and waved, like a queen on a walkabout amongst her subjects.

Vera's composure only faltered once for a brief second when

her gaze fell on Emma. She gave the smallest incline of her head before moving forward.

The entourage continued up to the head table. Once they had taken their places behind the chairs, Randall turned his attention to his guests.

"Thank you all for coming to help us celebrate this auspicious day for my daughter Corinne. My wife, Vera, and my younger daughter, Marianne, as well as my father-in-law, Harcourt Fenton, all welcome you and hope you enjoy the meal the chef has prepared."

Applause broke out, as did the murmur of voices as the guests began to talk amongst themselves. Chairs scraped the floor as people took their seats, but Emma remained rooted to the spot. Not once had her father even glanced her way, much less acknowledged her existence.

A hand closed around her upper arm. "Emma, love. Come and sit down."

She blinked and looked around, realizing she was the only one still standing. Gently, Jonathan guided her to their table and pulled out the chair for her.

The unwanted child, relegated to the back corner.

She took a seat and stared blindly at the china plate in front of her, trying to be happy for Corinne and not turn this evening into something about Emma's yearning to belong.

The servers appeared with multiple trays of food and began to distribute the salads.

"Emma? Have you met Mr. and Mrs. Ford?"

She turned her attention to Jonathan, who gestured to the couple on his left. The smiling woman looked vaguely familiar. As Emma focused on the other people at the table, she realized that most of them worked at the Faculty of Law. Apparently she'd been seated at the employee table.

"Hello." Emma did her best to summon a friendly smile.

"It's Betsy. I suppose you don't remember me. I work down the hall from you at the university."

"Oh, sorry. I still haven't put all the names and faces together."

"Not to worry. It takes some time. By the way, I love your accent." The woman chuckled. "Don't you, Herbert?"

Her husband grunted. Not a conversationalist apparently.

"We also attend the same church as Professor Moore," Betsy said. "Vera and I often serve on the same committees."

"That's wonderful." Emma took a hasty sip from her water goblet. Why did the woman feel the need to explain her connection to the family in such detail?

"You share the same surname as the professor. Are you any relation?" Curiosity brightened the woman's gray eyes.

"I . . . He's my uncle." The lie stuck in her throat this time. She took another gulp of water.

"Lucky you, being a part of that beautiful family." She paused. "I'm surprised you're not seated closer."

Emma followed the woman's admiring gaze to the front of the room. Yes, they certainly made a beautiful family: her father with his swarthy good looks and the three fair-haired beauties beside him. A storybook family to be sure.

One she did not seem to fit into—no matter how hard she tried.

The air stirred behind her as someone slipped into the empty seat across from her. Will! Emma smiled in welcome, happy to see at least one other familiar face.

"Sorry I'm late. Got held up at home." Will's cheeks were a subtle shade of red as he unfolded his napkin and laid it on his lap.

"You haven't missed anything," Jonathan told him. "They're just serving the salad now."

"I didn't make it to the ceremony though." Disappointment shone in his eyes. "How did it go?"

"Very well," Emma said. "Corinne looked so happy as she received her diploma."

Will turned to stare across the room where the family sat. Corinne was laughing at something, her face aglow. "I'm glad," he said quietly. "She deserves it."

Poor Will. The raw longing in his voice matched the angst on his face. He dropped his gaze to his plate as the server set down his salad.

The rest of the meal passed in companionable conversation with the others at their table. At least Emma would know more of the people she worked with after this. They all seemed intelligent and kind, and thankfully none of them seemed to resent her presence.

"Where's Doris?" Emma asked Will at one point in between courses. She would have loved having her company at the table. Over the weeks at the university, Emma had come to appreciate Doris's wit and take-charge attitude.

"She and her fiancé had to cancel at the last minute. Some family crisis came up," Will said. "Lucky for you, I guess. It meant there were two extra seats at the table."

Emma's hand stilled on her fork. So the only reason Randall had invited her was because he had two seats that needed filling.

Not because he really wanted her there.

Her appetite vanished. She pushed the rest of her meal away.

After the dessert dishes were cleared, the band started up again. Would they move the tables for dancing afterward? Emma normally loved to dance—however, tonight she didn't think she could stomach it. As soon as it was polite to do so, she'd ask Jonathan to take her home.

She reached into her handbag and took out the small wrapped gift she'd gotten for Corinne. It was a tiny silver scroll that she could wear on a necklace or a charm bracelet. Emma hoped it would remind her of this significant time in her life, marking her entry into adulthood. Emma fingered the ribbon with an inward sigh. The reality was that Corinne probably wouldn't like it. Perhaps Emma would keep it and give it to her in private. She didn't relish the thought of all these people watching. Best not to bring any more attention to herself.

Behind her, the double doors opened, and seconds later, a redheaded man entered her line of vision, a camera slung around his neck.

Emma's mouth fell open. "What's he doing here?"

"Wainwright." Will scowled.

Emma tightened her grip on her napkin. "That fellow has some nerve. Coming to the ceremony is one thing. But this is a private function." She jumped up from the table. Mr. Wainwright had gotten past her once. She wouldn't allow him to do it again.

"Emma, wait."

She evaded Jonathan's hand and marched over to the reporter. "Mr. Wainwright. What are you doing here?"

"Miss Moore. How nice to see you."

"This event is by invitation only, and I'm fairly certain you haven't been granted one."

He gave her a look of cool regard as he set his satchel down on the floor. "Actually, I'm here to take photos of the graduate."

"On whose authority?" Emma couldn't imagine her father hiring the man who was trying so hard to ruin his career, unless he'd adopted the ideology of keeping your enemies close.

"Mrs. Moore herself. Sorry to disappoint you." He gave her a cocky grin and removed the lens cap from his camera. "Now, if you'll excuse me, I'm on the clock."

Emma walked back to her table. "He says Vera hired him," she told Will. "I don't know if I believe him or not, but I suppose we'll know soon enough." Would her father throw the man out or would manners dictate that he go along with the ruse?

Surprisingly, Randall shook Mr. Wainwright's hand and gestured him toward Corinne. He didn't appear the least bit distressed, which meant he must have sanctioned his wife's decision to hire the man. Either that or he was an excellent actor.

Emma, along with the rest of the group who still sipped their tea and coffee, watched the man take an assortment of photos—first just of Corinne, who posed like a true model, and then of the whole family together.

Finally, he lowered his camera, then turned to look over his shoulder. Emma swore he stared right at her.

"Are you certain you don't want any other members of the family included in some of the pictures?" he asked in a voice loud enough to be heard at the back of the room.

Emma's heart stuttered in her chest. He wouldn't—

"You've got all the family right here, Mr. Wainwright." Her father's clipped response spoke to his dislike of the man.

"But surely you'd want your lovely niece included?" He pointed toward the back of the room. "After all, she's working in your office now, so you obviously think highly of the girl."

Heads turned in their direction. Emma wished she could slide under the table, especially at the furious look on Vera's face.

"I didn't hire you to give opinions, Mr. Wainwright." Vera's shrill voice echoed in the suddenly quiet space. "If you're done with us, you may leave."

Mr. Wainwright shrugged, seemingly unfazed by her reprimand. "As you wish, ma'am." He snapped the cap back on the camera and bowed to Corinne. "Congratulations, Miss Moore. I hope you'll be pleased with the photos. I'll contact you when I have them ready."

In his cocky manner, he strutted past the tables toward the door, stopping to nod at Emma. "So sorry, Miss Moore. I wasn't aware of the strained family dynamics. Until next time." He tipped his hat at her, then sauntered out the door.

Jonathan clenched his hands into fists and fought to keep from running after the arrogant oaf and decking him. Only because he didn't wish to cause Emma any more discomfort did Jonathan force himself to remain seated.

Emma sat frozen beside him, her cheeks ablaze. "Jonathan, would you mind taking me home, please? I'm suddenly feeling . . . indisposed."

"Of course. I'll get your wrap."

"I'll come with you." Emma slid a small packet across the table. "Will, would you be so kind as to give this to Corinne? I'd like her to have it tonight."

"Certainly. I'll pass on your good wishes as well." Will picked up the box and tucked it in his jacket pocket. He gave her a sympathetic smile.

"Thank you." She rose from her chair. "I hope you'll excuse me," she said to the table at large. "It was lovely sharing the meal with you." Her strained smile tore at Jonathan's heartstrings.

"Good evening, everyone," he said. Then he took Emma's arm and led her out of the room.

They crossed the hall to the coat check and retrieved Emma's wrap. He helped her put it on and proceeded farther down the carpeted corridor toward the bank of elevators.

"That Wainwright chap better not be anywhere around," he muttered under his breath. "Or I might be tempted to create a scene worthy of front-page news."

Emma shook her head. "He's not worth the trouble. In his own slimy way, he's just doing his job."

The elevator doors opened, and they stepped inside.

"You're much more forgiving than I am. He singled you out

in front of everyone on purpose, just to get a reaction from Randall."

"And he got what he wanted," she said. "He stirred the pot quite well." Emma wiped the corners of her eyes with her gloved fingers. "I don't know why I expected anything different. Just because my father invited me tonight doesn't mean he wanted to announce my existence to the world."

When the door slid open, they walked out into the lobby of the grand hotel. Jonathan scanned the area to make sure the vile reporter wasn't hiding in the wings, ready to jump out and take their photograph. But like a true snake, it seemed he had slithered away.

Emma was uncommonly silent during the cab ride back to the boardinghouse. Jonathan searched for the appropriate words that might bring her comfort. *Lord, help me say something to ease her pain.*

"I'm so sorry, Em. I know you had high hopes for tonight. I wish your father could appreciate the gift he's been given to have a daughter like you."

"It's all right, Jonathan. We don't know what type of pressure he's dealing with at home. I can't expect him to jeopardize his marriage and his relationship with his other children—not to mention his career—for a stranger he's just met." She turned to look at him. The sadness in her eyes made his throat ache.

"No, it's not all right. Doesn't he realize what he's doing to you?" Especially after Jonathan had made it abundantly clear to the man how much was riding on his acceptance of Emma. He blew out a harsh breath, then deliberately softened his features. "You say the word and we can take the next ship back to England and forget all about Randall Moore and his pretentious life." He wanted nothing more than to take Emma back home where no unfeeling father could hurt her again.

She stiffened on the seat beside him. "I don't want to forget about him. He's my father." Her voice quavered, and Jonathan mentally berated himself for succumbing to a moment of weakness. "I'll just have to be patient a while longer. He'll come around. Eventually."

He took one of her hands in his. "You're remarkable, you know that? I've never met anyone braver than you."

"I'm not brave. Simply stubborn."

He held her gaze. "Emma, no matter what happens with your father, please remember that you'll always have me in your corner."

"I know that, Jon. And I thank God for you every day. You've been my lifeline since I lost Grandad. I wish—" She clamped her lips together.

"You wish what?" he prompted gently.

She shook her head. "Never mind. Just know that I appreciate you more than you can imagine."

In the cocoon of the back seat, with her hand warm in his, he'd never loved her more. His heart beat an unsteady rhythm in his chest. If he moved just a few inches closer, their lips would touch. Would she welcome his embrace or push him away, as Will had done with Corinne?

Before he could act, the cab drew to a halt in front of the boardinghouse.

"One dollar and twenty-five cents, please," the driver announced.

Emma slid out of the back seat. By the time Jonathan had paid the man, she was standing just inside the front door, where she waved to him. "Good night, Jonathan. We'll talk tomorrow."

Biting back another flood of frustration, he waved back. "Sweet dreams, Em." He stuffed his hands in his pockets, lowered his head, and made his way around back to the garage, ruing another missed opportunity.

Randall Moore wasn't the only one not brave enough to claim Emma.

Would Jonathan ever gain the courage to bare his heart to her, no matter the consequences?

Time was running out for him to decide.

CHAPTER 17

Corinne stretched luxuriously in her bed and hummed to herself, remembering the wonderful events of the previous day. Her graduation from high school. The ceremony at the Academy and the grand party afterward.

It was everything she'd hoped for—except that she'd had no time alone with Will. In fact, she'd barely gotten to say hello or acknowledge the gifts he'd brought. One had been from Emmaline, which Corinne had pointedly ignored, gushing instead over Will's present: a new edition of the Oxford dictionary, inscribed *Affectionately yours, Will*.

Corinne glanced at her dresser, where the book sat beside the unopened box from Emmaline. Why had Papa even invited her? Didn't he realize that Corinne wouldn't want her there? At least he had the good sense to seat her at the farthest table, where she wouldn't interfere. That is, until that horrid photographer had pointed her out. Why did Mama hire *him* to take the pictures? Surely there were more qualified professionals she could have engaged. Knowing Mama, there was another reason why she chose him, though Corinne couldn't begin to fathom her mother's motives.

Fifteen minutes later, she headed down for breakfast, amazed to find her father at the dining table. The delicious aroma of pancakes and maple syrup filled the room.

"Good morning, Papa. What are you doing still home?" Even though it was Saturday, he usually went in to work for several hours.

He laid aside the newspaper and smiled at her. "I wanted to spend some time with my daughter. Is there anything wrong with that?"

Her father took the day off work to be with her? Excitement filtered through her chest. "Really, Papa? I'm so glad. What shall we do?"

"I thought we'd take a little drive around the city, then I'll treat you to an early dinner at Chez Marie's."

"That sounds wonderful." She took a seat and pulled a napkin across her lap. A maid appeared with the platter of pancakes and placed some onto Corinne's plate.

Papa cleared his throat. "Tell me, Corinne, do you still enjoy painting?"

"I haven't done much lately, but yes. Now that I have more time, I'd like to start sketching again."

"Wonderful. Then perhaps we should visit the museum today. I hear they have an amazing Impressionist exhibit on display right now."

"That sounds perfect." She leaned to one side while the maid filled her juice glass. "Thank you, Ellen."

Papa poured himself another cup of coffee, the rich aroma wafting over to her. "After that, perhaps we can drop in to the English department at the university. Collect some brochures and see what courses are available."

Corinne set her fork down with a clunk. "I thought I made myself clear. I have no desire to attend university." She reached for the teapot, annoyed to find her hands unsteady.

"If English isn't to your liking, I'm sure we can find something more suitable. Perhaps some courses in fine art?"

"No."

Papa's brows thundered together. "Then what do you plan to do with your time? You're far too intelligent to just sit around this house all day long."

"I intend to enjoy the summer, and in the fall I will join Mama with her charity work. She can always use the help." She glanced up at her father. "I also thought I could assist Will with your campaign. I think we'd make a great team." If she couldn't work with Will at the university, then this was her next best option. She hoped Papa would be thrilled with her interest in his political career.

However, his mouth pulled down at the edges, and he released a slow breath. "I don't know, Corinne."

"Papa, what on earth would I do with an English degree? Join Mr. Wainwright at the newspaper?" She gave a light laugh to cover her discomfort and smiled brightly, her tried and true method of getting her way with her father.

Sure enough, he shook his head and chuckled. "I guess you have a point. But my darling girl, you have so much potential. I want you to do something great with your life. Please promise you'll give the matter some serious thought."

"That's one thing I can do." She smiled again and took a quick sip of tea to hide the gleam in her eye.

Little did he know that she'd given her future a great deal of consideration and had come to one unavoidable conclusion: The only thing she planned to accomplish was becoming Mrs. William Munroe.

"I'm sorry I didn't get to spend more time with you yesterday, Emma." Marianne maneuvered her chair farther back into the hospital elevator car while Emma pushed the button for the third floor. "I wish you were at our table. Then we could have talked all night."

As the elevator jerked into motion, Emma banished her disappointment from the evening before and forced a smile. "It's a good thing that we have all day together today then. I was so happy when you asked me to come to your therapy session."

The girl's invitation had indeed lifted Emma's spirits considerably. She'd been in her room, attempting to write in her journal. Wallowing in her disappointment, Emma could barely put pen to paper, and instead had spent most of the morning staring out her bedroom window. She'd even briefly considered taking Jonathan's advice and booking a ticket back to England. After all, if her father was never going to accept her in his life, what was the point in staying where she wasn't wanted?

Two things stopped her. First, the idea of disappointing Marianne. And second, the subtle and disconcerting shift in her relationship with Jonathan. On two separate occasions now, she'd sensed he'd been about to kiss her. The jumble of emotions that had rioted through her both times had left her shaken and unsure of where their relationship stood.

Jonathan had always been her best friend, her honorary brother.

Then why did his nearness scramble her pulse lately? Make her palms sweat and her breathing shaky?

Now that she thought back, there'd been a change in Jonathan's reaction to her ever since he returned from the war. Heat warmed her cheeks as she recalled the embrace he'd given her upon their reunion at the train station, the way he'd held on to her as though she contained the very air that sustained him. He'd actually wept, which had rattled her, but Emma had simply put it down to the effects of surviving the atrocities of war. Could it have been more? And if so, how did she feel about that?

Her heart fluttered at the thought.

Until she had time to sort through her feelings, she could not commit to going back to England with him.

"Emma?" Marianne's voice broke through Emma's confused thoughts. "The elevator has stopped."

"Oh, I'm sorry." Emma grasped the handles of the wheelchair and steered Marianne into the hospital corridor. "Which way?"

"To the right. Follow the signs to the physical therapy room."

A few minutes later, they entered the designated area, and Emma was immediately fascinated with the array of equipment. When she glanced down at Marianne, however, the girl's face had drained of color, and she clutched the arms of her chair with white-knuckled anticipation.

"Are you nervous?" Emma asked softly.

Marianne shook her head. "I just don't like the exercises they make me do. They're painful."

Emma bent down to eye level. "I always find a reward helps me endure something unpleasant. How about we go for an ice cream sundae when you're finished?"

"With whipped cream and cherries on top?" The spark of life in her sister's eyes brought a smile to Emma's lips.

"Absolutely."

"And don't forget the nuts," a male voice said. "Sundaes aren't complete without crushed walnuts."

Emma straightened quickly to see a tall, handsome man dressed in a white coat enter the room, his gray eyes twinkling. He didn't appear much older than Emma, yet he must be to have finished medical school.

"Hello. I'm Dr. Hancock, Marianne's therapist." He held out a hand to Emma.

"Emmaline Moore, Marianne's . . . cousin." She shook his hand.

"And where is Mrs. Moore today?"

"She had an emergency board meeting to attend," Marianne said. "I asked if Emma could take me today, and Mama said it would be all right."

Dr. Hancock turned his smile on Emma. "I'm very glad she did." He pointed to a chair on the far wall. "You may have a seat over there while I get started with Marianne."

"I'd like to observe a little closer, if I won't be in your way," Emma said. "I thought that maybe I could learn some of the simpler exercises so I could practice with Marianne at home."

"Do you live with the family?"

"No," she replied quickly. "But I could come over several times a week and work with her, unless that would be stepping on anyone's toes." She looked at Marianne. "Does your mother like to help you with that?"

She wrinkled her nose. "No, Mama doesn't like to do anything physical. Sometimes Papa makes me do exercises, but only when he's not working or out at meetings."

"What about Corinne?"

"Heavens no." Marianne giggled. "She doesn't even like coming here with me."

"So I've noticed." The doctor grinned. "For a while I thought it was *me* she was trying to avoid." He wheeled Marianne's chair over to a set of parallel bars and a bench with some weights. "Let's get your muscles warmed up first."

The doctor elevated the girl's legs onto the bench. Then he opened the lid of a metal box, reached inside with a pair of tongs, and lifted out a towel. "We use heated towels to relax and loosen the muscles before we begin," he explained to Emma. He folded one towel and laid it across the length of one leg, then repeated the procedure with a second towel. "Now we wait five minutes for the heat to do its work." He winked at Marianne.

"This is the easy part," Marianne replied. "It's the rest that isn't so nice."

"I'll do my best not to hurt you." Dr. Hancock's features became solemn. "My mission isn't to cause you pain, but unfortunately a little discomfort is necessary to get the muscles to function again." He glanced over at Emma. "If you're willing to work with Marianne at home, her future sessions might go much easier."

"I'll do my best. If her parents allow it."

The doctor frowned. "Why would they object?"

Emma's back stiffened. How could she explain without telling him the whole ugly story? "I'm sure it will be fine." She smiled at him, hoping he'd let the matter drop.

He studied her, then nodded. "That would be a big help." He lowered his voice. "I've been suggesting they hire someone at home to do the exercises with Marianne, but I've sensed some resistance, which puzzles me. Why go through the trouble of bringing her here if they don't really want the treatment to succeed?"

"Why indeed?" Emma shook her head. So many of her father's attitudes remained a mystery to her. Would she ever get behind his façade and learn his true motivations?

"Sit or stand wherever you're comfortable, Miss Moore. And if you have any questions, you may ask at any time." The doctor turned back to Marianne and removed the towels.

The next forty minutes passed by in a flash while Emma watched with admiration as the doctor worked. True to his promise, he used the utmost gentleness with Marianne, backing off immediately as soon as he perceived the actions were causing too much discomfort.

"When will we try to stand again, Dr. Hancock?" Despite her fatigue from the draining exercises, Marianne still seemed optimistic.

"If you continue to work at home, we might be able to try in a few weeks. If I feel the muscles are strong enough." He patted her shoulder. "And don't forget to work on your arm strength as well. The next step in getting mobile would be metal leg braces and arm crutches. You'd have to be strong enough to bear your weight on your arms."

He turned his full focus on Emma. "Would you like me to write down some of the exercises you can do with Marianne?"

"That would be helpful. Thank you."

"My pleasure." His eyes crinkled as he smiled. "I'm glad Marianne has someone willing to work with her. I expect we'll start to see great improvements over the next few weeks."

Emma smiled but inwardly wondered at the battle she might face with Marianne's parents. Why wouldn't a mother do everything in her power to help her child walk again?

Perhaps she'd have a private conversation with Randall and let him smooth the way for Emma's assistance.

CHAPTER 18

Corinne followed her father into the Faculty of Law department, discreetly attempting to pat her hair into place on the off chance that she might run into Will. When Papa had told her after their visit to the museum that he needed to drop by his office for a few minutes, her heart had nearly stopped beating. What were the chances that Will would be there?

To her amazement, he was waiting by her father's door as though expecting them.

"Hello, sir. Good afternoon, Corinne." A flush graced Will's cheeks.

Papa turned to her. "I hope you don't mind, honey, but I asked Will to show you around campus. I thought you might enjoy it more with someone closer to your own age. And Will can give you an unbiased opinion of the institution." He winked at Will.

Corinne clasped her hands together, uncertain whether she should be ecstatic or suspicious at this turn of events. Was Papa trying to use Will to persuade her to his way of thinking?

In any event, it didn't matter. She was being given the opportunity to spend one-on-one time with Will, and she didn't care the reason.

"I don't mind at all, Papa," she said, smiling.

Even though Will had been at her graduation party, she hadn't had much chance to talk to him since the roller-skating debacle. She hoped that since he was such a gentleman, he wouldn't bring up the incident again.

"Good. And maybe afterward the three of us can dine at Chez Marie's."

Will took a step back, shaking his head. "That's not necessary, sir."

Corinne's spirits plummeted. Didn't he want to eat with her in one of the city's finest restaurants? It was the closest thing they'd get to an actual date.

"Don't turn down an offer like that, son. It may not happen again." Papa gave Will a long look, one that seemed to have more meaning than she could fathom. He looked at his pocket watch. "By then it will likely be closer to the dinner hour anyway."

"Please join us, Will." She held her breath, waiting for his response.

At last he nodded. "Thank you. I'd be honored."

Two hours later, after walking up and down the stairs in many different buildings, Corinne's shoes had begun to pinch her toes. If Will hadn't been her guide, she would have put a halt to this tour long ago.

Corinne slowed her steps as they crossed one of the university's lawns. "If you don't mind, could we go somewhere to sit for a while? My feet could use the rest."

"Of course. I should have thought of that sooner." Will guided her over to a bench under a tree and sat down beside her, leaving far too much room between them.

"Don't apologize. I've enjoyed our time together." She hoped he'd understand her meaning—not that she'd enjoyed the tour exactly, but rather his company.

"So, did any of the courses interest you?" Will splayed his hands flat over his thighs as if unsure what to do with them.

"Not especially." She leaned closer, near enough to catch the scent of his soap. "Can I tell you something?"

His breath seemed to catch in his throat, but he nodded. "Of course. You can tell me anything."

"I have no desire to attend university. But Papa seems to have his heart set on it for some reason."

"I see." Will studied her quietly. "Then what do you want for your future, Corinne?"

Her heart gave a strange little quiver. What if she answered him with the bare, unadulterated truth? Would he get up and race off? Better to soften her response. "You won't laugh?"

"Of course not." His green eyes were solemn. Trustworthy.

She drew in a breath. "After school finished, I was hoping to get the job as my father's secretary. But then he gave it to Emma."

Will's brows rose. "Did you tell your father that you wanted the job?"

"Not directly. But I hinted many times." She smoothed her skirt over her knees. "I thought he understood and was holding it open for me."

"I didn't know you could type." Will seemed to be having a hard time keeping his lips from twitching.

"I can't. But I'm sure I could learn. I picked up the piano fairly quickly."

He laughed, and his gaze held a glint of admiration. "I believe you could do anything you set your mind to. Although I never thought you'd be interested in office work."

She lowered her gaze to her lap. "I want to do something meaningful. And what better way than to help my father?" She peeked up at him. "I told him this morning that I also want to join his campaign team. Help him win the election."

Real approval shone in Will's eyes. "You would surely be an asset. I'd be happy to mention it to him again if you think it would help."

"Really? That would be wonderful." She beamed at him.

He swallowed and looked away.

Several seconds of silence passed. A few students walked by on the path toward the street.

"Can I tell you something in confidence?" Will said at last.

"Certainly." Corinne's breath tangled in her lungs. Was he at last ready to declare his feelings?

He leaned closer. "I'm very fond of Emmaline, but I don't think she's cut out to be a secretary. She's wasted more paper than anyone in the whole department."

Corinne covered her mouth to stifle a giggle. "Really?"

"It's true. If it weren't for her relation to your father, I'm certain he would have fired her long ago." He unbuttoned his jacket and let it fall open. "You might consider taking a few typing lessons in the event that the position becomes vacant again."

"That's a great idea, though I wonder if Papa will allow it. He may think it beneath me."

"Would he have to know exactly what course you're taking?"

"Why, Mr. Munroe, I didn't realize how devious you could be."

He laughed out loud. "I've had my share of practice in getting around a domineering parent."

"Then you understand my dilemma."

"All too well, Corinne." He cleared his throat and rose. "I need to get my bag from the office before we meet your father. Do you want to wait here or come with me?"

"I think my feet have sufficiently recovered." She held out a hand.

Slowly he took it and helped her to her feet. But he didn't release her right away. "I want you to know, Corinne," he said softly, "that I hold you in the highest regard. And if I could relive that moment at the roller rink over again, I would never have pushed you away." He raised her hand to his lips.

His mouth warmed her skin, and her heart leaped in her chest.

"I think very highly of you too, Will." She looked into his eyes, praying he would pull her into his arms now and kiss her. "In fact, I've been hoping you might ask me out." Her mouth went dry. She chewed her bottom lip, praying she hadn't gone too far.

He let out a sigh. "Believe me, if I were in a position to court you, I would do so without hesitation. But being your father's protégé, along with my studies and all my responsibilities at home, I'm afraid it's not feasible right now."

Her heightened spirits plummeted. "But I don't care about any of that, Will."

He gave a sad smile. "You deserve a man who can give you the world, Corinne. Not one with so many obligations weighing him down."

She fought for some logical argument to persuade him to her way of thinking. But nothing came to mind. Other than "I love you," which she doubted would sway him.

"Come on," he said. "We don't want to keep your father waiting."

They made a quick trip up to the law office. Corinne waited by Emma's desk while Will went to his area in the back. Resentment burned inside her as she ran her hand over the smooth desktop and rolled a pen between her fingers. This should be her spot. Her work area. Now more than ever, Corinne needed to have a job here so she could see Will on a daily basis. Surely then he would realize that the obstacles he mentioned weren't really obstacles at all.

She picked up a bottle of ink and twirled it absently. What she needed was a way to make Emma's departure happen sooner rather than later. Quietly, she opened the top drawer a few inches. Inside were some handwritten documents, as well as several typed pages.

Her throat tightened. Before she could let her conscience overrule her, she unscrewed the cap and tipped the ink out. It pooled in a dark puddle, soaking into the papers. She pushed the drawer closed just as Will approached.

"Ready?" she asked brightly.

"Sure am. I hope I don't look too out of place at this restaurant. I've never been anywhere so fancy before."

"Don't worry." She looped her arm through his. "I'll make sure you feel right at home."

CHAPTER 19

Jonathan opened the envelope and eagerly removed a letter from his Aunt Trudy. He'd been hoping for weeks now to hear from her again, and finally she'd answered his many letters. He only prayed she would be honest and not keep any unpleasant news from him.

Halfway through the missive, Jonathan's heart sank. Just as he suspected, his aunt was struggling both financially and personally. With him so far away and Felix gone, Aunt Trudy had lost both her support systems. Though fairly independent, she was still a somewhat fragile woman who needed help chopping wood for the stove, lifting some of the heavy bolts of material down from the higher shelves, and fixing the plumbing when leaks sprung up. Jonathan had spoken with their minister before he left, asking him to keep an eye on her and to send the parishioners over once in a while to keep her company or help out in the store.

Aunt Trudy didn't mention any such visits in her letter. But she did say that the bank manager had been harassing her again. All over that pesky loan, one that would have been paid off long ago if Jonathan hadn't been away at war. He sighed. If only he could be in two places at once, maybe then he wouldn't be plagued with such constant guilt.

What if the bank made good on their repeated threats and called in her loan? Aunt Trudy would lose her shop. And since they lived in the flat above the store, she'd also have to find a new home.

Jonathan couldn't allow that to happen. Ever since his uncle Truman had died twenty years ago, Aunt Trudy had put every penny into Trudy's Dress Designs, determined to earn a living for herself. And when Jonathan's family had perished in that fire, she hadn't hesitated for one second to take in the orphaned boy. Jonathan owed her everything, and because of that, he would never abandon her, never allow her to lose the store that meant so much to her.

He took out a piece of paper from the bedside table. He intended to write to the bank and ascertain their intentions. If at all possible, Jonathan would get them to leave his aunt alone, at least until he returned later in the summer to handle her finances.

Never had the weight of his responsibilities threatened to undo him. For as much as he owed Aunt Trudy, he felt an equal, if not greater, responsibility toward Emma. How could he leave her in this strange country with a family that barely acknowledged her existence? What would Emma do if Randall broke ties with her? How would she make a living here all alone? Would she come back to England, even though selling her grandfather's shop meant she no longer had a job or a home to return to?

Jonathan lowered his head. The only thing he could do was pray for a solution to his troubles and trust God to provide the answers he needed.

Lord, show me the right path to take, one that will allow me to take care of both the women who need me. I can't bear to let either one of them down.

On Monday morning, for the first time since she started her job, Emma considered faking an illness so as not to have to go in to work. Still smarting from her treatment at the graduation, she didn't know if she could set aside her hurt and continue as though nothing had happened.

But unfortunately, her grandad's mantra rang in her head: *"Never shirk your duty, Emma girl. If you're lucky enough to have a job, make sure you don't take it for granted."*

Heaving a sigh, Emma climbed the stairs to the office. Likely her father wouldn't even realize that Emma might be upset by what happened at the graduation. He'd probably never given it—or her—a moment's thought.

But for Marianne's sake, if nothing else, Emma would persevere.

"Good morning, Doris," Emma called as she reached her desk. She frowned, finding her chair somewhat askew. Had the janitor forgotten to put it under the desk when he'd finished cleaning?

"Morning, Emma." Doris held up her coffee mug in a silent salute and nodded toward Randall's door. "The boss is in early today."

With a sigh, Emma pulled her chair over and took a seat. This morning she had to finish the minutes from the law society board meeting. Mrs. Anderson had been kind enough to provide a longhand version of the minutes, knowing Emma would be asked to type them. And Emma had been so careful with each page, placing each one safely in her drawer as soon as she finished it. This was an important document, one that had to be error-free since it was going out to the university's board of directors. Emma was glad those secretarial courses she'd signed up for would start soon. Maybe then she'd begin to feel more competent at her job.

But when she uncovered the typewriter and then opened her

drawer to take out the documents, a shriek escaped her lips before she could stop it.

"What's the matter?" Doris crossed the aisle.

With a hand over her mouth, Emma pointed to the inky mess in her drawer.

"Oh dear. That's unfortunate." Behind her large glasses, Doris's eyes shone with sympathy. "Let me get something to clean this up."

She disappeared down the hall and came back moments later with a couple of large rags.

Emma fought back tears as Doris dabbed at some of the ink that was still wet. The rest, it seemed, had soaked right through all the papers underneath. How was she going to explain to her father that the whole document was ruined?

"What a shame. I don't think any of this can be salvaged." Doris held out the blackened stack of papers for Emma to see before she dropped the whole mess into the metal bin.

"What am I going to do?" Emma said. "He needs those minutes done by today."

"What if I help you? I can take one half and you do the other. If we're lucky, the professor won't ask you for it till later this afternoon. Do you have the original notes?"

Emma shook her head. "They were in that pile," she whispered.

Doris reached into the can and searched through the pages, pulling out the stained handwritten minutes. "It's no use. They're unreadable." She huffed out a breath and tossed the pages back into the trash.

"I didn't put the ink bottle in that drawer, Doris."

"What?" Doris paused from wiping her fingers on a clean rag. "Then how did it get in there?"

"I have no idea. But someone has been here since Friday. My chair was out of place, and"—Emma picked up a pen from the desktop—"this pen was moved, and the ink bottle was spilled in the drawer." She looked up at Doris. "If I didn't know better, I'd swear someone did this on purpose."

Doris threw the rag down. "Why would anyone do such a thing?"

Emma's mind swirled. Only one person came to mind. Well, two really, but she doubted Vera would stoop so low. It was entirely possible, however, that her daughter might.

"Good morning, ladies." Will entered the office whistling to himself.

Emma rose from her chair and followed him to his desk. "Good morning, Will." She attempted to keep her voice even. "Do you know if anyone was in the office either last night or on Saturday?"

He removed his cap and put it on the coat hook. "I was here on Saturday. Around dinner time. Why?"

"Did you see anyone lurking about?"

"Lurking?" He frowned. "No. Why? Is something wrong?"

Emma inhaled and lifted her chin. "Someone spilled a whole bottle of ink in my top drawer."

For a split second, Will's eyes widened, then he looked away, busying himself with his satchel. "Why would anyone do that? I'm sure it must have just tipped somehow."

"Was anyone else in the office, Will?"

He pressed his lips together. "I only came back for a minute to get my bag. I didn't see anyone in here."

Emma studied the streaks of red across his cheeks. He was lying to her, she was certain. But why? Surely *he* wouldn't have done such a thing. Would he?

The professor's door opened, and a scowling Randall poked his head out. "Is anyone here planning on working today?"

Will plopped into his chair, still not meeting Emma's eyes.

Emma hurried back to her desk. "Good morning, Professor," she said. "Is there something you need?"

Randall turned piercing blue eyes on her. "As a matter of fact, yes. I need those minutes from the board meeting. Have you finished them yet?" His irritated tone indicated that he thought she'd taken more than enough time already.

Her stomach sank. There was no escaping this now. "Unfortunately, there's been a slight accident."

His dark brows crashed down. All noise in the office seemed to cease.

"A bottle of ink spilled in the drawer." She lifted the trash can. "Everything was ruined."

He stared at the pile of ink-stained pages. "How could a bottle of ink spill on its own?"

"I have no idea. When I left on Friday, it was on my desktop. I don't know if one of the cleaners put it away or how it got in my drawer."

"The cleaners usually come in on Friday night," Doris said with an rueful glance at Emma. "But they never remove anything left out on the desk."

"Then I have no explanation for how this could have happened." Emma gave a miserable shrug.

Randall moved into the outer office. "Will, you were here on Saturday. Did you see anything out of the ordinary?"

"No, sir. Everything was fine when I was here." Will's voice was tight, and he barely looked up from his desk.

Randall's lips pinched until they were white. "I suppose the handwritten minutes were ruined as well?"

Emma nodded.

He blew out a loud breath. "Excuse me while I make some unpleasant phone calls." The door slammed behind him.

Emma sank onto her chair, any hope of impressing her father with her abilities now darker than the inky mess in her trash bin.

Randall replaced the receiver on the telephone and rubbed his temples. The board members were understandably upset that the minutes of their last meeting were ruined. The head of the faculty told him he'd call around to see if anyone else had taken notes. If they were lucky, they might get a rough outline of the topics discussed—enough for *his* secretary to transcribe, which is what Randall should have requested to begin with. The board usually took turns having the different faculty staff prepare the minutes. Randall should have been up-front about Emma's abilities and not given her something so challenging until she'd gained more experience or at least completed some secretarial courses.

He shoved away from the desk to look out the window at the grounds below. This was not the way he'd wanted the day to begin. His head already hurt from another argument he'd had with his wife that morning over hiring that good-for-nothing Wainwright to take pictures at the graduation. Randall had almost lost his cool when the man had walked into the room at the hotel. But Vera claimed that it was an effort to get on the man's good side, to garner favor in the hopes of getting him to cease his efforts to discredit Randall.

Sometimes his wife overestimated the power of money to get her own way.

Randall stared out at the peaceful scene below. Students walking across campus to their classes. Some reading on the benches beneath the trees. All so serene, while up here, Randall was gripped by unrest. He hated what he had to do next, but there was really no other choice.

He crossed to the door and peered out at Emma, who was trying to clean her drawer. "Emmaline. May I have a word, please?"

She lifted her head, misery swirling in her eyes.

He knew just how she felt.

He went back to his desk to wait for her. A few seconds later, she entered, notebook in hand, and took a seat across from him.

"I'm terribly sorry about the ink," she said immediately. "I don't know what could have happened."

Randall forced a smile. "I'm certain you never intended any harm."

"Of course not. I want to help you, not cause more problems. Yet that's all I seem to do." She lowered her head to gaze at the notebook on her lap.

"It's not your fault." He inhaled and then slowly let out his breath. "Do you remember the deal we made when I agreed to let you work here? That if either one of us found the situation . . . unsatisfactory, we'd be honest with the other?"

She nodded.

"I'm afraid that time has come." He straightened in his seat. "This arrangement isn't working, Emma, and not just because of the ink spill. You have many good qualities, but not ones suited to being a secretary."

Her shoulders slumped. She looked so defeated that he had to bite his tongue to keep from rescinding her termination. But common sense told him this was the best thing for both of them.

Perhaps he could salvage the situation somewhat by helping her figure out her next move. "Emma, what is it you envision for your future?" he asked as gently as he could.

She sniffed and took a handkerchief from her sleeve. "I-I don't know. I've never really allowed myself to think about it. I always assumed I'd be working with Grandad until the day I got married. Maybe even after that, if my husband didn't mind."

Randall studied her. On one hand, Emma was feisty and independent, yet in some ways she'd lived too sheltered a life. Why hadn't the Bartletts encouraged her to dream big, to spread her wings and leave that tiny town?

"Did you ever consider going to college?" he asked.

She shook her head. "Grandad depended on me to help run the shop. I never could have left him."

"All right. Let's look at this another way. If money were no object and there was nothing to stop you from doing what you wanted, what would you choose?"

She raised her eyes to him and blinked. "I suppose I'd be a bookkeeper. I love working with numbers."

"There. That wasn't so hard." Randall smiled. "You might consider taking a few accounting courses. That, combined with your previous experience, would put you in an excellent position to find a job."

"I suppose." Emma bit her lip, obviously still not convinced.

"Sometimes we have to be open to the different turns our lives can take," Randall said gently. "For instance, when I finished law school, I expected to become a top-notch attorney. Imagine my surprise when I found teaching made me the happiest." He picked up the letter opener with *The City of Toronto* engraved on the handle. "Of course, my interest in politics came later on, after I understood how local government worked and garnered some ideas as to how to improve conditions in the city."

"I'm sure you'll become mayor one day." Emma gave a tremulous smile.

"Enough about me. We're trying to figure out your next step." He tapped the blotter.

Emma tilted her head, a new spark of interest in her eyes. "I do have one thing I wanted to talk to you about."

"Why does that make me nervous?"

She laughed. "Jonathan always says the same thing. I hope you'll think my idea has merit." She fiddled with the notebook on her lap. "Marianne's doctor showed me some of the simpler exercises he uses and suggested I work with her at home, which I am more than happy to do. He believes the extra practice will strengthen her muscles faster and might even lead to her being able to walk with braces. Wouldn't that be wonderful?"

"It certainly would." The very thought of his little girl being able to walk at all made Randall's throat tighten.

Emma leaned forward on the chair. "Would you speak to Vera and see if she'd allow me to work with Marianne at the house?"

Instant tension radiated down Randall's spine. Doing battle with Vera was not something he enjoyed. In fact, he mostly deferred to his wife, simply because it was easier than fighting. They'd already had numerous arguments over Marianne's treatment, and each time he'd given in. Could he really bring up the issue again, this time with Emma in the mix? Yet how could he not try if it meant a chance to help Marianne?

"Very well. I'll see what I can do, but I'm not promising anything. Vera has set ideas about Marianne and her treatment. It took a lot to get her to concede to the therapy Marianne is presently receiving."

"That leads me to another question." Emma paused. "Why does the doctor seem to feel that Vera doesn't want Marianne to improve?"

Randall froze. "He told you that?" If so, the man was more astute than Randall gave him credit for, though the doctor wasn't entirely aware of Vera's motives and shouldn't be putting ideas in Emma's head.

"He implied as much, yes."

"It's not that she doesn't want Marianne to walk again," he said carefully. "It's more a fear of pushing her too far and causing a relapse. After almost losing her to that dreaded disease, we have become somewhat overprotective."

"But Marianne is older now. Shouldn't she have some say in the matter?"

"You have a point." He studied Emma, amazed at her resilience for someone who had just lost her job. His daughter had a lot of fine qualities. If only Vera could come to see Emma as he did. "I'll see what I can do."

The first true smile bloomed on Emma's lovely face. "Thank you. It means a lot to me."

Randall nodded. Maybe Emma's devotion to Marianne would be the key to unlocking his wife's hardened heart. Then he'd only have Corinne to worry about.

"Did you spill ink in Emma's desk the other day?" Will's question extinguished Corinne's excitement faster than a snuff to a candle.

She'd been thrilled to learn that he'd come over to the house on his lunch break, certain that he meant to ask her out on a real date. Every moment spent with Will on Saturday was etched with startling clarity in her mind. And even though he'd said he couldn't court her, the longing in his eyes told her he wanted to do just that. One way or another, Corinne was determined to change his mind.

But now, seated on the sofa in her living room, Corinne's palms grew damp. "Wh-what did you say?"

"You heard me," he said quietly. "Emma swears she left the bottle of ink on top of her desk. When she came in this morning, it had been spilled in her drawer."

Corinne dropped her gaze to the floor, clasping her hands together in her lap. How could she get out of this without lying to him?

"It ruined several valuable documents," he continued. "Ones that were very important to your father, and it got Emma in a whole pile of trouble."

Sudden outrage shot through Corinne's system. Why was he taking Emma's side over hers? She jumped to her feet. "If they were so important, she should have put them somewhere safer than a desk drawer. She's probably just trying to save face for ruining them."

Will stepped toward her, close enough for her to see the golden flecks in his eyes. "You were standing by her desk on Saturday. Did you perhaps knock the bottle over accidentally?" A frown furrowed his brow, but his eyes shone with sincerity. Was he trying to give her a plausible way to explain her actions?

A horrifying thought hit her. "You didn't tell my father I was there, did you?"

"Of course not. I wanted to talk to you first to find out the real story."

She bit her bottom lip and wrung her hands together, pacing away from him. Will was too honorable to lie to her father. He would eventually tell him of her presence at the office last night, and Papa would know what she'd done. How was she going to get out of this one?

The back of her throat burned. She stopped pacing and faced him. "Oh, Will. Something just came over me, and before I knew it, the ink was everywhere." Tears bloomed in her eyes, blurring his features.

With a sigh, he stepped forward and wrapped his arms around her. "Please don't cry, Corinne. It's going to be all right."

The tension eased from her muscles. He didn't hate her. He understood. She pressed her face into the wool of his jacket, drinking in the comfort of his embrace. The scent of his sandalwood soap mixed with a hint of smoke. "I'm sorry, Will. It was a foolish thing to do."

He rubbed a hand over her back in a soothing motion. "Everyone makes mistakes," he said in a gentle voice. "I'm sure if you explain it to your father—"

Tell Papa?

She jerked out of his arms. "Absolutely not. Will, you have to promise me you won't tell him. Please. Our relationship is finally getting better. If he thinks I did something to hurt Emma, it would ruin everything."

Will's shoulders sagged. He closed his eyes, let out a long breath, and then opened them. A mixture of sympathy and distress shone in their depths. "I'm pretty sure your father fired Emma this morning. Are you really going to let her take the blame and lose her job over something you did?"

Her lips trembled to match her shaking legs. She tried to answer but couldn't form the words. Did Will care about Emma more than her?

When he looked at her, the disappointment radiating from his eyes nearly stole her breath. "I've always admired your spirit, Corinne, but I never thought you'd be deliberately cruel to another person. And Emma is your sister." He shook his head. "I have to get back to work. I'll see myself out."

He picked up his hat and walked out the door, never once glancing back.

She rushed after him into the hall. "Wait, what are you going to tell my father?"

But it was too late. He'd already left the house.

Corinne walked back to the parlor and sank onto the sofa, a hand over her stomach.

What had she done?

She'd wanted to get rid of Emma, but instead she'd effectively destroyed any feelings Will might have had for her. What was she going to do now? Could she salvage the situation without earning her father's wrath?

"*You might as well be good, Corinne. Your sins will always come back to haunt you.*" Papa's words rang in her ears.

He was right.

This was one sin that surely would haunt her forever—especially if it cost her Will.

CHAPTER 20

"I don't know about you, but I had a rather interesting day." Emma leaned against the fence by the garden where Jonathan was digging up weeds. "I lost my job at the university."

For some reason, she wasn't nearly as upset as she'd expected to be over that occurrence. The one thing that did bother her was that someone might have purposely set her up to look bad in her father's eyes.

Jonathan's head jerked up. "What did you say?"

"My father sacked me."

"Oh, Em. I'm sorry." He brushed the dirt off his hands and straightened. "What happened?"

"A bottle of ink spilled in my desk and ruined some important documents. I have no idea how that bottle ended up in my drawer." She blew a curl off her forehead. "But I can't really blame Randall for firing me."

"Are you kidding? An accident is hardly grounds for dismissal."

She sighed. "The truth is I'm a terrible secretary. It takes me at least three tries to get one letter typed. And I can barely take dictation."

"He didn't give you very long to learn the ropes." Jonathan swiped the dust from his trousers. "What are you going to do now?"

She paused, recalling the conversation with her father. Despite the fact that he'd let her go, it hadn't ruined their relationship. "I'm hoping to work with Marianne to do physical therapy at home, if Randall can convince Vera to allow it."

"That's not what I meant. How will you make money? If you're going to stay in Canada, you'll have to earn a living."

"I'm not sure." She tilted her head, and the sun blazed into her eyes. "But I have an idea for a campaign project that might keep me busy, if Randall agrees. I haven't shared it with him yet. I didn't want to overwhelm him all at once."

Jonathan scratched his forehead, leaving a smear of dirt. "You surprise me, Emma. I would have thought you'd be devastated by this."

She shaded her eyes with her hand. "To tell the truth, I'm a little relieved. And after my father sacked me, we had a rather good chat. Discussed possibilities for the future. I think he felt bad for having to let me go."

"That's something, at least." He walked over to stand near her at the fence. He smelled of fresh earth and sunshine. Her gaze fell on his physique, so much fuller now after a few weeks of Mrs. Teeter's good cooking. His forearms and face were tanned from his hours spent in the garden. He radiated good health and . . . masculinity.

She looked into his eyes, and her mouth went dry.

He lifted a finger to her cheek. "You have a smudge of ink here," he said huskily.

A flutter of nerves invaded her belly, and for one crazy moment, she wanted to grab his face and kiss him. Instead, she gave a nervous laugh and stepped away. "What do you say we go out to dinner tonight? You can cheer me up and tell me more about your friend Reggie. And I'll tell you about my grand new idea."

Jonathan's eyes took on a mischievous look. "Are you asking me on a date?" he said with a wink.

"What if I am?" A rush of heat infused her cheeks.

He gave her a slow smile that made her heart beat faster in her chest. Then he threw his trowel on the grass. "Just give me twenty minutes to get cleaned up."

The fact that he was this giddy over one meal should have told Jonathan that he was living in a fool's paradise. But it was the end of June and he hadn't made any real headway with his plan to woo Emma. He had to make tonight count.

The fact that she'd seemed flustered by his presence a few minutes ago made his heart sing with hope. Could she slowly be developing romantic feelings for him? He offered a quick prayer heavenward that it might be so.

Changing quickly out of his work clothes, he washed up with a pitcher of water in his room. Then he pulled out his best shirt, waistcoat, and trousers, making sure to tame his hair and fix a perfect knot in his tie. On his way across the back lawn, he plucked a few of Mrs. C.'s flowers and twisted them into a posy for Emma. Instead of going through the kitchen, he went around to the front of the boardinghouse and knocked on the door.

Emma herself answered, her face brightening as she took in the flowers and his appearance. She was wearing a pretty striped dress that brought out the color of her eyes. Her freshly brushed hair shone under the entry hall light.

"For you, m'lady." He swept a bow, then held out the posy.

"Why, thank you, kind sir." She brought them to her nose and inhaled. "They're lovely."

"Are you ready to go?"

"I am. Let me get my purse." She disappeared inside for a minute, then returned with her bag. "I asked Mrs. C. to put the flowers in water for me."

"I hope she doesn't mind that I swiped them from her garden." He grinned as they strolled down the walkway.

"I don't know," she teased. "Your career as a gardener could be in jeopardy."

He laughed. "Where would you like to eat?"

"I thought we could try that Italian restaurant on King Street. It looks cute from the window."

"Do you mean Mama Vittore's?" Hopefully not, because judging by the tablecloths and candles, it might be expensive.

"That's the one." Her eyes lit up as she snaked her arm through his. "I think we deserve an elegant night, don't you?"

He smiled down at her. So much for his pocketbook. But with such excitement in her voice, he'd pay whatever it cost to keep her happy. "I must say, I'm amazed you're in such good spirits after what happened today."

"I was upset at first, but the more my father talked, the more I realized that he hated to disappoint me and, in fact, did everything he could to help me come up with a new plan."

They reached the restaurant, and Jonathan held the door open for her.

Inside, the enticing aromas of tomato sauce, garlic, and fresh bread surrounded them. Jonathan's stomach growled in response, and he suddenly realized he was ravenous after working in the garden all afternoon.

A hostess showed them to a table in the corner by the window. Almost instantly, a waiter appeared with a basket of bread and two menus. Once Jonathan had a chance to peek at the prices, he was relieved to see that they were quite reasonable after all.

After Emma had ordered the cheese tortellini and Jonathan had chosen the cannelloni al ragù, they finally had a chance to talk.

"What sort of therapy do you plan to do with Marianne?" Jonathan asked as he broke a piece of bread in half.

"Nothing too difficult. Her doctor gave me a few exercises I could help her with." She unfolded a pristine white napkin onto her lap. "He says that if Marianne works hard at home, as well as at her appointments, her muscles will strengthen faster and she might even be able to walk with braces. Wouldn't that be wonderful, Jonathan? To see her out of that chair?" Emma's eyes glistened in the candlelight.

"Yes," he said, his voice husky. "It certainly would."

"The only problem is Vera—and possibly Corinne." She paused in the midst of buttering her bread, knife in the air. "They still don't like me."

At that moment, she resembled the young eight-year-old girl she'd been when he first moved next door, sad because the girls at school were mean to her. Now, like then, he wanted to confront the bullies and make them play nice.

He reached across to squeeze her hand. "They don't know you well enough yet. Once they do, they won't be able to help but adore you."

Like I do. With effort, he refrained from adding that part.

She gripped his fingers. "Thank you. I wish everyone felt the same as you." Her features brightened. "The good news is that at least my father appears to like me."

"He should. He's your father, after all."

"That doesn't mean anything. Lots of parents don't get along with their children."

The waiter arrived with their entrées. He set their plates down with a flourish, then garnished the pasta with a heaping spoonful of grated cheese. "*Buon appetito.*" He bowed and hurried off.

Jonathan took the opportunity to change the subject slightly. "So, tell me about your grand idea. Does it have something to do with getting a new job?"

"Not exactly. More of a project I'd like to start." She speared a tortellini with her fork. "I want your honest opinion before I approach Randall about it." She placed the fork in her mouth and closed her eyes, savoring the flavor. "Mmm. This is delicious."

"I agree. Best cannelloni I've ever tasted."

"Back to my idea. I was thinking about the rally coming up. You remember the debate with Mayor Church?"

"I remember. Even Reggie is planning to attend."

"A debate is all well and good, but I think Randall needs something to show him interacting with the community in a positive light."

"What did you have in mind?"

She leaned forward, the flame from the candle casting a glow over her face. "A fundraiser for the children's hospital."

"The one Marianne goes to?"

"That's right. It's such a great institution. We could have games and pony rides and charge a small price for each. The money would go to the hospital. I'm sure the local papers would cover the event, and if Randall was photographed having fun with Marianne and mingling with families and kids, then the people would get to see him in a different light. Not just as a professor, but as a man who truly cares about all the citizens."

Jonathan set down his fork. "That's brilliant. Just what he needs to give him an edge: a more-rounded public persona."

"Exactly." She beamed at him. "Do you think Randall will like it?"

"He'd be crazy not to." He narrowed his eyes. "Does this mean you're joining his campaign team?"

"I'd like to. I don't think I'd get paid for it though, which wouldn't solve my employment issue." She took another bite of her pasta and washed it down with a sip of water.

Jonathan hated to dampen her enthusiasm, but she needed a

dose of reality to mix with her optimism. "Emma, what will you do if your father never claims you as his daughter and continues to say you're his niece? The election is a long way off. Can you really wait until next January before ending this masquerade?"

Her features clouded over. "I don't know."

He took her hand in his. "How about this idea then? If Randall agrees to do the fundraiser and the event goes well, you insist that he acknowledge you publicly."

She bit her bottom lip. "That's pushing a bit hard, don't you think?"

"His family has had more than enough time to get used to your presence. It's time to put yourself first for a change."

"I will. Soon, I promise." She smiled. "Let's wait and see how this idea goes over first."

Jonathan wanted to push her to stand up for herself. In other circumstances, she never had a problem with confidence. But when it came to her father, she was too afraid of alienating him to speak her mind.

Could he really blame her? After all, it was exactly the reason he'd been hesitating to reveal his heart to Emma. He was afraid of the repercussions.

"How have you been? Have you had any more . . . episodes lately?" Emma's quiet question brought him up short.

He stiffened. "No. Not for a few weeks now."

"That's good." She hesitated, then leaned closer. "Have you been able to talk about it with Reggie?"

His heart took on an uncomfortable palpitation. He shook his head.

"If it helps, you know you can tell me anything." Her earnest blue eyes held him captive.

Did he dare ruin the mood of the evening by sharing his guilt over the one event that tortured him the most? The one that she, more than anyone, had a right to know about? He took a sip of water to ease his suddenly dry throat. "There is something I need to tell you." He took in a breath. "It's about Danny."

Her brow furrowed. "Go on."

"I was there during the raid when he . . ." Jonathan swallowed. "We were running across a field. Danny was behind me when the explosion happened. I turned to look over my shoulder and . . ." He closed his eyes. "I saw Danny get hit. He stared right at me in horror as he flew backward." Jonathan wrenched his eyes open to clear the vision in his brain.

Emma sucked in a breath, but leaned closer, squeezing his hand.

"That's not the worst part." He could barely force the words from his throat. "If I'd gone after him, I might have been able to save him . . . but a wall of fire sprang up between us, and I couldn't make my legs move. I stood there like a statue until the rest of the squadron went in and retrieved his burned body." Unable to bear her anguish, he lowered his head, eyes fused to the bread basket.

"Oh, Jonathan." Her voice came out in a whisper. "How horrible."

"I live with that guilt every day. My fear prevented me from going to his aid."

She lifted a napkin to dab at her cheeks. "It doesn't sound like there was anything you could have done. And you might have ended up dead yourself."

"We'll never really know, will we? My best friend died while I watched." He swiped his fingers over his damp eyes, afraid to look up and see the disgust on her face.

Instead, her strong fingers gripped his hand. "Listen to me, Jonathan Rowe. You are not responsible for Danny's death. It was God's will, and as hard as it is, we must accept it."

He dared to look at her. "How can you say that when I cost you the life of your fiancé?"

Her gaze faltered, her expression pained. "If anyone has cause to feel guilty about Danny, it's me," she said quietly.

"Whatever for?"

"For agreeing to marry a man I wasn't in love with." She sagged back against her chair dejectedly. "The only reason I went along with the engagement was to give Danny a reason to come home."

Jonathan blinked. He'd tortured himself for months, thinking of Emma's pain at losing Danny. But she hadn't been in love with him at all?

"Don't misunderstand me," she said quickly. "I cared for Danny very much. His proposal came as a shock, and I probably shouldn't have accepted it. But it seemed cruel to end our relationship right when he was heading off to war."

Jonathan leaned back. How many times had Danny looked at Emma's photo and told him that she was the one thing keeping him going? That he would do everything in his power to return to her and their future together?

"I don't think it was a mistake," Jonathan said. "At least Danny's last days were happy, knowing you'd be waiting for him."

She shook her head and looked at him, an inexplicable emotion burning there. "I was far more worried about you being killed than Danny. Does that make me a terrible person?" She bit her bottom lip.

Jonathan's heart hammered in his chest. She'd worried more about him than her own fiancé? What did that mean? "You're not terrible." He reached for her hand. "It seems we've both been wrestling with our own demons over Danny." He smiled, a large part of his burden easing from his conscience. He might never fully get over his guilt, but at least now Emma knew the truth. "I'm glad we finally cleared that up."

An expression of relief washed over her features. "You don't hate me for treating your friend that way?"

"I could never hate you, Emma." The intensity of his feelings made his chest constrict, the air bursting in his lungs. He had to clamp his teeth together to keep from blurting out something she wasn't ready to hear.

A sudden movement beside them broke the moment. Their server stood smiling, waiting to clear the plates. Jonathan leaned back to allow him access to the tabletop. "Thank you. That was delicious."

"*Buono*." The waiter quickly stacked everything on a tray. "You have dessert and stay for the music, no?"

"What music?" Emma's eyes lit with curiosity.

"You wait and see." The waiter grinned and swept off with the dishes.

A few minutes later, two men walked up to a small raised platform at the end of the room, where a microphone had been placed. One rather stout fellow spoke in Italian, loud enough not to need any amplification. The people applauded.

Jonathan looked at Emma, who shrugged and laughed. Jonathan laughed too, relieved at the change in atmosphere. After all, this night was supposed to be fun, not maudlin or overly emotional.

The other man sat down on a stool and pulled out an ancient-looking accordion. After a few discordant notes, he got the rhythm down and began to play a lively tune. Then the stout man began to sing along in Italian.

Though Jonathan couldn't understand the lyrics, the foreign words oozed romance. Sure enough, several couples got up from their tables and began to dance in the small area near the platform.

Jonathan glanced at Emma, who seemed to be enraptured by the performance. Did he dare ask her to dance? His pulse sprinted hard. If he didn't make a move now, when would he ever?

He took a quick sip of water, then cleared his throat. "May I have the honor of this dance?"

A blush crept across Emma's cheeks, but she nodded.

Jonathan held out his hand and led her to the now-crowded dance floor. The group was a mix of ethnicities and ages. Old and young, short and tall, plump and thin. Within that circle, he and Emma could remain anonymous. Strangers on a first date in a foreign land.

The music changed tempo, and this time there was no doubt the man was singing a love song. The longing in his voice struck a chord deep within Jonathan. Anticipation and a touch of nerves spilled through his system when he placed a hand at Emma's waist and drew her closer. She fit against him perfectly. The floral scent of her perfume drifted up to him as they glided in time to the unfamiliar music.

He allowed his eyes to close, his cheek resting against the silkiness of her hair. Every sense seemed to come alive. The feel of her hand in his, the heat of their bodies touching, the intake of her every breath. He wished the music would never end, and they could stay locked together this way forever.

A perfect ending to a perfect date. Well . . . almost.

It would only be perfect if he got the chance to kiss her before the night was over.

Emma hummed to herself as she and Jonathan walked back to the boardinghouse. It had been a wonderful evening—more fun than she'd had in a long, long while. In fact, she could never remember having a better time with anyone.

Being held in Jonathan's arms had stirred something within her. Something magical and secret. Something she'd never dared examine before now.

Her feelings for Jonathan, once so staid and sure, were changing, and that confused her. She no longer thought of him as her brother—or even just her best friend. Best friends didn't cause one's pulse to skip or the nerves to jump in one's stomach. But lately, every time she was near Jonathan, the air around them fairly crackled with a strange sort of electricity. A type of anticipation. For what, she wasn't entirely sure. For their hands to brush, their eyes to lock, their lips to join?

She inhaled sharply. Was that really what she wanted? For him to kiss her? Not just a brotherly peck on the cheek, but a passionate kiss between a man and a woman?

Her heart quivered at the thought, but she couldn't deny it. Nor could she deny the fact that she'd never felt anything close to this with either Danny or Terrence. She'd dated Danny because he was the first boy who'd ever asked her out. And Terrence had been more of a safety net, a mature gentleman who would have made sure she was safe and protected—all the more important after Grandad died. But she'd never loved him. She knew that the moment he proposed. Yet she'd kept him dangling for weeks before she gave him her answer. Was the real reason for her hesitation the fact that she'd had feelings for Jonathan all along?

She tucked that idea away to examine later in the privacy of her room. For now, she planned to enjoy every minute of this magical night.

When they reached the boardinghouse, Jonathan unlatched the metal gate and escorted her up to the front porch. "Will you sit with me for a minute before you go in?"

"All right." She smoothed her dress under her as she sat down on the swing.

He took a seat beside her, so close that their legs brushed. Her mouth went dry, her breathing shallow. It was a beautiful summer evening, warm enough for her to be appreciative of the slight breeze. A multitude of twinkling stars dotted the dark night sky.

Very romantic. Maybe too romantic.

Jonathan's arm stretched behind her on the swing, and his fingers played with the loose ends of her hair. Surely, he must be able to hear the hammering of her heart.

She searched for something to say, but her mind was blank, fixated solely on the sensation of his fingers in her hair, brushing her neck.

The next thing she knew, he'd reached over with his other hand and caressed her bare arm, sliding down until his fingers entwined with hers.

"I had a wonderful time," he said quietly. "I wish this night never had to end."

She stared down at their joined hands. "I-I feel the same way."

In reality, she had no idea what she was truly feeling. Or what Jonathan was feeling. Was his pulse as erratic as hers? Was he having the same trouble breathing?

His hand came up to cup her face and slowly turn it toward him.

She lifted her eyes to his. The heat she saw there lit a match to her already chaotic pulse.

"Emma." The one word said everything.

Then he gently lowered his mouth to hers.

Her eyelids fluttered closed while her heart battled to escape the confines of her chest. His lips on hers became more demanding. Heat swirled through her system, and she leaned into him. Yearning, needing more. Every thought left her head as she kissed him back with an almost desperate desire. Her fingers found their way into his hair, while his arms tightened around her. She'd never felt safer, more cherished, more wanted in her entire life.

At last, he pulled away and rested his forehead against hers, his breath fast and warm against her cheek.

She didn't dare move lest she break the heavenly spell she was under. What had just happened?

She opened her eyes and pulled back a little to look at him.

"I've wanted to do that for a very long time now," he said in a husky voice. "To show you how special you are to me."

She didn't know what to say. He seemed to be waiting for her to admit to something she wasn't quite prepared to say. She hadn't even had time to examine this rush of new feelings.

"You're special to me too, Jonathan. You always have been."

He frowned slightly. It probably wasn't what he'd hoped to hear. But she couldn't give him more than that. Not yet anyway. This turn in their relationship seemed to be both a long time coming and happening overnight. She needed a bit of time to absorb it. To savor it. To see how it fit with the rest of her life.

"It's getting late. I should let you get inside." He brushed a quick kiss to her temple then rose.

The swing groaned in protest.

Emma stood as well, suddenly unsure what to do, what to say. "Good night, Jonathan. Thank you again for a wonderful evening."

"You're welcome." In the shadow of the porch, his eyes were unreadable. "Sweet dreams, Em."

She wanted him to pull her into his arms again, sweep her away with the sensations of his kisses. But he headed down the porch stairs and disappeared around the corner of the house, back to his humble room above the garage.

CHAPTER 21

The next day, Jonathan stopped at the door to the military hospital, willing his feet to keep moving. Was he making a huge mistake? He took in a breath, forced his mind to think of Emma and their amazing kiss last night and the reasons why he needed to conquer his inner demons.

She'd actually kissed him back, and for the first time, Jonathan had hope that they might share a future together. And if so, she deserved a whole man, not one broken on the inside.

"You need a minute before we go in?" Beside him Reggie leaned on his cane. He'd made great strides in wearing his new leg. Today marked the first occasion to wear it in public.

"I'm fine."

"There's no shame in being apprehensive. I think treating a physical injury is easier than what you're facing."

Jonathan agreed. He'd far rather be dealing with a gunshot wound, something tangible he could worry about. The horrors in his head were something he might never be able to erase. "You ever have flashbacks, Reg? Nightmares?"

His friend grimaced. "I did a few times, especially right after that last battle. But I think the fact that I was hit from behind and blacked out right away saved me." He gestured to Jonathan.

"You saw everything—the bodies and the destruction. I escaped all that."

"Maybe so." For a moment, he envied his friend and immediately hated himself. Reggie had lost his leg and his fiancée. "You don't have to come in with me, you know. I'll be fine."

"Hey, it's like I told you. You were there for me. Now it's my turn."

"Thanks." Jonathan inhaled deeply. "Let's go."

They took the elevator to the third floor, where the main offices were located. They found the right place and entered a comfortable-looking waiting area, entirely different from Dr. Clayborne's dingy office in the basement. Plush chairs sat around the perimeter of the room, flanked by tables with a variety of newspapers and magazines. At least Reggie would have a nice place to wait.

Jonathan gave his name at the reception desk, then sat down.

"It was nice of Doc Clayborne to get you in with his own doctor." Reggie flipped through a magazine. "He must be good if he fixed the doc."

Jonathan threw him a wry glance.

"Not that you need fixing." A flush invaded Reggie's cheeks.

"No, mate. You were right the first time. I do need fixing. I'm just not sure if that's even possible."

"You're in the best of hands, if that's any comfort."

"It is. Thanks again for coming with me."

"What are friends for?" Reggie tossed the magazine down with a grin. "While we're waiting, why don't you tell me more about your fabulous date with Emma?"

Emma watched her sister attempt to lift her leg. "That's it, Marianne. Five more repetitions on that side."

While she waited, Emma could barely resist the urge to twirl about in the middle of the room as a way of expressing the joy bursting inside her. Life could not be going any better. This morning, when Emma had approached Randall, he had whole-heartedly agreed to her idea for a fundraiser at the children's hospital. In fact, he'd been so enthused by the concept that he'd already started making phone calls and plans.

To make this day even sweeter, he'd smoothed the way for Emma to work with Marianne twice a week after Marianne's tutoring in the afternoon. She could tell that Vera hadn't readily given her consent, and that he'd had to put down his foot about the matter. Yet Emma was determined to win the woman over—if not by helping Marianne, then by assisting Randall with his campaign. After all, wasn't one of Vera's worries, and Mr. Fenton's as well, that Emma posed a threat to Randall's career? By joining efforts to improve Randall's public image, they would see how sincere she was in her desire to help her father achieve his dream.

And then there was Jonathan . . . Her pulse sped up just thinking of him.

"Emma, I've finished that exercise. Which one is next?" Marianne's question pulled Emma from her daydreams.

"Sorry, love. I got distracted." She crossed the room to remove the weights from Marianne's legs. They'd been using the music room as their exercise studio, mainly because of the wooden floors and open space. Other than a grand piano and a music stand, the room was virtually empty. Marianne told her that Corinne also used the room for her dancing lessons and for her oil painting, since the large windows afforded great light in the area.

"You're doing wonderful, Marianne. One more set and then you can rest."

The girl smiled, but the perspiration shining on her forehead bore evidence of the effort the exercises were taking.

"Don't push her, but at the same time don't go too easy on her," Dr. Hancock had said. *"Slowly increase the repetitions until she can do each exercise with little exertion. At that time, I'll give you some new ones to implement."*

Emma grabbed a wooden chair and moved it over to the bench where her sister sat. "I'm going to assist you with this one," she said, taking a seat. She lifted one of Marianne's legs and took her foot in her hand. "I want you to push your foot as hard as you can against me. Almost as though you were trying to push me off my seat."

Marianne giggled. "That wouldn't be very nice, would it?"

"Don't worry about being nice. Or about hurting me. I'd be thrilled if you actually knocked me over." Emma smiled. "All right, whenever you're ready. And hold it as long as you can."

After ten minutes of Marianne's valiant pushing, with one leg proving stronger than the other, Emma set her foot down. "Very good. Now you rest and I'll get you a drink of water."

"Wait, Emma."

She stopped, worried that she'd overtaxed her sister. "What is it? Are you feeling all right?"

"I'm fine." But Marianne's cheeks seemed a touch too red.

"Shall I help you into your chair?" Emma fanned the air in front of her. "Let me get you that water."

Marianne shook her head and threw Emma a pleading look. "I want you to help me stand up."

The air whooshed from Emma's lungs. As much as she'd love to grant Marianne's every wish, something told Emma it was too soon. "Oh, honey, I'm not sure that's a good idea. You need more time to strengthen your legs before you attempt that. It would defeat our purpose if you fell and hurt yourself."

Marianne jutted out her chin. "I've done it once before. I know I can do it again."

"But that was with Dr. Hancock, right?"

The girl nodded.

"He's more qualified to know if you're ready. Why don't we wait until next week when you go to see him again?"

Marianne frowned and scooted toward the end of the bench.

Emma reached out to place her hands on the girl's shoulders, just in case she had the notion to try standing on her own. "You don't want to undo all the hard work you've put in. Come on, let me help you back into your chair."

"Emmaline is right, Marianne. Your muscles have worked hard today and need time to recuperate."

Emma stiffened at Vera's cool voice. She offered up a quick prayer of thanks that she'd followed her instincts and not tried to help Marianne stand up.

"Cook has a snack ready for you in the kitchen. I'd like to talk to Emma in private, please."

"Yes, Mama." Marianne's thunderous look didn't match the meekness of her reply.

Emma wheeled the chair over and helped her sister into it, glad she was now adept at doing so. "I'll come in and say good-bye before I leave." Emma smiled brightly, yet her stomach jumbled at the thought of being alone with Vera.

As soon as Marianne wheeled out of the room, Emma braced herself for what was to come.

"I'm sure you know I was against you working with my daughter," Vera said in a clipped voice. She folded her arms over her chest, her rope of pearls bouncing at her neck.

"Yes, and I want to thank you for allowing me to. I only want to help, and at the same time, get to know Marianne better." Emma smiled. "She's a wonderful girl."

The rigid planes of Vera's face softened a fraction. "Thank you. She is indeed a special child." Vera went to move the chair Emma had been using back against the wall. "Randall accuses me of babying her too much. I can admit that he's right about that."

Emma rushed to help Vera lift the piano bench Emma had used for Marianne's therapy.

"I came by to make sure that you didn't overdo these exercises." Vera set the bench down by the piano. "Thank you for not giving in to my daughter's request."

Emma straightened. "Don't worry, Mrs. Moore. I promise I'm following the doctor's instructions to the letter. Although I will admit I was tempted by her pleas."

"She does have a way of making you want to grant her every wish." Vera smiled, and it struck Emma that she was actually a very attractive woman. "There's another topic I'd like to discuss."

"Yes?"

"Randall told me about your idea for the hospital fundraiser."

Emma held her breath. Would Vera veto the whole project?

"I think it's a fabulous idea. An event like that would give my husband the right kind of attention to boost his image."

"That's exactly what I thought. People need to see him as more than just a law professor."

Vera tilted her head. "You're a very astute young woman. I was worried that you being here might derail Randall's career. But I'm seeing now that you could actually be an asset."

Emma's heart soared. Had she really won the woman over at last? "That's all I ever wanted. To get to know my father and to help him in any way I can."

"Randall has already received approval from the hospital board to go ahead with the event. He's asked for my assistance in getting this project off the ground, which is going to require a Herculean effort on everyone's part since the only date the hospital had available was July 19." She studied Emma. "Would you be willing to work with the campaign team on this?"

"I would love to." Emma hardly dared to breathe.

"Good. Let's schedule a meeting with the committee so we can all put our heads together." She led Emma out into the hallway. "We'll need all the help we can get to pull this off within such a short time frame."

"I'm ready and able. I'll do anything I can."

"Excellent. I'll be in touch."

The next morning, Mrs. Chamberlain entered the dining room where Emma sat sipping the last of her morning tea. "You seem very happy this morning," she said. "Anything you care to share?"

Emma laughed. "Did my silly grin give me away?"

"That, and the humming I heard earlier." Mrs. C. set a tray on the table. "Does this have anything to do with your dinner with Jonathan the other night?"

Heat climbed into Emma's cheeks. "That's part of it." Another smile bloomed. "The other is that I'm finally making headway with my father and his wife." Emma had recently confessed to Mrs. Chamberlain the true nature of her relationship to Randall.

"That's wonderful, dear. I've been praying hard for just such an outcome." She loaded the rest of the breakfast dishes onto the tray.

"You and me both, Mrs. C." Emma set down her cup. "Jonathan kept telling me it would just take time. I guess I was too impatient."

"As Reverend Burke is so fond of saying, the best things in life are worth waiting for." Mrs. C. chuckled. The woman seemed extremely fond of the minister, often inviting him over for tea and scones. He, and now Jonathan, were the only men Mrs. C. let in the house.

Emma stood and placed her cup on the tray. "Speaking of Reverend Burke, you two seem awfully chummy. Anything *you* care to share?"

"Good gracious, child. At my age?" Mrs. C. chortled. "No,

we're merely friends. After each of us lost our spouses, we took comfort in our shared grief. But he has his life, and I have mine."

"You could have a fine life together."

For a moment Emma thought she saw a wistfulness pass over her landlady's face. "I think it's too late in the game for that. Now you, on the other hand, have many wonderful years ahead with that young man of yours."

Emma opened her mouth to protest. It was the years ahead that were the problem. To acknowledge her feelings for Jonathan would mean that he would likely expect her to return to England with him. And with her relationship with her father finally improving, Emma was not prepared to walk away from the family she'd just begun to know. Yet how could she deny her longing for Jonathan?

"Take some advice from a woman who's lived a good life: Don't let a fine man like Jonathan get away. It's clear to these old eyes how much he cares for you. A gift like that is rare indeed."

The doorbell rang, and Mrs. C. hurried down the hall to answer it, leaving Emma somewhat disturbed by the woman's words. It was almost as if she knew Emma had been having mixed emotions since her date with Jonathan. While she got light-headed at the mere recollection of their kiss, she was unsure how to act around him now. Part of her wanted more romantic moments, more wonderful kisses. The other part worried that if something went wrong, their friendship might never be the same again. And that thought terrified her.

"Emma, there's a young lady to see you. She's waiting in the front room."

Emma frowned. Who could that be? Maybe Doris had come to see how she was doing after being let go from her position at the office.

"Thank you, Mrs. C." She walked slowly down the hall and entered the parlor, then stopped in surprise.

Corinne stood by the fireplace, her purse clasped tightly in her gloved fingers. Though immaculately dressed in a peacock-blue skirt and white blouse, tension radiated from her frame. Her features were pinched, her lips pressed together.

"Corinne. Is everything all right?" Alarm leapt into Emma's throat. "Is Marianne—"

"She's fine." Corinne's voice was flat. "I came to speak to you about something else."

Emma gestured to the sofa. "Please sit down."

"No, thank you. I need to stand."

A surge of compassion rose in Emma's chest. No matter how unkind the girl had been to her, she was her sister after all, and still so very young. She walked over to Corinne. "I can see that something is upsetting you. What can I do to help?"

Instead of accepting Emma's gesture, sudden anger seemed to rise in Corinne's eyes. "Nothing. And after you hear what I have to say, I'm sure you'll want to rescind your offer."

Emma bit back a sigh and said a quick prayer for guidance. "Go on."

Corinne lifted her chin with an air of defiance. "I was the one who spilled the ink in your drawer."

Emma's mouth fell open. Even though she'd suspected Corinne might have been responsible, hearing it stated so blatantly was a shock. And from the girl's tone and body language, Emma knew it had been no accident. "Why, Corinne? Why would you do something like that?"

The girl shrugged and shifted from one foot to the other. Emma waited for more of a response, but Corinne remained stubbornly silent.

A flash of heat rose in Emma's chest. "Why do you dislike me so much? I've never done anything to you. All I wanted was to get to know my family."

Corinne's head jerked up. "We're not your family." The furious words erupted from her. "Papa is *my* father. Marianne is *my* sister. The job at the university should have been mine too." Corinne's cheeks blazed red and her body shook.

Emma stiffened at the sheer force of Corinne's anger. But she held her ground, determined to get the animosity out in the open once and for all. "I see," she said slowly. "You feel threatened by me. That I might take something that belongs to you."

"You've already done that." Corinne stalked across the room to stare out the front window. "Papa caters to you, Marianne dotes on you, and I'm forgotten. Nobody cares how I feel."

Though the girl was exaggerating, her hurt was real. Hurt that had started, Emma suspected, long before she ever showed up. Yet Emma had to acknowledge that while she'd been trying to win Randall's favor, she'd never taken the time to consider Corinne's point of view. Never thought that Corinne might be vying for his attention too. Or that perhaps she suffered from feeling less important.

A wave of sympathy rose, replacing the momentary anger. "I'm sorry, Corinne. I had no idea. I suppose I've been a trifle selfish. And, to be honest, somewhat jealous too."

Corinne whirled around. "Jealous? Of who?"

"Of you . . . and Marianne. You got to grow up with a mother and a father—my father—while I believed myself to be an orphan. All my life, I longed for the type of family you have." She smiled sadly. "Perhaps I've been trying too hard, hoping that one day I might belong—like you."

Corinne's mouth fell open. She blinked several times but said nothing.

Emma took a hesitant step toward her sister. What was done was done, and in truth, Emma didn't really want her job back anyway. She had nothing to lose by being generous. "Now that I'm no longer working at the university, perhaps you can talk to your father about getting the position. If he hired me on a trial basis, I don't see why he wouldn't give you the same chance."

A hardness returned to Corinne's features. "He won't after you tell him what I did. That I'm responsible for your getting fired." She flung out her hand in the direction of the door. "I'm sure you can't wait to run over and tell him."

Emma remained still. She'd assumed that Randall had sent Corinne over to confess. If her father didn't know, what had prompted this visit? "What made you come here today, Corinne?"

She stared at the floor. "Papa says if we wrong someone, we have to admit our mistake and make amends."

"But he didn't make you come. And I'm having a hard time believing you had a sudden attack of conscience. What's the real reason?"

Corinne's bottom lip trembled. "It's Will." The words rushed out, and moisture glistened in her eyes. "He figured it out and"— she gulped in some air—"he won't even speak to me now." Tears broke loose and slid down her cheeks.

Emma took her by the arm and guided her to the sofa. She handed the girl a handkerchief and waited while she sobbed. Emma sighed, and not knowing what else to do, bowed her head. "Lord, I ask for your guidance and wisdom. Corinne needs your help to fix this situation, to atone for her mistakes. Please show her the best way to do that. And help me to understand and forgive my sister. Amen." Then she reached out and took one of Corinne's hands. "Everyone makes mistakes. It's how we handle them that shows our true character."

Corinne blew her nose. "I-I'm sorry for ruining your work and getting you fired."

An actual apology. Could Emma be making a tiny bit of progress? "It's all right, Corinne. I forgive you."

The girl's head snapped up. "You do?"

Emma nodded. "I don't think I'm meant to be a typist anyway. I tried so hard to do a good job, but for the life of me, I couldn't seem to get through one letter without making a hundred errors."

Corinne's lips twitched. "Will said you wasted a lot of paper."

"More than a lot." Emma laughed. "You're welcome to take the position, if your father agrees."

For the first time, Corinne's features relaxed. "You're not going to tell Papa?"

Emma held Corinne's hopeful gaze. "From what I understand, being a tattletale is a cardinal sin among siblings, is it not? We sisters have to stick together."

"I-I don't know what to say . . . except thank you." Corinne squeezed Emma's hand.

Emma swallowed a rise of emotion. "You're welcome." She paused. "And if you think it would help, I could talk to Will. Tell him that you're truly sorry and that you apologized to me."

Hope fluttered over the girl's face. "You would do that after I've been so horrible to you?"

"Of course I will. If you'll do something for me."

A shadow of suspicion flashed over Corinne's features. "What is it?"

"Will you help me with Marianne's exercises when you're able? That way all three of us can get to know each other better." Emma held her breath. She hoped Corinne would want to spend time with her, not feel forced out of some guilty sense of obligation.

"What if I say no?" Her chin jutted out.

"Then I'd be disappointed. But I'll still talk to Will and put the poor man out of his misery."

A flicker of hope sparked in Corinne's brown eyes. "You think he's miserable?"

"I'd bet my last shilling." Emma grinned. "After all, he's quite smitten with you, in case you haven't noticed."

Corinne let out a long breath and gave a tentative smile. "Maybe having an older sister won't be such a hardship after all."

CHAPTER 22

MID-JULY 1919

The next few weeks passed by in a blur. Emma threw all her energies into helping to organize the hospital fundraiser, keeping so busy that she barely had time for Marianne's exercises.

Vera proved to be an invaluable resource with all her charitable connections and her experience over the years in arranging many types of fundraisers. She was able to get the permits signed, the vendors in place, and the volunteers to help distribute the event flyers. Emma worked on obtaining the entertainment for the children, hiring clowns, ordering prizes and balloons, and arranging for rides and games. The rest of the committee filled in the gaps. The date was coming up soon, and they all prayed the weather would be good, since everything was to be set up outdoors on the hospital grounds.

The one thing that marred this blissful time for Emma was that Jonathan seemed even more preoccupied than she. With what, she wasn't certain, but she thought he was spending a lot of time with Reggie. Although she was glad he'd found such a good friend, part of her couldn't help but wonder if he was avoiding her. Did he regret kissing her after their date? Had he come to the realization that he'd rather just remain good friends and was too scared to tell her?

When she asked him about his noticeable absence, he assured her everything was fine, that he and Reggie were just busy working on a project.

Emma didn't know what to think. Or what to believe. What kind of mysterious project could the two of them be working on?

Finally, on the morning of the fundraiser, Emma rose early and went to find Jonathan. He knew how much this day meant to her and had promised to attend. She wanted to make sure he hadn't forgotten or made other plans.

Emma found him tending the garden, picking beans and putting them into a large basket, his shirt-sleeves rolled up past his elbows. She stared at the dark hairs on his forearms as he worked, the tanned skin of his neck, the taut pull of his shirt across his shoulders. Her heart pulsed to life in her chest as memories of being held in those arms came roaring back, and she realized how much she'd missed him.

She cleared her throat. "You're at it early this morning." For some reason, her voice sounded shaky.

He turned with a grin and pushed his cap back on his forehead. "It's a big day, or so I've been told. I thought I'd get my chores out of the way so I can spend as much time at the fundraiser as possible."

Under his affectionate gaze, the air in her lungs grew shallow. "Oh good," she said with forced cheerfulness. "You haven't forgotten."

His brow furrowed. "Why would you think that?"

She toed a pinecone on the grass. "You've been so busy lately, I thought it might have slipped your mind. Reggie must be keeping you very entertained."

"I told you he's been helping me with something, which I want to tell you all about very soon." He stepped out from the rows of vegetables. "It seems we've both been caught up with our own . . . interests."

"True enough. I'll be glad for a rest once this day is over."

Jonathan set the basket on the ground and wiped his forehead with a handkerchief. The temperature was already quite warm, and Emma hoped the heat wouldn't deter the guests from enjoying the day.

He moved closer to her and her pulse sprinted, making her a little light-headed. Would he touch her? Maybe kiss her again? It seemed so long since they'd shared any such closeness.

"I've missed you," he said huskily. "Is everything still going well with your father and your sisters?"

The question seemed laced with a meaning Emma didn't understand. Wasn't he happy that she'd broken through their reserve, that she'd found some semblance of acceptance in the Moore household? Or did he resent all the time she'd been spending with them? "Things are going very well," she said. "Even Vera has been nice to me."

Jonathan nodded. "I'm glad you're so happy, Em."

But to Emma's ears, he didn't sound glad. Not at all. "Is something wrong, Jonathan?"

A slight breeze stirred the fabric of his shirt. He watched her with an enigmatic expression. "I've been thinking that the summer is slipping away. It will soon be time to book my passage home." He picked up the basket and started across the lawn.

A wave of disappointment rolled in her chest as she watched him retreat. Despite their kiss, their unspoken feelings, nothing had really changed. He still intended to leave her. Why had she ever imagined he might choose her instead?

She followed him to the rear door. "Is there no way I can convince you to stay?" she asked. Her heart raced at the boldness of her request. She knew how much she was asking of him, but if he truly cared for her, wouldn't he be willing to make a sacrifice to be with her?

He stopped and slowly turned around. "I have to go back, Em. You know that. I've already paid a good portion of my tuition. And then there's Aunt Trudy to consider."

Emma's legs shook. She twisted her hands together, searching for the words to sway him. "Trudy managed without you all the time you were at war. I'm sure she'll be fine now. And you could go to school here. You said Reggie is enrolled at the university. Why couldn't you do the same?" Her words tumbled out, falling over each other in her haste. "Unless . . ."

She bit her lip. Her stomach churned on a roll of nausea. This was not the conversation she wanted to be having this morning. But somehow once it got started, there seemed no way to stop it. "Unless I've misread the change in our relationship?"

Jonathan set the basket down and reached for her hand. "You haven't."

She gripped his fingers hard, a bud of hope blooming. "Then stay. Give us the chance to see what happens."

He studied her with an intensity that unnerved her while his thumbs caressed her palms. "Marry me, Emmaline. Come back to England and be my wife. We could have a great life there."

She froze, every vertebra in her back stiffening. They'd had one date, one kiss—and now he was talking marriage?

He stood there in the bright morning sun, his eyes the color of melted chocolate, watching her with such hope on his face that she couldn't breathe.

"Jonathan, I . . . I don't know what to say." A hard ball of emotion lodged in her chest. Oh, how she wished the circumstances were different. That she could joyfully accept his offer and that he would sweep her into his arms with another breath-stealing kiss. But it was far too soon in their newly budding romance to consider such a huge step.

She let out a long breath. "I can't leave right now. Not when I'm finally getting somewhere with my family." Her eyes pleaded with him to understand. To make sense of this craziness. Perhaps he'd tell her it was all a joke. They'd have a good laugh and everything would be fine between them again.

But a shutter came down over his features, and he dropped her hand. "You can't leave and I can't stay. England is my home, Emma. Do you really expect me to give up Oxford when I've finally achieved my goal?"

She took a step back, stunned by the resentment that laced his words. Her voice quavered. "Aren't you asking me to do the same? To give up the chance to have a real relationship with my father and sisters?"

If he cared about her, how could he ask that of her? And if he wanted to marry her, how could he think of leaving her behind?

Yet hadn't she known all along that he would?

He looked at her with such sorrow that she couldn't stand it.

She squeezed her hands into fists, fighting against the sting of tears. She wouldn't cry in front of him. Not this time. "I have to go now or I'll be late."

Then she turned and strode around to the front of the house before a single tear could fall.

Two hours later, Jonathan made his way to the children's hospital, dread dogging his steps. The event he'd looked forward to because it meant so much to Emma now held little appeal. Not after their fight earlier, which had forced him to face the reality that their relationship was doomed.

What on earth had made him blurt out a marriage proposal like that? He was never impulsive or spontaneous, and he knew it was far too soon to suggest such a thing. Emma had just started to think of him as a possible suitor. Now he'd gone and ruined every chance of her returning to England with him.

"You could go to school here. You said Reggie is enrolled at the university. Why couldn't you do the same?" Emma's plea had tugged at his heartstrings. How he'd wanted to give in, but if he stayed under those conditions, he would forever come second to Randall Moore and Emma's sisters.

For the past three weeks, Emma had been so busy arranging this fundraiser for her father, she'd scarcely had two minutes to spend with Jonathan. He'd thought they'd made such headway with their relationship after their date, after that kiss . . . a kiss that had sent him soaring to the highest peaks of ecstasy and made him believe for the first time that Emma might love him enough to go back with him.

"I can't leave right now. Not when I'm finally getting somewhere with my family."

Yet Emma's cavalier dismissal of Jonathan's proposal came as a cruel reminder that he could never overcome the lure of her new family.

Jonathan kicked a pebble onto the grass. What sort of heel was he to be jealous of Emma's relationship with Randall? Of course he was happy for her—it was just that she always gave one hundred percent to whatever she decided to focus on. And right now, that was her father. Which left no room at all for Jonathan or romance, let alone marriage.

Jonathan looked up from the sidewalk to see hundreds of gaily colored balloons bobbing in the morning breeze. The sound of children's laughter drifted over to him, such a happy, wholesome sound that it lifted the chains around his battered heart.

This day would bring so much joy to the little ones, and it was all because of Emma. Despite his frustration, a wave of pride rose inside him. Emma was meant for greatness. Who was he to stand in her way?

When Jonathan rounded the corner to the hospital property, the sight there took his breath away. Among the rows of booths, a vibrant array of clowns colored the grounds. Throngs of children of all shapes and sizes milled about, some in wheelchairs or on crutches. Some had shaved heads after surgery, and most were in pajamas, but all sported ear-to-ear grins. The more energetic ones ran and played, balloons trailing out behind them, hands glued to gigantic lollipops.

His chest swelled. Emma had done a brilliant job in helping to arrange this. Her father would surely have to acknowledge her now. Jonathan tried hard to be happy about that—that her dreams were beginning to come true. As much as he couldn't give up Oxford, Emma felt the same way about her family. How could he resent her for that?

Jonathan moved into the crowd, his spirits rising on the waves of pure joy that surrounded him. In the midst of all the chaos, he spotted Emma, wearing a smile so big he could see it from across the lawn. At least their argument hadn't ruined the day for her.

He waded through the people, intent on reaching her. He'd promised to help her and no matter how hurt he was he wouldn't go back on his word.

From the corner of his eye, he spotted Giles Wainwright snapping pictures of a group of children on the pony ride. Immediately, Jonathan's hackles went up as his protective instincts kicked in. He'd keep a close watch on this character to make sure he didn't bother Emma. The man had ruined Corinne's graduation. Jonathan wouldn't allow him to do the same at this event.

At last, he made it to Emma's side. With considerable effort, he pushed his hurt and disappointment down deep and forced a smile. "Congratulations, Em. You've done a marvelous job."

Her startled gaze met his, then skittered away. "Thank you. But we've already hit a few snags."

"Anything I can do?"

Her brows rose. "You'd help me after our . . . disagreement?"

"Yes, Emma," he said in a measured tone. "I promised to help, so here I am. Now, what needs fixing?"

"There's a problem at the Ring-the-Bell game. The bell's stuck, which is making for some very frustrated players."

"I think I can handle that. One bell about to be unstuck." He smiled, but she didn't return his banter. He was going to have to work hard to get their relationship back on track, even if it was only a return to their former friendship.

With a sigh, he headed in the direction she pointed, a little unsettled to notice that Wainwright had the camera aimed at them now. As Jonathan worked on fixing the bell, he kept watch on the reporter's every move. He always seemed to be hovering near Emma, except when someone called him to go elsewhere. If Jonathan didn't know better, he'd think the bloke was sweet on her.

With the game once again operational, Jonathan strolled about the hospital grounds, taking note of where there was an extra-long line or where a booth needed more attention. He reported his findings back to Emma, who seemed grateful for his observations.

Randall spent his time posing for pictures with the families in attendance. Jonathan spotted Corinne pushing Marianne through the area. Vera, he assumed, must be working behind the scenes.

A while later, Jonathan bought a hot dog and a cold lemonade from one of the booths and went to sit under a tree in the shade. The afternoon sun had the sweat dripping from his forehead.

"There you are, buddy. I thought I'd never find you." Reggie lowered himself gingerly to the grass beside him and lay his crutches down.

"Hey, Reg. Glad you could come." He'd invited his friend but hadn't been certain he could make it. "Not wearing your leg today?"

"I didn't want to risk it with all these people. Still taking it slow."

"That's probably smart."

Reggie grabbed Jonathan's lemonade and took a swig. "Have you seen all the booths and games yet?"

"Most of them, I think."

"I'm a little disappointed." Reggie waggled his brows. "I was hoping there would be a kissing booth. One with lots of cute nurses on hand."

"You are incorrigible. What about the nurse at the military hospital?"

"Ah, she still hasn't succumbed to my charms. But there's always hope." Reggie leaned back on one elbow. "How are things with Emma?"

The lemonade soured in Jonathan's stomach. "Not good. I made a muddle of it this morning. We had a huge row."

"By *row* do you mean fight?"

Jonathan nodded. "I asked her to marry me and go back to England."

"Good grief!" Reggie straightened. "What did she say?"

"That she couldn't leave her father. I think I shocked her, since I just sort of blurted it out. Not my finest moment, that's for sure."

Reggie scrubbed a hand over his face. "Have I taught you nothing, man? A marriage proposal must be well rehearsed. Every detail planned out. Flowers, a ring, and of course, a declaration of undying love."

Jonathan scowled and crumpled his hot dog wrapper.

"Wait a minute. You did tell her you love her, didn't you?"

"Not exactly. But for Pete's sake, I wouldn't have asked her to marry me if I didn't love her."

Reggie shook his head and looked at Jonathan as though he were a simpleton. "Women need to hear the words. It's little wonder she turned you down."

"Thanks for that vote of confidence." Jonathan pushed up to his feet, his mellow mood ruined.

Reggie reached out a hand, and Jonathan helped him up.

"Don't worry, pal. You can always try again. Only this time, take my advice, and she won't be able to resist."

"I don't think there'll be a next time. Emma's made it quite clear she's not leaving Toronto."

Reggie positioned the crutches under his arms. "It seems to me," he said in a serious voice, "that if you truly love Emma, you'd be willing to give up Oxford for her. I know I'd follow the love of my life anywhere if it meant we could be together."

His wistful tone snapped Jonathan back to the present. For all Reggie's talk of nurses, maybe his friend wasn't really over his former fiancée. Perhaps underneath all his cheerfulness and swagger was a heart still broken by Elsie's rejection.

"Hey, who's that guy taking all the pictures of your girl?" Reggie pointed across the grounds.

Jonathan frowned, surprised Reg even recognized Emma. He'd only met her once briefly when he came to pick Jonathan up for an appointment. "His name is Giles Wainwright. He's a reporter. A real pain in the posterior, if you know what I mean. Seems to be wherever Emma is."

"Maybe he has designs on her."

"More like he's trying to sniff out a story about her father." Jonathan tossed his wrapper in the trash. "I think I'd better make my presence known. See you later, Reg."

CHAPTER 23

The hot sun beat down on Emma's back. She blew a curl off her forehead and wished for a parasol. At home, she was far more used to the cool mists that hugged the English countryside and rarely had to worry about being out in such extreme heat. Unbidden memories of sitting on the riverbank with Jonathan jumped to mind, of them relaxing at their favorite spot by the bridge in Wheatley, the place where they used to share their innermost thoughts.

A spasm of pain hit her chest. She rubbed at the ache and resolutely pushed away all thoughts of Jonathan. She had a job to do and couldn't afford to be distracted. She'd figure out what to do about him tomorrow when the fundraiser was over.

Spotting Corinne pushing Marianne toward her, Emma pasted on a forced smile. A bunch of balloons tied to the handles of Marianne's wheelchair streamed out behind them.

"Emma!" Marianne called, waving some pink cotton candy. "Look what Corinne bought for me."

"How lovely," Emma said. "Are you having a good time?"

"A wonderful time."

"And how about you, Corinne?" Emma focused her attention on her other sister, noting the pinched lines around her eyes.

"I'm fine."

"But you wish you were elsewhere?" Emma guessed. "Or that a certain someone was here with you?"

Corinne nodded and leaned closer. "Will said he'd try to come and bring some of his brothers and sisters, but I haven't seen him yet."

"I'm sure he'll do his best." Emma smiled. Ever since she'd told Will about Corinne's confession, it sounded like the relationship had improved between the pair. Yet, according to her sister, Will still hadn't asked their father for permission to court her. Emma made a mental note to discover what was holding him back.

"Good afternoon, ladies. May I take your photo?" Giles Wainwright came up behind Emma.

She fought back a grimace. Mr. Wainwright wasn't the only reporter here, but he was the only one who seemed to be in her path every time she turned around.

"To go in the newspapers?" Marianne asked excitedly.

"Possibly. I can't promise which ones will be selected for print, but if this one turns out well, I'll do my best to persuade my editor to include it." He winked at Corinne, who blushed. "With such lovely subjects, I'm sure he'll say yes."

Emma folded her arms in front of her. She wasn't fooled by his false charm for a minute. "You two go ahead. I have to see to more pressing business."

"Wait, Miss Moore. I was also hoping to interview you since I understand this fundraiser was your brainchild."

"I came up with the initial idea, but a whole team has worked hard to make it a reality. I deserve no more credit than anyone else."

"Ah, beautiful and modest too. A stunning combination."

Irritation prickled along Emma's already frayed nerves. "Excuse me." She peered past the man and his enormous camera. "I'll see you girls later. Have fun. Don't eat too much candy, Marianne."

She pushed on ahead, intent on finding her father to make

sure he was prepared for his speech, which was slotted for three o'clock. She also wanted to ensure the dais and the microphone were in place, and that the hospital board members were on hand as well. Knowing Vera, she would have matters well under control.

As Emma made her way through the crowd, she heard someone calling her name. Frowning, she looked up. A woman dressed in a white blouse and dark skirt lifted her hand from the handle of a large pram and waved at her.

"Grace? Is that you?" A wave of pure delight rushed through Emma.

"It is." Her friend hurried forward and enveloped her in a hug. "I can't believe we finally found each other. Every time I've come to visit Mrs. C., I seem to miss you somehow."

Emma hugged her again. "How have you been? I was so sorry to hear about your sister." Mrs. C. had told Emma the tragic news of Rose's death.

"Thank you. It was indeed a shock." Grace gave a sad smile. "But being with Christian is helping with the grief." She took Emma's hand and led her to the pram. "Isn't he precious?"

Inside, a beautiful child lay asleep, long lashes fanning his cheeks.

"He's marvelous." Emma straightened. "How did you come to be his nanny?"

Grace shook her head and glanced around, as though expecting someone to appear. "It's a rather long story, one I'll tell you when we have more time. Right now I'm afraid I have to get back to the house."

"Of course. And I should get back to work. This fundraiser is part of my father's campaign for mayor."

Grace nodded. "That's what Mrs. C. said." She looked around. "Is Jonathan here?"

Emma fought to keep her smile in place. "He's around somewhere. Well, I'd love to chat longer, but I need to find Randall. It's almost time for his speech."

Grace leaned in for another quick hug. "Good luck with everything. I hope we can get together soon and have a proper visit."

"Count on it."

As Grace pushed the pram down the sidewalk, Emma gave a wistful sigh. The renewal of her friendship would have to wait. Right now, she had to attend to more important matters.

Jonathan followed Wainwright past the booths, past the pony ride and the games until the man disappeared around the back of the hospital.

An urging in his gut propelled Jonathan forward. Why had he left the activities to come here? Maybe he only wanted a smoke away from the kids, yet somehow Jonathan sensed a more underhanded reason was afoot.

As quietly as possible, he rounded the corner where Wainwright had disappeared and entered an alley that seemed to be a loading area for hospital supplies.

Wainwright was talking to another fellow, one who looked vaguely familiar. Their heads were bent close together as they spoke.

Jonathan moved closer, keeping to the shadows of the far wall.

"You're not going soft on me over that girl, are you?" The second man's voice grew louder. "Because unless you want to pay back the money I've already given you—"

"No. I just need more time." Wainwright actually sounded nervous, his usual bravado nowhere to be found

"That's the problem. We're running out of time. We need to stop Moore's momentum now so the mayor can recover any lost support."

Jonathan's pulse spiked as he recalled why the man looked familiar. He'd seen his picture in the papers. He worked for Mayor Church. What was he paying Wainwright to do?

"If you can't get that girl to talk, we'll find someone with more persuasive talents to make her."

"That won't be necessary." Wainwright sounded even more nervous. "I'll get the info you need. Don't worry."

Jonathan backed out of the alley and returned to the festivities, his instincts telling him that he didn't need to be discovered overhearing this conversation. His mouth went dry thinking of the menacing tone of the other man's voice. By "that girl" did he mean Emma? He must. That would explain Wainwright's dogged determination to get her to reveal something about Randall.

The instant the reporter approached the outskirts of the hospital grounds, Jonathan walked up to him and stood toe-to-toe. "I don't care who you're working for," he said, his voice so low that only Wainwright could hear. "I'm warning you to stay away from Emma. I won't allow you to use her as a pawn in whatever game you're playing." He poked Wainwright in the chest. "Take your pictures of the event, but leave Emma alone."

His hard gaze pinned the reporter to the spot. Beads of sweat stood out on the man's forehead, but he remained silent, his mouth a grim line. Then, grasping his camera, Wainwright took off into the crowd.

Emma scanned the area, relieved that for the moment there was no sign of Wainwright. Perhaps he'd gotten enough photos and left, though she doubted he'd leave before the speeches. She blew out a breath as Vera and Randall came walking toward her.

"All set?" Emma asked her father.

"Ready as I'll ever be." He draped an arm over his wife's

shoulders. "I must congratulate you both. This has been a wonderful day for the community."

"Thank you, darling." Vera smiled at him. "I'm only happy I can be of such help to you."

"You've always been my biggest supporter." He brushed a kiss to Vera's cheek.

Emma stood in front of them, trying hard not to let envy gain a hold of her. "We have chairs on the platform for some of the board members. I'm not sure if the mayor will be able to make it, but I have a seat for him just in case."

"You invited the competition?" Vera's tone hinted disapproval.

"Protocol, my dear." Randall patted her arm. "But if we're lucky, he'll be too busy to attend."

"Oh, a word of warning," Emma said. "There are several reporters here, and Mr. Wainwright is among them."

A flicker of irritation crept over her father's face. "Good to know. Always wise to be aware of the enemy's position. Come, Vera. Let's get everyone in place."

Vera threw her an enigmatic look before she followed her husband to the stage.

Emma scanned the group of people again and this time spotted Wainwright leaning against a pole. For once, he didn't seem his usual overly confident self. Instead, he wore a worried frown as he mopped his forehead with a handkerchief.

An undercurrent of unease seemed to hang in the air, sending tingles down Emma's spine. Why did she get the feeling that something was about to go horribly wrong?

Jonathan found a spot on the edge of the crowd, where he could keep an eye on both Wainwright and Emma without too much difficulty. He suffered through the rather boring speeches by the hospital board members until Randall himself came to the podium. Emma's face shone with pride as she listened to her father speak. The audience responded with thunderous applause, indicating that this fundraiser had done wonders for his public image, just as Emma had hoped. Despite their argument this morning, Jonathan was glad the rest of the day had turned out so well for her.

The speeches were just ending when Wainwright broke away from the other reporters who were taking pictures and headed right over to Emma.

Instantly, Jonathan's senses went on alert. Had his warning to the man gone unheeded?

Wainwright took Emma's arm and leaned in to whisper something to her. She frowned and shoved his hand away. But he persisted, blocking her path and standing over her in an almost threatening manner.

Fury ripped through Jonathan. Without thinking, he charged through the bystanders until he reached them.

"If you don't leave this instant," Emma was saying, "I'll have security remove you." Her voice quavered, with anger or fear Jonathan didn't know.

Wainwright lowered the camera, wielding it almost like a weapon. "There's no law against taking someone's picture."

"There might not be a law, but there's common decency." Jonathan grabbed the guy and jerked him away from Emma. "You've been harassing her all day. Now she's asked you to leave. If I were you, I'd listen." Still gripping Wainwright's arm, Jonathan glowered at him.

"It's all right, Jonathan." Emma's voice was laced with tension. "I'm sure Mr. Wainwright has taken enough photos for today."

Wainwright pulled free of Jonathan's grip. "Not quite. I still need one of you, as well as that interview you promised."

"I never agreed to an interview. If you want a quote for your paper, then speak to my—" Emma stopped, the color draining from her face.

"To who, Emma?" Wainwright practically pounced on her.

"My Uncle Randall. Excuse me." She went to move away, but once again Wainwright blocked her path.

"Come on, Emma. Admit who he really is to you."

The look of panic on Emma's face lit the fuse of Jonathan's temper, igniting it to a full-blown inferno.

He spun the man around. "I warned you to leave her alone. You should have listened."

Wainwright's face registered shock a split second before Jonathan plowed his fist into his jaw. Emma shrieked as the reporter flew backward and landed with a thud on the ground, the camera crashing down beside him. Blood spurted from his lip.

A bellow of rage erupted from Wainwright as he shot to his feet and attacked.

Jonathan ducked the fist and whirled in time to see Wainwright coming at him again. This time Jonathan wasn't quick enough. The blow glanced off his cheek, sending him spinning to the grass.

"Stop it!" Emma's cry barely registered as he pulled himself upright.

His anger roared in his ears as he lurched toward Wainwright again. They circled each other like two feral animals, fists up and ready. Wainwright made the first move, but Jonathan dodged the blow. Then he charged at the reporter, locking his arms around the man's waist in an attempt to take him down.

Someone tugged hard on Jonathan's shoulder, trying to separate him from Wainwright. With a growl, Jonathan elbowed the unwanted interloper and pushed him off.

A familiar scream tore his attention away from his opponent.

Flashes from the reporters' cameras momentarily blinded him. When his vision cleared, he recognized Emma sprawled on the ground, a shocked expression on her face.

"Emma, are you—"

Pain exploded in his left cheek, the force of the blow knocking his head to one side. Wainwright pounced on him, fists flying. Jonathan deflected the shots as best he could, but several found their mark. On a last surge of energy, he threw the man off him and their roles reversed. Through a haze of red, Jonathan pummeled the rat until someone again attempted to haul him off from behind.

A crowd had formed around them. Jonathan struggled against whoever had a hold of him, swiping his sleeve across his bleeding mouth. One of his eyes had already started to swell shut. His breath came in ragged gasps, and beads of sweat dripped off his face.

Wainwright rolled over on the ground and groaned. Someone came to help him sit up. His fingers grappled for the strap of his camera, and he looked down in disbelief. "You broke my camera, you heathen." He pointed at Jonathan. "You're going to pay for this." He stumbled to his feet and staggered away.

Pain radiated through Jonathan's skull, but all he could think about was Emma.

He needed to go to her. Comfort her. Make sure she was all right. He stumbled toward her. Tears stood out in her blue eyes, and her lip was swollen.

"You knew how important this day was, and this is how you behave?" she cried, her trembling fingers hovering over her injured mouth. "How could you do this to me?"

"Someone had to teach that bloke a lesson." He blinked his one good eye, the anger draining as he realized in horror that he was the one who'd struck her. "I'm sorry, Em. I didn't know it was you. You know I'd never deliberately hurt you."

She shook her head, disgust evident in her eyes as she walked away.

"Emma, wait!"

Behind him, a hand gripped his shoulder. "Let her go, pal," Reggie said. "She's too angry right now."

Jonathan watched Emma push her way through the crowds that were now starting to disperse. A groan ripped through him. He'd just ruined everything Emma had worked so hard to achieve—and hurt her physically in the process. Would she ever speak to him again?

"Come on." Reggie nudged him. "Let's go get that face looked after."

"He's not going anywhere except down to the police station."

Jonathan's stomach sank as he turned to see a burly constable standing behind them with a smug-looking Wainwright at his side.

The constable tapped a baton against his palm, his eyes hard. "You're under arrest for assault and battery."

CHAPTER 24

The next morning, after tossing and turning all night, Emma dragged herself down to the dining room. Her jaw still throbbed from the blow of Jonathan's elbow when he'd pushed her off him. After several applications of ice, the swelling of her lip had receded, but nothing could banish the ache in her heart.

Mrs. C. sat at the table, as though waiting for her. "Good morning, dear. How are you feeling today?"

"Exhausted." Emma reached for the coffeepot and poured a mugful. Tea would not do this morning. "I didn't get much sleep."

"No doubt. I'm so sorry how it turned out yesterday." Mrs. C. rose from the table and put her cup and saucer on the sideboard. "I do hope you won't let that unfortunate episode ruin all the good that happened. Reverend Burke and I had a wonderful time, as did everyone else who attended. Especially the children."

Emma tried hard to hold on to that fact and remember the joy on the children's faces. But the cloud would not lift from her soul.

"That's kind of you to say. Unfortunately, the only thing everyone will remember now is the brawl." Emma sipped the bitter brew, not even bothering to doctor it with milk and sugar. "Speaking of which, has the morning paper arrived?"

Mrs. C. looked away, busying herself with a platter of eggs. "I don't think so."

Emma frowned. "You needn't bother to hide it. I can walk down to the next street and buy one."

The woman released a long breath. "Very well, but it will only ruin your mood."

"It can't get much worse." Emma held out her hand.

Mrs. C. opened the top drawer in the sideboard and removed a folded newspaper.

Bracing herself, Emma opened it to the front page and just stared. Never had she imagined seeing herself on the front page, especially not in such an unflattering manner. The picture had captured her right after Jonathan had shoved her. Emma's face was contorted in an ugly grimace, and Jonathan's wild eyes gave him a deranged appearance. His face was twisted with anger, his fist raised. Underneath, a smaller photo showed Randall's horrified reaction.

The headline, however, was worse. *Family Drama Ruins Event for Mayoral Candidate Moore.* In smaller letters underneath, it read, *Niece Assaulted in the Fray as Her Lover Attacks Member of the Press.*

Emma's mouth fell open. *Lover?* That made her sound like some sort of harlot. And it made Jonathan sound like a jealous fool. She skimmed the article, which indeed made it seem that the men had been fighting over her in a romantic skirmish.

Emma laid the paper down. "You were right. It's worse than I imagined." She put her head in her hands with a groan. What must her father think of her now? She'd been so ashamed when the police had hauled Jonathan away, but to have the whole sordid ordeal splashed on the front page of the paper was enough to send her scurrying to her room.

"Did Jonathan spend the night in jail?" her landlady asked. "Mrs. Teeter was watching for him but said she didn't see him come home."

"I don't know." Emma sighed, attempting to push away the niggle of guilt.

"You didn't go to see him? Or call the station at least?" Mrs. C. looked appalled.

"After what he did?" Emma still couldn't believe he'd struck her. Granted, he hadn't realized it was her, but that didn't excuse his boorish behavior. She lifted her chin. "His friend Reggie said he'd go. I'm sure he took care of him."

"That poor boy. You know he'd never hurt you on purpose."

"Poor boy?" Emma stabbed a finger at the newspaper. "He made me look like a fool in front of all those people. And he ruined the day for my father."

Mrs. C. set her cup on the table. "When everything settles down, I hope you can find it in your heart to forgive him. Remember what Jesus said: 'Let he who is without sin cast the first stone.'"

Emma pressed her lips together, her indignation slowly fading. She'd been guilty of allowing her temper to get the best of her in the past, and she knew that if their positions were reversed, Jonathan wouldn't hesitate to forgive her—he'd done it often enough over the years. She released a sigh. Even though she wasn't ready to let go of her outrage just yet, she ought to at least make sure he was all right. She'd go down to the police station as soon as she finished her breakfast.

A loud knock sounded.

"Goodness, who can that be?" Mrs. C. bustled off to answer the door.

Emma listened from the dining room, certain it must be Jonathan come to make amends. She rubbed her aching jaw. Was she ready to accept his apology?

"I don't think Miss Moore cares to speak with you," Mrs. C. said in a loud voice.

Emma frowned. She couldn't believe her landlady would turn Jonathan away.

Mrs. C. appeared in the doorway. "Mr. Wainwright is asking to see you."

Hot tingles coursed through Emma's system. Of all the nerve for him to come here.

"I wouldn't have let him in, but he says it's about Jonathan." Her landlady gave her a serious look.

"Fine. But stay close by, Mrs. C., in case we need to call the police again." Emma swept down the hall to the parlor.

Giles Wainwright stood with his back to her, staring out the window.

Emma paused to gain a foothold on her already raw emotions, then entered the room.

"I don't know what you could possibly have to say to me," Emma said.

He turned around, and Emma fought a gasp. Dark purple bruises marred his jaw and cheek. One eye was swollen, ringed in red.

"I came to apologize for my part in the fiasco yesterday," he said quietly. "It was never my intention to ruin the day." He seemed sincere, but Emma didn't quite trust him.

"Yet you're determined to ruin the professor's reputation. A bigger man would have reported on the benefit of the day for the community, not run gossip on the front page."

He stared at her, and it reminded her of when she'd caught a glimpse of him before her father's speech began, when he appeared to have removed the mask he always wore. "It was my editor's decision, not mine. You probably won't believe me, but I tried to make him change the headline and the picture. He wouldn't listen."

"You're right. I don't believe you." She walked to the middle of the room, her arms folded in front of her. "My landlady said you wanted to talk about Jonathan."

His features hardened. "Right. I have a proposition for you." He paused. "I'll drop the charges against Mr. Rowe for doing this"—he pointed to his face—"and for ruining my best camera if you will do something for me."

Goose bumps erupted on Emma's arms. She wished she could refuse outright, but she had to at least see what this rat wanted. "Such as?"

"Grant me an interview and give me the honest story about your relationship to Professor Moore."

Not this again. "You already know everything. There's nothing more to tell." She turned her head and went to move away.

In a flash, he was in front of her, so close she could smell the coffee on his breath. "We both know that's not true, Emmaline. I will uncover the truth, and when I do, you'll be sorry you didn't accept my offer to tell it your way."

Emma tore her gaze from his and stalked to the fireplace, indecision eating at her. What if she granted his request? She could slant the facts of the story in her father's favor, make him look like a martyr, a man who'd lost his true love and gave up his child in order for her to have a better life. How could that hurt his image?

Perhaps she could finally tell the truth, and by doing so, help Jonathan go free. Even though she was still incredibly angry, she wouldn't want to see him in trouble with the law.

Emma bit her lip, her stomach clenching. But could she really trust Wainwright not to distort the facts to make her father look bad? She turned around, praying she was doing the right thing. "I'm afraid I can't agree to your terms, Mr. Wainwright."

He came closer and reached out a finger to touch one of

Emma's curls. "That's too bad, Miss Moore. I guess your boyfriend will have to suffer the consequences."

She sucked in a breath, ready to argue, but realized it would be a waste of her breath.

Wainwright dropped his hand and moved swiftly to the door. "Have a pleasant day." Then with a tip of his cap and a return of that smug smile, he was gone.

Emma lowered herself to the closest chair, her legs suddenly weak. Should she have sacrificed her father's image to save Jonathan? What was the punishment for assault? Would Jonathan go to jail? Maybe she hadn't fully thought through this decision.

She could ask her father. If anyone would know what type of punishment Jonathan might be facing, Randall would. However, the thought of going to speak with her father, of seeing the disappointment shadowing his eyes after recently gaining his approval, was almost too much to bear.

But she couldn't sit by and do nothing. No matter how convoluted her feelings were toward Jonathan, he didn't deserve that. If she found out he was still in jail, she'd swallow her pride and ask Randall for help.

Jonathan spent the night on Reggie's sofa, ice packs on his eye and jaw. After being surrounded by drunkards for several hours in a jail cell, Jonathan had finally been released once Reggie paid his bail.

Another debt Jonathan would need to repay. At this rate, his tuition fund would be nonexistent by the time he got back to England.

Plus, the constable had made it clear that Jonathan would be expected to reimburse Wainwright for the cost of a new camera. Jonathan groaned. Why hadn't he kept his fists to himself?

Fighting with Wainwright hadn't solved anything. In fact, it had only made everything much worse.

"You doing all right, pal?"

Jonathan opened his good eye to see Reggie staring down at him.

"You need some aspirin? More ice?"

"I'm fine. But I wouldn't turn down a cup of strong coffee."

Reggie grinned. "Coming right up."

When Reggie crutched off to the kitchen, Jonathan pulled himself to a sitting position, the movement making his face pound. Ice might be a good idea. Maybe he'd just dunk his whole head in a bucketful.

He rose from the sofa and crossed the cramped living area to the warped mirror hanging near the door of the apartment. Reggie must have gotten all his parents' hand-me-downs for this place. Either that or he shopped at a secondhand store. The sofa had definitely seen better days, and the coffee table had more dents and scrapes than Jonathan's face. However, Jonathan was grateful that his friend had recently moved into his own flat, since it would have been doubly embarrassing to have to impose on Mr. and Mrs. Wentworth in this condition.

He peered at himself in the glass and groaned. With his hair sticking up at odd angles and bags under his eyes, he could scare small children. But that was nothing compared to the purple bruising on his cheek and eye. The swelling had at least gone down, though he couldn't quite open his eye. No wonder the drunkards in the cell had left him alone. He looked like a demented prizefighter.

All things considered, it was probably good that Emma hadn't come to see him at the police station. Looking this rough certainly wouldn't have helped his cause.

In reality, however, Jonathan's heart felt more battered than his face. He'd prayed that Emma would realize he'd only been trying to protect her from that blackguard, that he never intended to hurt her. He'd imagined her being so distraught over learning of his arrest that she'd rush over to the station and demand to see him. He imagined her pressing her face against the metal bars, tears in her eyes, telling him she forgave him.

Maybe even admitting she loved him.

He snorted. Right. There he went deluding himself again.

Face it, mate. She doesn't love you the way you love her. And she never will.

He touched a finger to his cheek and winced. A half-mad derelict stared back at him. Was this the sort of man he'd become? Someone driven by enough jealousy and frustration to perpetrate physical violence?

He blew out a long breath and turned away, too disgusted to look at himself any longer.

"Coffee's here." Reggie's cheerful voice didn't help Jonathan's foul mood. "And I brought you some aspirin in case you changed your mind."

Jonathan went over to take the cup from him. "Thanks."

Reggie lowered himself onto a chair, then pulled a bottle of pills from his pocket and set it on the table. "Any word from Emma?"

Jonathan's chest squeezed. "No."

"Aw, she'll come around. She just needs time to cool off."

"I don't think so." Jonathan sank onto the sofa and took a long swallow of coffee. "There's no point in fooling myself any longer." He sighed. "I think it's time to go home."

Reggie studied him. "Are you sure? You're welcome to stay here for as long as you need."

Jonathan shot him a wry glance. "As much as I loved sleeping on your lumpy sofa, I do have to go. Though I might need to bunk here for a few days until I can make arrangements for the trip back."

"Stay as long as you like."

"Thanks, Reg," he said. "You've been a real friend."

"A real friend would have stopped you yesterday before you punched that reporter. I should have hooked you with my crutch and toppled you." Reggie laughed, and Jonathan couldn't help but join in.

Then the laughter faded and silence hung in the room.

Reggie scratched his chin. "On a serious note, what about your sessions with the doctor? You said they were helping."

"They are. Don't worry, I'll find someone to continue with back home." Jonathan leaned back against the cushions. "Maybe Dr. Clayborne has a colleague in England."

Reggie groaned. "I don't know what I'm going to do when you're gone, Jon. You've made life bearable around here."

"I'll miss you too, mate." Jonathan hated the thought of relegating their friendship to a letter every couple of months. But unfortunately, it was the way it had to be. He cleared his throat. "Could you do me one more favor?"

"Name it."

"Could you check on Emma every now and then to make sure she's doing all right?" Jonathan's heart felt like a deflated balloon at the idea that he'd never again have the privilege of doing that job himself. "In case her relationship goes sour with her father, I'd feel better knowing she had you."

"You got it, pal."

"Thanks, Reg. I knew I could count on you."

CHAPTER 25

On Sunday afternoon, Corinne got off the streetcar at the stop nearest Will's address, careful not to drop the armload of textbooks she carried. Even though school wouldn't start for a month, she was on her way to tutor Will's younger sister with her math and English. Will had told her that Kate needed a tutor, but they couldn't afford one on the family's limited income. And with Will's own studies and his chores at home, as well as his job at the university, he simply didn't have the time to do it himself.

Seeing an opportunity, Corinne had offered to do it for free, glad to have a chance to meet Will's family and get to know them. Each step would bring her closer to Will until one day, she hoped, he would have the courage to face her father and ask to court her.

Though they weren't dating, Will had at least accepted her offer of friendship. She owed that much to Emma. Whatever she'd said to him, Will had totally forgiven her for the spilled ink incident and had even come by to take her on a couple of walks. For that reason alone, Corinne would be forever in Emma's debt.

Somehow that thought didn't bother her as much as she once imagined it would.

Corinne turned onto a side street, the events of the previous day returning to trouble her. For the first time since Emmaline had darkened their doorstep, Corinne actually felt sorry for her. She'd worked so hard on the hospital fundraiser only to have it all end in disaster. One look at the front page of the morning's paper told Corinne that nothing would salvage the situation—for Emma or for Papa. Mama had taken the whole incident as a personal affront, almost as though Emma had purposely ruined the event to make Mama look bad.

Corinne sighed. Now that she'd spent more time with Emma while working with Marianne, she'd come to realize that Emma bore her family no ill will. She simply wanted to be a part of their lives in some small way. Corinne could even admit that Marianne had made astounding progress since Emma had taken an interest in her therapy. And now that Corinne had started to participate, she was finding she enjoyed helping too. That common bond had drawn the three sisters together.

In fact, it had been Emma who had first remarked that Corinne would make a good teacher. That seed of an idea had been germinating lately and had prompted her offer to Will. One she hoped would serve both Kate Munroe and herself equally well.

The street curved, and Corinne stopped in front of the house number Will had given her. She stared at the sight before her, certain she must have the wrong address. The small walkway was overgrown with weeds. The wooden steps leading up to the narrow front door looked cracked and rotting. How did Will, always so meticulously dressed, live in such a run-down place?

She climbed the steps and knocked on the door. Several seconds later, the sound of running feet could be heard. The door flung open, and two faces peered out at her.

"Hello. Who are you?" a fair-haired moppet demanded, while her brother looked over her shoulder.

"I'm Corinne, a friend of Will's. Is he here?"

"He's in the backyard. But he said you can come in." The older boy, who looked to be about eight or nine, steered his little sister out of the way so Corinne could enter.

The inside of the house, though stark, was much cleaner than the exterior. The floors looked freshly swept and the furniture recently dusted.

"What are your names?" Corinne asked, eager to learn everything she could about Will's family.

"I'm Albert, and this is Chrissy."

"Nice to meet you. I'm actually here to see your sister Kate."

The boy nodded. "Chrissy, go upstairs and fetch Katie. She's probably doing her hair or something girly."

Chrissy giggled, then scampered off.

Albert motioned to an armchair. "You can sit down. I'll go see what Will's doing." He disappeared toward the back of the house.

Corinne set her books on the chair and walked over to a table by the wall that held a group of framed photos, the largest of which was of a handsome man in uniform. That must be Will's father, a boat captain who'd died in some type of storm at sea. Will had only been seventeen at the time, and his father's death had changed his whole life, thrusting sudden responsibility on his young shoulders. With several younger siblings and his mother expecting another child, Will had stepped up to take on the role of the man of the household.

"That's my Pa, but I don't remember him." Chrissy's voice came from behind her. "He died before I was born."

Corinne turned around. "That's too bad. He looks like a very nice man."

Chrissy skipped across the room. "Mama says Will is just like him." The girl smiled up at Corinne.

Corinne smiled back, instantly charmed by the child's blue eyes and freckles.

"Corinne. I'm sorry I wasn't here to answer the door." Will appeared, looking somewhat disheveled. There was dirt smudged on his cheek, and the knees of his pants were stained. "I was outside in the garden." He took out a handkerchief and wiped his forehead and hands. "Chrissy, did you tell Kate that Corinne is here?"

"Yes, I did."

"Good. Now you can go help Albert pick some carrots for dinner."

As soon as Chrissy left, Will turned to Corinne, his eyes solemn. "I meant to warn you about the porch stairs. The landlord has been promising to fix them for weeks." His gaze slid away. "As you can see, we live in a less affluent area of town. Nothing like what you're used to."

"It's fine, Will."

But his eyes betrayed his discomfort. "That's why I didn't want you to come. I thought you'd take one look around and realize we come from two very different walks of life." He reached for her hand. "I wasn't kidding when I said I had nothing to offer you."

Warmth spread up her arm. She smiled at him. "My father started out with nothing when he came to Canada. But he made his way in the world, and so will you."

"He didn't have a mother and five siblings to look after."

"Does your mother work too?" she asked. Surely everything hadn't landed on Will's shoulders.

He nodded. "She cleans houses and takes in sewing. The money helps, but if it weren't for my job at the university, we'd be a lot worse off."

"Well, I admire you. Not many men would be willing to take on such responsibility. Your family is lucky to have you." She smiled up at him.

"Thank you. That means a lot." His voice was gruff with emotion.

And the approval in his eyes made Corinne feel like a queen.

"I hope I'm not interrupting anything."

Corinne turned to see an attractive girl in the doorway, arms crossed in front of her. If she weren't frowning, she might even be beautiful. Her chestnut hair was fixed in a cascade of ringlets over her shoulder, and she wore a yellow dress that highlighted her lightly tanned skin.

Will stepped forward. "Corinne, this is my sister Kate. Katie, this is Miss Corinne Moore."

"It's nice to meet you, Kate." Corinne gave the girl her best smile.

"Likewise. I only wish it wasn't for this reason." Kate came farther into the room and shot a glare at Will. "I don't see why I have to study now. School doesn't start until September."

"You barely passed your last grade," Will said. "You need decent marks in order to get a good job when you graduate."

Corinne picked up the textbooks. "Think of it this way. We'll do some studying before school begins, and then you'll find your courses so easy that you'll pass with flying colors."

The creases in Kate's brow lifted. "You really think so?"

"Absolutely. Now, where can we work?"

Two hours later, Corinne was pleased with the girl's progress. Kate caught on quickly once Corinne explained the concepts.

"I think that's enough for one day." Corinne gathered her papers and pencils. "Would you like to meet again next week?"

"Sure." Kate closed one of the books. "May I keep this book until then? I'd like to work ahead."

"Of course. One less book to carry home." Corinne pushed away from the dining room table, glancing back through the arched opening into the living room where Will was sitting.

He rose from the chair by the fireplace. "Katie, will you watch the younger ones while I walk Corinne to the streetcar? I think they're out back. Have them come in and wash up for dinner."

He spoke with such authority in his tone, Corinne had no trouble picturing him in front of a class full of students.

"Yes, Will. See you next time, Corinne."

"Good-bye." She turned to Will. "You don't have to walk with me. I'll be fine."

"I'm sure you would. But I'm going anyway."

She smiled, loving the hint of protectiveness in his voice. He'd changed into a fresh shirt and clean pants while she'd been tutoring Kate and now resembled the meticulous Will she was used to seeing.

Once he donned his hat, they set out. "Thank you for doing this," he said as they walked. "I can tell Katie likes you, which is good, since she'll be more inclined to want to learn."

"I like her too." Corinne ducked under a stray branch hanging over a fence. "I like all your family."

Will smiled. "Thanks. I do too."

They turned a corner and soon came to the streetcar stop. The breeze swayed the branches of an overhead maple tree. The street was uncommonly empty for this time of day, making Corinne feel like she and Will were alone in their own little universe.

"You shouldn't have to wait too long for the next car." Will shoved his hands in his pockets, almost as if he were nervous.

Corinne wished she were bold enough to take the next step, but even now the fiasco at the roller rink still weighed on her mind. "I'll come back next week," she said to fill the silence. "However many times Kate can stand me."

"Thank you." Will put a hand on her arm. "The fact that you're willing to help my sister means a lot."

Her pulse skipped as she looked up into his eyes. "I'd do almost anything for you, Will." Her voice was breathless.

He bent closer to her, his eyes locked on hers. Then ever so softly, his lips met hers. She didn't dare move, in case she scared him off. But then he gave a soft groan, and his arms came around her, pulling her tight against his chest. Her heart took flight, batting against her ribs. His mouth moved more firmly on hers. He tasted of coffee and smelled of herbs from the garden. She thought she might swoon from the headiness of the sensations coursing through her system.

Then the loud grinding sound of metal on metal broke through their haze as the streetcar approached.

Will pulled back and cleared his throat. "I'm sorry, Corinne. I should never have taken such liberties with you. Please forgive me." His green eyes flashed with regret.

She shook her head and smiled. "There's nothing to forgive. I was hoping you'd kiss me."

The streetcar stopped in front of them.

Reluctantly, she moved away. "Good-bye, Will. I'll see you again soon."

He didn't answer, just stared at her as she boarded the car. She grabbed a seat by the window and turned to wave at him, smiling brightly to assure him she didn't regret their kiss one bit.

Instead of smiling back, however, he had misery on his face that almost broke her heart.

How would she ever get him to see that their differences didn't matter to her?

Nothing mattered as long as she could stay in the shelter of his embrace and be guaranteed of another kiss like that one day soon.

CHAPTER 26

Jonathan snapped the lid of his worn leather valise shut and straightened to take a final look around the room. Despite its rustic nature, he'd grown fond of this tiny flat over the garage, his home away from home. He would miss it, as well as the vegetable garden in the yard below that had flourished under his care.

But he'd always known that his sojourn here was temporary, and he'd already stayed far longer than he ever anticipated, unwilling to concede defeat.

Hope was a funny thing. It kept you dangling by a thread until the last possible moment, even when the odds weren't in your favor. But the time had come to sever that thread, face reality, and go back home where he belonged.

He put on his cap and jacket, despite the balmy temperatures, and picked up his case, the part he dreaded most still to come.

How would he ever say good-bye to Emma? His throat cinched shut at the very thought. But this was how it had to be. He couldn't cling to a fantasy forever.

It was time to let go and let God take over. Whatever the Lord had in mind for Emma, it was clear that Jonathan would not be included. Somehow he'd have to learn to accept that and move on with his own life.

With a heavy heart and a still-throbbing cheek, Jonathan crossed the back lawn and entered the kitchen where, much like his first day here, Mrs. Teeter stood at the stove.

"You're either late for lunch or early for dinner," she called over her shoulder.

He set his bag down. "I'm neither, Mrs. Teeter. I've come to say good-bye."

Her spoon banged to the countertop as she whirled to face him. "You're leaving?"

"I'm afraid so." Jonathan tried to smile without wincing.

Her eyes widened as she saw his bruised face, and she rushed over, tilting his chin upward. "What on earth happened to you?"

"I guess you've not seen the newspaper. I'm sure it was all over the front page."

"You've been brawling." She shoved her hands onto her hips. "I hope the other fellow looks worse than this."

"I imagine he does." Jonathan attempted another smile. "I want to thank you for everything, Mrs. Teeter. You've been more than kind to me. You took me in and made me feel at home."

She heaved a great sigh. "Having you here made the loss of my nephew almost bearable. I'll miss your cheery face in my kitchen, that's for sure." Then, without warning, she grabbed him for a hard hug.

After a moment, Jonathan swallowed and stepped back.

"What's going on in here?" Mrs. Chamberlain entered the kitchen, eyebrows raised. She looked at Jonathan's bag, then back at him.

"I've come to say good-bye," he said. "And to thank you for hiring me on like you did so I could be near Emma."

A look of confusion crossed the landlady's face. "Emma didn't say anything about leaving. In fact, she's in the parlor, writing in that journal of hers."

"Emma's not going with me." The words were like broken

glass on his tongue. "She wants to stay now that she has family here." He avoided the woman's frown by looking down to pull a piece of paper from his pocket. "I'll be bunking with a friend for a few days until I can make arrangements for my trip home. Here's his address in case you need to reach me. He doesn't have a telephone."

Mrs. Chamberlain took the slip and pushed it into her apron pocket. "If you're leaving because of what happened at the fundraiser—"

He shook his head. "It's about much more than that, Mrs. C. Thank you so much for your kindness and your hospitality." He bent to kiss her cheek. "Take good care of Emma for me."

"You're not leaving without seeing her, are you?"

"No. I could never do that." Even though it would be the hardest thing he'd ever have to do. Harder than when he shipped off to war. At least then, he knew if he survived, he'd be coming home to her.

This time, however, the odds were high that they'd never see each other again. And Jonathan didn't know how he was going to bear that.

Emma closed her journal with a decisive snap and set it on the seat beside her. Usually words came so easily to her, but today she seemed incapable of capturing her thoughts and feelings. They were too jumbled. Too filled with contradictions to express adequately.

After the fiasco and the horrible headlines, she was hiding from reality, unable to face her father's disappointment or deal with Jonathan's unusual behavior—his out-of-the-blue marriage proposal and the brawl at the hospital. She still trembled with anger when she recalled the way he'd attacked Wainwright.

At least he wasn't still in jail. A constable at the police station told her that a friend had posted his bail and he'd been released late last evening. Emma assumed he'd then stayed with Reggie overnight, since Mrs. Teeter hadn't seen him come in.

Before the war, Jonathan never would have acted with such hostility and rage. After experiencing the type of violence he must have during combat, she guessed it was to be expected that he'd change. Yet part of her mourned the loss of the innocent young man he'd been before he left.

She rose to look out the parlor window at the street outside. Perhaps a walk would clear her head, chase away these morose thoughts. Maybe she'd go over to the church and spend some time in prayer. If Reverend Burke was around, she could seek his advice on how to go forward from here. She always found his sermons on Sunday a great comfort, and she could use a little of that comfort now.

"Hello, Em."

Emma jumped and whirled around, hand at her throat.

Jonathan stood just inside the door, wearing his good suit jacket, which was unusual given the temperature of the day. Then she focused on his face and had to suppress a gasp at the sight of the ugly purple bruises on his cheek and eye.

Forcing back all traces of sympathy, she crossed her arms. "If you've come to apologize for yesterday, you needn't bother. I'm still too angry with you."

"I *have* come to apologize," he said quietly. "I feel terrible for ruining your day and for hurting you. There's no excuse for my abominable behavior, and I regret it more than you know."

She hesitated, wanting to tell him she understood, yet not quite ready to grant absolution. Something about his demeanor sent a spurt of alarm through her chest.

He stood very still, staring at her. "I've also come to say good-bye."

"What do you mean? Where are you going?"

"Back to England, as soon as I clear up the legalities with Wainwright. Until then"—his gaze slid to the far wall—"I'll be staying with Reggie."

Her mouth opened, but nothing came out. She took two steps forward and stopped. "Why?" she finally whispered. "Why not stay here?"

He looked at her then, misery swirling in his brown eyes. "Being here is not doing either of us any good. I'm only creating more problems for you, and . . ." he trailed off. A nerve jumped in his jaw. He seemed to be working hard to keep his emotions tamped down. "It's time to go home where I belong."

Emma's hands began to shake. She clasped them together hard enough to crack a bone. *Don't leave me*, she wanted to beg. But that was foolishness. Jonathan didn't want to live in Canada. He'd made his position abundantly clear.

He walked toward her, an unreadable expression on his bruised face. Without a word, he bent and brushed his lips over hers—just long enough to make her want to cling to him. Then he moved away. "Take good care of yourself, Em." His voice sounded like a broken phonograph needle scratching over a record. "I pray you find the love and acceptance you're looking for with your family. You deserve that . . . and so much more."

Her breathing grew shallow as panic set in. She wasn't prepared for this final farewell. She needed more time. "We . . . we don't have to say good-bye yet. I'll see you before you leave."

"No." The harsh word erupted from him. "It's best to sever ties now. It will be easier that way." His eyes burned into hers with a thousand unspoken words.

This couldn't be the end of their friendship. The last time she'd ever see him.

On a strangled cry, she threw her arms around his neck and hugged him. The familiar smell of his soap met her nose. She inhaled, trying to memorize the scent. His arms came around her and squeezed so tightly she could barely catch her breath. Her throat burned, her eyes stung.

How could she let him go?

"You don't have to leave," she whispered into his neck. Tears brimmed over and rolled down her face. *If you loved me, you'd stay.*

"I'm afraid I do." Gently, he pried her arms away and set them at her side. "We want different things from life. I see that now, and that's why I have to let you go—so you can be free to live the life you were meant to live. The one God intends for you." He ran a finger down her damp cheek and smiled sadly. "I'll always love you, Emmaline. Don't forget that." With a final searing look, he strode out the door.

Choking back a sob, she followed him into the hall, only to see the front door close behind him. She rushed back to the parlor window and pressed her hand to the glass, straining to catch the last glimpse of him until he was out of sight.

Then she laid her forehead against the windowpane and allowed the tears to flow in earnest, certain that nothing in her life would ever be the same again.

CHAPTER 27

Randall wasn't accomplishing a single thing today. He might as well have stayed home. But to do that would look like he had something to hide, something to feel bad about, and he would take no responsibility for the fight that had ruined the fundraiser.

The blame for that lay squarely on Jonathan Rowe and Giles Wainwright. What on earth had possessed Emma's friend to attack the reporter like that?

Someone knocked on his door, despite the fact that he'd asked not to be disturbed.

"Come in."

Will entered. "Good afternoon, Professor. Is this a good time to talk?"

Randall frowned. "I suppose so." He set down his pen. "What can I do for you?"

Will cleared his throat, his hand loosening the knot in his tie. "I'd like to speak with you about . . . Corinne."

Randall stared at him for a second, then nodded. "Please sit down." He took in Will's nervous demeanor and suddenly had a very good idea what Will wanted. Randall had not been looking forward to this conversation.

"Thank you." Will took a seat across the desk.

"Now, what about Corinne?"

A sheen of sweat shone on Will's brow. "I've grown quite . . . fond of Corinne, and with your permission, sir, I'd like to start courting her." He rubbed his palms on his pant leg.

"I see." Randall gave thanks for his training in the courtroom that allowed him to school his emotions. "Do I presume my daughter would be agreeable to this arrangement?"

"I believe so, yes."

"I take it you would be leading up to an eventual marriage proposal?"

"That would be my intent."

Randall steepled his fingers together. Will was one of his best employees. His protégé. He would have to handle this request in a most delicate manner in order not to alienate him. "You're still living at home with your mother and siblings, correct?"

"Yes, sir."

"And you're still providing for them financially."

"Yes." The lad shifted on his seat.

"You know I want only the best for my daughter," Randall said slowly. "How do you intend to provide for Corinne while supporting five siblings? Even I would find that challenging."

Will cleared his throat. "By the time we wed, I expect my situation will have changed and my family will be in a better position. Two of my sisters should be working by then, which would relieve the burden considerably."

"But you'll always feel responsible for them. At what point will Corinne become your priority?"

Will frowned. "My wife would always be my main priority. But only a cad would turn his back on his family."

He couldn't really fault the boy for his loyalty. However, that type of sacrifice wasn't what Randall wanted for his daughter. Nor would Vera. Though she was all in favor of Corinne marrying, she had high standards for a future son-in-law.

"I don't mean to be insensitive," Randall said, "but my daughter is used to an affluent lifestyle. Can you guarantee her the same standard of living?"

"Not right away." Will straightened on his seat and looked Randall in the eye. "But as I recall from your stories, you were around my age when you came to Canada with nothing more than the clothes on your back. Did that stop you from pursuing your wife?"

The boy had gumption, Randall would give him that.

"When I met Vera, I was further along in my career than you. And I had the support of my future father-in-law."

"Which is what I'm attempting to gain now. You know I have aspirations for a career in law, and that I'll eventually be able to offer Corinne a very comfortable life."

"Ah, the 'eventually' part is what worries me. How long will that take? Five years? Ten?" Randall pushed his chair back on a sigh. "You know I hold you in high esteem, Will. You're smart and principled. But I don't think you're ready for courtship or marriage. Perhaps we can revisit this conversation in a few years, if Corinne is still unattached by then. Maybe then your family situation will have changed and your career will be on a more solid footing." He rose and crossed the room to open the door.

With a defeated air, Will slowly stood up.

Randall clapped a hand on his shoulder. "Nothing personal, son. If all goes well for you, I'll be more than happy to have you as part of the family."

Will stared woodenly at the floor, clearly unhappy with the direction the conversation had taken.

"Thank you for your time," he bit out before exiting the office.

Randall closed the door behind him and blew out a breath. He'd only had Corinne's best interest in mind, so why did he feel like he'd done something that would cost him not only his daughter's respect but Will's as well?

"You're doing very well, Kate. Only one wrong answer this time." Corinne smiled at the eager girl seated beside her. She'd really improved in her equations since Corinne had started tutoring her.

Kate beamed at her. "You make it seem so easy, Corinne. I wish my teachers could explain everything as simply as you do."

Corinne's chest swelled with the unexpected praise. "Why, thank you. That's a wonderful compliment." Her pulse quickened, the girl's words seeming to confirm the idea that she'd been toying with for days. Could she have found her calling in life?

"Have you ever thought of becoming a teacher?" Kate's question had Corinne's breath catching in her lungs.

"I hadn't before," she said. "But I must admit there's something very satisfying in helping a person learn."

Kate leaned forward. "I've always wanted to be a teacher, only my marks were never good enough. Mama keeps telling me I have to get a job to help support the family." She bit her lip, twirling her hair around her fingers. "Do you think I could raise my marks enough to get into college?"

Corinne was struck by the irony. Her father was practically begging her to continue her education and she'd had no interest, and yet Kate wanted to and circumstances denied her that right. "I think you can do anything you set your mind to, Kate. If you study hard, there's no telling what you can do."

The girl's shoulders slumped. "Even if I bring my marks up, we'd never be able to afford it."

"You could get a part-time job to help earn funds. If you really want something bad enough, you'll find a way to make it happen."

"Well said."

Corinne swiveled on her chair as Will entered the room. Instant heat bloomed in her cheeks. "Will, hello. I didn't hear you come in." Had he overheard their conversation? What would he think of his sister's ambitions?

He leaned against the doorframe, a thoughtful expression on his face. "How is Katie doing?"

"I was just telling her how much she's improved." She paused. "It seems she might want to become a teacher."

Will nodded, studying his sister. "That would be great, if we could find the money to pay for it." He turned his green eyes on Corinne. "Speaking of teaching, you're a natural."

"Thank you. I really enjoy working with your sister."

"Are we done for today, Corinne?" Kate had started to gather her papers together.

"I think so. You know which questions to do for next time, right?"

"I do." She smiled at Corinne. "I'll be ready for our quiz. I'd better go and start dinner. See you on Thursday."

Corinne picked up her books and put them into her bag. As usual, Will waited to walk her to the streetcar.

Today, however, he seemed unusually somber as they walked. She sensed something was occupying Will's thoughts. Something more than Kate's studies.

"How was your day?" she asked to break the somewhat strained silence.

"I went to see your father," he said abruptly. He stared straight ahead, his forehead wreathed in lines.

Corinne's pulse skipped. "What about?"

"I asked permission to court you."

Her heart did a slow roll in her chest. The fact that he didn't look at all happy made her think it hadn't gone well. "What happened?"

"He said no."

Her stomach sank to the walkway, though she didn't know why she had expected anything different. "What were his reasons?"

"He said I wasn't ready for such a commitment due to my family obligations." His lips pressed together.

Corinne waited for him to continue.

"He said I had nothing to offer you. And he's right."

"No, he's not, Will. You have many wonderful qualities that any girl would be proud to have in a suitor."

Will turned to look at her. "He didn't refuse me outright. Just told me to wait a few years until my situation has changed." His eyes grew sad. "I tried to warn you that this would never work. I guess I was a fool to think it ever could."

She tugged on his sleeve. "We're both young. We have our whole lives ahead of us. Maybe it wouldn't hurt us to wait a while."

She could hardly believe she was saying that. But with a newfound confidence in Will's affections, she believed their relationship could withstand a period of waiting.

He frowned. "What are you trying to say?"

"I've been thinking that maybe my father was right about me going to college." She peered up through her lashes. "Since working with Kate, I've been thinking of becoming a teacher."

His eyebrows rose. "Really? So my idea wasn't anything new?"

"No. But it helped confirm what I was already thinking." She leaned her shoulder against a lamppost. "We could have an unofficial courtship while we both go to school. Once we graduate, your circumstances might be more favorable for us to consider something more serious." Her heart beat in her chest as she tried to gauge his reaction. Maybe he wouldn't want to wait that long to marry.

He shook his head and stuffed his hands in his pockets. "I can't ask you to put your life on hold until my circumstances improve. Besides, you'll likely meet someone else before then."

She weighed her words while her heart beat an erratic rhythm in her chest. "I'm not interested in anyone else, Will. I'll wait as long as it takes—within reason, of course." She smiled at him, hoping to lighten the mood.

The leaves overhead fluttered in the breeze, causing a host of shadows to dance over his features.

"Are you sure? That seems too much to ask of any woman, much less the daughter of such a prominent member of society."

"I'm no different than any other girl, despite my father's political ambition." She gave him her most serious stare. "Do you think I'm worth the wait, Will? Because I think you are."

His pupils darkened, the only warning she had before he swept her into his arms. "I think you're the most amazing woman I've ever met, Corinne Moore." His mouth captured hers in a long kiss.

Every nerve in her body came alive, every sense attuned to his touch. All too soon, he set her away from him. This time, however, a huge smile brightened his features. At least he didn't regret kissing her again.

Yet one thought still worried her. "You wouldn't object to a wife who wants a career?"

"Not at all. I think it's most admirable that you want to teach."

She reached up to place her palm against his chest. "Thank you for believing in me, Will."

"I'm the one who should be thanking you. I never dreamed a girl like you would want anything to do with me. How did I ever get so lucky?" He brushed his fingers across her cheek. She shivered at the goose bumps chasing along her spine.

"I think God has big plans for you, Will," she said. "I'm just happy those plans brought us together."

He gave her a crooked smile, then wrapped his arm around her waist as they continued on toward the streetcar stop. By now they would have missed the one she usually took, but Corinne didn't care. She was floating on a wave of pure bliss.

Will came to a stop under the streetcar sign. "We'll have to thank your sister. Emma was the one who encouraged me not to give up hope." He studied her. "Do you think you can ever overcome your animosity toward her?"

Corinne smiled. "I already have," she said softly.

"That's my girl." And he kissed her again.

CHAPTER 28

The next morning, with fresh trepidation crawling up her spine, Emma knocked on her father's front door. If she hadn't promised Marianne that she'd be over to continue their exercises today, Emma would have stayed holed up in her room until the whole hospital fiasco blew over. But she couldn't bring herself to disappoint her sister.

Besides, keeping busy might be the only way to keep her mind off Jonathan's departure and the gaping hole in her soul.

The housekeeper answered her knock. "Good afternoon, Miss Emmaline. Miss Marianne is waiting in the music room for you."

"Thank you, Mrs. Beck." Emma stepped into the hallway.

"That was a lovely event at the hospital the other day," the housekeeper said. "Everyone seemed to enjoy themselves tremendously."

"You were there?"

"I was indeed." She smiled.

"I'm so glad you enjoyed it." Emma glanced toward the study and bit back the urge to ask her father's whereabouts.

"A shame what happened at the end. But that doesn't take away from the rest of the day."

Emma forced a smile. "I hope you're right."

High heels tapped down the hall. Vera appeared and gave Emma a cool appraisal. "I'd like a word before you go in to see Marianne, if you don't mind."

Emma swallowed a sigh. So much for taking her mind off her problems. "Of course."

"We can talk in the parlor." Vera nodded a dismissal to Mrs. Beck and led the way into the room. They each took a seat on opposite sides of the coffee table.

"How bad has it been?" Emma asked before Vera could say a word.

"Bad enough. Randall has been fielding questions for two days now, trying to undo the damage that article in the paper created."

"I'm terribly sorry. I don't know what got into Jonathan. He's never been one to initiate a fight before."

"Too bad he started now," Vera said, a wry twist to her lips. "However, what's done is done. What I want to discuss now is how we move forward from here."

Emma clasped her hands together on her lap. "Whatever I can do, just let me know."

"I might have an idea about that." Harcourt Fenton strode in through the arched doorway.

A tremble of anxiety rolled through Emma's belly, but she pushed it aside. "I'd welcome your opinion, especially if you have any thoughts on how to get rid of Giles Wainwright. That man is a constant source of friction. It seems like every time I turn around, he's there."

Mr. Fenton took a seat in an armchair, crossing one ankle over the knee of his perfectly pressed trousers. "And therein lies the problem, Emma. Wainwright is like a bloodhound sniffing out a scent—*your* scent. And until we remove the object of his obsession, I doubt the problem will be resolved." He stared at her with piercing eyes.

Emma pressed a hand to her midsection. "What are you saying?"

He leaned forward. "I'm saying that if you care about your father as much as you claim, you'll disappear for a while. Preferably until after the election."

Disappear? Her hand moved to her throat, her chest tightening. "But the election isn't until January."

"I realize that." He continued to stare.

Emma glanced at Vera, hoping for a glimmer of support, but she only nodded. "I agree with my father. I'm sure you mean well, Emmaline, but it has been nothing but chaotic in our household since your arrival." She heaved a sigh, running her fingers over her strand of pearls. "Randall would never ask you to go, but we wish to appeal to your generous nature. For his sake, the altruistic thing to do would be to leave."

Emma's muscles grew slack, and she fought to stay upright on her seat. "But where would I go?" she whispered. "I have no home to go back to."

"Canada is a large country, my dear. You could go anywhere you wished." Mr. Fenton gave her a pointed look. "We'd be willing to help you financially if necessary."

Emma swallowed back a thousand protests, her mind swimming. Her mouth was so dry she feared she couldn't speak.

"It's a fair offer." Vera straightened a book on the coffee table. "Think about it and let us know. I'd be happy to help you make arrangements."

Emma squeezed her fingernails into her palms. She would not make any rash decisions, especially since she had no idea how her father felt about the whole matter. She looked from Vera to Harcourt, their animosity almost palpable in the room. With a curt nod, she rose. "I'll have to get back to you. Now, if you'll excuse me, Marianne is waiting for me."

Jonathan walked out of the police station onto the sidewalk, his mouth set in a grim line. Wainwright had agreed to drop the assault charge as long as Jonathan paid to replace his camera, which amounted to an outrageous sum that would cost him half his savings.

Seeing the smug look on Wainwright's face, it took all of Jonathan's willpower not to punch him again.

Fortunately, Jonathan had come prepared with his wallet and had begrudgingly paid off the miscreant. With the legalities settled, Jonathan was now free to leave the country. And at least Reggie would get his bail money back. A minor consolation, if that.

Jonathan jammed on his hat and continued walking. With what was left of his funds, he planned to buy a train ticket to Halifax, where he hoped he could trade his open-ended return passage for the next available steamship.

Thankfully, he'd left the second installment of his tuition with his aunt back home. She assured him she would deliver it to Oxford on the due date. That amount would cover his first term, and if he was extremely fortunate, he hoped he could find a job on campus where he could earn a little money on the side while he studied.

All those details, however, would have to wait until he arrived home.

In the meantime, perhaps he'd treat Reggie to dinner tonight as a final farewell before he left Toronto. He wished he could convince his friend to come to England and find his fortune there. Jonathan would miss his companionship, his words of advice, and, most of all, his offbeat sense of humor. Reggie could always get Jonathan to see the bright side of any situation.

Except for this one.

The sooner he left the shores of Canada behind him, the

sooner he could put Emma out of his mind—and his heart—once and for all.

Maybe then he'd stop feeling the tug of her presence constantly weighing on him.

Maybe then he'd at last be able to face a future without her.

CHAPTER 29

Although Emma had considered Mr. Fenton's request that she leave town, she refused to make any radical decisions before the rally, which was scheduled to take place at the end of the week. This big debate with Mayor Church would be a defining moment in her father's campaign—a benchmark in gauging the city's support for Randall in the next election. She prayed his soaring popularity had not suffered due to the incident at the hospital.

Emma could not imagine missing the rally. She'd been looking forward to it since she first saw that flyer on the university campus. On her walk with Jonathan.

Her footsteps faltered on the way up to the second floor of the law building. She grasped a newel-post to steady herself, feeling a tightening in her chest, which was now merely a hollow concave where her heart used to reside. Every now and then without warning, the grief snuck up on her, rendering her almost incapable of functioning. It took every bit of strength to face each day without him.

Her heart ached at the recollection of Jonathan's promise to go with her to the rally. The first promise he'd failed to keep. But no matter. She would go alone.

After she accomplished one important thing first.

Emma stared at her reflection in the office window, firming her resolve. It was time to face her father, and in an effort to avoid another unpleasant conversation with Vera or Mr. Fenton, she'd decided to seek Randall out at work. Hopefully, now that everything had settled down, he would be in a frame of mind to put the fundraiser behind them and look toward the future.

Emma had dressed with great care for her first time returning to her old workplace. As she hovered in the outer hallway, however, she realized it was going to be harder than she'd imagined to face her former colleagues. Would there be a new girl at her desk or was the job still open?

Nerves swirled in her stomach as Emma entered the room, smiling at everyone in the vicinity to mask the confidence she didn't feel.

Right away, Doris jumped up and rushed over to hug her. "Please tell me the professor has reconsidered and taken you back."

"No," Emma said with a laugh as she nodded to the empty desk. "I guess that means he hasn't hired anyone yet."

Doris shook her head and pushed her glasses higher on her nose. "He's interviewed one or two candidates, but that's it." She took Emma by the arm. "I miss you so much. It's far too dull here without you around."

"I'll take that as a compliment." Emma looked up to see Will coming forward, his hair tousled, his shirt-sleeves rolled up to the elbow. "Hello, Will. It's good to see you."

"You too, Emma." His easy smile reminded her a little too much of Jonathan.

"How are things with you?" She'd almost said *with Corinne*, but thought the better of it. He likely didn't want everyone to know of his feelings for his employer's daughter.

"Very well, thank you." He gave her a serious look and lowered his voice so that people at the desks behind them couldn't hear. "I understand I missed a lot of drama at the hospital fundraiser."

Emma raised a brow and glanced over at Doris. "I'm sure you both saw the papers the next day."

"Sure did." Doris perched on the edge of her desk, swinging one leg in the aisle. "If I'd been there, I would have applauded your friend for decking Wainwright. Sad that I missed it."

"Don't be. It was a disaster. I never dreamt Jonathan would do such a thing."

"That's all in the past now," Doris said briskly. "Maybe, if we're lucky Wainwright will be too mortified to show up at the debate tomorrow."

"Don't count on it." Will shoved a pencil behind his ear. "Knowing him, he's bragging to anyone who'll listen about the fight. He'll be there. I'd bet a week's wages on it."

"Speaking of the debate . . ." Emma darted a glance at Randall's door. "I wanted to see my . . . uncle. Is he in?"

"Afraid not." Doris angled her head. "Won't be back until later today from what I understand."

"Oh. That's too bad." Yet Emma's muscles suddenly relaxed. She'd been prepared for a tense conversation, which would now have to wait. Maybe she'd go to his house this evening after all. Or maybe she'd just show up at the rally and take matters from there. "I guess I came by for nothing then."

Doris shot up from the desk. "Not necessarily. I was just about to go on my lunch break. Care to join me at the diner across the street?"

Emma paused to consider. If nothing else, she could use another friend, and she'd always enjoyed Doris's company. "Why not? I'd hate to waste this outfit." She smiled. "What about you, Will? Can you join us?"

He grinned but shook his head. "You two ladies enjoy yourselves. I'll hold down the fort here."

"You're a true gentleman, Will Munroe." Doris laughed as she pulled her purse from her desk drawer. "Be sure to watch out for any pesky reporters."

Ten minutes later, Emma sat in the booth across from Doris and sipped a glass of water while they waited for their food to arrive. The small restaurant vibrated with energy. Waitresses hustled back and forth with trays of food and drinks. A row of patrons seated along the counter laughed and chatted.

"Thank you, Doris. This is just what I needed. A distraction from my worries." The smell of grilled hamburgers and apple pie made Emma realize she'd had nothing for breakfast other than coffee, and now her stomach rumbled loudly.

Doris gave her a sympathetic look. "What's troubling you, honey? Is money an issue? Because I can help you look for another job, if you want."

A waitress appeared with their sandwiches and set the plates down.

Emma sighed. "I'm not even sure what type of work I'm suited for. I'm certainly not cut out to be a typist."

"It helps if you like what you're doing." Doris grinned as she picked up her ham sandwich. "What did you do back in England?"

A sudden rush of homesickness seized Emma, and she released a wistful breath as the memory of her old wooden desk in the corner of Grandad's shop surfaced. Her lips curved softly. "I did bookkeeping for my grandfather's watch business. I've always loved working with figures. Grandad said I had a talent for it."

"That's perfect." Doris reached for a napkin. "There must be lots of that type of work in a city this large."

Emma's mood brightened at the thought. "The professor did suggest I take a few accounting classes, which he thought might be beneficial. Perhaps I'll look into that."

She'd initially dismissed the idea, but the more she thought about it, the better the idea seemed. She had more than enough savings from the sale of the watch shop to tide her over while she took whatever courses might be required. That way, no matter what happened with her father, she'd have a decent job and the means to remain independent without draining her savings.

Doris lifted her glass of soda. "What will Jonathan think of your new career?"

"He won't care. He's heading back to England any day now." She winced at the bitterness in her tone and set down her sandwich with a sigh. "That's not true. He'd be thrilled if I found a job that made me happy."

Jonathan had always been her biggest champion, always wanting what was best for her. Without him now, her world echoed with a new emptiness.

"I'm sorry he's leaving. According to Will, Jonathan is a hard worker and a gentleman. Too bad I'm off the market." She flashed her engagement ring and winked. "But I do have two sisters."

Emma couldn't bring herself to join in Doris's banter. She pushed her half-eaten sandwich aside, sudden anxiety ruining her appetite.

"Hey, I was only teasing. Judging by the way Jonathan went after Wainwright on your behalf, I'd say his heart is already spoken for." Doris wiped her fingers on her napkin. "Which begs the obvious question: Why is he going back to England without you?"

Emma stared out at the restaurant patrons, avoiding Doris's intense gaze. She'd love nothing more than to explain the whole thorny issue to her friend. However, with Doris working in Randall's office, she didn't think it fair to get into all the details about her and Jonathan's disagreement over her father. It would put Doris in an uncomfortable position.

"I'm afraid the answer to that," Emma said at last, "is complicated." Oh, how she wished it wasn't. That her relationship with Jonathan could have remained the same as when they were young. That their feelings hadn't changed. Instead, what she feared would happen had come to pass. She'd literally lost her best friend.

"Men are always complicated, my dear. That's what makes them so fascinating." Doris glanced out the window. "Speaking of complicated, there goes the professor now. Maybe you'll get to speak to him after all."

Randall removed his hat and jacket and placed them on the coatrack. He needed to get in touch with Emma before tomorrow's debate, yet he dreaded that conversation with every fiber of his being. For he knew no matter how he framed his request, it would hurt his daughter's feelings.

Emma had worked so hard to help with the hospital benefit in order to improve his image. And for the most part, she'd succeeded. Except for that crazy incident with the reporter at the end of the day, everything had gone without a hitch. Unfortunately, all anyone remembered after that ugly front-page pictorial was the brawl—with Emma right in the middle.

A fact Vera and Harcourt delighted in reminding him.

A knock sounded on his door. What now?

"Come in."

Emma's head poked inside. "Hello, Randall. Could I speak with you, if you have a minute?"

The hesitant look on her face made his chest ache. They'd been making such headway in their relationship.

"Of course. I'm glad you're here, Emmaline. Please sit down."

She smiled, a measure of relief easing the tension on her lovely face. In a cheery red hat and dress, she lit up the room. "I'm sorry I didn't come to see you sooner," she said. "I'll admit I was hiding out after the embarrassing fiasco and that dreadful article in the newspaper."

"Let's hope that's all behind us now." He leaned back in his chair and attempted to keep his expression light. "Vera has been after me to speak to you."

Right away, Emma's smile faded.

"I take it you have some idea about her concerns."

She nodded. "She's already talked to me. She and Mr. Fenton." Emma's lips pinched together.

Randall held in a sigh. There was no easy way to come out with this. "Then what I'm about to say won't come as a surprise." He tried to soften his features as he met her wary gaze. "I think it would be in everyone's best interest if you stayed away from the rally tomorrow." He paused. Best to get it all out at once. "Not just the rally actually. From the family too."

She shrank back, her frame crumpling as though the air had leaked out of her.

"This is just a temporary measure," he continued quickly, hoping to lessen the damage of that statement, "until we can figure out a way to deal with Wainwright. He's always been a bother, but for some reason you seem to have sparked a new obsession in him."

"I don't know why. I've never done anything to warrant such interest."

"A beautiful woman like you doesn't have to do anything, Emma. You attract notice whether you want to or not. Unfortunately, sometimes the attention is negative." He smiled. "But don't worry. I have some of my campaign staff working on a solution."

"I see." She stared at her lap, misery darkening her features.

"So," he said gently, "can you do me that favor and stay away for a while?"

Her head snapped up, an unusual flare of heat flashing in her eyes. "Exactly how long is a while? A week? A month?"

He straightened in his chair. "Naturally, I hope it won't take that long. Why does the amount of time matter?"

Emma pressed her lips together. She seemed to be weighing how to answer his question. Finally, she said, "I thought by now, after everything I've done for you, that you'd have . . . you'd have told everyone who I really am."

When her sorrowful gaze met his, his gut twisted. How he wished it were that simple. "I realize it's a frustrating situation. With a political career, you have to weigh every move before you make it. Can I ask you to be patient a while longer?"

She let out a long breath. "I guess I don't have much choice."

"Thank you." Relief flooded his chest. "Once this rally is over . . ." He paused, not willing to make false promises.

She shook her head. "Once this is over, there'll be another event or another speech. It won't end until the election is over."

He'd never heard her sound so defeated. Though he wished he could reassure her, he couldn't dispute her claim. "As soon as we get this Wainwright character contained, we'll revisit our options." A lame attempt to appease her, but he couldn't leave it like this. "Why don't you and Jonathan do something together tomorrow night instead? Maybe go out for a nice dinner? My treat."

She looked at him, her eyes dull. "Jonathan isn't . . ." She took a breath. "He's gone to stay with a friend for a while." She grasped her handbag and stood. "Good luck with the debate."

Randall rose as well, regret clawing at him. "Emma, I'm sorry. Really I am."

She shook her head again, her dark curls swinging about her shoulders. "If you were truly sorry, you'd do something to fix this." Then, with a sharp inhale, she squared her shoulders. "You know where to find me, should the need arise. Good-bye, Randall."

When the door shut behind her, the breath left his lungs with a whoosh. He longed to chase after her, to tell the whole world she was his daughter, but he couldn't risk destroying his career for good. He'd worked far too hard to throw it all away now.

He only hoped that one day Emma could understand his reasons and forgive him.

CHAPTER 30

The next day, Emma threw herself into helping Mrs. C. around the boardinghouse with uncommon vigor. Anything to burn off the sting of her growing anger. The more she thought about the conversation with her father yesterday, the angrier she became. Like a slow burn, her defeat turned to annoyance, which had then begun to smolder, and by the morning, she'd worked herself up to a fine blaze of temper.

Randall had some nerve, demanding that she sever ties with him and his family for the foreseeable future. She'd had to disappoint Marianne already today by cancelling their therapy time together.

"Is everything all right, dear?" Mrs. C. asked from the door of the dining room, where Emma had taken to scrubbing the walls. "I didn't expect you to do such a . . . thorough cleaning."

Emma swiped her arm across her forehead, dislodging a curl from beneath her kerchief. "I'm just trying to keep busy. Working off some frustration."

Mrs. C. came farther into the room, a dustcloth in hand. "Would you like to talk about whatever's bothering you? I'm a good listener."

Her landlady's sympathetic expression made Emma want to heap all her troubles on those petite shoulders. But until Emma had sorted through her own feelings, she wouldn't do that to the kind woman. "Thank you, Mrs. C., but I can't talk about it. Not yet." Emma rinsed her rag in the bucket of water and wrung out the cloth.

"Is it anything to do with Jonathan's leaving?"

The soft question tore a strip off Emma's flayed heart. She missed him every hour of every day. She couldn't even go out to the garden or sit on the porch swing anymore because it hurt too much. "That's a large part of it." She scrubbed a stubborn mark on the faded wallpaper, trying to ignore the weight of Mrs. C.'s regard.

"Well, don't tucker yourself out, dear. You'll want to save some energy for the big rally tonight." She flicked her dustcloth over the dining room chairs.

Emma sat back on her heels. Another sore topic. "Are you going?" she asked cautiously.

"I wouldn't miss it. Reverend Burke is coming by to pick me up."

Emma bit her lip. "Do you think a lot of people will show up?"

"I expect so. They're holding it at Convocation Hall, which seats over a thousand people." She frowned. "You are going, aren't you?"

"I'm not sure." How could she tell Mrs. C. that her father had basically banished her from the event?

"You're welcome to join Geoffrey and me if you don't want to go alone."

Emma swallowed an unexpected rise of emotion. "That's kind of you. But I don't think I'll be attending."

Mrs. C.'s hand stilled on the back of the chair she was cleaning. "Did you and your father have a falling-out?"

"Not exactly. But after the fundraiser disaster, he doesn't want me there." Emma got off her knees and stretched out her back.

"Surely he can't blame you for that. You had no control over the actions of those two men."

"I'm afraid he believes otherwise. He fears my presence could cause some other disaster to ensue." Emma moved the bucket to a spot farther down the wall.

"That's hardly fair." Mrs. C. frowned. "Besides, the event is open to the public. He can't bar you from going."

Emma paused as the truth of Mrs. C.'s statement sank in. Her landlady made an excellent point. After all, she didn't have to bow to her father's wishes. The choice was hers to make.

She threw the rag into the bucket with enough force to cause the water to slosh out. "You're absolutely right, Mrs. C. After all, this is a free country." And she planned to take advantage of that freedom. She was tired of hiding, tired of pretending, tired of letting Randall dictate every aspect of their relationship.

This debate was the buzz of the city—a very big deal, or so the press made it seem. As an honorary Torontonian, Emma had every right to attend. She would do as Jonathan had suggested when they'd initially planned to go together.

She'd stay in the background. Remain anonymous.

No one would even know she was there.

That evening, Emma ignored the ripple of nerves in her belly as she moved along the outer edges of the enormous auditorium, skirting the mass of people who spilled from the rows of seated spectators. She'd waited until the debate was in full swing before slipping unnoticed into the back of the hall. Now, she took a moment to catch her breath and survey her surroundings.

Convocation Hall was indeed impressive. The seats surrounded the stage in tiers. From Emma's vantage point, all she could make out was a sea of colored hats below. Above her, in the balcony, people leaned over the rail for a better view of the speakers. Directly in front of the stage, about a dozen reporters jotted notes on pads of paper, while others held cameras at the ready. Emma recognized one man in particular from his profile. The one man she needed to avoid at all cost.

From the expensive-looking camera draped around his neck, Emma surmised that Giles Wainwright had replaced the equipment broken in the scuffle at the hospital. Just seeing him point his lens made Emma's blood boil.

She ran a hand over her tight chignon, mostly hidden under the floppy brown hat she'd borrowed from one of Mrs. C.'s boarders. Tonight, it was imperative to not draw any undue attention to herself. Even in the simple outfit she'd donned— a coffee-colored skirt and plain ivory blouse—Emma didn't care to test Mr. Wainwright's powers of observation.

She kept to the back wall, shifting every now and then to an aisle that afforded her a better view of the platform below. From what Emma could ascertain, Mayor Church was giving a rebuttal to Randall's challenge about the deplorable state of the Ward, an area of the city where many immigrants lived in squalor. In true political fashion, the mayor was avoiding saying anything concrete, merely explaining how it wasn't the city's fault that the people ended up living in these conditions.

A light flashed and popped. Of all the reporters, it appeared Wainwright was the only one snapping pictures during the speeches, and he seemed to time his flashes to the moments Randall stepped up to the microphone. Was he purposely trying to unnerve her father and distract him from what he wanted to say?

At the far right of the podium, Mr. Fenton, Vera, Corinne, and Marianne sat with their hands folded on their laps. Mayor Church, on the other hand, had a handful of his employees seated on his side. As a bachelor, he had no wife or children to offer the picture of the perfect family.

Applause broke out over the auditorium. Emma hadn't been listening, so she wasn't sure whom they were applauding. At the lectern, Mayor Church frowned, his cheeks a mottled shade of red, while Randall wore a satisfied expression. Obviously, those in attendance supported his view on the subject of immigrant poverty.

With all the doors shut, the air in the room had become increasingly stuffy. Perspiration snaked down Emma's back. The starched collar of her blouse bit into her neck, making it difficult to breathe. She wished she could undo the top buttons and rid herself of this suffocating sensation.

The back door of the auditorium opened, and a welcome rush of fresh air entered the room. A stir of movement disrupted the spectators standing along the back as a man squeezed by them.

Will!

Never had Emma been so happy to see a familiar face. She felt a certain kinship with Will, for in some respects, he was in the same untenable position as she—yearning to belong to the Moore family but always seeming to be relegated to the sidelines.

Will carried a stack of flyers, which he stuffed into his satchel as he walked. He must have been manning the information table outside. When he moved by without greeting her, she tapped his shoulder. He turned, a confused frown on his face. "Emma? Why are you way back here?"

She raised her brows. Did he really need an answer to that?

"Oh." Understanding dawned. "Trying to avoid a certain reporter?"

"Exactly."

"Is Corinne here?" He strained to look at the stage below.

"She's seated with the rest of the family. Doesn't she look lovely?"

He released a breath. "Beautiful." The longing in his voice was unmistakable.

"When are you going to speak to Randall about her?" Emma kept her voice low, so as not to disturb the other spectators.

"I already have."

"Will, that's wonderful! Corinne must be thrilled."

"Not quite." He scowled. "Her father refused my request. Said I have nothing to offer her." His eyes fixated on Corinne. "Trouble is he's right."

"No, he's not." A hot flush rose in Emma's cheeks, indignation on Will's behalf renewing her annoyance. What gave Randall the right to try to control everyone's lives? "You have the most important thing of all—love. Anything else you can build together."

The irony of her words struck like a fist to the midsection. Why couldn't she have taken this advice before she'd ruined everything with Jonathan? Why had she put her father first, believing him to be noble and loving, the hero she'd always imagined?

A wave of unease rose through the audience, pulling Emma's attention back to the stage. It seemed the question-and-answer portion of the evening had started, and some of the topics were inciting heated discussions.

Will leaned toward her. "Come on. Let's get a little closer. We can still avoid Wainwright if we keep to the far right-hand side."

Emma stiffened. "I don't want to risk it."

"Don't worry. You can stay behind me. No one will see you." He took her hand and tugged her into motion.

Against her better judgment, Emma followed him along the curved wall and down the tiered stairs. Her unease grew as he kept going until they were almost at ground level. She did her best to stay behind Will's shoulders, hoping to remain obscured.

The moderator of the debate rose to announce they were nearing the last questions of the evening. A ripple of movement ran through the spectators as a certain reporter plowed his way to the front, hand in the air. "I have a question for Professor Moore."

The moderator barely suppressed an eye roll. "Go ahead, Mr. Wainwright."

"One of your chief platforms, sir, is your relatability to the immigrants of Toronto since you yourself were once one. You also flaunt your family status, priding yourself on being a morally upstanding husband and father."

Randall moved to the microphone. "That's right. I believe a strong family support system is a definite asset."

"Does that include the love child you left behind in Britain?"

A loud gasp rose from the crowd. All the color seemed to drain from Randall's face.

Emma shrank back against the wall, her lungs seizing, trapping the air within.

Dear Lord, surely he doesn't mean me?

Randall cleared his throat. "I don't know what you're trying to insinuate, but you're very much mistaken."

"I think not. I've done my research."

The air in the auditorium fairly crackled with suspense.

Panic clawed at Emma. Wainwright was not going to give up until he'd created another scene, possibly worse than the one at the hospital.

A sense of urgency rose within her, and Emma tugged on Will's sleeve. "Get me out of here," she whispered.

His lips pressed in a grim line, he nodded and took her hand, starting toward the side door. But before they could make their escape, Wainwright turned and looked right at Emma. "There she is now." He pointed an accusing finger at her. "Do you deny this woman is your daughter?"

As much as Emma wanted to flee, her feet froze to the floor. Against her will, her gaze flew to Randall. He looked trapped, his hands glued to the podium.

Even still, an unbidden bubble of hope rose in Emma's chest. This was the perfect opportunity to tell the world that she was his daughter. Surely now he would defend her honor and set the record straight.

"Of course I deny it." Randall's voice boomed over the room. "Just as I would deny any unfounded accusation."

"Unfounded? Really?" Wainwright flung a hand in her direction. "Even though the resemblance is undeniable? The same hair color, facial structure, and identical blue eyes?"

Heat flooded Emma's cheeks, the curious gaze of the audience piercing her like a thousand needles.

This was it. Randall would have to realize there was nothing left to say. It was time to tell the truth. Time to show the world that he had another daughter, one he was proud to acknowledge at long last. With her heart thudding in her chest, Emma waited in silent anticipation for the signal to join her father on stage.

Randall pulled himself up tall, his jaw taut. A vein pulsed in his neck. "Emmaline is not my daughter," he said firmly. "She is my niece."

The lie reverberated through the room, echoing loudly over the sound system against an unnatural quiet.

Not my daughter. Emma struggled to breathe. The weight of betrayal sat like an anvil on her chest, threatening to collapse her lungs. Not only had he failed to defend her, he'd outright denied her existence.

"Your niece, you say?" Mr. Wainwright narrowed his eyes at Randall. "Tell me, how does someone with no siblings come to have a niece?" The reporter's smug expression matched his arrogant tone. "Admit it, Professor. This woman is the illegitimate love child you abandoned twenty-two years ago before you fled the country."

Mr. Fenton dashed forward and smashed a fist onto the wooden dais. "You, sir, are a liar and an agitator. You'll do anything to discredit the mayor's chief opponent, especially since he's favored to win. Did Mr. Church pay you to say this?"

"I refuse to answer such a ludicrous question," Wainwright sputtered.

The murmurs in the audience became increasingly loud. Chairs squeaked as people began to rise, pushing their way into the aisles. Some raised their fists and shouted at the stage.

Emma could make out nothing that was being said over the roar in her ears. Another reporter's flash went off near her face, momentarily blinding her. She brought up a hand to shield her face, a strangled cry dying in her throat. When her vision cleared, her focus remained locked on her father, silently begging him to rectify the situation. He, however, made a point of intentionally ignoring her, while Mr. Fenton continued to shout.

At that moment, something shifted within her. All-consuming anger broke loose and rushed into her throat, swamping her senses in a sea of red.

"Enough." The word erupted with such intensity that it overcame the cacophony of noise.

Another hush descended over the gathering as though everyone held their breath.

"Emma. Don't." Will's panicked whisper barely registered.

She pushed away from him toward the raised platform where the Moore family stood, mouths agape. "It's time to stop the lies." Emma pulled the annoying hat from her head as she climbed the stairs to the stage, her focus zeroed in on the stricken man before her. Neither the whispers of the spectators nor their scandalized stares mattered. Weeks and weeks of suppressing her feelings, burying her hurt, and doing her best to give this man the benefit of the doubt had all been for nothing. Her father didn't love her, didn't want her to be part of his life. She was a dirty secret he wanted to keep hidden away.

Ignored. Buried.

That stopped now. She would no longer be party to his deception.

When Mr. Fenton made a move toward her, she halted him with one withering glare.

Then she circled the podium to face her father. "Do you have any idea what I sacrificed to come here? I gave up *everything* for you. Everything." The word came out as a near screech from her raw throat. "I sold my grandad's shop, left my home, and crossed an ocean in order to meet you—all in the naïve hope that my *father* might actually want to know me. Yet all you've done from the moment we met is deny my very existence."

Her eyes grew hot. Her limbs shook. But she couldn't stop the tide of words spewing forth.

"Do you know what it was like to grow up without a mother or father? To believe that I was an orphan?" She pointed to Vera, Corinne, and Marianne huddled together. "Why did *they* get to have you? Why did *they* merit sharing your life and your love, and not me?" A sob strangled her. All the pent-up resentment she'd repressed for weeks spilled out in a flood of tears.

Someone touched her arm. She shook it off.

Randall came closer. "Let's go somewhere private to discuss this," he said in a tense whisper.

"Ah, at last the truth comes out." Wainwright's voice, smacking of disgust, rang over the stage. "At the very least you owe the girl an explanation."

Randall faced the reporter. "For once, you're right, Wainwright. I owe her the truth. But I owe you nothing." He took Emma by the arm and guided her off the stage.

After purging her outrage, she was left numb. Hollow. She allowed herself to be led down a back corridor to a small room. Randall brought her inside and closed the door, then remained still, not moving.

Emma stumbled against the wall, the reporter's words repeating in her brain. *Illegitimate love child.* A dark cloud of suspicion surfaced.

"What did Wainwright mean by *illegitimate*? He was making that up, wasn't he?" Her voice shook, her mind scrambling to remember the story her grandparents had told her. Her parents had eloped, they'd said.

His back to her, Randall's shoulders went rigid. Slowly he turned and raised haggard eyes to hers. He appeared to have aged ten years in the last few minutes. "Technically, he's correct. I never married your mother."

Emma blinked, certain she hadn't heard right. All the air seemed to leave the room, and mustiness surrounded her. She clawed at the neck of her blouse. There were no windows in the tiny space, just a stack of boxes and a mop and bucket.

"That's why your grandparents hated me," Randall said. "That's why they told you I was dead. I'm sure they wished it was so."

Her muscles seized as coldness invaded her core. She'd been born out of wedlock, an illegitimate and unwanted burden.

All her romantic illusions about her father's grand love for her mother shattered in one ugly moment. Theirs hadn't been a fairy-tale love.

It had been . . . sinful.

"Why didn't you marry? Didn't you love her?"

He came forward, the blueness of his eyes more intense. "I may have lied before, but please believe this. I loved Loretta and wanted to marry her. But we couldn't agree on either a Catholic or a Protestant church, and she refused to go to a justice of the peace. Then the pregnancy got difficult, and she was forced to stay in bed. We planned to get married as soon as you were born, but then . . . well, you know the rest." He squeezed the bridge of his nose.

"So that's why you left." Emma struggled to process this different version of her history.

"What I told you was true. I had no way to look after an infant. Your grandparents stepped in immediately and took you to their home."

Her brain buzzed. "Why am I a Moore then? Why didn't my grandparents name me Emmaline Bartlett?"

"It was the one demand I insisted upon in order to relinquish my parental rights."

That made no sense at all. Why insist on her having his name when he never intended to see her again? She raised her disbelieving gaze to his. "How could I ever have thought you were so noble and self-sacrificing?" A harsh laugh that sounded slightly hysterical escaped her dry throat. "I couldn't have been more wrong."

A knock sounded at the door, and Will's worried face appeared. "Is everything all right?"

Emma's lungs relaxed their death grip, allowing her to draw a full breath. Will would get her to safety. Away from her father's lies. "No, it's not. Can you get me out of here, please?"

Will shot a glance at Randall, then nodded. "Of course. We can go out the back. I know a shortcut."

Without another word to her father, Emma blindly followed Will's lead, grasping his hand like a lifeline keeping her from drowning. She had no idea how far they went before Will slowed to a stop. He'd found a secluded alcove at the side of one of the buildings where they could avoid the last of the people who were filing out of the auditorium.

"Are you all right?" he asked quietly.

She shook her head, certain she'd never be all right again. She was an illegitimate child. A dirty secret. Unwanted. Unloved. She rubbed at the ache in her chest. "I just want to go home."

At that moment, she wasn't sure if she meant the boardinghouse . . . or England.

"Come on. I'll take you."

As she trudged along the street beside Will, the burden of her father's lies weighing on her spirit, Emma had never missed Jonathan more.

CHAPTER 31

Emma awoke the next day and couldn't muster the energy to move her feet to the floor. Instead, she lay in bed and stared at the ceiling. Her eyes were dry and scratchy after a night of weeping. Her insides felt hollow as though her river of tears had emptied her out, leaving a void she doubted anything could fill.

The day loomed ahead of her with nothing but bleakness.

She'd come to Toronto with the highest of hopes for her future, filled with unbridled optimism that here, at last, she would find her place in the world with the father she'd longed for.

Now all her hopes had turned to ashes.

The idealized version of her father she'd held since childhood had died with them. Gone was the daydream of the man who had loved her mother with such intensity that he couldn't live without her. The man who would cherish Emma with the same unconditional love.

Instead, he hadn't even bothered to marry her mother. No wonder he was able to abandon their child so easily.

All through the sleepless night, three dreaded words kept echoing in Emma's brain. *Illegitimate love child.* How would she ever hold her chin up in public again?

She pulled the covers over her head. If only Jonathan were still in his flat above the garage, she'd go and talk to him. He'd know how to cheer her up. He'd help her figure out where to turn next.

But even if he were still in Toronto, he'd made it clear he didn't want to see her again. A tear trickled onto the pillow. How had she ruined everything so completely?

A knock sounded. "Emma? You didn't come down for breakfast. Are you feeling all right?" Mrs. Chamberlain's voice sounded worried.

How could she even ask that question? If she'd been at the rally last night, she must have witnessed Emma's public humiliation. Along with a thousand other people.

"I'm a bit tired. I thought I'd lie in a while this morning."

A few seconds of silence followed.

"That's fine, dear. You rest. A letter arrived for you. I'll just slip it under the door." A rustle of paper sounded.

Emma held her breath until the footsteps receded down the hall. Probably a note from Randall trying to justify his actions. She had no stomach for his meaningless words.

But what if the note was from Jonathan? She sat up in bed and peered over the footrail. What if he'd heard about last night and was reaching out to her? A faint flutter of hope propelled her out of bed to retrieve it.

She tore open the envelope, and her stomach dropped at the sight of the handwriting. It was from Aunt Trudy. Her lip trembled. How she missed this dear woman and her motherly advice. Emma could use some of it right now.

She moved to the window seat and scanned the brief note, her heart pinching more with each word.

Dearest Emmaline,

I'm sorry I've been so remiss in not writing more often since you left. I've recently had a letter from Jonathan. He says that you intend to stay in Canada. While I'm happy you've found your father—and sisters too—I must admit that selfishly I'm grieving your loss. I miss you both more than I thought possible. Thankfully Jonathan will be returning home soon. I'd always hoped you and he would end up married and give me lots of babies to spoil. Must be the romantic in me. However, we must follow God's will for our lives, and knowing you, I'm certain you're doing just that. I wish you nothing but happiness, my dear. You'll always be like a daughter to me and are always welcome here.

All my love,
Aunt Trudy

Emma let out a slow breath and brushed the tears from her cheeks. If only she could go to Trudy now and pour out her troubles to her. She might not have any answers, but her arms would provide shelter and her love would be a balm to Emma's battered soul, just as it had been after Gran's death.

In the distance, the faint toll of a church bell could be heard. Emma opened her window to allow the morning air into the room. The mournful tones resonated with her, yet as she breathed in the fresh air, she dug deep for her determination. Her grandparents would want her to be strong, and so would Aunt Trudy. Emma had been through worse in her life and had survived. With God's help, she could do it again.

She rose and took some notepaper from her night table. She would answer Trudy's letter and take it to the post office. Then, on the way back, she'd pay Reverend Burke a visit.

Perhaps some divinely inspired advice was exactly what she needed right now to pull her out of her despair and help her determine what to do next.

Later that day, Emma sat in Reverend Burke's kitchen, a cup of tea in front of her. Upon finding her on his doorstep, the dear man hadn't hesitated for a moment to invite her in.

"I've just come back from a meeting at the church and made a fresh batch of cinnamon buns," he'd said. "Must have had a feeling I'd be having company."

Though the buns smelled delicious, Emma had only been able to pick at the treat, barely managing to swallow a few sips of tea.

After finishing his own bun, the minister wiped his fingers on a napkin. "I'm sensing you're in need of an ear this morning," he prompted gently. "Harriet and I left the rally right after all the drama erupted last night. Is that what's troubling you?"

"That's only the tip of the iceberg." Emma attempted to smile but failed miserably.

"Why don't you start at the beginning, and let's see if we can make sense of the situation."

Haltingly, Emma poured out the entire sordid tale, ending with the revelation of her illegitimacy. "I thought finding my father would fill all the empty spaces inside me," she said. "Now I feel even worse. Like I'm a stain on both sides of the family." She looked up. "I'm so ashamed of the way I barged into my father's family as though I was entitled to be there. Instead, I'm the nasty secret he's been running from his whole life."

Reverend Burke handed her a napkin. "The situation is indeed unfortunate, but my dear girl, you are in no way to blame for the sins of your parents. You were born an innocent babe, and I've no doubt that if your poor mother hadn't passed away, she and your father would have wed and provided you with a wonderful family." He lifted the enormous teapot to pour himself another cup. "But your childhood wasn't so terrible for you, was it? You had two devoted grandparents who raised you in a loving home and gave you everything you required. Why was this not enough?"

Emma's gaze slid to the striped tablecloth. He made her sound like the most ungrateful girl in the world. But how could she begin to make him understand the gaping emptiness that existed within her?

An emptiness she'd been sure finding her father would fill.

"I just wanted a normal family," she whispered. "The same as everyone else had growing up." Long-held visions surfaced of her friends being greeted by their parents. Fathers who lifted their daughters in their arms and twirled them in the air, gazing at them with undisguised adoration.

Reverend Burke studied her in a way that made her squirm. "Is it a family you're really seeking, Emma? Or is it the need to be loved and accepted? To be valued for the wonderful person God created you to be?"

Emma hesitated. Did she dare utter the truth she'd never divulged to anyone—not even to Jonathan? "My grandparents loved me as best they could," she said slowly. "But somehow it wasn't enough." She felt selfish admitting that out loud. "I wanted a parent, a father, specifically. Someone to love me more than anyone else in the world."

She didn't dare look at the minister for fear of seeing the disgust on his face.

"May I share some hard-earned wisdom with you?"

She nodded.

He scratched his chin in a thoughtful manner. "There's only one parent's love you truly need: your heavenly Father's. And the good news is you don't have to earn it, and you don't have to prove yourself worthy to receive it. You are loved for exactly the person you are, with all your faults and flaws. In His eyes, you are a masterpiece. His own wondrous creation."

Emma bit back the protest on her tongue. She was anything but a masterpiece—more like a disaster.

"Learn to accept that love, Emma. Breathe it in and let it fill

303

your soul. You'll be amazed at what a difference it can make in your life." He leaned forward and laid his hand gently on her arm.

Emma sighed. "I know God loves me, Reverend."

"You know it in your head, but do you know it in your heart—where it matters? Because only when you've fully accepted His love can you begin to accept the love of others." He smiled, his eyes kind. "Love is a gift to be given freely and received without condition. It's up to you to choose what you do with that gift."

Jonathan's face sprang to mind. Emma blinked hard, fighting the sting of tears. Jonathan had always loved her without condition, without judgment. Always putting her needs first. Then, when he'd given her the gift of his heart, she'd rejected it in order to keep chasing after a man who was too self-centered to ever give her the validation she craved. Now Jonathan was gone, and she needed to figure out how to survive on her own.

"Emma? Are you all right?"

The minister's voice startled her from her thoughts, and she became aware of the tears streaming down her face. "Not yet. But I think I will be." She swiped the moisture from her cheeks. "Thank you, Reverend Burke. I'm going to do my best to be content with God's love, and hopefully that will be enough."

He patted her arm. "Start with prayer and reflection. Reach out to the Lord, Emma. I promise He won't disappoint you."

CHAPTER 32

Despite the rainy afternoon, the boardinghouse parlor glowed with soft lamplight, cocooning Emma in her spot on the sofa. She had the room to herself, as the rest of the boarders were busy with their day. Emma blinked in an attempt to refocus her tired eyes, and she laid her Bible on the table. She had been reading for several hours, and her back muscles protested her lack of movement, so she rose and stretched, then crossed to the front window. Outside a light rain continued to drizzle, streaking the pane with moisture. People walked by on the sidewalk, huddled under black umbrellas. Somehow the weather mirrored her mood—gray and damp, yet with a glimmer of light peeking through.

The memory of the rally still haunted Emma, and though she grieved the loss of her dream, many hours of prayer and reading her Bible had brought her a measure of peace. Not enough yet to fully forgive her father, but enough to let her know that, given time, she would be able to let go of the hurt and shame. In the meantime, Reverend Burke's advice had been helpful. She'd immersed herself in God's Word and allowed her faith to fill the hollow parts of herself, the messages of love and hope starting to be a balm to help heal her wounds.

Mrs. C. entered the parlor and with a loud huff sank onto her favorite chair.

At the window, Emma let the curtain fall back into place. "What's wrong, Mrs. C.?"

"I was just talking with Grace on the phone." Mrs. C. shook her head. "I feel so sorry for her. The young man she fancies is marrying someone else in a few weeks' time."

Emma frowned. "Andrew is getting married?" Grace had told Emma of her budding feelings for her nephew's guardian, but Emma hadn't given it much thought. Clearly, she should have paid more attention.

"Yes, and he's taking that sweet baby away from her by moving all the way to Ottawa. So, on top of everything else, Grace will be left without a job."

"That's terrible." For the first time, Emma's problems seemed trivial compared to her friend losing her sister, the man she loved, and now her nephew. "Do you think she'll go back to England?"

"I imagine she will. There won't be much point staying here if she can't be part of little Christian's life."

Emma swallowed a sudden rush of tears. The same thought had been circling in her brain for two days now, since Aunt Trudy's letter and Emma's talk with Reverend Burke. What reason did she have to stay in Canada? Her father certainly didn't want her in his life. And though she loved Mrs. C., the boardinghouse wasn't exactly a permanent residence.

"What about you, dear?" Mrs. C. asked gently. "Will you be heading back home as well?"

She blinked hard and swallowed. "I don't have a home anymore, Mrs. C." She resumed her seat on the sofa. "Maybe I made a mistake selling my grandfather's shop so quickly. At the time, I was so angry at Grandad for not telling me the truth about my father. I think I acted out of spite."

"A perfectly understandable response. You were hurt and grieving."

"Jonathan and Aunt Trudy tried to talk me out of it, but I was so stubborn. I wouldn't listen. I should have known my grandparents would never do anything to harm me." Emma swiped at the moisture gathering in her eyes. Now that her anger had faded, she could see that her grandparents had given her a wonderful home. How could she have let her anger erase all they had done for her? "I think I understand why they kept the truth from me. They never wanted me to feel the burden of illegitimacy."

Mrs. C. came to lay her hand on Emma's shoulder. "Your grandparents would understand why you did what you did. Besides, you couldn't really have run the shop alone, could you? And now you have the funds to do whatever you like, either here or back home."

Home. The word was a constant ache in Emma's chest. "But I have no home or family anymore, Mrs. C. How do I start over?" Her voice cracked, and she pressed her lips together.

"I know how you feel." The landlady smiled sadly and took a seat beside her. "As someone who's had to find a new home far away from the land where I grew up, I learned that family is not always the people you're born to. Sometimes they're the people God places in your life. The ones who choose to love you." She took Emma's hand in hers, and warmth surrounded Emma's fingers. "Home is somewhere safe, somewhere you can be yourself and know that there everything will be all right. But home is not just a physical place. It's where your heart lives. It's where the people you love live. For me, that was Mr. Chamberlain. The moment we met, I knew I'd found my home."

"He must have been a wonderful man," Emma whispered.

"Ah yes. My husband was a rare jewel among men." She paused. "Much like your Jonathan."

Emma inhaled sharply. Her muscles tightened as though trying to shield her from the truth and the heartache of Mrs. C.'s words.

"Emma, dear, I recognize love when I see it. And Jonathan was most definitely in love with you. What really happened to make him leave so abruptly?"

A painful spasm hit Emma's midsection. She wrapped her arms around her waist as the memory surfaced of how dismissive she'd been of his feelings. "Jonathan asked me to marry him and go back to England," she whispered. "I didn't know what to do. My father was just beginning to . . ." She trailed off, realizing how lame that sounded now. Was she the only one who couldn't see Randall's true nature?

"So you chose your father over Jonathan?"

The quiet question held no recrimination and no judgment, yet a wave of shame shimmered inside her. "Yes."

"And now that you know the truth, do you still feel the same? Do you still expect to find acceptance and love and a home with your father?"

"No."

"Does your father make you feel loved and protected? Or is it really Jonathan who does that for you?"

Emma forgot to breathe as tears spilled down her cheeks. Jonathan had always been her haven, the place where she felt cherished and safe.

Jonathan was her home.

He had been since they were children. With him, everything about her world made sense. Without him, her world had fallen into chaos. Her hopes and dreams were in shambles around her.

"It's where the people you love live."

She remembered their night at Mama Vittore's, their romantic dance, the kiss on the porch swing. The way she'd felt so alive, so protected, so cherished. Her throat swelled with the truth she could no longer deny. A truth she'd come to realize that night in his arms.

She loved Jonathan. Not just as a brother. Not just as a best friend. She loved him the way a woman loves a man she wants to share her life with.

Why had it taken her so long to admit that? Why had she been fighting so hard against it?

Emma raised her eyes. "Oh, Mrs. C. I think I know where I belong. But I'm afraid it may be too late."

Mrs. C. squeezed her hand. "You'll never know if you don't try. Maybe he's still staying with his friend." She reached into her apron pocket. "I happen to have the address, if you're interested."

Emma took the paper and rose, laughing through her tears. "Thank you, Mrs. C. You're an angel. Do me a favor? Say a prayer for me."

"Already taken care of."

⁓ ⚬⚬ ⁓

In a rather shabby hallway, Emma peered at the wrinkled piece of paper Mrs. C. had given her to ensure she had the right apartment, then knocked loudly on the door. Her heart beat an unnaturally fast rhythm in her chest, while her lungs seemed unable to take in a full breath.

Please, Lord, let him be here. Please let him not have left for England yet.

A shuffling noise sounded from within. "Just a minute."

Emma's stomach swooped. Not Jonathan's voice, but he could still be inside.

The door opened. A groggy Reggie stood there, balancing on one crutch. "Emma." His sandy brows rose and he rubbed a hand over his short hair. "This is a surprise. Come in." He moved back and opened the door wider.

Emma entered a sparsely furnished living room. The dull beige walls were bare, except for a warped mirror by the entrance. A rather lumpy-looking sofa occupied the middle of the room, along with an armchair and a scarred table that had seen better days. It appeared Reggie hadn't lived here too long. Either that or he needed decorating help.

"Sorry. I just woke up from a nap. Please sit down," he said, gesturing to the sofa.

"Thank you, but I won't be staying long. I just . . ." She clasped her hands together, peering down the short hall. "Is Jonathan here by any chance?" Her lungs squeezed with expectancy. Would Jonathan hear her voice and come out to see her? What exactly was she going to say if he did?

"Hello. How have you been? I love you."

But Reggie's eyes filled with sympathy. "I'm so sorry, Emma. He left on a train to Halifax three days ago."

"Oh. I see." The strength seemed to leave her legs. She sank onto the sofa and stared at the worn rug beneath her feet, dimly aware of Reggie hobbling away.

Jonathan was gone. He'd left town before the rally and had no idea of the devastating revelations that had occurred or the way her life had fallen apart.

But it was all her fault. She'd waited too long, her realization coming too late. *Why, Lord? Why couldn't I have figured this out sooner?*

Because she'd been so obsessed with earning Randall's affection, she'd forfeited the one person who'd always been there for her—first as a friend, but then as so much more.

No wonder his leaving to join the war had hurt so much. She must have loved Jonathan even then, but hadn't let herself admit the truth, hiding instead behind her engagement to Danny. Danny had been the safe choice. She was fond of him, but not so consumed with love that the loss of him terrified her. That's why she'd been so devastated when Jonathan had enlisted. But she'd been too afraid to let him see her heart, too afraid to acknowledge the depth of her feelings for him.

Despite everything, he'd come with her all the way to Canada, and when he'd finally got up the courage to offer her his heart, she'd turned him down.

Her chest grew tighter. What was wrong with her?

"Here. Drink this." Reggie handed her a glass of water, then lowered himself somewhat awkwardly to the armchair beside her.

With trembling hands, she lifted the glass and drained its contents, then set it on the table in front of her. "I've been such a fool," she said softly. "And now he's gone."

Reggie let out a sigh. "I tried to get him to stay. Told him our university was just as good as Oxford, but he wouldn't have it." He scratched his head. "I think it was too painful for him here, to be so close to you and not be with you the way he wanted."

Emma closed her eyes until the wave of sorrow passed. She opened them and looked at Reggie, surprised to find no condemnation in his eyes, only compassion. "I was so busy chasing after my father that I didn't see what was right in front of me all along."

A dull silence filled the room. Emma knew she should go but couldn't quite make herself leave the one person who shared her connection to Jonathan. Who probably missed him as much as she did.

After several seconds, Reggie leaned forward, elbows on his thighs. "You know, when we were in the hospital in France, Jon told me all about you. How you were the one thing that had kept him going through all the torment he'd experienced. And he vowed that as soon as he got home, he was going to tell you how he felt."

She blinked. "He never said a word. Not until just recently."

311

"Apparently when he arrived home, you were involved with 'some rich bloke,' as he put it." Reggie smiled sadly. "Seems there was always something holding Jonathan back. Some reason to put your happiness ahead of his own."

"I've made such a muddle of everything," she whispered. "What am I going to do now?"

Reggie leaned back in his chair. "I guess you have a choice to make. You can stay here and keep hoping your father will change, or you can go after the man who truly loves you. Who would do anything for you." He paused to give her a pointed look. "Even let you go."

Emma sniffed, determination returning to her spirit. "You're right. It's time I put Jonathan's happiness first." She walked over and bent to kiss Reggie's cheek. "Thank you for being such a good friend to him."

"It wasn't hard, believe me." Reggie struggled to get to his feet. "Good luck, Emma. I hope it works out for you both."

She smiled. "Thank you, Reggie. And if it does, I'll send you an invitation to the wedding."

CHAPTER 33

Jonathan shifted his bag from one shoulder to the other as he made his way down the street toward home. He shrugged deeper into his jacket, trying to ignore the steady stream of rain that dripped off the brim of his hat. Having gotten used to the mostly sunny days in Toronto, he'd forgotten how much rain his homeland experienced.

But it was the differences in the street around him that really caught his attention. How could so much have changed in the two months he'd been gone?

His gut clenched. All traces of Felix Bartlett's store had vanished, and in its place a sign reading *Peter's Apothecary* was proudly displayed. The front window, which had once contained Felix's prized clocks, now contained an antique mortar and pestle surrounded by an array of colored bottles.

Did Emma know this was what the new owner had intended to do with the property? Not that Jonathan had anything against apothecaries. The shop would at least attract customers who might wander next door to order a new dress.

Jonathan pulled his collar closer to his hat, yet the moisture still seeped down his neck. With a last look at the shop, he resolutely put Emma out of his mind. He hadn't come back here to dwell on the past. He needed to see his aunt, and then tomorrow he'd go and register at Oxford.

Focus on his future.

Jonathan moved on to his aunt's store, where an even more disturbing sight met his eyes. A red *For Sale* sign hung in her front window.

Heat filled Jonathan's chest and streaked up his neck. Why on earth would Aunt Trudy be selling her business? Hadn't he left enough money to cover her expenses? Or had something else come up that she hadn't told him about?

He charged inside, causing the bell on the front door to swing wildly. The shop was empty and the shelves were almost bare, save for a few bolts of material. The mannequins still wore the same dresses he remembered from before he left.

"Aunt Trudy?" he called, shaking the raindrops from his hat and coat. Since when did she leave the counter unattended?

"Jonathan!" She came rushing out from the back room, clutching her shawl about her shoulders. "Is it really you?"

Relief filtered through his system. For a moment, he'd feared something terrible had happened to her.

"It's me. Home at last." Jonathan dropped his bag and swept her into a tight hug. He allowed himself a moment to experience the pure pleasure of being back with the woman who loved him more than anything. "I've missed you so much."

"Not nearly as much as I missed you." Her thin frame shook in his arms. She pulled back, swiping at the tears rolling down her face. "Let me look at you." She held him at arm's length, shaking her head. "You look tired. And thinner."

He shrugged. "Turns out I don't make a very good sailor. Although the trip over was much worse. At least this time I was only sick for the first two days."

She raised a hand to his cheek, her light blue eyes searching his. "You're not only physically sick, are you? You're heartsick." She let out a sigh. "So Emma really didn't come back with you?"

He sucked in a breath, her name like a punch to his gut. "She wanted to stay with her new family." He ducked down to retrieve his bag and hoisted it onto his shoulder, avoiding the eyes that already saw too much. "Let me go wash up, and then you can tell me why you're selling our home."

She covered her mouth, and tears welled up again. "I'm sorry, honey. I tried my best to keep everything running, but I'm afraid I've let you down."

"It's not your fault." He pulled her against him again and dropped a kiss to the top of her head. "Tonight I'll get a good night's sleep, and tomorrow we'll come up with a plan."

"There's nothing to be done, I'm afraid." Her gaze fell away. "I owe a lot of money that I can't repay."

"What happened at the bank? Did the manager call in the loan?"

She opened her mouth, then closed it and patted his arm. "We don't have to get into all the details your first few minutes home. Let's go upstairs, and I'll make you a nice cup of tea. I'm sure Canadian tea is nowhere near as good as ours." She headed toward the back room. "And I made an apple pie this morning."

Jonathan chuckled. He'd get to the bottom of everything soon enough. For now, he'd let his aunt enjoy their reunion.

The next day, Jonathan awoke before dawn, his system not sure what time zone he was in. He allowed himself a few moments to savor the comfort of his bed. Between the cot at Mrs. Chamberlain's, Reggie's lumpy sofa, and the cabin in the steerage section of the ship, he hadn't had such luxury in a long time.

He rose and dressed, thankful for the hot bath his aunt had prepared for him last night that had made him feel human again. Minutes later, he found Aunt Trudy in their small kitchen, frying eggs and bacon. The delicious aroma teased his senses, reminding him of Mrs. Teeter's kitchen, which of course led to thoughts of Emma. Resolutely, he pushed the sharp pang away.

His aunt turned and caught sight of him. "You're up early. I thought you might lie in a while today."

"You know me. Always up with the birds." He kissed her cheek and grabbed a chipped cup from the shelf. As usual, the large ceramic teapot was filled and hot. He poured himself a cup, then took his spot at the small table.

"What's on your schedule for your first day back?" She slid a plate of eggs in front of him.

"I think I'll get a haircut, then head over to the university." He bit into a piece of bacon.

Her spatula clattered to the floor, but Aunt Trudy hastily retrieved it. "The university? Isn't it a bit early for that?"

"Not really. I want to make sure everything is squared away for me to start classes." First, he'd check in at the admissions office to confirm that his tuition was up to date, then perhaps wander about the grounds to get a sense for the layout of the buildings. Maybe he'd even find the bookstore and buy his first textbook. That thought buoyed his spirits considerably. "Speaking of which, did any mail come for me while I was gone?"

"Yes. I put it all on the desk." Aunt Trudy turned off the stove and came to sit across from him, a worried expression wrinkling her brow. "Jonathan. There's something you need to know."

He swallowed a mouthful of eggs, unease rising in his chest. "What is it?"

She picked up a napkin and smoothed it on her lap. "I wasn't able to pay the next installment of your tuition."

Jonathan's lungs seized. What did she mean? He'd left the money in a marked envelope for her to deliver on the date it was due, knowing he likely wouldn't be back from Canada in time. She'd assured him it was no trouble to take it in for him, as she often went into the town of Oxford to shop.

"What happened? Did you forget?" If business had been chaotic in the store, it would have been easy enough to forget the date.

She shook her head, her gaze fused to the tablecloth. "I used the money to pay the interest on the bank loan," she said, her voice barely a whisper. "I thought I'd have enough time to earn it back before your tuition was due." She paused to release a shaky breath. "But then business went from bad to worse. Two of my best customers cancelled their orders. Two others deferred payment. This war has put everyone in a very cautious mood."

Jonathan inhaled slowly, attempting to ignore the clutch of panic. "How much of it did you use?"

Moisture brimmed in her eyes. "More than half."

Half. Jonathan mentally calculated how much money he had left after his trip and what he remembered he had in his bank account after he'd paid for his overseas passage.

"I'm so sorry, Jonathan." She gripped his hand. "But as soon as I sell the shop, I'll have more than enough to pay you back."

He zeroed in on her anxious face. "Don't tell me you're selling because of that."

"That's one of the reasons. I owe too much money to keep going. I can't even afford material anymore, and without fabric I can't fill any orders." She pushed up from her seat and moved to the sink. "I do have one person interested in buying the shop. He's supposed to get in touch with the bank by tomorrow."

For a second, Jonathan put his own troubles aside. "What are you going to do if it sells? Where will you live?" At least he would have lodging on campus, if they still let him attend. Hopefully, once he explained the reason for the mix-up, he and the administrators could figure out a solution.

"I've asked Rita if I can stay with her until I get my feet back under me." Trudy scraped the drippings from the frying pan into the dustbin.

"Rita?" Her distant cousin lived on the outskirts of London. "I thought you didn't get along."

Trudy shrugged. "Can't be picky under the circumstances. She has an extra room in her flat now that Gina's married. It'll do until I find a job."

This didn't make sense. How could business at the shop deteriorate so quickly?

Unless . . . it hadn't.

"You knew the situation was dire before I left, didn't you?"

She didn't answer, continuing to scour the frying pan.

"Why didn't you say anything?"

"I didn't want to hold you back. Then, after you told me Emma was staying in Canada, I thought you might end up staying with her. Even if you didn't, you'd be moving out to attend school. I figured I could ride out the problems until then." She brushed a lock of gray hair off her forehead. "If it hadn't been for that horrible Mr. Martin at the bank, I might have been able to keep the shop going. But he wouldn't extend my loan. Said money was tight all over the country and he couldn't afford to be sentimental."

Jonathan pushed his half-eaten meal aside. He hoped the people at Oxford didn't share that feeling or he could be in as much trouble as his aunt.

After gathering the tuition envelope with the meager amount of cash inside, Jonathan put on his best tweed suit and combed his hair, which would have to stay slightly shaggy for a while longer. He left his room, then on a sudden whim, went back inside and picked up the book on his nightstand. He took out the tattered Oxford acceptance letter and tucked it in his jacket pocket, the familiar feel reinforcing his confidence. Then he descended the back stairs to the alley below, where he pulled his bicycle out from behind the shed and brushed the cobwebs off the seat. Tugging his cap more firmly over his eyes, he began the forty-minute bike ride into Oxford.

Thankfully, the rain from the day before had stopped, though he still had to avoid several large puddles along the way. Despite the bad news of the morning, Jonathan managed to focus on the greenery of the countryside as he pedaled. He breathed in the fresh smell of the dew-filled grass, the passing scent of roses, and the slight murky smell of the nearby river.

It was wonderful to be home. Though Toronto was a beautiful city, nothing beat these familiar roads, these old stone walls, or the friendly greetings of neighbors as he passed by. Wheatley might not be everyone's ideal place to live, but to him it would always be home.

Once he got into Oxford proper, excitement mounted in his chest as he caught sight of the majestic university buildings. Soon, God willing, he'd be attending classes within these hallowed walls, living and breathing the same air as some of the greatest academic minds in the country. Smiling, he drove under the Bridge of Sighs, and when he reached the administrative offices, he parked his bicycle out front and made his way inside.

A woman looked up as he reached the counter. "May I help you?"

He put on his most charming smile. "I hope so. I'm here to pay a portion of my tuition."

The woman frowned. "Tuition was due several weeks ago."

"I realize that. However, I was overseas for two months and left the money with my aunt. Unfortunately, she fell on hard times while I was away and wasn't able to come here to pay it as she intended. I'm here now to settle the matter." He smiled again.

"What's your name?"

"Jonathan Rowe."

"Wait here while I check the files."

"Thank you, ma'am. I appreciate your help." Jonathan fought the urge to pace the room. *Lord, if you have a minute, please let these people understand my plight and find compassion for my situation. I can't have come so close to my dream to lose it now.*

Five minutes later, the woman returned with a beige folder in her hands. "Mr. Rowe, I see that you paid the first installment back in May. I spoke to my boss, and he said that he will extend you a period of grace if you pay the required amount in full today."

Jonathan's heart beat against his ribs. He removed the envelope from his pocket and handed it to the woman.

She counted it out, then peered over her spectacles. "This is not the full amount. It's not even half."

He wet his lips. "I promise I'll get the rest to you by the end of the week."

"I'm afraid that won't do. Unless you can pay the entire amount today, you will be removed from the student register." She placed the money back in the envelope and slid it toward him.

His stomach sank. Even if a bank manager agreed to see him today, he'd never be able to secure a loan that quickly. He blew out a breath. "Sadly, I don't think that will be possible."

"There's always next term." The woman gave him a sympathetic smile.

He reached for the envelope on the counter. "I suppose that's all I can hope for at this point."

"We'll hold on to your tuition deposit for now, which will keep your file open. If at some point you decide to withdraw your application altogether, we'll refund that sum, of course."

"Thank you. I sincerely hope that won't be necessary."

With feet as heavy as his heart, Jonathan made his way back to his bicycle. What a first-class chump he'd been. He'd failed to live up to his responsibilities here while he chased Emma halfway around the world. Now Aunt Trudy was in dire straits and his dream of Oxford in serious jeopardy. What if he wasn't able to come up with the required tuition money before the next term started?

The letter in his pocket rustled as he climbed onto the bike. Jonathan reached in and fingered the paper, recalling the moment he'd first opened the envelope. He'd cried tears of joy, wishing he could share the good news with his father and let him know that he'd finally fulfilled his dream. His dad had always told him, *"Education, son. It's the most important thing there is. Once you have your degree, no one can take it away from you."*

Jonathan lifted his chin. He wasn't ready to give up yet. This was a temporary setback. But right now, he had a more pressing problem. He had to figure out a way to earn some money fast, because if Aunt Trudy sold the shop and moved to London, he soon wouldn't even have a roof over his head.

CHAPTER 34

Emma approached Randall's front door, a mixture of emotions churning in her system. She couldn't help but remember the first time she'd come here, filled with such excitement to meet her father. Fueled by an unrealistic sense of optimism, she now realized.

Jonathan had been right to warn her, to try to make her understand that it might not turn out as she'd planned. Back then, she couldn't heed his words, couldn't allow herself to imagine a bad scenario. Yet here she was, facing the worst possible outcome: her dreams in tatters, conceding defeat.

Her cheeks heated every time she thought of her emotional display at the debate and the devastating revelations of that night. If she could, she'd have preferred never to face her father again, but that would mean leaving without saying good-bye to Marianne and Corinne, something she couldn't even consider, for they should not have to pay for Randall's shortcomings.

A tremble of nerves rolled in Emma's stomach. What would her sisters think of her after the scene she'd caused the other night? She prayed they wouldn't hold her outburst against her. Though she held little hope of Vera doing the same.

A somber-looking Mrs. Beck answered the bell and admitted Emma to the foyer.

Emma forced a bright smile. "Good morning. Are Corinne and Marianne at home?"

"I believe they're out on the back terrace, if you'd care to join them there." Though the woman didn't smile back, her eyes radiated sympathy.

"Thank you, Mrs. Beck. I know the way." Emma slipped down the hallway to the rear of the house, found the door, and exited onto the patio. She shielded her eyes from the sun and peered across the lawn.

Corinne was tossing a ball to Marianne in her chair, while a black-and-white puppy raced in circles around them.

Emma couldn't help but smile at the sight. Shoring her courage, she walked toward them and waved when Marianne spied her.

"Emma! Look! Papa bought us a puppy. Isn't he cute?" The sheer joy in Marianne's voice brought a lump to Emma's throat.

How she would miss her sisters, especially this brave girl. Emma rued the fact that she wouldn't be here to see Marianne take her first steps out of that wheelchair or watch her mature into the wonderful young woman she would certainly become.

"He's adorable. You're very lucky. I always wanted a puppy when I was young." The animal stopped to sniff Emma's shoes, and she bent to stroke his soft head. "What are you going to call him?" She looked up at Corinne in an attempt to gauge the older girl's mood.

"We're not sure yet," Corinne said with a light laugh. "It's between Sparky, Duke, or Grover." She tossed the ball, and the dog took off across the grass.

Emma laughed too, glad to avoid the topic that weighed on her. To pretend that nothing was amiss, for even a few minutes. "All very nice choices. Although he's acting a bit like the Mad Hatter right now."

"What's a mad hatter?" Marianne asked.

"Don't tell me you haven't read *Alice's Adventures in Wonderland*."

"Afraid not." Corinne came closer, twisting a curl around one finger in an almost unconscious manner.

"It's a marvelous story. You'll have to get a copy and read it together." *Once I'm gone.* Emma blinked against the sudden sting of tears that came at the thought that she would no longer get to share such moments with them.

"What's the matter, Emma?" Marianne wheeled closer. "Are you still mad at Papa?"

Emma swallowed hard and pasted on a smile. "No, I'm not. And I've come to apologize to you both for my bad behavior. There's really no excuse for it."

"I think there is." Corinne gave her a solemn look. "Papa hasn't treated you very well since you came here. Neither has Mama, or me either for that matter."

The puppy ran up with a ball in its mouth and dropped it at their feet.

"It's not your fault." Emma sighed. "I did rather force myself on everyone. I should have handled the whole affair differently from the beginning. But the one thing I'll never regret is getting to know my sisters." She forced a trembling smile to her lips.

Frowning, Corinne crossed her arms. "Why does that sound like you're saying good-bye?"

Emma swallowed. "Because I am. I'm going back to England." She scooped up the little dog to avoid the looks on her sisters' faces. The tiny creature squirmed and licked her cheek.

"Why are you leaving?" Marianne asked, her brow puckering. "Papa said you were staying in Canada."

"I intended to, but . . . I've changed my mind." Emma couldn't stand the sadness on Marianne's face, the tears welling in her eyes.

"It's because of him, isn't it?" Corinne said quietly. She'd matured so much over the summer that Emma almost didn't recognize her as the same hostile girl she'd first met.

Emma met her grave stare and nodded. "It's my own fault though. My expectations were too high when I came here. Life isn't a fairy tale. You can't make people feel how you'd like them to." She kissed the puppy's head and deposited him on Marianne's lap.

Silent tears rolled down the girl's cheek. "Who's going to help me with my exercises now?"

A stab of guilt sliced through Emma. Was she wrong to have started something she couldn't finish? To give her sister false hope? "I'm sure Corinne will be happy to take over. She knows what to do." It took all Emma's strength to keep her emotions contained. She had to be strong for all of them.

"But it won't be the same without you. I don't want you to go."

Emma's heart cracked open at the sorrow on the girl's face. She bent to gather her sister in a fierce hug. Marianne's slim frame shook with the force of her sobs, and she sniffed into Emma's shoulder.

There was no holding back the tears now. They dripped off Emma's chin and onto Marianne's fair head. "I'll be back one day," Emma promised, her voice scraping her throat. "In the meantime, we can write to each other. I've always wanted a pen pal." She rose and wiped the tears from Marianne's face, holding on to her composure by a thread. Then she turned and held a hand out to Corinne. "That goes for you too, if you'd like."

Slowly Corinne put her hand in Emma's and nodded. "I'd like that very much."

Emma pulled Corinne into an embrace. If only they'd had more time together. Now that she'd gotten past Corinne's hostility, they'd come to understand each other. "You'll have to tell me what happens between you and a certain young man," she whispered as she released her. "With any luck, he'll come to his senses soon."

Corinne flushed and blinked back actual tears. "Actually, we've decided to put our relationship on hold for a while. I want to go to school and become a teacher. Will has been very supportive."

"That's wonderful." Emma squeezed her hand. "I have no doubt you'll make an excellent teacher."

"I have you to thank for it." Corinne's eyes, though teary, were solemn. "If I hadn't started helping Marianne, I would never have volunteered to tutor Will's sister. Working with her made me realize how satisfying it is to help others."

"I'm very happy for you, Corinne." Emma's heart swelled with joy, yet it was bittersweet, since she wouldn't be here to witness her sister grow into her full potential. "If Will cares about you as much as I think he does, he'll be waiting for you when you graduate."

"Thank you. I hope he will be."

Emma straightened her spine. "Well, I'd best go say good-bye to your parents. Be good, the both of you. And if you ever want to visit England, you'll always be welcome." She leaned over to kiss Marianne one more time, clinging to the girl for just a bit longer than necessary, before she gave them a watery smile and set off across the lawn.

When she reached the patio, the French doors opened, and her father stepped out. "Hello, Emmaline."

She came to an abrupt halt, causing her skirt to swish about her legs. Instant tension seized her muscles. "Randall. I was just coming to find you." She lifted her chin, dragging a breath into her lungs. No matter how many times she'd rehearsed this moment, she still wasn't prepared. "I've come to say good-bye."

"You're leaving?" For an instant, he looked stricken, as though her departure might actually mean something to him.

"Yes. I'm going back to England."

"I see." Brackets formed beside his mouth.

She waited for the usual stoic expression to return, but he just stared at her.

Her stomach churned with a confused mixture of emotions. Regret, sorrow, and beneath it all, an underlying anger that had not fully dissipated. She'd have to spend a lot more time in prayer to fully forgive Randall for everything he'd put her through.

She squared her shoulders, realizing that this could be the last time they saw each other. She met his eyes. "Despite everything," she said, "I do wish you the best. I hope you achieve your goal of becoming the next mayor." She paused. What did she do now? A hug didn't feel right. Did she offer to shake hands?

"Before you go, there's something you should know." He moved forward to grip the back of one of the chairs. "First, I found out that Wainwright was being paid by Mayor Church's campaign manager to dig into my past and find some way to discredit me. I confronted the mayor about it, and he seemed genuinely shocked. I believed him when he said he had no knowledge of their collusion, and, in fact, he fired his manager on the spot."

Emma nodded. "I'm glad the mayor wasn't involved, although if that had come to light, it might have guaranteed you the election."

Randall cleared his throat. "That's a moot point now after everything that's happened. For many reasons, I've decided to pull out of the mayoral race." A soft breeze stirred the hair on his forehead as he looked at her. "Even if my reputation hadn't been sullied, you've made me realize I've placed far too much emphasis on my career and not enough on my family."

"I think that's a wise decision," she said quietly. "I know two young ladies who will be very happy to have more of your attention."

"Only two?"

She met his eyes, for once without expectation. "I'm afraid it's a little late for that." And because she no longer held any illusions where her father was concerned, she could speak the truth. "I don't regret coming here, and even though it didn't turn out as I'd hoped, I'm glad I met you. Mostly I'm grateful for getting to know my sisters." She smiled sadly. "Our failed relationship is as much my fault as yours. I had no right to demand more of you than you were capable of giving."

His features crumpled, and he took a step toward her. "Emma, won't you stay and give us another chance?"

Fresh sorrow clawed inside her. What she wouldn't have given for him to utter those words weeks ago. But too much had happened for them to make a difference now. "Perhaps I'll come back someday for a visit, but I need to go home. I have to try and make amends to the one person who has always had my best interest at heart. If I'm lucky, maybe he'll be able to forgive me."

"Jonathan."

She nodded.

"He left because of me, you know." A muscle worked in Randall's jaw. "He told me he never wanted to make you choose between us. He left so you wouldn't have to."

Emma swallowed. "I made a terrible mistake. But I intend to make it up to him somehow. If he'll let me."

A small smile played across Randall's lips. "With your tenacity, I have no doubt you'll win him over in the end." He came closer, regret shadowing his features. "Can I give you a hug before you go?"

She bit her lip and nodded, steeling herself for the one embrace she'd longed for her entire life.

Tentatively, he put his arms around her. "I do love you," he whispered into her hair. "I'm sorry I wasn't a better man. Sorry I wasn't able to be the father you deserved."

An unexpected sob caught in her throat. Tears she thought

she'd finished with flooded her eyes and spilled down her cheeks. She pressed her face into the wool of his jacket and clung to him, memorizing his scent for the years to come. Then she sniffed and pulled back. "I love you too." Despite everything, she did.

As Reverend Burke told her, love was a gift meant to be freely given, whether it was deserved or not, and without expectation of anything in return.

Movement behind them caught Emma's eye. Vera stood watching her with a hostile expression. "So, you've done your damage and now you're leaving?"

Emma winced as the accusatory tone hit its mark. Perhaps she hadn't handled everything in the best way, but she wasn't the only one to blame for the events that had transpired. She looked Vera in the eye. "It was never my intention to cause problems. But I'm not the only one responsible for what happened. If I'd known the truth from the beginning, things could have been a lot different."

The woman's stare didn't soften. Emma wished she could rewind to the days before the fundraiser, when everything had been going so well. But that was impossible. The best she could hope for was that, in time, the wounds left behind would heal.

"You have a wonderful family, Vera. I hope you appreciate them and realize how lucky you are." Emma turned her gaze to Randall. "And I hope one day your dream of becoming mayor comes true. Perhaps a dream deferred will be all the sweeter when you finally achieve it."

"Thank you, Emma." He swallowed hard. "I wish the same for you."

Emma forced another smile. Then, with one final glance at her sisters on the lawn with their puppy, Emma turned and left.

CHAPTER 35

Jonathan got off the train at Piccadilly Circus and stood still among the rush of the people surrounding him. A temporary job had brought him to London—too close to his childhood home not to go back and visit his old neighborhood. He scanned the street, attempting to find a familiar landmark among the throngs of people and vehicles. Something that would remind him how to find the bookstore his father had owned and the flat above it where they'd lived for the first ten years of his life.

Until that fateful night that had destroyed everything.

After several blocks, the buildings began to look vaguely familiar. Jonathan stopped in front of Hatchard's Bookshop, his father's biggest rival. If memory served, his former home was a few blocks east.

The likelihood was high that someone would have rebuilt the store by now, since it was situated in one of the prime retail areas of London. His steps slowed as he neared the spot where he believed Rowe's Books had once stood. When his gaze fell on the tobacco shop to the left, a long-forgotten memory of his father buying pipe supplies swam to the surface.

His heart began to beat faster. This had to be the right place, though nothing remained of the bookstore. The sign above the door now read *Fine's Haberdashery*, and the window sported an impressive array of women's and men's hats. Jonathan smiled to himself. With Emma's penchant for outlandish headwear, she would have loved this place. He rubbed a spot on his chest where a perpetual ache resided, reserved solely for her.

The door to the tobacco shop opened, and a white-haired gentleman emerged. From the full-length apron the man wore, Jonathan surmised he worked there. "If you're considering a new cap, son, I can recommend Mr. Fine's wares. Best quality I've seen."

"Thank you, but I don't need a hat."

The man walked closer and took a pipe out of his pocket. "Then may I ask why you've been standing there staring at the building for so long?"

Jonathan swallowed and turned to look at him. "I thought this used to be a bookstore."

"It was. Burned down about ten or twelve years ago. Terrible tragedy." A shadow of grief passed over his ruddy features.

"Fifteen."

"What's that?"

"It burned down fifteen years ago."

The man squinted at him. "You seem quite certain."

"I am." He looked back at the building, his muscles tensing as memories of that horrific night intruded into his thoughts. Flames everywhere. Smoke and heat. His father carrying him out, depositing him on the sidewalk, telling him to stay there. Jonathan clinging to his father's arm, begging him not to go back inside.

"You wouldn't be the young Rowe lad, would you?"

Jonathan's manners kicked in. He extended his hand. "Yes, sir. Jonathan Rowe."

"Ronald Barber." He pumped Jonathan's hand. "It's good to see you again, son. Always wondered how you made out after that terrible night."

So, this man had likely been there. How many others had witnessed the spectacle? Jonathan wished he could remember more, but only trauma stood out in his mind.

"My aunt took me in," he said. "She owns a dress shop over in Wheatley."

"Ah. I'm glad you didn't end up in a workhouse." He peered at Jonathan. "What brings you by now after all this time?"

"Attempting to make peace with the past." Jonathan stuffed his hands in his pockets. Why had he expected that some remnant of his home might still be here? Something that would bring him the closure he craved?

"I'll never forget that night." Mr. Barber ran a hand over his jaw. "I had to hold you back to keep you from following your father inside."

Jonathan frowned, struggling to recall that particular detail. He vaguely remembered someone grabbing him from behind as he screamed for his dad, but he'd had no idea who it was.

"Felt so bad for your father. He had an impossible decision to make: stay out here and keep his son safe, or go back into the inferno for his wife. I'll never forget the tortured look he gave me before he went in." Mr. Barber shook his head. "In the end, neither choice would have ended well."

The lump in Jonathan's throat swelled. "At least we would have had each other. I wouldn't have been alone."

Mr. Barber took a thoughtful puff on his pipe and blew out the smoke. "Lord knows I love my children, but if it had been my Effie inside, I'd have moved heaven and earth to get to her." He glanced at Jonathan. "Could you hang back and let your wife burn to death without doing everything in your power to save her?"

Jonathan pressed his lips into a hard line, his fists clenched at his side. What would he do if Emma were ever trapped in a burning building? Play it safe and wait for the fire brigade, or rush into the flames to get to her? The air seeped from his lungs as the hard truth dawned. Even with his fear of fire, if it were Emma, he knew he could never sit back and do nothing. He would risk everything, face any demon to save her. Just as his father had.

For the first time, Jonathan was able to view his father's actions through the eyes of an adult and not an orphaned boy.

He dashed the back of his hand across his eyes. "You're right, Mr. Barber. If the woman I loved was in jeopardy, I'd have done the same thing."

Mr. Barber squeezed Jonathan's shoulder. "Doesn't mean it didn't rip your father's heart out to leave you."

"I know." And for the first time, Jonathan really did. Perhaps he could finally make peace with the fact that he'd been left an orphan. Finally forgive his father for leaving him.

"Care to come inside for a few minutes?" The man's kindly eyes studied him. "I'd love to share some stories with you about your father and how he got his business off the ground."

Jonathan looked at his pocket watch. He had time to spare before he needed to go.

His chest expanded with a pull of fresh air. "Thank you, Mr. Barber. I'd like that very much."

Randall leaned on the wall of the back patio, watching the sky change from gold to pink, the setting sun casting fanciful shadows over the lawn. Even the beauty of a summer sunset couldn't lift his mood tonight.

After twenty-two years, his worst fears had come true. His sordid past had returned to haunt him, effectively ruining his future in politics. All because the child he'd forsaken years ago had wanted to find him.

It would be easy to place all the blame on Emmaline for

the downfall of his career, but to be fair, she'd come here in good faith to forge a relationship with him. How was she to know the secrets he'd kept hidden all these years? He'd been a fool to think they'd never be discovered. If he'd been less of a coward, he would have told her—and his family—the truth from the very beginning. Maybe then he could have avoided the ensuing disaster.

He drew in another lungful of smoke from his cigar, let it linger for a second, then expelled an opaque cloud that hung in the air before dissipating. Even this activity brought him no pleasure tonight, no easing of his tension. The fact that Harcourt had declined to join him for their usual after-dinner ritual spoke volumes about the man's disappointment with him. No one had wanted Randall to succeed in politics more than his father-in-law, likely because Harcourt's own political aspirations had never come to fruition.

The back door opened and familiar footsteps crossed the patio.

Vera came up beside him and laid a hand on his sleeve. "You're very pensive this evening, darling. Is everything all right?"

He turned to look at his wife. "What do you think? I'm the subject of the city's latest gossip mills. I've disappointed everyone I know, including you."

She sighed. "I'll admit I was angry when this all blew up at the rally. But I understand why you would keep such a secret. It's a scandal today. I can only imagine how much worse it would have been twenty years ago."

Bitterness coated his tongue. "Enough to make my own mother disown me."

"I'm so sorry, Randall." She squeezed his arm. "But this will die down. Another year from now it will be old news, and if conditions appear favorable then, you could try your bid for mayor again."

His lips twitched. "Thank you for your support, as always, my dear."

She laid her head against his shoulder. "For the record, I'm also sorry about Emmaline. Although I can't say I'm sorry she's gone. She created nothing but chaos."

The tip of his cigar glowed red in the waning daylight. He tossed it down on the patio stones and crushed it underfoot. "Again, it was my fault. I held back from truly embracing her, from allowing her to get too close, because I knew the secret would come out eventually." He sighed. "I should have been upfront with her right from the beginning—and with you. Perhaps then we could have avoided this whole mess."

"No use dwelling on what might have been. We must focus on going forward now."

A slight cough sounded from behind them. Randall turned to see Corinne approaching with a hesitant smile. At least this daughter didn't seem to hate him.

"Papa. Mama. Could I speak to you both for a minute?"

"Certainly, darling." Vera motioned for her to join them.

Corinne came up beside them at the stone wall. "I have something I'd like to tell you."

For a moment, a jolt of panic hit Randall's midsection. He prayed his daughter hadn't done something foolish, like gotten herself pregnant. If so, he might have to murder Will Munroe. He would not allow history to repeat itself.

"What is it?" Vera asked. "You sound serious."

"I've made a decision that I hope you'll be pleased about." She looked directly at Randall. "You in particular, Papa."

"Go on."

She clasped her hands together as though nervous. "I'd like to go to college after all." She hesitated. "I want to become a teacher."

Randall drew in a breath. Finally, a bit of good news.

"A teacher?" Vera asked, her voice thin. "What made you suddenly decide this?"

"Emma was the one who first suggested it. When I was helping her with Marianne's therapy, she remarked how good I was with her, how patient, and that I might make a good teacher. It was just a passing comment, but it got me thinking. Then I started tutoring Will's younger sister."

"When did this happen?" Randall frowned. How had he missed so much that was going on with his family?

"A few weeks ago. The point is that I really enjoyed helping someone learn. And Will seemed to think I had a knack for it too." She gave a tremulous smile. "So I'd like to look into courses at the university, if that's all right with you both."

Vera remained unusually silent, which likely meant she wasn't thrilled about Corinne's choice to pursue a career instead of look for an eligible husband. It was another issue she and Randall had disagreed upon regarding their children.

Randall dropped a kiss on the top of his daughter's head. "You know that I want you to further your education, so I'm thrilled about this. I'd be happy to take you to register."

"Thank you, Papa." She beamed up at him.

"But don't you want to get married, Corinne?" Vera said at last.

"Of course I do, Mama. That leads me to my next topic." A slight gust of wind came up, and Corinne rubbed her arms. Then she straightened to her full height. "I intend to marry Will Munroe once we've both finished our schooling."

"Will? But he's not—" Vera clamped her mouth shut.

Randall knew exactly what his wife had been about to say—that Will wasn't of the right social standing. That he was only taking courses as he could afford them, and thus it would take a long time to complete his degree. That Corinne would be an old maid by then.

Randall laid a hand on his wife's shoulder. "No need to panic, Vera." He turned his focus to Corinne. "As you know, I think the world of Will," he began. "And I told him when he came to see me that once he's finished his degree and gets a better position, we will revisit his . . . suitability at that time."

Vera's shoulders relaxed under his fingers.

However, Corinne's chin jutted out in a way that they both knew too well. "I didn't ask for permission, Papa," she said. "I *will* marry Will one day, as long as he still wants me. In the meantime, we will be courting—unofficially." She looked from him to her mother. "I love him, Mama. And he loves me. Maybe that will change over the next few years, I don't know. But we intend to see where it takes us."

Vera moved to sit on one of the patio chairs, running her pearls through her fingers as she did when agitated.

"Is Will in support of your intended career?" Randall asked carefully. He'd already alienated one daughter. He didn't want to risk losing another.

"He is."

"I see." Randall scratched his chin. "In that case, as long as you are always well chaperoned or see each other in public places, I will accept your decision."

A tentative smile bloomed. "Really, Papa?"

He nodded. "I've noticed a new maturity about you lately. It's time I trust you to make some decisions for yourself."

She leaned in to hug him. "That means a lot, Papa. Thank you." She drew back. "There's one more thing."

Vera threw up her hands. "What now?"

"It's about Marianne."

His wife stiffened as though preparing for a blow.

"I intend to keep helping her with her therapy, as Emma did." Corinne went to lay a hand on her mother's arm. "I think we owe it to Marianne to help her get out of that chair one day."

Vera bit her lip.

"It's time, Mama. Time to let go of your fear. Marianne is strong. She can do this. And we have to support her. Emma showed me that."

Vera reached out for Corinne's hand and, without a word, nodded.

Randall cleared his throat. "You're right again, Corinne. I've let fear control too many aspects of my life. It's time to change that."

His wife and daughter looked up at him with such trust and admiration that his chest swelled.

Despite the turmoil Emmaline's arrival had caused, it seemed he and his family had much to thank her for as well. In the short time she'd been with them, she'd forced them to take a hard look at their lives and brought about some needed trans-formations. Because of her, Randall's career may have suffered a setback, but his family would reap the benefit of his renewed commitment to them and to their future.

He prayed Emma would find happiness back in England, and that one day, God willing, their paths would cross again.

Maybe then he could make up for all his mistakes.

CHAPTER 36

Emma entered the front door of Peter's Apothecary, her grandad's old shop, and stopped short, letting the door bang shut behind her. Despite her eagerness to find Jonathan, to beg his forgiveness and hopefully start to heal the wounds she'd inflicted, she couldn't pass her childhood home without going inside.

The very doorway beckoned her to enter. To remember. To grieve her loss anew.

But instead of anything remotely familiar, a multitude of foreign sights and smells assaulted her, overwhelming her with the harsh reality that Grandad was truly gone. Not only him, but every shred of evidence that he'd ever run a watch repair shop here.

Tears burned at the back of her eyes. Slowly, she edged farther into the store, trying to picture how it used to look. Now, with its counters filled with jars and ointments, she could almost believe she was in the wrong place. Only Grandad's old wall sconces and the same creaky floorboards told her she wasn't mistaken.

Fighting a lump in her throat, she walked past a man examining an item under a glass magnifier and headed directly to the back room. Maybe there she would find some trace of her grandfather, even if only the lingering smell of his favorite pipe tobacco. The room, however, was filled with jars of herbs and liniments that lined a long table against one wall. She scanned the space until she spied a familiar item in the corner. Her chest tightened. Grandad's old desk still sat in the same spot. In an almost numb state, she crossed the space and ran her fingers over the scarred surface, a thousand memories hurtling back. She and Grandad working together, him fixing clock springs, her filling out the ledger, the two of them trading stories of their day.

"Hey, what are you doing back here? This area's off limits."

Emma whirled around to see a man in a white coat charging toward her. "I'm sorry, I—" She swallowed, unable to continue. "Excuse me." Ducking her head, she scurried by him, through the main shop, and out the front door. She leaned against the stone wall and attempted to regulate her breathing against the wave of grief that swamped her.

Had she made a terrible mistake coming back here? To a place where she no longer belonged? A place so foreign she could barely reconcile herself to its former appearance?

She took several deep breaths and moved away from the stones. Resolutely, she forced herself to think about Jonathan, the true reason she'd returned. She needed to find him and make amends. Figure out where they would go from here.

On shaking legs, she proceeded next door to the dress shop. Once again, she paused at the door, her heart pulsing in her throat for a different reason this time. Would Jonathan be inside, or had he moved to Oxford already? Her stomach churned more now than during the sea voyage home. As Emma reached for the door, she froze, her gaze falling on a sign in the corner of the window.

For Sale? There had to be some sort of mistake. This dress shop was Trudy's life. She would never sell it.

Emma twisted the door handle and pushed inside, all thoughts of Jonathan banished for the moment. As she had in the apothecary shop, she stood and gaped at the difference in the space. Several bare mannequins lined one wall where there had normally been shelves of material. The bins of thread, ribbons, and buttons were empty, save for a smattering of items. A heavy velvet cloth covered the ornate cheval mirror that graced the left side of the store.

From the back, the sound of soft weeping could be heard. Emma followed the sound to the room where Trudy usually spent most of the day creating her fabulous dresses. Emma pushed the curtain aside and stepped into the room.

Trudy sat at her sewing table, her head in her hands.

Emma moved closer, alarm rising in her. "Aunt Trudy, what's wrong?"

The woman's head snapped up. "Emma? Is that you?"

She forced a smile. "Yes, I've come back." Back to a universe where everything was different.

Trudy rose and rushed to gather Emma in a warm hug. "I'm so happy to see you. I thought you were staying in Canada."

"I changed my mind." She took the older woman's hands. "Why are you crying? Is everything all right?" She couldn't form the words to ask if something had happened to Jonathan.

Trudy returned to her seat and took out a handkerchief to blow her nose. "I had some upsetting news earlier. A prospective buyer for the store changed his mind and rescinded his offer."

Emma frowned. "But I don't understand. Why are you selling your store?"

A loud sigh escaped as Trudy fingered the fabric she was sewing. "I've made a terrible muddle of the finances." She shook her head. "It was bad before you left, and I knew Jonathan would feel obliged to stay and help me, so I made sure he didn't realize how much money I owed." She folded the material and set it on the table. "I've made my peace with losing the shop. But what I can't live with is knowing I cost Jonathan *his* dream."

Emma went still. "What do you mean?" She held her breath, not entirely sure she wanted to hear the rest.

"I used Jonathan's tuition money to make a loan payment. I reasoned that I could earn the amount back before the tuition was due. But instead I ended up robbing Peter to pay Paul."

Emma's blood seemed to slow in her veins. "Are you saying that Jonathan isn't going to Oxford?"

Trudy raised the handkerchief to her nose. "No. At least not right now."

"Oh no." Emma clutched the back of a wooden chair to steady herself. Whenever her guilt had risen to shame her over the way she'd treated Jonathan, she'd comforted herself with the fact that she hadn't ruined his life, that he was living his dream at Oxford, probably not really missing her much at all.

"What is he going to do now?" Emma whispered.

Trudy plucked several spools of ribbon from the messy array of shelves behind her. "He's looking for full-time work so he can save money and maybe reapply next term. In the meantime, he's been doing odd jobs for people—handyman repairs, deliveries, gardening."

Gardening. Emma's heart cinched at the memory of him happily tending Mrs. Teeter's vegetables. The sunshine glinting off his dark hair, the streaks of dirt on his cheek.

"That's the main reason I wanted the shop to sell quickly. I thought if I could repay his tuition money, the university might be willing to make an exception and grant him late acceptance." She moved to a long table and began to unfold a bolt of fabric. "None of that matters now since the one person interested has backed off."

"If you sell the shop, where will you go?" Emma glanced toward the rear staircase that led to the living quarters upstairs. Trudy had done such a good job of creating a cozy home for Jonathan and herself.

"I'm not sure. I'll stay with my cousin in London until I figure that out."

"London? But you hate the city."

She shrugged. "There's a better chance to find work in the dress shops there."

Emma put an arm around the woman, who seemed much frailer than she remembered. "I'm sure God has a plan in mind. We just have to hold on to our faith."

"I'm trying, dear. I really am." She straightened her spine. "But enough about my problems. What about you? Why aren't you in Canada?"

Heat bloomed in Emma's cheeks. Perhaps it was a little too early to tell Trudy about her hopes concerning Jonathan. "My relationship with my father got rather unpleasant after Jonathan left. It made me realize that I had pinned all my hopes for the future on a man who doesn't really want me in his life."

"Oh, honey. I'm so sorry." She gave Emma a quick hug. "The man doesn't deserve a daughter as wonderful as you."

"Maybe not." Emma smiled, amazed that the sting of rejection had lessened now that there was an ocean between them.

"Let's go upstairs, and I'll make you a nice pot of tea." Trudy headed toward the back stairs.

Emma glanced at the clock on the wall, one her grandad had given Trudy as a gift. "Can we delay that for a bit? I have an errand I need to run before the shops close for the day."

An idea that had started to gnaw at her now pressed against her temples with an urgency that defied logic. She dropped a kiss on the woman's cheek. "I'll be back soon." She paused, her hand fluttering to her throat. "Is Jonathan going to be here later?"

"I don't think so. He's gone into the city for a few days on a job."

Emma pushed away a twinge of disappointment. But that

might be better after all. She'd have time to see if her plan might work.

"Guess it will just be us girls for dinner," Trudy said with a smile. "We'll make it a proper welcome home party."

Two hours later, Emma walked back through the streets of Wheatley, buoyed by how easily her idea had come to fruition. It had to have been divinely inspired for that to happen.

Now if only she could convince everyone else of her plan's merit.

This time, when Emma entered the dress shop, a very different Trudy met her. Her eyes shone with excitement. "Emma, dear. You'll never believe this. The bank manager just called to tell me that someone has made an offer on the shop. I have a buyer after all."

"That's wonderful news."

"And the best part is the new owner wants to take over right away. If we can get all the paperwork done, I might even have my money by tomorrow." She clasped her hands together like a happy child. Then a sudden cloud came over her features. "In all the excitement, I forgot to ask how much time I'd have to vacate the place. It will take me a few days to pack everything. I suppose I'll have to ship the furniture. . . ." She paused, staring around the room as though doing a mental inventory.

"I don't think the new owner will be too worried about that. In fact, I suspect you may not have to go anywhere."

"Well, of course I will. Even if he was willing to rent me the upstairs rooms, I would still have to find a job to support myself."

"What if the new owner wanted to hire you as the head seamstress of the dress shop?" Emma tilted her head, biting her lip to contain a smile.

Aunt Trudy's eyes widened, then quickly narrowed. "What do you know about this, young lady?"

Emma laughed out loud with pure glee. "You're looking at the new owner of Trudy's Dress Designs."

Instead of the delighted response Emma had anticipated, Trudy's eyes filled with tears. "You bought my store?"

"I did. Isn't that wonderful?" Emma twirled around in the middle of the floor. "Now you can stay here and keep making your beautiful creations."

"But it won't be mine anymore." She slumped onto a stool behind the counter. "I don't think I can stay on as an employee."

Emma's heart sank to the toes of her shoes. She'd expected some resistance from Jonathan once he learned, but she'd never anticipated a negative reaction from Trudy. She approached the counter, ready to use all the arguments she'd given the bank manager. "We can make this work, Trudy. You're not good with figures, but I am. I handled the books for Grandad and made sure he was never in the red. I'm good at following up with customers and collecting the money they owe. And I've got lots of ideas how we can improve the shop and bring in more business. All you'd have to worry about is the sewing. Together, we could form a partnership and turn this store into the success it was meant to be."

Trudy shook her head. "I don't have the capital to become your partner."

Emma reached over the counter and took Trudy's hands in hers. "But you will. As of tomorrow, you'll have all the capital you need. You'll be able to pay off your debts, with hopefully a fair bit to spare. If you want to use some of that money to invest as my partner, we can discuss that option. Or we can draw up an agreement that at any time you wish to buy me out, I will sell the shop back to you. For the same amount that I paid."

Trudy covered her mouth. "That sounds very reasonable," she whispered. Hope brimmed in her pale eyes.

"There's one aspect you may not agree with." Emma hesitated, then plunged on. "I want to renovate the back rooms to include a living space for me."

Trudy just blinked.

"I've taken out a small loan to do that and to update the interior as well. Make a true fresh start. What do you say, Trudy? Are you in this with me?"

Trudy rose, a smile flickering over her face. "I'll be able to pay Jonathan back."

Emma grinned. "Exactly. Maybe we could discuss an idea I have about that over dinner?"

Trudy didn't answer but walked out into the middle of the shop and slowly looked around. She ran her fingers over the fabric of one of the last bolts of material with a sigh.

Emma's palms grew itchy. What if she had misjudged the woman's wishes? What if she simply wanted to leave it all behind? "You do still want to run the shop, don't you?"

Trudy turned around, tears glistening on her cheeks. "Oh, Emma. You've given me new hope for my old dreams. How can I ever thank you?" She moved in to clasp Emma in a tight embrace.

Emma squeezed her back, her own eyes watering. "Just seeing you so happy is thanks enough for me." She laughed out loud with sheer delight. "Although I do have one thing I could use your help with."

"You name it, dear. I think I could take on the whole world right now."

CHAPTER 37

Jonathan couldn't wait to have a hot bath. To soak his stiff muscles and rid himself of the city's soot. As he entered his aunt's shop through the rear door, though, the enticing aroma of fried meat, potatoes, and onions met his nose. His stomach grumbled, reminding him how many hours it had been since his last meal. Maybe a quick wash-up would do until he'd eaten. After almost a week in London, he looked forward to a good home-cooked dinner.

"I hope that's your shepherd's pie I smell," he called as he climbed the stairs to their flat. "I'm hungry enough to eat the whole pan myself." Grinning, he walked into the kitchen and came to an abrupt halt.

The kitchen table was draped in his aunt's best tablecloth, one usually reserved for Christmas and Easter, with two settings of her good china on top. A long taper candle glowed in the center beside a vase of wildflowers. He looked around the empty room. The kitchen was spotless, every dish washed, a covered pan sitting on the stovetop. In the adjoining living area, the furniture fairly gleamed, every blanket folded, every book in its place. His aunt must have been bit by the cleaning bug.

Or had Jonathan forgotten a special occasion? He wracked

his brain to think what it could be. His birthday wasn't until next month. Trudy's not until December.

He removed his cap and jacket and hung them on the peg on the wall.

"Aunt Trudy?" He crossed to the sink to wash his hands and face. "Why the good dishes? Are we celebrating something?"

A movement from the hall flickered at the edge of his vision. But when he turned to greet his aunt, he froze, the words dying in his throat.

"Hello, Jonathan. Welcome home."

Emma! His heart chugged to a painful halt in his chest. How could this be? Clearly, he must be hallucinating.

He blinked, staring in disbelief. But the image didn't change. She stood there in his kitchen, a vision in a silky blue dress, her hair piled on top of her head with a few long curls framing her face. For one ecstatic moment, a blast of pure joy soared through his system. His heart took off at a crazy speed, beating so fast he couldn't seem to catch his breath or feel his limbs.

Until reality came rushing in, dousing him with a delayed sense of self-preservation. This was the woman who had rejected him. Who'd chosen her father and a life in Canada over him. What made him think anything had changed?

He took a breath and forced the walls back up around his heart. "Emmaline," he said. "What are you doing here?"

"Your hands are dripping." She came forward to hand him a towel. "That's a rather long story. One I'll tell you while we eat." She flashed him a bright smile, yet he could tell she was nervous by the way she wouldn't quite meet his gaze.

"I hope you like the meal I made. Trudy gave me her recipe." She lifted the lid of the pan on the stove, then reached for a serving spoon. "Please, sit down. You must be tired after your trip."

He dried his hands and face, then took a seat, his mind still reeling over her presence here. "Where is Aunt Trudy?"

"She had a potluck at the church tonight." Emma ladled the food onto a plate and set it in front of him.

The familiar scent of her floral perfume wafted by him, taunting him.

Seconds later, she fixed her own plate and sat down across from him. The table was so small, their knees brushed.

The nerves in Jonathan's stomach jumped. He scraped his chair back to avoid contact with her.

Why was she here wearing fancy clothes and serving him food on good china? He couldn't eat one bite until he knew what was going on.

"What's that scowl for?" Emma laid a napkin on her lap.

"I want to know what you're doing here."

"Can't we just enjoy our meal first? I thought you were hungry."

"Not until I make sense of this. You said you were staying in Canada with your family. Now, three weeks later, here you are. What happened?"

The candlelight flickered over her delicate features, creating a glow in her eyes. No, he could not relax and pretend this was just an ordinary meal, not without an explanation first.

Her brows crashed together. "Fine, have it your way." She jutted out her chin. "It became apparent that it was never going to work out with my father. So I decided to come home."

He knew her well enough to recognize there was much more she wasn't saying. "What brought about this sudden realization?"

Her gaze slid to the table top. "Must we discuss all that unpleasantness now? After I spent hours cooking for you?"

"Emma." He pinned her with his fiercest stare.

She huffed out a sigh. "All right. I'll tell you the whole story. But first, why don't you open your mail?"

A diversionary tactic if ever he'd heard one. He glanced down at the envelope beside his fork and frowned at the sight of the Oxford emblem. "What is this?"

"Open it and see."

Alarm bells blasted in his head. Her smile was a bit too smug for his liking and every instinct shouted that he was not going to like this, whatever it was.

Reluctantly, he slit open the envelope and pulled out a sheet of stationery. He scanned the typed words, his frown becoming deeper by the moment. "This says that my tuition has been paid in full, and I'm to report for classes as soon as possible." He raised his head. "Is this your doing?"

"Indirectly." Her eyes danced. "Isn't it wonderful? Aunt Trudy sold her shop and was able to pay your tuition after all. She went down to the admissions office and apparently created quite a scene. Eventually, because she paid for the full year, they relented and allowed you back on the roster."

Suspicion buzzed through his brain. "A new buyer must have come up very suddenly. Before I left, negotiations for the sale weren't going well. I hope Aunt Trudy didn't lower the price too much." His mind whirled, trying to fit the pieces together. "But how are you involved?"

A grin spread over her face. "You're looking at the new owner."

"What?" He couldn't possibly have heard her correctly.

"I bought Trudy's shop."

He stared, his mouth falling open. Heat flooded his system, blasting up his neck. Then he shoved his chair back and surged to his feet. "Why on earth would you do such a thing? You no more want to sew dresses than I want to shovel manure."

Her smile faded, confusion clouding her features. "I thought it was a brilliant idea. A solution to everyone's problems."

Jonathan stalked over to the living room, raking a hand through his hair. Having Emma here, not only in Wheatley but in the very place he lived, was *not* a solution to his problem at all. In fact, it would be intolerable.

She came up behind him. "Why are you angry? I thought

350

you'd be thrilled to finally have your dreams come true." Hurt laced her words.

When he looked at her, her eyes shone with unshed tears.

Jonathan bit back a curse. Emma always had wonderful intentions, but she jumped into things without considering all the ramifications.

"Trudy gets to keep her store and her home," she said slowly. "You get Oxford, and I—"

"What, Emma? What do you get, other than an empty pocketbook?"

Emma recoiled. She'd never seen Jonathan so upset, never heard him speak so harshly. "I get my own business to run. I have lots of ideas how to increase sales by bringing in new designs and new customers. Plus, if you'd bothered to let me explain, I would have told you that Trudy can buy in as a partner if she wants. Or she can continue as the head seamstress and invest the rest of her money elsewhere. She'll have options now, rather than going to live with a cousin she doesn't get on with." She allowed herself to look at him fully. "I thought you'd be happy about that."

She'd thought he'd be happy to see her too, but she'd obviously been wrong. She should have remembered that surprising people rarely turned out well.

He shook his head. "I am glad that Aunt Trudy doesn't have to move, but—"

"But what?"

He threw out his hands, his eyes almost panicked. "Where are you going to live? I can't have you staying under my roof."

She crossed her arms and glared. "It's my roof now. Or it will be once the paperwork is filed. But don't worry, I'll only be in your space until I can build my own quarters at the back of the store."

His hands fisted at his side, and he uttered a coarse word. Could he really not stand the sight of her now?

"That's it, isn't it? You hate that I own your home." Or maybe he just hated her.

"It's more than that." He blew out a breath. "But it's my problem, not yours. As you pointed out, it's your roof now. I'll just have to learn to deal with the situation."

Emma held back any further attempts to convince him of her plan's merit. She'd shocked him by showing up out of the blue and then surprising him with her purchase of the shop. One thing Jonathan was not and that was spontaneous. He always mulled a scenario over six ways to Sunday before he made a decision. Once he'd had time to digest the new turn of events, Emma was sure he'd see the benefit. Maybe then she could tell him how she felt about him.

Tonight was obviously not the right time for that.

Jonathan paced the braided rug in front of the fireplace and seemed to struggle to regain control of his emotions. He finally stopped and turned his intense brown eyes on her. "What really happened in Toronto that made you decide to come home?"

She bit back a sigh. The last thing she wanted was to rehash that painful event. At least not yet. "Can we not save that conversation for another time?"

"No, Emma. Something must have happened with your father to make you leave. I want to know what."

She hesitated, but realized from the stubborn set of his jaw there was no point in putting off the inevitable. "Fine. If it's a confession you want, I'll tell you the ugly truth." She crossed the room to the window that looked over the street below and gathered her courage. She'd never really considered what Jonathan's reaction might be to learning the real story about her birth. Only one way to find out. "It all fell apart the night of the rally. Against everyone's wishes, I went to see my father debate the mayor. Wainwright showed up, and the night turned into a disaster."

"What did that lowlife do this time?"

"Actually, he did me a favor. He exposed my father for the coward he is." She gripped her shaking hands together and turned to face him, needing to see his reaction to what she was about to say. "Not only did Randall deny that I was his daughter, it turns out he'd been lying to me all along." She drew in a breath. "He never married my mother. That's why my grandparents let me believe he was dead. They didn't want me to know that . . . I was illegitimate. The product of a sinful union, not a romantic fairy tale after all." Fresh tears burned her eyes. How humiliating to admit that everything she'd believed about the man had been false.

For a moment, she thought Jonathan was going to take her in his arms. Tell her it didn't matter to him.

But instead he shoved his hands into his pockets. "I'm sorry, Em. You must have been terribly upset."

She nodded. "I finally realized I was wasting my time. My father was never going to love me the way I wanted, since I'm nothing but a reminder of his sordid past. His dirty little secret now exposed. That's when I decided to come home." She held her breath. Would Jonathan let his guard down at last? Tell her he was happy to have her back? That he'd missed her?

But his face went blank, the light of compassion fading from his eyes. He gave a laugh that sounded more like a sneer. "It all makes sense now. Your father let you down, shattered the last of your illusions, and you ran away."

The harshness of his tone twisted her heart like wet laundry through a wringer. Her lungs ached. Her throat burned. She took a jerky step back. "I didn't run away. I came back because I finally figured out where I belong."

He stared at her warily, like she was a stranger. When had she lost his trust?

"I came back," she said slowly, "because I'm in love with you. And I needed to tell you that."

She swallowed, her pulse beating wildly in her throat. This was not how she imagined revealing her feelings to him. It was supposed to be a happy moment over candlelight and shepherd's pie. She blinked away the moisture in her eyes, willing him to understand that she was telling the truth.

He closed his eyes, his face awash with pain. Tired lines formed around his mouth.

"Don't you see, Emma?" he said wearily. "I'm always your second choice. Your father broke your heart, and you beat a hasty retreat home to the next best thing. Good old Jonathan. Always there when you need him." His jaw tightened. "Sorry, but I'm not willing to settle for second best anymore."

She inhaled sharply, her hand fluttering to her neck. "You're wrong, Jonathan. I chose you over my father. Randall wanted me to stay. He even pulled out of the election to focus on his family. But I told him it was too late because I'd finally realized where my heart belonged. Where it's always been. With you."

He stared at her for a few long seconds, his brown eyes now filled with what looked like pity. Then he shook his head. "Tell Aunt Trudy I'll stay at the inn tonight and be back for my things in the morning."

Then he turned on his heel and left her standing alone, the smell of her untouched dinner lingering in the air, as the sound of his retreating footsteps echoed down the stairs.

CHAPTER 38

In the lavatory at the Cricket Bat Inn, Jonathan sluiced cold water over his head, shivering as the droplets slid down his neck and chest. The frigid tiled floor added to his discomfort, but he welcomed the pain. After an agonizing night spent reliving the horrid day before, he couldn't stay in bed for one more second. Now in the predawn darkness, he toweled himself dry and considered his next move.

Too early to go home. Knowing Aunt Trudy, she'd likely put Emma in his room while he was away in London. He'd wait until later in the day to go back there, but for now, he needed clarity and perhaps some divine guidance. He hoped to find that in the solitude of their parish church.

Jonathan returned to the room he'd rented, got dressed, and vacated the premises, welcoming the hush of the morning that enveloped the streets as he walked.

After about twenty minutes, when he reached the old stone building, he quietly let himself inside and slid into one of the pews. Kneeling, he bowed his head and waited for God's presence to wash over him, anticipating the measure of comfort it would provide.

Lord, help me to understand why you brought Emma back into my life. I'd made peace with the fact that I'd never see her again. I'd dealt with the grief and the heartache, believing it was your will for me. But now . . . now I'm not sure of anything. What would you have me do?

He waited, listening for the still, small voice inside him.

Love. The word floated into his consciousness.

Yes, he loved Emma. Probably always would. But he couldn't be sure the feelings she now professed for him were real. Her timing was more than suspect. If she'd told him back in Canada when he asked her to marry him that she loved him, he might have believed her.

But she hadn't said a word. Only cited the reasons why she couldn't leave Canada. Was it so wrong for him to want to come first for once?

You're mine.

The random thought jarred him. "Yes, I know," he muttered aloud. "I'm a child of God. But so is everyone. How does that make me special?"

"It doesn't."

Jonathan's head whipped up, and he expected to see the vicar. Instead, an older gentleman stood in the aisle, leaning on a broom. He wore a burlap apron over a beige shirt and red suspenders. The caretaker, most likely.

"Sorry. Didn't mean to interrupt your conversation." The man's chest shook with a chuckle.

Curiosity won out over Jonathan's desire for solitude. "What did you mean when you said it doesn't make me special?"

The man entered the pew and sat down beside him. "Everyone is equal in the eyes of God. If you're looking for Him to make you His favorite, you'll be waiting a long time."

Jonathan gazed ahead at the cross on the wall. "Actually, I'm more interested in being the favorite of someone here on earth. Unfortunately I came in a dismal second."

"A woman?"

356

"How did you know?"

"Just a hunch." The man folded his hands over his belly. "May I offer a word of advice?"

Jonathan sighed and nodded.

"Love should never be viewed as a competition. Take it from a man who's been married nearly forty years. Love requires compromise and sacrifice. There's no place for an ego in marriage. Whenever I get caught up in anger or resentment, I try to remember my favorite verse from Ephesians: 'Be completely humble and gentle; be patient, bearing with one another in love.'" His voice rang with certainty over the cavernous space. Then he turned kind eyes on Jonathan. "Do you think you can put your pride aside and simply love this woman without expecting anything in return?"

A thousand emotions flooded Jonathan's chest as the truth resonated within him. His ego *had* gotten in the way. It had swelled like a bloated river, wiping out the pureness of his devotion. He'd loved Emma unconditionally for so long without asking anything of her. Yet recently, he'd turned their relationship into a contest, a battle of wills and self-righteousness.

He hung his head. "You're right. My pride did get the better of me, and I did something I said I'd never do. I made her choose. When she didn't choose me, I left her. And when she changed her mind, I punished her." A hot wave of shame engulfed him. He was no better than Randall, rejecting her that way.

"Don't be too hard on yourself, son. Selfless love is difficult to achieve. Even after all these years, I still struggle with it." The older man chuckled again.

"What do I do now?" Jonathan's voice scraped over his raw emotions.

"I guess you have to ask yourself one important question." The caretaker stood and looked down at him. "Is she worth it?"

Jonathan closed his eyes, allowing the walls to fall away and love to surface. "She is. Most definitely."

"Then that's all you need to know." The man nodded. "You have a nice day now."

Jonathan watched him push his broom up the aisle and disappear from view. The fellow was right. What did it matter how Emma had come to the realization that she loved him? Didn't he owe it to himself to explore the possibility that her feelings were genuine?

He said one more round of prayers, asking for God's guidance, before he grabbed his cap off the pew and set out for home.

Emma awoke with the thrum of a headache. Little sleep after hours of crying would do that to a person. She shifted to her side and inhaled Jonathan's scent on the pillow. Why was she torturing herself this way? Tonight, she would find a new pillow with a freshly laundered case. Maybe then she'd be able to forget Jonathan long enough to get a decent sleep.

Lord, please take this heartache away. Allow me to let him go, to wish him well at Oxford while I get on with my new venture.

Releasing a heavy sigh, she dragged herself out of bed. Jonathan would be returning soon to pack his things. And she needed to be out of the flat when he did. She'd go for a long walk through the village. Maybe catch up with some old friends and neighbors while she was at it. Hopefully that would take her mind off Jonathan and the pain he'd inflicted last night.

What about his pain? The unwelcome thought mocked her.

She could only imagine how hurt he'd been the day she'd dismissed his marriage proposal. If only she'd been ready to accept his love then, how different it might have been. But there was no use in wasting time on regrets.

After dressing quickly, Emma went out to the kitchen, prepared to tell Trudy her plans. But there was no sign that she was up yet. So Emma jotted her a quick note and propped it against the vase of now-wilted flowers.

After grabbing her shawl to ward off the morning chill, she descended the stairs. Outside, she paused to breathe in the wonderful heather-scented air before heading down High Street, where she passed the butcher shop, Franny's bakery, and the post office. Realizing it was still too early to call on anyone, she turned down the dirt road that led toward the river. Her pace increased with a sudden urge to reach her favorite spot—the sloping banks near the old stone bridge. There, under the ancient willow that bent toward the water, was Emma's sanctuary. The place she felt safest, the place that brought her closest to God.

Emma made her way past the low branches and sat down. Even though the grass was damp, she didn't mind. She tucked her skirt around her ankles and inhaled the cool air, allowing some of her tension to seep away. For a minute, she could almost pretend that nothing had changed, that Grandad was alive, and that her friendship with Jonathan was still strong.

"Oh, Grandad," she whispered. "Did I do the wrong thing buying Trudy's shop? I only wanted to help her . . . and Jonathan."

She swallowed a lump in her throat and stared out over the water, watching a pair of ducks bob for food. Gradually her muscles relaxed as she soaked in the calming atmosphere. She drew in a few deep breaths and dug deep for her usual optimism. No matter how it turned out with Jonathan, Emma would do her best to help Trudy make the dress shop a success. And eventually Jonathan would forgive her. They might never get back to their former closeness, but in time, she prayed they could at least get past the hurt and remain friends.

"I thought I might find you here." Jonathan's voice came from behind her.

Emma jumped, her pulse sprinting like an overwound watch.

What was he doing here? Was he too seeking peace in their old haven? Or had he purposely come to find her?

She glanced over her shoulder as he descended the slope. When he reached her, he pointed to the space beside her. "May I?" Haggard lines hugged his cheeks. It looked like he hadn't gotten any more sleep than she.

Emma nodded, pulling her shawl tighter across her shoulders. A breeze teased strands of hair out of her braid. "Why are you here, Jonathan?" she asked quietly.

"I wanted to talk to you. When you weren't at the flat, I knew you'd be here."

She faced out over the water, her heart hammering hard against her ribs. He seemed somewhat wary, but at least not openly hostile like the previous evening. She'd wait for him to say his piece and then attempt to make amends.

"I've been doing a lot of thinking," he said at last, "and I believe I owe you a long-overdue apology."

"What for exactly?" she asked cautiously.

"To start with, that terrible marriage proposal back in Toronto. That was no way to go about asking you to marry me." A nervous energy surrounded him. He plucked a stone from the grass and tossed it into the river.

Unconcerned, the ducks floated past them on the rippling waters.

Emma drew in a shaky breath. "It did come rather out of the blue."

"Seems you're not the only one given to impulsive actions." He gave a rueful smile. "I had no right to expect you to drop everything to marry me. Since that day, I've let my pride override all common sense and turned our relationship into a competition, which is the opposite of what it should be."

Jonathan reached for her hand, and her heart jumped in her chest. With the warmth of his fingers engulfing hers, she couldn't seem to draw a full breath. She turned to look at him, and her insides relaxed for the first time in days. Because in the depths of those chocolate-brown eyes, she found her old Jonathan. Her best friend. The one she could always rely on.

"I need to start at the beginning," he said. "You see, I've known for a long time that my feelings for you were more than friendship, but I was afraid to say anything." He shrugged. "Then you started seeing Danny."

Her breath caught. He'd loved her even then? Her mind went back to the day she'd agreed to marry Danny, recalling how Jonathan hadn't seemed happy when he heard the news. She'd thought it was due to the timing with the men leaving for war. In reality, he must have been dying inside. Her throat constricted. "You didn't say anything because you didn't want to hurt us."

"You were both too important to me to risk losing either one of you." Jonathan's thumb caressed her palm in mesmerizing circles. "Then I planned to tell you when I got home from the war, but you were involved with Terrence, and again, the timing wasn't right. You had enough to deal with without me creating more problems."

"Oh, Jonathan." What could she say? She'd had no idea he'd been in love with her for so long.

"When you said you were going to Canada, I couldn't let you go by yourself. Part of me hoped that during our shared adventure"—one brow quirked up—"you'd fall madly in love with me."

She covered her mouth with her free hand. How could she not have seen the clues? The fact that he'd insisted on coming with her, then stayed in the room above the garage so he could be near her, and then done everything possible to help her get close to her father. She recalled the excitement on his face when they'd gone out for dinner. The romantic dance. The kiss on the swing. She bit her lip. How could she have been so insensitive to his feelings? It had been all new for her, but it was a culmination of years of yearning for him.

"I'm sorry I wasn't more considerate." She stared down at their joined hands. "That I took you for granted."

He squeezed her fingers. "You had no idea what I was feeling until I blurted everything out in that rash proposal. Reggie was quite annoyed with me for that, by the way."

Emma gave him a watery smile. "Did I ever tell you how much I adore Reggie?"

"Not too much, I hope."

She laughed and shook her head.

A soft breeze stirred around them, blowing some hair across her face. He reached over and gently brushed the strands away. "What I'm trying to say in a horribly roundabout fashion is that I love you, Emma. Plain and simple. And I won't rescind that love if your feelings don't match mine." He gazed into her eyes and drew in a long breath. "No matter what happens, I know now my love for you will never end."

Her heart beat too hard in her chest. She blinked furiously to hold her tears at bay. After everything she'd done, all the pain she'd caused him, he still loved her. It was more than she deserved. More than she'd dared hope for. But now she had to make him believe she felt the same.

"I love you too, Jonathan. It took me a while to recognize that my feelings were changing—to understand why I was suddenly nervous around you, and why I knew the moment you came into the kitchen every morning, and how my day didn't seem complete until I'd shared everything with you." She shook her head. "I pushed my feelings aside, too concerned about winning my father's affection when I should have been paying attention to you. Can you ever forgive me?"

He moved one hand up to caress her cheek. "Already done."

There were no words for the joy that entered her heart. She

placed her hand over his and looked deeply into his eyes. There, she found the look of adoration she'd always craved.

It had been there all along. She'd just been too blind to see it.

He lowered his head toward her, and then very slowly, his lips met hers.

Her soul sighed on a wave of pure love. She wrapped her arms around his neck and drew him closer. He tasted of acceptance and hope . . . and home.

A groan rumbled through his chest. "You have no idea how much I've missed you," he whispered.

"I think I do." She pulled back to look at him. "For the first time since I left Canada, I feel like I can finally breathe again. When I thought you hated me, I couldn't bear it." A tear slipped down her cheek.

He leaned his forehead against hers. "I never hated you, Em. Not even for a second. I'm sorry if I made you feel that way." With his thumb, he wiped the tears from her face. Then he tenderly kissed her again.

When they finally drew apart, he gave her a serious look. "Are you certain you really want this dress shop? Because if not, we can figure out another solution."

He was doing it again. Thinking of her first. Giving her a way out if she needed it.

"Of course I do. I'm excited and happy to help Trudy. I have so many ideas how to bring in new business." She reached up to caress his face, relishing the scrape of stubble against her palm. "I promise if it doesn't turn around the way I anticipate I'll discuss it with you both, and we can all decide what to do from there."

"Agreed." He teased her lips with his, making her head spin. "Only one problem remains," he said. "When I come home between school terms, how will I bear having you living right downstairs? The temptation might be too much to handle."

She laughed. "We'll have your aunt as a chaperone. But I suppose I could get a very big lock for my door."

He grinned, then grew serious. "I don't want to wait until I graduate to marry you, Emma. That is, if you want to marry me." He groaned. "There I go again. You deserve a proper proposal with romance and flowers and—"

"I would love nothing more than to marry you." Happiness broke free inside her, bubbling up, ready to spew outward like a geyser.

"You would?" His smile widened.

"I would."

He kissed her again, pulling her so close that she was almost on his lap. She laid a hand on his chest where his heartbeat thrummed under her hand. At last, he drew back, and with a sigh, she laid her head on his shoulder.

"There's one more thing I have to say," he said quietly.

He sounded serious, almost troubled.

She lifted her head to look at him. "What is it?"

"Do you remember the project Reggie was helping me with?"

"Yes." For an instant, a thread of fear wound through her, but she pushed it away. She would let nothing ruin this happy moment.

"I'd been seeing a doctor at the military hospital about my anxiety issues. Reggie came for moral support."

Of everything Emma could have imagined them doing, she never would have guessed that. "Jonathan, that's wonderful. Did it help?"

"It did. And I've continued with a doctor here since I've been back." His gaze was sober. "I don't know if I'll ever be fully cured, but I'm able to manage my symptoms better. I haven't had an episode in a long while now."

"I'm so glad. And so very proud of you." More tears brimmed over her lashes. "It took courage to seek help that way."

"I did it for you," he said gruffly. "I wanted to be whole again, to be the man you deserved."

"You've always been the man I deserved. I'm sorry it took so long to realize it."

The worry left his face. "Better late than never, my love." He brushed her lips with the most reverent of kisses.

Emma's heart filled with a love she'd only dreamed of. One better than any fairy tale she could have imagined. How ironic that she'd traveled thousands of miles, searching for home, for love and acceptance, when it had been with her all along.

Then, under the wispy shadows of the willow tree, Jonathan sealed his promise for their future with yet another kiss.

One of many more to come. Enough to last a lifetime.

EPILOGUE

The faint scent of lilacs covered the village of Wheatley on the morning of Emma's wedding. She peered out of the open window of her bedroom with a smile, inhaling the sweet fragrance. How she loved her new living quarters. The renovations had been completed just prior to Christmas, and now she and Jonathan would have their own private area off the back of the dress shop.

A knock sounded on the main door of the flat. Emma tied the sash on her robe and went to answer it.

"Who is it?" If it was Jonathan, she wouldn't open the door, not willing to incur any bad luck on this special day.

"It's Trudy. I have your dress ready."

Excitement bubbled through Emma's system. She could hardly wait to see the finished product. Trudy had been working on the dress for weeks now, and after the last fitting, Emma was not allowed to see it until her wedding day.

Business had certainly picked up for Trudy's Dress Designs over the past nine months, and with a rash of upcoming weddings, Trudy had been kept hopping—so much so that now she was considering specializing in nothing but wedding attire.

Emma opened the door and Trudy bustled in, arms full.

They walked through the living area and straight to the bedroom, where Trudy laid the garment on the bed. "Happy wedding day, my dear. I'm so excited for you, and more than that, I'm thrilled to officially welcome you into our family." She reached out to squeeze Emma in a tight hug.

"Not as happy as I am."

"Before you get into your dress, a telegram arrived for you this morning." She pulled a piece of paper from her pocket.

A sudden flare of alarm chilled Emma. Telegrams usually meant bad news.

"I'm sure it's nothing to worry about." Trudy patted her shoulder. "Likely a note of congratulations."

Emma's fingers trembled as she broke the seal. "Dearest Emma and Jonathan. Blessings on your wedding day. With you in spirit. Love, Mrs. C."

A lump of emotion rose in Emma's throat. "Wasn't that thoughtful?"

Yet she couldn't help the pang of sorrow that arose. Why hadn't her father or sisters bothered to wish her well on this momentous occasion? She'd sent them an invitation as a gesture of goodwill, knowing they'd likely not come. But for them to not at least acknowledge the day in some way hurt more than Emma had thought possible.

She swallowed hard and laid the telegram on her vanity table, alongside the other good wishes she'd received from Grace and Quinten. She would not allow her father to ruin one minute of this special day. "Let's get this fabulous gown on, Aunt Trudy. I don't want to keep Jonathan waiting."

Aunt Trudy insisted they take a taxi to the church. Emma was more than happy to accept her offer, and now as she got out in front of the stone building, she lifted the hem of the white satin high above her ankles to keep the material pristine.

Once inside the vestibule, she released the volumes of fabric. The pungent scent of fresh roses met her nose. From the open doors at the back of the church, Emma could see that small bouquets of flowers adorned every pew. A smattering of guests gathered near the front of the church, some seated, some talking in the aisles.

Emma turned to see what was keeping Trudy. The minister would want to start the ceremony on time.

A man in a charcoal-gray top hat and tails entered the church doors. He came to a stop and smiled as Emma's eyes met his familiar blue ones.

"I understand there's a bride here requiring an escort." Randall gave a nervous laugh. "I'd like to offer my services—if you'd allow me the privilege."

Emma's throat seized. She couldn't seem to draw air into her lungs. Her father had actually come all the way to England for her wedding?

"I'll understand if you refuse, since I haven't done much to deserve the honor." Regret radiated from his features as he extended a hand toward her.

She couldn't speak, couldn't think. But somehow she managed to take a halting step toward him and place her hand in his.

They stood, gazes locked for several seconds, until Randall cleared his throat. "I hope you're not mad. Jonathan wrote to me about the wedding. I told him you'd sent an invitation, but I doubted you really expected me to come. Yet he seemed to think you might want me here. I wasn't sure, but I decided it was about time I took a risk for you."

Silent tears slid down Emma's cheeks. He drew her to him in a gentle hug.

She laid her head on his shoulder. Her eyes closed, and she

released a deep sigh. "Thank you, Randall. I'm very glad you're here."

He drew back with a smile. Then he held her at arm's length to look her up and down. "You're breathtaking, Emma. Jonathan is a very lucky man."

At last, the adoration she'd waited for all her life glowed in his eyes.

Yet, for Emma, it couldn't compare to the look of love Jonathan gave her every day.

"Oh, I almost forgot." Randall held up a finger, then disappeared around the corner.

Emma's heart sank. Had he brought Vera with him? If so, she'd try to be gracious.

When Randall returned, however, he had two beautiful girls on his arms. Corinne looked stunning in a long pink gown, her blond hair piled high. But it was her younger sister who made Emma gasp.

Supported by her father, Marianne walked toward her, one arm in a metal brace attached to a cane, a big smile on her freckled face. "Hi, Emma. Are you surprised?"

Warmth spread through Emma's chest, tightening her throat. Marianne was out of her wheelchair. "Surprised? I'm stunned." A laugh gurgled up through her tears. "Look at you. You're walking. And you're here." She bent to kiss Marianne's cheek, then gathered her in a tight hug. "This is the best wedding present I could have received."

The girl hugged her back, and when Emma straightened, Marianne grinned. "Corinne helped me with the exercises until Dr. Hancock said I was ready for braces." She lifted the hem of her dress to reveal the metal bands on her legs.

"That's wonderful. I'm so proud of you." Emma turned to Corinne. "And Corinne. You look gorgeous." Emma kissed her other sister. "I can't believe you came."

"We wouldn't miss it," Corinne whispered, her eyes dancing with pleasure.

"Speaking of which," Randall said, "we'd better get started. Jonathan must be dying a thousand deaths up there. Corinne, will you help Marianne to her seat? I have a bride to escort."

Aunt Trudy bustled forward then with Emma's bridal bouquet. Sniffing back tears of her own, she gave Emma a hug and kiss before arranging the lacy veil in front of her face. "Congratulations, my dearest girl. You know I've always considered you the daughter I never had. Now we're truly a family."

Emma squeezed her hand. "I love you, Aunt Trudy."

The organ music started. Randall offered his elbow, and on his arm, Emma fairly floated up the aisle. Halfway to the altar, she caught Jonathan's gaze and mouthed, "Thank you."

He beamed at her, tears glinting in his eyes.

In his tailored morning suit and striped tie, Emma had never seen him look more handsome. Her heart swelled with such love, she feared it might burst from her chest.

As best man, Reggie Wentworth stood tall beside the groom. Jonathan had been thrilled that his friend could make the trip. He'd even come a week early so he and Jonathan could spend time together before the wedding. Jonathan had enjoyed showing Reggie his hometown, especially the hallowed halls of Oxford.

When Emma reached the altar, her father lifted her veil and handed her over to Jonathan. His fingers wrapped around her trembling hands, steadying her with their strength as they always did. She smiled up into his beloved face, the one she knew better than any other.

Theirs would be an everlasting love, she was certain. One forged from a common childhood, solidified by friendship, and strengthened by the challenges that had come their way. A love refined through many tests and that would withstand many more to come.

The minister welcomed everyone and began to read a passage from the New Testament. "'Love is patient; love is kind. Love is not envious or boastful or arrogant or rude. Love bears all things, believes all things, hopes all things, endures all things. Love never ends.'"

Jonathan squeezed her hand, his eyes brimming with emotion, and Emma smiled at him through her tears. She knew without a doubt that God had taken all her hopes and dreams and given her the gift of this wonderful man. A man who would provide her with the family she'd always desired.

On a wave of pure joy and gratitude, Emma pledged her life to her best friend, to the one who would hold her heart and keep it safe for all the years to come.

ACKNOWLEDGMENTS

Dear Friends,

Can you imagine being told your father was dead when he was really alive all along? That is the true life story of my maternal grandmother, Irene, whose mother died in childbirth and whose aunt raised her. She'd been told by her family that her father had died of a broken heart soon after her mother passed, but in reality he lived not far away, remarried with other children. My grandmother went her whole life never knowing that her father was alive. We don't know why "Auntie" brought my grandmother to live in Canada when Irene was twelve, but part of me suspects she was worried that Irene's father might come back into her life and create trouble.

It wasn't until I began researching our family tree in 2007 that I discovered the truth about my great-grandfather (who outlived Irene, by the way), and I started thinking: What if Irene had found out while she was alive that she had a father? Would she have gone back to England to find him? Demand answers as to why he abandoned her? I figured she probably would have. This, then, became the premise of Emmaline's story!

Many people helped bring this story to fruition:

I'd like to thank my agent, Natasha Kern, for all her support, both in my writing life and in my personal life. Your prayers are greatly appreciated!

Thank you to David Long and Jen Veilleux, my editors at Bethany House. You really work hard to make my books the best they can be!

A special thanks to Rachel Hauck, who helped me flesh out Emmaline and Jonathan's story during the Deep Thinker's Retreat in Florida. Just being around such brilliance, watching Rachel and Susie May Warren create magic with their stories, was so inspiring. The addition of Private Reggie Wentworth in the book is due to a suggestion from Rachel that Jonathan needed a friend. Reggie popped into my mind, fully formed and ready to go, and I love the depth he adds to the story!

As usual, my sincere gratitude goes to my two amazing critique partners, Sally Bayless and Julie Jarnagin, who give such great advice and help make me a better writer.

And, as always, I'm grateful to my family for their love and support.

Thank you to my wonderful readers and influencers. I appreciate you all so much!

With hugs and good wishes until next time,
Susan

To learn more about my books, please check out my website at www.susanannemason.net.

Susan Anne Mason describes her writing style as "romance sprinkled with faith." She loves incorporating inspirational messages of God's unconditional love and forgiveness into her characters' journeys. *Irish Meadows*, her first historical romance, won the Fiction from the Heartland contest sponsored by the Mid-America Romance Authors chapter of RWA.

Susan lives outside Toronto, Ontario, with her husband and their two grown children. She loves red wine and chocolate, is not partial to snow even though she's Canadian, and is ecstatic on the rare occasions she has the house to herself. Learn more about Susan and her books at www.susanannemason.net.

Sign Up for Susan's Newsletter!

Keep up to date with Susan's news on book releases and events by signing up for her email list at susannemason.net.

More from Susan Anne Mason

In the aftermath of tragedy, Grace hopes to reclaim her nephew from the relatives who rejected her sister because of her social class. Under an alias, she becomes her nephew's nanny to observe the formidable family up close. Unexpectedly, she begins to fall for the boy's guardian, who is promised to another. Can Grace protect her nephew ... and her heart?

The Best of Intentions
CANADIAN CROSSINGS #1

You May Also Like . . .

Englishwoman Verity Banning decides to start a business importing horses and other goods the residents of the West Indies need. This trade brings her to New York, where she meets revolutionary Ian McKintrick. As a friend to many Loyalists, Verity has always favored a peaceful resolution. But when a Patriot lays claim to her heart, she'll have to decide for what—and whom—she will fight.

Verity by Lisa T. Bergren
THE SUGAR BARON'S DAUGHTERS #2
lisatbergren.com

A female accountant in 1908, Eloise Drake thought she'd put her past behind her. Then her new job lands her in the path of the man who broke her heart. Alex Duval, mayor of a doomed town, can't believe his eyes when he sees Eloise as part of the entourage that's come to wipe his town off the map. Can he convince her to help him—and give him another chance?

A Desperate Hope by Elizabeth Camden
elizabethcamden.com

BETHANYHOUSE

More Historical Fiction from Bethany House Publishers

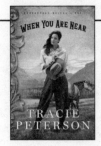

In 1900's Montana, Lizzy Brookstone's new role as manager of an all-female Wild West show is rewarding but difficult. However, trials of the heart and a mystery to be solved prove more daunting. As Lizzy and two other show members, costume maker Ella and sharpshooter Mary, try to discover how Mary's brother died, all three seek freedom in a world run by men.

When You Are Near by Tracie Peterson
BROOKSTONE BRIDES #1
traciepeterson.com

With a Mohawk mother and a French father in 1759 Montreal, Catherine Duval finds it easiest to remain neutral among warring sides. But when her British ex-fiancé, Samuel, is taken prisoner by her father, he claims to have information that could end the war. At last, she must choose whom to fight for. Is she willing to commit treason for the greater good?

Between Two Shores by Jocelyn Green
jocelyngreen.com

Daphne Blakemoor was happy living in seclusion. But when ownership of the estate where she works passes to William, Marquis of Chemsford, her quiet life is threatened. William also seeks a refuge from his past, but when an undeniable family connection is revealed, can they find the courage to face their deepest wounds and forge a new path for the future?

Return of Devotion by Kristi Ann Hunter
HAVEN MANOR #2
kristiannhunter.com

◈ BETHANYHOUSE